THE EDGE OF ETERNITY

(THE WIZARD OF TIME — BOOK 3)

G.L. BREEDON

KOSMOSAIC BOOKS

This is a work of fiction. Any resemblance of characters to actual persons, living or dead, is purely coincidental. The Author holds exclusive rights to this work. Unauthorized duplication is prohibited.

Copyright 2014 by G.L. Breedon
All rights reserved.

This book is available in print at most online retailers.

For more information:
Kosmosaicbooks.com

CHAPTER 1

A cloud of black arrows arced through the sky, reaching their apex before falling like a storm of slender hail, driving toward the earth below.

Gabriel ducked, arrows flashing past his head and clattering against stone, bouncing off armor, and sinking deep into human flesh.

Screams of pain and anger and military orders filled the air.

Gabriel glanced around and wondered, as he had nearly every second for the last half-hour, if coming to this place had been such a good idea.

It had been his idea.

"Are you certain they can't see us?" Marcus rubbed his bald head where a ricocheting arrow had grazed him.

"There are thousands of them." Sema crouched beside Marcus, her face a mask of concentration and fear. "I am doing the best I can."

"Are you sure this is the place?" Teresa clamped her hand on Gabriel's forearm as she looked around at the chaos surrounding them.

A phalanx of Chinese soldiers in hardened leather armor ran past. Nearby, a battery of archers returned fire, loosing a wall of arrows at their enemies below.

"This is the place." Ohin knelt beside Gabriel and Teresa. "The anchor point is close."

"Yes," Gabriel said, reaching out again with his space-time sense, searching for the mysterious point that had brought them to the top of the Great Wall of China on the 27th of May, 1644 — in the midst of the Battle of Shanghai Pass.

Gabriel still found it confusing that the battle and the wall were nowhere near Shanghai but actually in Shanhaiguan, some 870 miles to the north on the western edge of the Bohai Sea. The battle being fought around them would determine the course of Chinese history for the next several hundred years, resulting in the definitive end of the Ming Dynasty and the founding of the Qing Dynasty. Troops loyal to Qing Prince Regent Dorgon and General Wu Sangui, formally of the Ming

Dynasty, now defended the wall against the rebel, self-proclaimed emperor Li Zicheng, who had taken control of Beijing only days before. Zicheng would eventually lose the Battle of Shanghai Pass and return to Beijing, fleeing in advance of Wu Sangui's army. Nearly six months later, on November 8th, Prince Regent Dorgon would help install a six-year-old Qing Prince Shunzhi as Emperor. The Qing Dynasty would continue to rule China until 1912.

A volley of cannon fire sounded below, the stones of the Great Wall shuddering with the impact of the metal balls. Gabriel tried to blot out the battle around him and focus his mind on the faint distortion of space-time nearby. It felt very close — in time as well as space. They would not need to wait long, but they *would* need to wait somewhere else.

"It's this way, I think." Gabriel pointed to the east, past a line of archers, to an open space in the wide stone bricks lining the top of the wall.

"I'll shield us." Ling took a quick look over the parapet of the wall and turned back to the rest of the team. "Now!"

Gabriel and the Chimera team leapt to their feet and dashed along the top of the Great Wall, dodging the running soldiers of General Wu Sangui's army and their fallen comrades. Sema's Soul Magic rendered them largely unseen, the magical amulets at their necks camouflaging their appearance to make them indistinguishable from the soldiers around them if her magic wavered.

As Gabriel ran, the sound of intermittent gunfire echoed along the stone ledges of the Great Wall. The Chinese armies of the seventeenth century possessed matchlock rifles, reverse engineered from the muskets of the Portuguese sailors who arrived in the mid-sixteenth century. Gabriel flinched as a musket ball froze in midair beside him. He glanced back at Ling as he ran.

"Thanks!"

"What kind Wind Mage would I be if couldn't stop a few bullets?" Ling smiled as the team reached the unmanned section of the wall and once more ducked down to safety behind the parapet.

"I feel like a canary in a shooting gallery." Rajan crouched down beside Ling.

"It's a duck in a shooting gallery." Teresa laughed at Rajan. "Canaries are for coal mines."

"Dead birds either way." Rajan frowned as an arrow pierced the air beside his head and shattered on the far parapet atop the wall.

"Not long now." Ohin closed his eyes in concentration.

"This is definitely the spot." Gabriel sensed it clearly now — an event in space-time that would flower into being at any moment. An event that could not be a natural occurrence. An event linked to one they had witnessed a little over a week ago.

An anchor point.

That was the name Elizabeth had given the phenomenon in her coded notebook. It had taken most of a year for Gabriel and Teresa to decode the notebook. Doing so had involved repeated trips to the Indus Valley civilization. While the text of the actual Rosetta Stone, written on the first page of the notebook, had allowed them to decode Elizabeth's secret script, it had only revealed phonetically written text in the ancient Indus language. They had needed to learn the language to decipher the decoded text.

While Teresa's facility with languages proved to be every bit impressive as she had boasted, the vagaries of dialect throughout the Indus civilization, over time and between geographical regions, made translating the notebook a more complicated affair than either she or Gabriel had anticipated. That, of course, had been Elizabeth's intention — to make it as difficult as possible for the notebook to be read by the wrong people.

In the end, it had required seven separate excursions to the Indus Valley at various places and times between 2600 and 1900 BCE. The entire Chimera team had accompanied Gabriel and Teresa on their educational missions. Between expeditions they would return to help construct new forts in the far past to house the Grace Mages who had survived the attacks of the Apollyons and Kumaradevi during the destruction of the Council's Windsor Castle.

As a measure of security, they had agreed never to write down a direct translation of the notebook's contents. If Elizabeth had gone to such trouble to protect its revelations, it would be foolish to render it readable to anyone but themselves. There were members of the Council who had been upset with this decision, but unless they were willing to learn ancient Indus, there was little they could do about it. In the end, Gabriel became nearly as fluent in Indus, and as adept at reading and writing Elizabeth's code, as Teresa.

His findings so far were few, but what they had gleaned from the translated notebook proved to be invaluable. While they were aware from their spying on the Apollyons that the Great Barrier of Probability had apparently been constructed through the use of both Grace and Malignancy Magic, Elizabeth had investigated this discovery and unveiled another revelation even more surprising. By closely examining the Great Barrier, the magical wall that made time travel into the future beyond the year 2012 impossible, she had discerned that the magic holding it in place possessed a negative aspect. As a Grace Mage, she sensed only half of the magic she knew must be in use to exert its existence. She had also sensed something else — that the Barrier did not simply exist at all possible places in space at the specific moment in time on October 28, 2012 at 4:45 p.m. Greenwich Standard Time. Aspects of it seemed to link to other places and times. However, while able to sense the linkage, she had not been able to sense a location. She described it in the notebook as similar to trying to find a specific tree in the midst of a mist-shrouded forest.

Fortunately, the experience reminded her of a strange phenomenon she had witnessed nearly a hundred years prior. In the middle of a mission to sever the connections between one of Kumaradevi's concatenate crystals at the Battle of Ceresole in 1544, she had stumbled across a strange inversion of the space-time continuum. For exactly thirty-seven seconds, a sphere of space-time the size of a small house became a vortex of impossibly stable probability. It wasn't that time did not flow correctly in that space for those thirty-seven seconds, but that the very nature of space-time seemed upended. For those thirty-seven seconds, unlike the rest of the Primary Continuum, the course of time in that short, bizarre bubble of space-time could never be altered.

Only upon learning that the Great Barrier of Probability seemed to be linked to other points in space-time did it dawn on Elizabeth that what she had assumed to be a unique, but naturally occurring abnormality was, in fact, part of a purposefully created series of disturbances. When she returned to investigate the phenomenon more closely, she uncovered a vital clue to the Great Barrier's construction. A tendril of nearly imperceptible magic connected the first disturbance to two others, one nearly a century further in the future and another even further into the past.

Elizabeth named these phenomena *anchor points* and believed there were more of them, stretching from the moment of the Great Barrier at intervals back through time into the far past, binding them all to something, somewhere, that made the Great Barrier possible. Unfortunately, she had only been able to uncover three anchor points before the attack on the castle, and the Apollyons dark curse upon her mind had left her trapped in the unshakable sleep of a deep coma.

The anchor point at the top of the Great Wall of China in the middle of the Battle of the Shanghai Pass in 1644 was the second of the two that Elizabeth had discovered. Gabriel and the team hoped to be able to sense another anchor point further into the future, closer to the Great Barrier, with the eventual goal of charting all the anchor points. The more they understood about the creation of the Barrier the better they would be able to defend it against the intended destruction by the army of duplicate Apollyons.

A stray arrow shattered into bits of black wood on the parapet wall across from Gabriel. He blinked to clear his mind of the distraction and focused on extending his space-time sense as far as possible while sliding his grandfather's pocket watch into his hand.

"It's close." Gabriel closed his eyes, trying to shut out the sounds of warfare echoing along the ancient stone wall beneath him.

"You keep saying that, and they keep shooting at us." Teresa ducked as another volley of arrows coursed through the air above their heads.

"Shush." Ohin shot Teresa a stern look and closed his eyes again.

Gabriel's space-time sense began to vibrate in his mind like a plucked string oscillating at high frequency. Any moment now. Any second. The vibrations reached a crescendo as a sphere of space-time seemed to solidify around him. Gabriel opened his eyes to look down at the pocket watch, tracking the second hand even as his space-time sense observed the bubble of non-probability surrounding him. The anchor point existed in a perfect sphere a hundred feet in diameter — this one a little larger than the one linked to it in the past. Gabriel narrowed his concentration until he perceived that tenuous connection to the anchor point several decades previous. As he did so, he discerned another connection, a twin of the first, a wispy, vaporous trail of slightly twisted space-time proceeding onto the future.

"I feel it, but I can't see the terminus." Gabriel glanced down at the pocket watch again. "Only fifteen seconds left."

"We'll find it." Ohin placed his hand on Gabriel's shoulder. "Calm your mind."

Gabriel exhaled slowly and pushed the anxiety and annoyance from his thoughts. As he breathed in, he saw an image of the future anchor point in his mind.

Another battlefield. Several warring armies. Their uniforms looked familiar. So did the landscape behind them. He tried to bring the mental image into greater focus. Just as he thought he saw a flag, the images winked out and the space-time distortion of the anchor point ceased.

"Did you see?" Ohin opened his eyes to stare at Gabriel.

"Yes." Gabriel let out a long breath. "Another battlefield. I couldn't figure out which one though."

"The Siege of Namur in 1695." Ohin's mouth curled in a rare smile. "Nearly sixty years from now."

"I think the anchor points may be getting closer together as they get nearer the Great Barrier." Teresa seemed almost as excited by the successful location of the next anchor point as Gabriel.

"Yes, all very fascinating." Marcus glanced over his shoulder to a squad of Chinese archers running along the wall toward them. "However, I can be fascinated somewhere a bit less congested."

"I thought you liked a good battle," Ling teased.

"When I'm on the winning side, not when I'm stuck in the middle of it," Marcus said.

"You know I rarely agree with Marcus, but I really am at the limit of my ability to hide our presence for much longer." Sema glared as a passing soldier nearly crushed her foot beneath his boot.

"Yes." Ohin flinched as the wall of the parapet near him exploded in a hail of stone fragments under the impact of a stray bullet. "Someplace quiet is a very good idea."

Space-time bent around Gabriel as the blackness of time travel descended and Ohin took them away from the Battle of Shanghai Pass.

CHAPTER 2

Even in the momentary darkness between moments, Gabriel sensed their movement backward by years and miles. When the white light signaling the end of their brief time travel journey faded, he and the others still crouched behind the parapet of the Great Wall of China. Ohin had used the monumental structure as a relic to guide them to a time and place along its path where no people might observe them.

Gabriel stood with the team, looking along the roadway atop the massive wall, admiring the construction of the stone barrier undulating over the rolling hills of the land to the west and back again, eastward toward the sea. Emperor Qin Shi Huang, first emperor of China, may have intended the earth-packed walls of 220 BCE to have a very practical purpose in keeping out the Mongol tribes to the north, but as the wall changed and grew over the centuries, particularly during the Ming Dynasty in the years from 1567 to 1570, the resulting edifice became as much a marvel of architecture and engineering as a defensive stone barricade.

"This is much better." Marcus put his hands out and leaned against the edge of the wall. "No arrows."

"And no people." Sema turned to face Marcus. "I'm certain someone must have seen us."

"I sensed no potential bifurcations in the Continuum," Ohin said. "You did well. All of you."

"How many more times will we need to do that?" Ling swung the strap of a canteen from her shoulder and unscrewed the cap to take short swig of water.

"A hundred and six." Teresa gratefully accepted the canteen from Ling. "A hundred and five if we count the Great Barrier as the first anchor point."

"I still don't see how you can be so sure there are a hundred and eight anchor points in total." Rajan briefly touched the amulet at his neck, his armor shimmering as it changed to reveal his true attire of a dark blue tunic and pants. The others, whether from conscious or unconscious mimicry, gradually did the same.

"A hundred and eight anchor points would make sense if it took a hundred and eight mages to create the Great Barrier," Teresa said.

"We don't even know where that legend of one hundred and eight mages creating the Barrier came from," Rajan said.

"In the notebook, Elizabeth wrote that she thought it may have started with Vicaquirao." Gabriel licked his lips in anticipation as Teresa passed him the canteen. He swallowed urgently at the cool water. He hadn't realized how thirsty the events of the last few hours had left him.

"All mysteries lead back to Vicaquirao," Marcus said.

"I can ask him about it next time I see him," Gabriel said.

"You have plans to see Vicaquirao?" Ohin frowned in concern.

"No plans, but he has a way of turning up." Gabriel frowned, as well. Thinking of Vicaquirao always elicited mixed emotions. Was he a friend or foe or somehow both? "The real question is whether the Apollyons haven't attacked the Great Barrier yet because they haven't created enough duplicates, or because they *have* and they're not yet sure how to destroy it." Gabriel took another drink from the canteen to cover the sudden uneasiness his question had evoked.

"What a pleasant puzzle." Sema grimaced as she folded her arms.

"But why a hundred and eight?" Rajan gazed up into the blue sky as he thought out loud. "A hundred and eight turns up in Hinduism and Buddhism and a few other places as an important number, but why that number specifically? Why not a hundred and nine? That's a prime number at least."

"Look at you, mentioning prime numbers like you know what you're talking about." Teresa smiled at Rajan as though staring at a trained horse that had counted to ten.

"I'm with Akikane," Ling said. "Some things are the way they are because that's the way the universe works. The speed of light. The number Pi. Plank's constant."

"Have you two been taking math and science classes while I wasn't paying attention?" Teresa blinked in amazement as she looked between Ling and Rajan.

"The real question isn't how many anchor points there are or why." Ohin stroked his chin. "The important question is whether, by discovering how the Great Barrier of Probability was created, we can learn how it might be destroyed. Once that secret is known, it will be imperative to keep that information from the Apollyons."

"And we've been so successful keeping secrets from them in the past." Ling snorted in disgust.

"Unless they are close to discovering the secret themselves." Gabriel's stomach clenched at the notion. "In which case, if we don't know how it was created, we won't be able to defend the Barrier against them."

"A conundrum." Marcus sighed and handed he canteen to Sema. "I hate conundrums."

"Particularly when the entire Continuum hangs in the balance." Sema took a sip from the canteen.

"Well I love conundrums." Teresa smiled and threw her arm around Gabriel's shoulder.

"Wait. What?" Gabriel scrunched his face in confusion and turned to Teresa. "Are you implying something?"

"No implications are necessary with you, I'm afraid." Teresa laughed and kissed him quickly. The others laughed, as well.

"We should compare notes and be on our way," Ohin said. He knew how to take advantage of a positive shift of mood within the group.

"Yes," Teresa said. "Tell me everything you could sense."

"Well, firstly, I think it was slightly larger than the last one." Gabriel reached into his pants pocket and removed Elizabeth's red leather notebook. Teresa handed him a pen as he flipped to the last page to begin recording the day's discoveries in ancient Indus.

"It wasn't significantly larger, but I agree." Ohin said. "Maybe only a few feet."

"But still a perfect sphere?" Teresa asked.

"Yes," Gabriel replied. "And still thirty-seven seconds in duration."

"Another repeating number we don't understand." Rajan leaned over to watch Gabriel scribbling across a blank page of the notebook.

"It's possible that the nature of probability is somehow linked to the number thirty-seven," Teresa said. "It takes thirty-seven hours for the latent probability of a bifurcation to collapse into reality, and these time bubbles, or anchor points, seem to nullify probability for thirty-seven seconds."

"That makes sense because the anchor points feel like the inverse of a bifurcation." Gabriel squinted at the page, then looked up to Teresa, an idea flittering at the edge of his mind like a butterfly strenuously avoiding the net of his concentration. As he looked at Teresa, his frustration froze, replaced by a chill along his neck, the reluctant idea fading away as alarm filled his mind.

"What is it?" Teresa asked.

"Someone's coming." Gabriel spun on his heels, shoving the notebook into his back pocket and reaching over his shoulder to draw the Sword of Unmaking from the sheath across his shoulders, grasping its imprints as he clasped its handle.

"Two groups on either side of the roadway," Ohin shouted as a cluster of black-uniformed men and women appeared in an instant along the eastern road atop the Great Wall. "Gabriel, Teresa, and Rajan, to the east. Marcus, Sema, and Ling with me to the west." Ohin whipped around as six more interlopers materialized in a clump in the middle of the western side of the road.

Gabriel stared at the six Dark Mages facing him, Teresa, and Rajan as he claimed the imprints of the seven linked concatenate crystals in the pouch at his belt. Their backs to one another, the members of the Chimera team formed a tight circle against their enemies.

Gabriel recognized the six faces sneering at him from across the ancient stones of the roadway atop the Great Wall. He had seen them recently — the Dark Mages who had tortured him daily for month after month in Kumaradevi's private arena. Malik and his cohorts had found Gabriel and the Chimera team a week previous while investigating the other anchor point. They had defeated the Malignant Mages and made numerous time jumps to ensure they would not be found again. Apparently, Malik possessed considerably more skill at ghosting and tracking time trails than either Gabriel or Ohin had anticipated.

"You don't look happy to see us." Malik laughed. A string of seven concatenate crystals draped his shoulder like a bandolier glittering in the sun. "You'll be even less happy when we're through with you."

Gabriel had a brilliant retort ready to shout at his adversary, but it died in silence as the air and stone around him exploded in lighting and a space-time seal fell in place around the Chimera team. Gabriel deflected the lightning and the other magics assailing him and the team as Teresa created a massive wall of flame between them and their attackers.

"Focus on the time mages," Ohin shouted over the roar of the flames.

Gabriel sensed Ohin's magic pressing against the space-time seal put in place by Malik and his fellow Dark Time Mage. The seal held firm. Gabriel assumed each of the seven concatenate crystals Malik possessed linked to seven more elsewhere. Even though the imprints they connected to originated in Kumaradevi's evil alternate reality, and thus were weaker than imprints from the Primary Continuum, they still allowed for a formidable amount of magic.

While the Council had made finding positively imbued artifacts and creating concatenate crystals a priority, there were few available for teams in the field. Fortunately, the Chimera team's expeditions took precedence in the distribution of imbued objects. Unfortunately, the crystals Gabriel held didn't link to any others. Kumaradevi's soldiers outmatched his team.

"I can't see through the flames," Rajan shouted in frustration.

"That was the point." Teresa turned sideways, extending one hand in each direction, the wall of flame splitting into two enormous fireballs that engulfed each group of Dark Mages.

The Dark Fire Mages countered the flames, causing them to sputter out of existence. Gabriel used the distraction to focus all of his magical powers in attacking Malik. Ohin was right. If they disabled even one of the two Dark Time Mages, the team would be able to break the space-time seal and escape.

Malik sank to his knees under a crushing magical weight and clasped his head as Gabriel's Soul Magic blazed in his mind. Lightning arced around Malik as a tornado of fire surrounded him. The other members of Malik's unit broke off their attacks and focused their attention on defending their leader.

Gabriel knew only a moment remained for action. Even as he watched Teresa and Rajan mirror and multiply his attacks toward Malik, he reached out with his magic-sense and will, attempting to wrest control of the imprints the Dark Mage held. Gabriel struggled for control of the malignant imprints of the concatenate crystals in Malik's possession. It was not as easy as Gabriel had hoped. He had used the same trick the week before to escape the Dark Mage. Malik came prepared this time. He managed to repel Gabriel's attempt to usurp his mastery of the dark imprints in his power as his fellow Malignant Mages turned their attention to thwarting Gabriel's magical attack.

"Not this time, boy," Malik wheezed, his face contorted in concentration. "This time I kill you."

A scream pierced the air behind Gabriel. He risked a glance over shoulder to see Sema collapsing to the ground, holding her side. Marcus wrapped an arm around her, guiding her to the ground even as he cast a flesh-eating curse against the Dark Fire Mage who had felled her.

Gabriel turned back to Malik, still struggling to take control of the man's imprints. As he pressed on, Gabriel began to lose hope. They needed to flee as soon as possible. They could not allow themselves, or the notebook, to be captured. Unless he managed to claim hold of the malignant imprints at Malik's command, or wounded the man with an attack, it would be very difficult, if not impossible, to break the space-time seal around the Chimera team. They were trapped like an insect in amber.

Or, were they?

Gabriel and Ohin could not take the team through time or space, but that did not mean the team could not move at all. If they got far enough away, beyond Malik's magical reach, they would be physically outside the space-time seal. Ling would not be happy, but it might work.

As Gabriel continued to joust for control of the imprints of Malik's concatenate crystals and attack him and his companions with various magics, he reached out with Wind Magic, gently grasping Teresa, Rajan, and the other team members with an invisible hand.

"Goodbye." Gabriel smiled at Malik as he and the entire Chimera team shot upward into the sky. He heard Ling cursing behind him as he pushed them through the air at incredible speed, out above the rolling hills north of the Great Wall. He sensed the space-time seal trying to expand to encompass them, and he rushed them forward even faster. Glancing back, he saw Malik and the other Dark Mages in the distance, still standing on the wall. If Malik and the other Dark Time Mage jumped through space and closed the distance between them and Gabriel, they could maintain the space-time seal.

Gabriel waved the Sword of Unmaking in the direction of the Dark Mages, copying Teresa's earlier magic and creating a bubble-shaped barrier of sky-high flames in front of the Great Wall. A Time Mage could only jump through space to someplace they had been or could see directly.

"Flying and fire!" Teresa shouted. "That's why I love you!"

Gabriel watched as Teresa added her Fire Magic to his own, the intensity of the blazing dome encircling Kumaradevi's soldiers, flaring white-hot. The space-time seal faded and Gabriel thrust the Chimera team to the ground. He tried to guide their decent but they needed to land fast. A time travel jump while in motion could be unpredictable and dangerous. And Malik might reestablish the space-time seal at any moment.

They landed harder than Gabriel had hoped, everyone except himself and Ling falling to the ground. She had managed to wrap herself in a protective field of gravity at the last moment.

"This is why I hate flying!" Ling spat into the grass as she helped Ohin to his feet.

"Tend to Sema." Ohin nodded to where Marcus knelt beside Sema, his hands held against her ribs, healing her.

Gabriel sensed Ohin warping the fabric of space-time and the blackness of a time jump begin to form. They were free and would be safe in moments. They had escaped death once more. However, they needed to be more careful in the future. And better armed with imprints.

Gabriel frowned as the blackness wavered and flickered and faded away as yet another space-time seal slid into place around the Chimera team. This seal appeared different than the last. Stronger. Tighter. More impenetrable.

Teresa gasped behind him. As he turned toward her, his stomach clenched and the air seemed to freeze in his lungs. He had expected to find that Malik and Kumaradevi's other soldiers had breached the blazing dome to confront the Chimera team and restore the space-time seal.

Instead, he faced six black-clad Apollyons standing on the hillside above, their hatred-filled stares stabbing him like flaming swords.

CHAPTER 3

A strange silence seemed to cling to the small valley beneath the rocky hills. In the distance, the fiery sphere encasing the Great Wall of China blinked out of existence. Gabriel and Teresa's concentration rested entirely upon the six Apollyon duplicates confronting them.

"Any brilliant ideas?" Teresa's voice cracked as her breath quickened.

Gabriel's mind felt as empty as the cloudless sky above. "Not really."

A cloud of voices suddenly filled that emptiness within his mind.

"Come with..."
"Come with us..."
"And bring..."
"With us..."
"The notebook..."
"Bring..."
"And we will allow..."
"Come with us..."
"The notebook..."
"The others to live..."
"To live..."

"No." Sema's voice sounded firm and demanding. Gabriel saw Marcus helping her to her feet. She had also heard the voices. "You can't, Gabriel."

He had no intention of going with the Apollyons or giving them the notebook. Before he could state this firm conviction, the warping of space-time nearby drew his attention. Malik and the other eleven minions of Kumaradevi appeared on the opposite hillside from the Apollyons.

Gabriel sighed. He and his friends were surrounded. Again.

"The boy is ours." Malik's voice echoed among the rock-strewn hills. "Retreat now."

"Your mistress..." One of the Apollyons began to speak.

"Oversteps herself." Another Apollyon finished the thought.

"Leave this place…" A third Apollyon began.

"Or die." All six Apollyons uttered these last words in unison.

"Brave words for a mad man." Malik sneered at his adversaries.

"I have an idea." Rajan glanced between the two factions of Dark Mages flanking the team. "Duck!"

Dozens of magical attacks between the Apollyons and Kumaradevi's soldiers shattered the air around Gabriel and the team as the ground beneath his feet fell away. Gabriel and his team plunged down into a suddenly erupting sinkhole formed from Rajan's Earth Magic. They landed in a plume of earthen dust.

"Your idea is to bury us in a hole!" Teresa brushed a falling clod of dirt from her face.

"Better down than up." Ling's eyes were raised, like everyone else's, to the magical battle twenty feet above their heads.

"We're trapped either way." Marcus held his hand out to help steady Sema on the constantly shifting earth beneath their feet.

"We may only have a few seconds to come up with a plan." Gabriel tried to sense how the battle above them progressed. Which side was winning? How long would it take for a victor to emerge?

"Can you move us sideways through the earth the same way you brought us down?" Ohin stared hard at Rajan.

"I can move the ground, but I can't move us." Rajan looked to Ling.

"Which way do you want to go?" Ling turned her eyes to Ohin.

"That way." Ohin pointed uphill, between the two groups of Dark Mages above them. "Through the side of the hill."

Ohin barely finished speaking when the wall of rocky earth beyond his fingertip exploded inward, a ten-foot-wide tunnel burrowing into darkness under Rajan's Earth Magic. Ling's Wind Magic lifted them slightly into the air and then thrust them down the dark, continually expanding tunnel. Teresa raised her hand, and several globes of glowing white light blinked into existence, illuminating their progress.

Gabriel ignored the temptation to assist either Rajan or Ling with their subterranean retreat. He kept his mind focused on the magical warfare above ground while seeking out the edge of the space-time seal still restraining their escape. The seal seemed to be moving with them, expanding as they got further away from the Apollyons. They would need to flee quicker if they hoped get outside the reach of the space-time seal.

Daylight showered Gabriel's face, and clouds of dusty earth swirled in the air as the team broke through the topsoil on the opposite slope of the hillside and into the open. Even as Ling set their feet down upon the tall grass, two Apollyons appeared on either side of the hill. A moment later, the other four Apollyons materialized, forming a circle around the team. The space-time seal the Apollyons held in place would keep Malik from being able to teleport himself and his soldiers back into the fight.

"It was worth a try," Rajan said.

"Inventive…" one of the Apollyons said.

"But pointless," another concluded.

"You will come with us…"

"Now."

Gabriel didn't bother trying to keep track of which Apollyon spoke. They all shared the same thoughts — and nearly a single mind. It didn't matter which one spoke. He needed to figure out how to respond. He couldn't try to steal the Apollyons imprints the way he had with Malik. Their power came not from imbued artifacts, but from copies of themselves, stationed at places in time where malignant events had transpired.

"I'll go with you…on one condition." Gabriel had no condition, but he needed to stall for time. Time to think of a way out.

"No conditions." The Apollyons spoke in rapid succession, their words blending into a single sentence.

"Conditions…"

"No negotiations…"

"Negotiations…"

"We will take you…"

"Take you…"

"Just like this…"

The notebook flew from Gabriel's back pocket. He clutched at it with his free hand as he turned, focusing his Wind Magic on the little red leather tome as it tumbled toward one of the Apollyons. He sensed

Ling add her magical energy to his own, but they could not match the power of six Apollyons jointly using a single form of magic. Gabriel ground his teeth as he focused all of the imprints he possessed toward reclaiming the notebook, only to watch as it moved evermore quickly toward the Apollyon with an outstretched hand.

The Dark Mage did not try to touch the notebook. He, or his brethren, had made that mistake before with a booby-trapped decoy. The Apollyon formed a hand of Wind Magic and opened the cover of the book.

"No!" Gabriel shouted as the notebook exploded in a ball of flame.

The Apollyon screamed and covered his face as the charred lump of paper and leather fell to the ground. A wave of sadness washed over Gabriel.

"Another trick?" The burned Apollyon spat as he focused his Heart-Tree magic on making the blisters across his face recede.

"Another decoy?" a different Apollyon queried.

"Will you, too…"

"Burst into flame…"

"When we take you?" an Apollyon behind Gabriel said.

Gabriel couldn't imagine what he'd do when they took him, and it looked more and more like he would not be able to stop them from doing so. The sadness clinging to him spread, like a net pulling him beneath turbulent ocean spray.

It had not been another decoy notebook. It had been the real notebook. And now it was gone. All their efforts to recover and decode it turned to ash. Ohin had insisted that Gabriel and Teresa make sure no one but them could use the notebook. Only Gabriel or Teresa could touch it without it bursting into flame. And the same happened when it was opened without one of them touching it.

As Gabriel began to form a reply to the Apollyons, a bolt of lightning struck the duplicate Dark Mage, still recovering from his burns. Gabriel turned to see Kumaradevi's soldiers flying through the air above the hilltop the Chimera team had recently tunneled through. Malik and his troops once more attacked the Apollyons. Gabriel noted there were fewer of them than before. They had lost two mages in the previous engagement.

"Join the attack on the Apollyons," Ohin shouted. However distasteful the idea, by working with Kumaradevi's soldiers, they had a chance of defeating the Apollyons. And if they did so, there would likely be fewer of Kumaradevi's soldiers to deal with afterward. It seemed like the least worst option from an extensive array of bad choices.

Gabriel added his magic to the assault of Kumaradevi's soldiers against the Apollyons. He targeted one of Apollyons and tried to use Soul Magic to sever the man's mental connection to his fellow duplicates. The Apollyon glared at him and rebuffed his attack. They knew what to expect and how to deflect the magic that might make them individuals. Without access to more imprints, Gabriel couldn't attempt that sort of offensive again.

As he drained every calorie of heat energy from around one of the Apollyons, instantly chilling the air to an extreme subzero temperature, it occurred to Gabriel that at least one option might be open to him. It wasn't a sure bet, but it might work. However, if it did, and he survived, he'd be lucky if Teresa didn't try to kill him.

He turned toward Teresa as arcs of white-hot plasma shot from her hands toward an Apollyon beset by two of Kumaradevi's soldiers.

"I'm sorry." Gabriel looked away before she answered.

"Sorry about..." Teresa turned as Gabriel cloaked himself in Wind Magic and thrust himself upward into the air.

The wind whipped around him as he rocketed skyward. Malignant Wind Magic began trying to arrest his assent, and he focused all his power on defeating it. He looked back as he soared westward, away from the battle behind him. He had more of a notion than a plan, but he knew that if he lured the Apollyons away, his friends, Teresa especially, might have a chance at escape. With the notebook destroyed, his value to the Apollyons became immeasurable.

As he stared back at the warring mages on the hillside beside the Great Wall of China, Gabriel saw something that made him realize his imprudence. While one of the Apollyons took to the sky in pursuit of Gabriel, two others dragged Teresa through the air with Wind Magic just as they had done moments before with the notebook.

Gabriel pulled upward in a steep climb, curving back toward his friends, where he had abandoned them. Abandoned Teresa. He saw her, flailing in the air as she tumbled toward the two Apollyons, her motion only slightly impeded by Ling's attempted use of Wind Magic to save her. His foolishness had left her unprotected. Foolish not simply because he loved her, but because she understood, as much as anyone, the nature of the Great Barrier of Probability and the potential ways it could be destroyed.

Gabriel completed his aerial arc and pointed himself back toward Teresa and the others, directly into the path of the Apollyon pursuing him. Gabriel thrust the Sword of Unmaking out in front of him and channeled all of his magical energy and willpower into becoming a living missile. He didn't bother mounting a magical attack toward the rapidly approaching Apollyon. He doubted the man had ever played chicken.

The Apollyon tried to use Wind Magic to halt Gabriel's flight, but to no avail. Gabriel's immense momentum voided any attempts to arrest his motion. He would not be stopped. Gabriel managed to erect a sphere of gravity around him as he collided with the Apollyon, sending the Dark Mage spinning earthward. As Gabriel rushed toward the ground, he saw the two Apollyons grasp hold of Teresa's arms.

A blinding white light suffused Gabriel's vision. A miniature star of incalculable intensity flashed into existence between the two Apollyons. Teresa had taken a page from the notebook's demise and turned herself into a massive human fireball, brighter than the sun.

The Apollyons near her fell back in agony, struggling to mount magical defenses that would keep their flesh from melting and their bones turning to ash. The blast wave and incredible brilliance of the ongoing explosion that was Teresa stunned everyone nearby, forcing them to the ground, where they raised their hands to shield their eyes.

Gabriel, too, raised his hand to protect his eyes. As the pain in his optic nerves subsided slightly, he noticed something more important than slowing his decent or attacking the Apollyons trying to capture Teresa — the space-time seal had vanished. Teresa's blast had stunned the Apollyons enough to offer them all hope at an escape.

In a dangerous gamble that Gabriel trusted would not prove deadly in its recklessness, he struck the ground, feet first, using Wind Magic to cushion the effects of his impact upon his own body, even as he amplified it upon the ground around him. A shockwave of air and soil rippled out around his feet, slamming everyone back to their knees, even as they attempted to recover from Teresa's blast of heat and light. Gabriel used this momentary distraction to his advantage, grasping every Dark Mage in sight with Wind Magic and throwing them into the air and into each other with a bone-cracking crash, a screaming mass of arms and legs, plummeting down into the tunnel Rajan and Ling had created minutes before.

Gabriel spared a second to use Wind and Earth Magic to seal the tunnel entrance before wrapping himself and Teresa and his friends in the comforting folds of Time Magic, carrying them into the darkness between every moment and away from the Great Wall of China

CHAPTER 4

"Because you're an idiot."

Teresa crossed her arms as her feet dodged a rain puddle in the dirt-packed street.

"I was trying to lead them away from you." His attention fixed on Teresa, Gabriel planted his foot firmly in the middle of the puddle. He grimaced and shook the water from his shoe as he raced to catch up with her.

"You ran off and left me behind — again." Teresa turned a corner around a large log building and into the central courtyard of Fort Aurelius.

"I finally do what the Council ordered me to do, to abandon everyone at the first sign of real danger to myself, and now everyone's upset." Gabriel sighed as he tried to keep up with Teresa's pace. He had surpassed her in height in the last year, but she still had long legs, and she seemed intent on walking as fast as possible.

"No one is mad at you except me. They all know you were trying to be a *hero*." Teresa frowned with her final word.

"I thought the Apollyons wanted *me*." Gabriel tried to keep his voice calm. This was the first time they had fought in months. As usual, their arguments revolved around Gabriel's tendency to try to protect Teresa from the danger of being near the Seventh True Mage.

"And how did that work out?" Teresa sneered in Gabriel's direction.

"Not at all like I planned." Gabriel couldn't restrain himself from sighing again.

"When are you going to realize that every time you try to run off and protect me, one of us nearly gets killed?" Teresa stopped in the street and stared at Gabriel. "We're safer together. Me and you. We need to watch each other's backs."

Gabriel tried to ignore the people passing through the courtyard even as he noticed them trying to disregard him and Teresa clearly arguing while standing in the middle of the lane. Everyone in the fort knew they were a couple. Probably every Grace Mage in the Continuum knew they were a couple. The Seventh True Mage and his girlfriend were the closest things to celebrities that most mages would ever see. As he tried to push the embarrassment from his mind, he wondered how long this public display of disaffection would take to rattle through the magically-twinned tea cups and mugs that helped keep the twelve Council forts in contact with each other.

"I thought it would keep you safe." Gabriel stared into Teresa's eyes.

"I'm not going to be safe." Teresa ran her fingers through her hair, brushing it back from her face. "The Apollyons know I helped you with the notebook. And they must know enough about me by now to guess that I have the entire thing in my head." She tapped the side of her skull for emphasis. "Now that the notebook is destroyed, we are the next best thing."

"Yeah, well..." Gabriel's face grew hot as he shifted his gaze down to his muddy feet. "That didn't occur to me at the time."

"Hmmpf."

Teresa's stare seemed to burn into his head, but by the time he had collected the courage to meet her eyes, her gaze rested elsewhere.

"Teresa..." Gabriel wasn't sure what thought might follow her name, but he understood he needed to say something.

"I should go." Teresa sighed as a couple holding hands passed along the street. "I promised I'd help Ling. We need to set up for the ceremony. I'll see you later."

"Okay." Gabriel watched Teresa as she turned and walked toward the front gate.

Gabriel stood in the middle of the street for several seconds as Teresa walked away, a light breeze pushing her hair up around her shoulders. It took him a moment to realize she had not kissed him. That could not be a good sign. They always took every opportunity to kiss each other. Greetings and departures were particularly important. Not kissing Gabriel could only mean that she was far angrier with him than she appeared. And she appeared thoroughly annoyed with his attempt to save her life by abandoning her. Which, he had to admit in hindsight, had not been one of his more dazzling notions. It had, in fact, been a nearly disastrous idea with potential consequences too painful to fully contemplate. His stomach soured, and a strange, uncomfortable sensation radiated throughout his body. As the heat of the early morning summer sun baked the back of his neck, he broke out in a damp sweat. He hated arguing with Teresa.

"Morning."

Gabriel's mind snapped back to the present moment and he had just enough time to nod a greeting to the mage walking by him in the courtyard. "Morning," he managed to say before the man had completely passed him.

Gabriel started walking, not sure where to go, but knowing he needed to stop standing around in public places, mooning after the girl he had just had an argument with. He assumed it looked ridiculous.

He hated looking ridiculous. Even more, he hated the fact that it seemed to happen more often the older he got. Particularly where Teresa was involved. She could probably come up with a mathematical equation to explain the inverse relationship of aging and ridiculousness. Then again, she might simply suggest that it was a natural side effect of being a teenage boy. She had made similar comments more than once. How she managed to avoid the problem as a teenage girl eluded Gabriel. He suspected she might imply that it was *because* she was a girl that she avoided that particular predicament.

Then again, maybe she felt ridiculous sometimes, and he never noticed because of how much he loved her. Or, and this thought nearly arrested his motion once more, maybe he never noticed when she felt ridiculous or insecure or inadequate because he didn't pay enough attention to her feelings. Maybe he stayed so wrapped up in his own thoughts and emotions that he never became fully aware of hers.

Gabriel forced his feet to plod ahead. Such thoughts were better contemplated in private than while walking through public spaces. He ambled through the heart of Fort Aurelius trying to think of something to keep his mind occupied rather than ruminating about his argument with Teresa. Surely she saw that he had her best interests at the heart of his actions, even if those actions put her in more danger. A pallid consolation, but the best he could offer.

As Gabriel passed a row of log cabins, which functioned as barracks and housing for the Grace Mages of the Fort, Teresa's words careened around his mind, knocking loose the thoughts he had tried to avoid since the team's return to the fort the previous night.

His best intentions were simply not good enough to keep Teresa safe. Luring the Apollyons away had seemed like the right choice at the time, but it nearly resulted in the death of Teresa and his friends. Maybe her words held more truth than he cared to admit. Maybe they were safer together. He knew better than anyone that time could not be turned back, not really. Now that Teresa held the contents and subsequent discoveries of the notebook in that photographic mind of hers, the Apollyons would be nearly as happy to capture her as Gabriel himself. Moreover, it would be almost as dangerous for the rest of the team to be around her as to be around him.

How could you keep the person you loved safe when being near you made them less safe, but being separated might be even more dangerous? This aspect of his life reminded him of the Zen koans Akikane often gave him to ponder, like some sinuous time paradox that resisted all attempts at logical unraveling.

Thoughts of Akikane brought some relief from his mental turmoil. With his return to the fort came the resumption of his training sessions with the elder True Mage. However, his lesson would not commence for another hour. He needed to find something to do until then. By chance, or subconscious inclination, he found himself standing outside a long, barn-like structure which served as the fort infirmary. He turned and stepped through a wide wooden door. At least in the infirmary he could do something that felt useful, even if it might have no discernible impact.

He forced himself to smile and wave at the attendant sitting behind a desk in the narrow foyer that led to the patient rooms down the hall. He didn't feel like smiling, but recognized what it would look like and the rumors that would erupt if the Seventh True Mage went around sulking. The attendant, one of the four Heart-Tree Mages who shared the daily rotation to staff the infirmary, waved back. He visited regularly enough to make his presence uneventful.

Gabriel's shoes clattered against the roughhewn wooded floorboards and echoed along the slat-walled hallway of the building. Like most of the structures in the fort, Earth and Wind Mages had constructed it entirely from trees felled in the nearby forest. No nails were used to connect beams and boards, only superior woodworking and a bit of magic when necessary. Back before he had begun the year-long journey to learn the Indus language and decode Elizabeth's notebook, Gabriel had helped build much of the fort, as well as the walls surrounding it. The loss of the notebook still stung his pride. As much as he wished for possession of the notebook again, he held an even greater desire that its author awaken from her coma to chide him for his carelessness.

Unfortunately, the dark curse of the Apollyon duplicates still clung to Elizabeth's mind and brain. While the Heart-Tree Mages kept her healthy with a blend of intravenous fluids and Magic, not even Nefferati's skill with healing had been able to affect the curse. Marcus and Sema still checked on her regularly to assess her status, but it had been largely accepted among the Grace Mages of the fort that she would not recover without some significant magical discovery.

As though materializing from his thoughts, Gabriel found Sema and Marcus seated beside the perpetually sleeping Elizabeth when he walked into her small room. They each held a hand on Elizabeth's forehead, fingers touching, their other hands clasped together. With their eyes closed and concentrations focused on Elizabeth, neither seemed aware of Gabriel's presence. He reached out with his magic-sense to follow their probing of Elizabeth's mind and body. He still had not found the time to learn the more subtle aspects of healing with magic. He simply spent too much time trying to learn how to defend himself to allow for more study of how to repair the damage he might potentially do.

Sema and Marcus blended their magic as they examined Elizabeth. This melding of magics still fascinated Gabriel. As a True Mage, he rarely needed to conjoin his magical power with other mages. Yet another thing he had not managed to find the time for.

"Gabriel?"

Gabriel looked up to see Sema hastily disengaging her fingers from Marcus's hand. The use of his magic-sense to follow their work must have finally alerted her to his presence. He actually found himself surprised she hadn't detected him earlier. She usually sensed his mental signature from a distance. Her concentration on Elizabeth must have been considerable.

"Gabriel?" Marcus opened his eyes at the sound of Sema's voice and blinked in surprise at Gabriel, frowning a bit as he released Sema's hand.

"I was walking past and thought I would stop in." Gabriel stepped closer to the bed, observing the flustered look on Sema's face and the pinkish tint to Marcus's cheeks. It wasn't until he reached the foot of the bed that it occurred to him why they might seem so disconcerted by his sudden arrival. While they did their best to hide it, from themselves as much as everyone else, it was the worst kept secret in the fort that Sema and Marcus were in love. Teresa had, of course, pointed it out to Gabriel, who had been doing his best to remain oblivious to the glances and whispers and soft laugher the two exchanged between bantering conversations. While it was not strictly necessary for two mages joining their magic to hold hands, it had not struck Gabriel as odd to find Sema and Marcus doing so until he saw the embarrassed looks on their faces when he stepped up to Elizabeth's bedside.

"So..." An uncomfortable heat rose to Gabriel's cheeks as he pointedly looked away from Sema and Marcus and stared intently at Elizabeth's slumbering face. "...Any change?"

"Unfortunately, no." Sema stood up, smoothing the wrinkles of her pale violet tunic.

"But she's no worse, either." Marcus stood as well, stepping sideways to put a respectable distance between himself and Sema.

"I just wanted to check on her. I'll leave you two..." Gabriel paused as he tried to figure out how to finish that statement. "...To continue."

"Oh, we're done." Sema patted the nonexistent wrinkles of her tunic once more.

"We were just..." Marcus thrust his hands in his pockets as he seemed to consider how to complete his sentence. "No Teresa this morning?"

Gabriel frowned and sighed, glancing down as he shuffled his feet. "No. She said she needed to help Ling."

"She'll come around," Marcus said, his voice reassuring.

"I'm sure she'll see that you thought you were doing the right thing," Sema added in a comforting tone.

"Even if you did nearly get us all killed." Marcus laughed and Gabriel's eyes snapped up from the floor. "It's a joke, lad. You did what you thought was right at the time."

"Sometimes what is right is not always evident." Sema shot a glance at Marcus. "Or easy to act upon."

"And sometimes you find what's right by listening to your heart." Marcus pulled his hands from his pockets and tightly clasped them together. "One thing you can say for Gabriel is that he has no trouble listening to his heart."

"One needs to listen to one's head as well as one's heart." Sema turned slightly toward Marcus.

"Life isn't always about strategies and tactics." Marcus shifted to face Sema. "Sometimes we need to worry about happiness."

"And every potential happiness must be weighed against the possible sorrows." Sema brushed a stray hair from her face.

"Sorrows are sometimes better lived and shared than avoided," Marcus said.

"I'm not suggesting that..." Sema began to say.

"Yes, that's all very good advice." Gabriel raised his voice as he interrupted. His face had become so hot listening to Sema and Marcus that rivulets of sweat tricked down through his hair. He wiped his forehead with the back of his hand. "I'll be sure to take that all into consideration the next time I consider abandoning everyone to the Apollyons."

"Yes, well..." Marcus licked his lips and paused.

"We're glad we could be..." Sema blinked as she steadied her breathing. "...Of assistance."

"We should let you get on with your visit." Marcus began to back away toward the door.

"Yes," Sema said, following Marcus out of the room. "We'll see you later."

Gabriel opened his mouth to say something in reply, but Sema and Marcus departed before he could form any words that didn't seem like they would exacerbate the cloud of embarrassment permeating the room.

Alone with Elizabeth, he sighed, slung the sheathed Sword of Unmaking from his shoulder, and sat down in the chair next to her bed. He leaned the sword against the bedpost. It never left his side. An attack might happen at any time.

Out of habit more than hope, he opened his mind to his magic-sense and embraced the imprints of the silver pocket watch. He began to scan Elizabeth's mind and brain with Heart-Tree and Soul Magic. He did not expect to find anything that far more skilled mages such as Sema, Marcus, and Nefferati had not. Elizabeth would be just as she had been the last time he had visited.

It had been nearly three weeks since he last sat by her bedside and stared at her unmoving features. In the days since, he and the Chimera team had traveled through time to hunt down the clues from Elizabeth's notebook and unravel the mysteries she had hinted at in her cryptic, coded passages. Enigmas like the anchor points.

Gabriel released the imprints and leaned back in the chair, sighing once more as he let his magic-sense fade. He found the feelings in his heart slowly tumbling forth as words spoken aloud.

"I wish you could help us. Help me. I could use your advice. The council of the Council Woman. I feel things...coalescing. I can sense something close. It feels like it did back when I had dreams about the future. Back before all this started. It feels like something inevitable is about to happen. Like the tremors before a volcano erupts, or the change in air pressure before a storm.

"But I don't know what it is. Is it the Apollyons? The Great Barrier of Probability? This is what I've been training for, but I don't think I'm ready. I don't know if I want to be ready. I'm afraid. Afraid I'll make a mistake. A mistake that kills Teresa. A mistake that kills someone else I care about. A mistake that lets the Apollyons win. Or a mistake that destroys the Primary Continuum.

"Everyone has advice, but I don't know if they are right or wrong. It's not like anyone can give me advice on something that's never happened before. Or on how to be someone who has never existed. I feel like one of those explorers who set out to sail the ocean without knowing where they were headed or what they might find. Maybe what I need is a compass. I suppose that's what Akikane and Ohin and Nefferati and everyone else are trying to give me with all their advice and training. An internal compass. Maybe I need to find true north.

"Maybe Teresa can be my true north."

Gabriel sat, watching the gentle rise and fall of Elizabeth's chest as she dreamed whatever deep and inescapable dream that occupied her slumber. He let his mind wander back through the thoughts he had uttered aloud, circling through the probabilities and potentialities of his future, trying to bring the unfocused, nameless sentiments into some kind of clarity.

After half an hour, he had obtained no more insight than when he sat down. With a deep sigh, he resigned himself to the fact that he would need to wait for whatever the future held to be revealed before he decided how to react to it.

He stood up and leaned over the bed, resting his lips briefly on Elizabeth's forehead.

"Thank you for listening."

Gabriel grabbed the Sword of Unmaking and left the infirmary. He walked to the Council Hall, a medium-sized log building at the western end of the fort. The Council Hall acted as a meeting place for Council-related governing business, as well as the place where Akikane conducted work and trained his students. Akikane and Nefferati had taken joint leadership positions on the Council. As a precaution against a catastrophic attack, like the one that had destroyed the Council's Windsor Castle, Nefferati, Akikane, and all of the surviving council members each took responsibility for governing one of the twelve forts. As the largest of the outposts, Fort Aurelius acted as the de facto seat of power for the Council, and most of the meetings were held in the Council Hall.

Between missions, Gabriel and Akikane resumed their daily lessons — training in meditation, mastering the sword, and the use of multiple magics. Gabriel stepped into the Council Hall and found it empty. Akikane usually cleared the room for training, but tables and chairs were still scattered, as though a meeting had been interrupted.

Gabriel suspected where Akikane would be. Whenever his mentor had in mind a more dangerous magic for the lesson plan, he and Gabriel retreated to a field far outside the fortress walls to guarantee they would not accidentally destroy anything or injure anyone.

Gabriel grasped the imprints of the sword across his back and twisted the fabric of space-time slightly, transporting himself to the middle of the familiar meadow, several hundred yards from the fort.

He found Akikane sitting in the tall grass of the field, meditating. As Akikane opened his eyes and stood up, Gabriel released the imprints of the sword and walked toward his mentor.

"Good, good." Akikane smiled as he strode through the knee-high vegetation. "You are on time."

"I'm not always late." Gabriel joined Akikane in a clearing where the grass had been matted down in a large circle.

"No, no," Akikane said. "Only when you are arguing with Teresa."

"Does the whole fort know we're fighting?" Gabriel unslung the Sword of Unmaking from his back and placed it in the grass beside two wooden boken practice swords.

"Perhaps, perhaps," Akikane said, standing in the center of the circle. "All things travel quickly in a small space, especially gossip."

Gabriel sighed and removed the pouch of concatenate crystals from his waist, placing it beside the Sword of Unmaking. He frowned at his sigh, realizing how often he seemed to be sighing lately. He needed to find a less annoying expression of his frustration. Sighing in front of Akikane only made him feel ridiculous again.

"What's the lesson today?" Gabriel smiled, trying to force himself into a better mood as he joined Akikane in the center of the clearing. As he did so, he discerned something. It was not that he saw or heard anything to attract his attention, but he perceived his body leaning forward ever so slightly, as though edging away from something unseen.

"Good question, good question." Akikane's smile seemed both radiant and mischievous. "Today I have a surprise for you."

Gabriel had learned to appreciate Akikane's surprises, especially when his mentor's smile seemed like it might take flight from his face and burst into the sky in an attempt to replace the sun. His magic-sense tingled slightly. Following some instinct too swift for conscious thought, he dropped to the ground and rolled away, reaching out his hand as he grasped the imprints of the pocket watch still in his pants. As he leapt to his feet, one of the wooden boken swords flew to his fingers in a cradle of Wind Magic. He brought the edge of the sword up before his head as he spun around, the crack of wood against wood ringing through the still air of the clearing, the impact vibrating down through his arm.

Gabriel jumped back, grasping the sword handle with both hands and turning slightly to discern the location of his invisible attacker. His magic-sense prickled again as the air shimmered to reveal Nefferati standing before him, a wooden sword in one hand and a steely glint in her eyes.

"You're right." Nefferati glanced briefly at Akikane. "He is getting good."

"Hello?" Gabriel wasn't sure what to say as a greeting to Nefferati after her unexpected attack. He hadn't seen the ancient True Mage since before he had left to find the anchor points. Now she had appeared from behind an invisible shield of Wind Magic to swing a wooden sword at his head.

"Akikane and I have been speaking." Nefferati turned her full attention to Gabriel. "We may find ourselves in total agreement for the first time in decades."

"That's good. I suppose." Gabriel did not take his eyes from Nefferati's sword.

"Before we discuss it with you, I wanted to see how your training has been progressing." Nefferati smiled and lowered her sword. "It seems to be going well, indeed."

"Thank you." Gabriel returned Nefferati's smile and let his sword fall to his side. Only as the wooded blade reached the nadir of its downward arc did he realize his mistake.

Nefferati's blade whipped out toward Gabriel's head. He stumbled backward, raising his sword and trying to regain his feet to fend off her next attack. It came swiftly after the first, a thrust toward his stomach. Gabriel parried the strike and each that followed. Nefferati held her sword in one hand, her body turned slightly sideways like a fencer. Gabriel found himself surprised at how much force her arm put behind each blow and how quickly she delivered them.

Nefferati jumped through space once, attacked, jumped again, her blade whirling around Gabriel, striking at him from every angle. He had upended a wasp's nest, Nefferati's sword a massive stinger seeking to pierce his flesh. He repelled her attacks, holding his ground and using his Time Magic not to bend space-time and leap away, but instead turn instantly in one spot as he deflected the impacts of her blade.

Nefferati's Wind Magic pressed suddenly against his chest, blasting him across the clearing toward a clump of nearby trees. Gabriel warped space-time around himself just before striking a tree trunk, appearing a moment later behind Nefferati, the momentum of her magical push still affecting his body as he spun around and swung his sword toward her side. He realized as he followed the trajectory of the blade that this would be his first offensive move since Nefferati had engaged him. So far, he had only defended against her attacks. Now she would need to defend against his. She turned at the last second, leaning away from his blade and knocking him back with another gravity-filled burst of Wind Magic.

Gabriel hit the ground, letting himself roll into the high grass and out of sight before jumping through space to hang upside down in the air above Nefferati and attack her from overhead. She jumped through space as Gabriel's blade swung through the air where her head had been.

As Nefferati appeared ten feet away, Gabriel reached out with Earth Magic, making the ground beneath her explode. As she again jumped through space, Gabriel began his own similar short journey, straining his space-time sense to intuit the end point of her transit. As his space-time sense flared, he split his Time Magic to warp space in two distinct directions at once. He appeared at the same time in the same place as Nefferati, his sword extended, the tip of the wooden blade hovering just beneath her chin.

"Hmmm." Nefferati frowned. "I didn't sense that movement."

"I sent my shoes over there as a distraction." Gabriel nodded to where his shoes sat in the dry grass.

Nefferati looked down a Gabriel's bare feet and laughed. "You're getting to be as devious as our smiling friend. However, I think he has another lesson for you."

The grass beneath Gabriel's feet burst into flame. He yelped and hopped back just in time to dodge a wooden sword blade heading toward his arm. Gabriel had no time to reflect upon the minor pain flaring across the soles of his feet. The multiple sword strikes from both Akikane and Nefferati demanded the entirety of his attention.

He tried leaping through space to escape the onslaught of their blades, but as he did so, a space-time seal locked in place around him. Ducking a swing from Nefferati and parrying a thrust from Akikane, Gabriel used Wind Magic to launch himself into the air. As he rose to the level of the treetops, the combined Wind Magic of his two instructors sought to pull him back to the ground.

As his blistered feet touched the matted grass of the clearing, Akikane and Nefferati appeared on either side of him, pressing their joint attack. Gabriel formed a mental sword of Fire and Wind Magic, wielding it with his left hand to keep Nefferati at bay while he fended off Akikane's blindingly fast strikes with the wooden sword in his right hand. It took only seconds for a wooden blade to find his ribs. A moment later, another blow caught his right arm, the boken falling to the ground. A blow struck his leg before another punched into his stomach. He let the magical sword of fire evaporate and created a shield of Wind Magic around himself to repel any more attacks.

Akikane and Nefferati both leveled their swords at Gabriel. He clutched at his stomach, wheezing as he fought to catch his breath.

"Good, good." Akikane's brilliant grin almost made Gabriel forget the pain of his burnt feet, aching arm, and tender stomach. He didn't spend any time worrying about his injuries. A practice session with magical combat inevitably led to burns and bruises, and often much worse, all of which could be healed with the application of Heart-Tree Magic. Besides, the damage he had suffered in Kumaradevi's training arena made everything thereafter seem like a mild inconvenience.

"What lesson have you learned today?" Akikane lowered his sword and Nefferati followed suit.

"Don't take my shoes off in a fight." Gabriel straightened up and stretched his arm as he used Heart-Tree Magic to heal his blistering feet. He sighed as the pain dissipated.

"Besides the obvious." Nefferati narrowed her eyes at Gabriel.

"That I need much more practice against two opponents," Gabriel replied.

"Less obvious, less obvious," Akikane said.

Gabriel thought about this a moment. The lesson wasn't about what it appeared. Not with Nefferati joining in. What had she said before she had attacked? That she thought she might agree with Akikane. What would they have been in disagreement about?

"That two skilled opponents can outflank and force a third to surrender." Gabriel recognized this lesson related to the war at large and not to his own personal combat training.

"Much better." Nefferati smiled and leaned on the wooden sword like a cane.

"Are you sure that's such a good idea?" Gabriel frowned as he tried to tease out the implications and possibilities of what Nefferati and Akikane seemed to be suggesting. "Will the Council even agree to something like that?"

"Possibly not, possibly not." Akikane's smile faltered for a moment. "Time will tell, as they say."

"So who are you thinking we try to ally ourselves with, and who are we going to try and outflank?"

"We are not in the position of having too many choices, are we?" Nefferati looked as though she just had eaten something sour that might come up again at any moment. "We are essentially in a state of truce with Vicaquirao. He seems to be as interested as we are in keeping the Great Barrier of Probability intact. We must maintain the Great Barrier at all costs, which means that defeating the Apollyon duplicates must be our foremost objective. That leaves us only one person to ally ourselves with."

"Yes, yes." Akikane's smile had completely faded.

"Kumaradevi." Gabriel found that speaking her name left a bitter taste in his mouth.

"If we can convince her that saving the Great Barrier is in her best interests, she might agree to a temporary alliance to destroy the Apollyons." Nefferati's voice sounded confident, but the look on her face spoke of deep uncertainty.

"What will she want in return for her help?" Gabriel found a list of possibilities suddenly flooding his mind — himself, Nefferati, and Elizabeth appearing at the top.

"Who knows, who knows," Akikane said.

"We're not going to reward her for her help like some mercenary," Nefferati said. "We need to appeal to her sense of self-importance as much as her sense of self-preservation. We need to present the alliance as something we both require and will both benefit from. Then we must confess that we have no hope of success without her and her army."

"Do you believe that?" Gabriel's stomach tightened at Nefferati's suggestion.

"No, I don't." Nefferati sighed. "But our odds are not great alone. However, if we can weaken her forces while destroying the Apollyons, that will put us in a better position for the future of the war and preserving the Great Barrier."

"Indeed, indeed," Akikane said. "And Kumaradevi will surely know the same to be true of our forces at the end of such an alliance."

"It is a risk." Nefferati looked up at the clouds above. "No one is more loath to contemplate a truce and partnership with Kumaradevi than I am. I spent years in a state of hell while captive to that woman. But this is not about my desires, or even hers. This is about preserving the Great Barrier of Probability. About saving the Primary Continuum from an unknown and unknowable catastrophe."

"Yes, yes." Akikane allowed his gaze to follow Nefferati's upward. "And it can only be a matter of time before the Apollyons discover how to destroy the Barrier. They attacked you at an anchor point. It will not take them long to realize what the anchor points imply and to begin seeking them out."

Gabriel said nothing. He waited for Akikane and Nefferati to lower their eyes from the sky and settle on him. He didn't like this idea, but he had to admit that it made a dark and mad kind of sense. Even if they knew how and where to attack the Apollyons, there were too few Grace Mages left after the battles at Windsor Castle to mount a successful assault. Even mustering every Grace Mage alive, they would still not likely manage to prevail in a fight against the Apollyons. He hated the plan, but saw its strategic wisdom. The question wasn't whether they should attempt this alliance. A better question lurked behind Nefferati and Akikane's proposal.

"Why tell me?" Gabriel looked between the faces of his two mentors, seeing for the first time how old they looked. They had both lived for centuries, but Gabriel had never before sensed their extreme age when in their presence. Now they seemed not merely old, but tired as well.

"For the same reason we always come to you." Nefferati reached out and placed her hand upon Gabriel's shoulder. "We need your help."

CHAPTER 5

"Help?" Gabriel blinked at the thought. "How can I help?"

"By being you," Nefferati said.

"Just so, just so." Akikane smiled broadly again.

"The Council is unlikely to be swayed by the logic of our suggestion," Nefferati said. "They have been at war with Kumaradevi far too long to see her as a potential ally, if even for a short time."

"Too long, too long," Akikane said. "They will not willingly support this plan."

"They have to listen to the two of you," Gabriel said. "You agree on this. That has to mean something."

"Less than you would think," Nefferati said.

"Much less, much less," Akikane said. "But they will listen to you."

"Why would they listen to me?" Gabriel asked. "I'm a fifteen-year-old kid."

"True, true," Akikane said. "But you are also the Seventh True Mage."

"And you can threaten them," Nefferati said.

"Threaten them?" Gabriel shook his head, confused by the idea. "Threaten them with what?"

"With your absence," Nefferati said. "They all believe you are the key to winning this war. You can threaten to leave and have nothing to do with it."

"Like you did?" Gabriel saw Nefferati's lips curl downward ever so slightly.

"Not exactly, not exactly," Akikane said.

"I left because I could not accept what needed to be done to win the war," Nefferati said. "I needed to learn to reconcile being a warrior with being a human being."

"Just so, just so," Akikane placed his hand on Nefferati's arm as he turned to Gabriel. "A lesson we must each embrace."

"What if I threaten to leave and they call my bluff?" Gabriel bit his lip, wondering how he always ended up at the center of the war.

"Simple." Nefferati laughed. "Don't bluff."

"What do you mean?" Gabriel shifted his gaze between his two mentors.

"Run away, run away." Akikane joined Nefferati's laughter.

"I can't leave the war." Gabriel felt oddly dizzy at the thought, as much because he desired to abandon the war as because he believed it to be impossible without abandoning those he loved. "Can I?"

"You can, you can," Akikane said. "At least as far as the Council is concerned."

"What about the Great Barrier, and the Apollyons and…everything else?" Gabriel's dizziness increased as he considered the idea of leaving the war and all its concerns and dangers.

"You don't have to leave the battlefield simply because you disobey orders from the general." Nefferati stared hard at Gabriel. "Particularly if the general's orders are likely to lose the battle."

"So I would still fight the war, but on my own?" The tension within him relaxed and he marveled at how uncomfortable the idea of deserting the war made him. The very notion seemed wrong. He could no more allow the Apollyons to destroy the Great Barrier of Probability than he could have ignored the kids drowning in the bus at the bottom of the river that fateful day.

"Not alone, not alone." Akikane glanced at Nefferati as though suddenly unsure of himself. That glance worried Gabriel more than anything in the conversation so far. "Others would follow you. Gladly. Myself, Nefferati, your team."

"I doubt there'd be more than a handful of Grace Mages throughout the forts who wouldn't follow you." Nefferati looked back to Fort Aurelius in the distance as she spoke. "Men and women in battle want a leader. Not merely the head of a council. They have been waiting for a leader, a true leader, for years and years. They have been waiting for the Seventh True Mage to lead them to victory."

"I'm a teenager, not a battle commander." Gabriel saw where this idea would lead and didn't like the destination.

"Not so, not so." Akikane's eyes narrowed in emphasis of his words. "You are nearly sixteen. A man in many times and cultures. And men your age have led whole nations."

"Joan of Arc was only a little older at the Siege of Orleans," Nefferati said.

"She ended up burnt at a stake." Gabriel swallowed at the analogy.

"Yes, yes." Akikane shook his head at Nefferati. "Not a good comparison."

"Not the way it ended, no," Nefferati agreed. "But the way her story began is similar. Prophesies of a woman warrior to lead the French people to victory. Nearly every Grace Mage sees the Prophecy of the Seventh True Mage in the same way."

Gabriel sighed, shaking his head in annoyance for having done so. He looked down at the grass as he considered what Nefferati and Akikane suggested. After a moment, he looked up to find them still staring at him.

"You want me to threaten the Council into following this plan to ally with Kumaradevi in order to defeat the Apollyons and save the Great Barrier, and if they don't agree, you want me to stage a coup."

"No, no," Akikane looked aghast at Gabriel's words. "If the Council will not agree to this plan, we are not suggesting that you seize power, rather that you leave and ask others to follow you."

"And they will follow you." Nefferati clapped Gabriel on the shoulder. "We all will."

Gabriel's mind reeled with a strange absence of cognition. He could not seem to make the words tumbling through his consciousness coalesce into concrete notions. He knew why. And that frightened him.

Akikane and Nefferati's suggestion didn't merely disturb him into interior silence. Their words reconfirmed something. Something he had been avoiding. He was the Seventh True Mage. He would need to lead this war at some point. He recognized this the same way he knew he loved Teresa. Every molecule in his body vibrated with that truth. His destiny had begun to catch up with him. He might be able to avoid it, might be able to convince the Council to follow the plan to join forces with Kumaradevi against the Apollyons, but even if he did, it would only postpone the inevitable moment when he would need to assume the mantle of leadership.

He sighed again, enjoying for once the sound of the air escaping his lips. He had infinite choices available to him as the Seventh True Mage, but the very nature of who he was as a person left many of them so unpalatable as to be impossible. He could not turn away from his duty, even if fate assigned him the task rather than choosing it of his own free will. The concept of duty reminded him of his conversations with Aurelius. His friend, lost now to the future beyond the Great Barrier of Probability, would have understood Gabriel's predicament and his decisions completely. He may not, however, have understood the convulsive fit of laughter that suddenly gripped Gabriel.

"I thought you might swear, but I didn't expect you to laugh at us." Nefferati furrowed her brow at Gabriel.

"Sorry." Gabriel wiped tears from his eyes. "It's easier to accept my fate with laughter than with curses."

"Good, good." Akikane laughed, as well. "Then you agree."

"I don't really have any choice." Gabriel took a deep breath as the last of his laughter faded away.

"I wish I had come to that realization as quickly." Nefferati smiled.

"When do we approach the Council?" Gabriel asked.

"Tomorrow, tomorrow," Akikane said.

"After the wedding," Nefferati added, glancing at the sun in the sky. "Which we should get ready for. Especially you." She turned to Akikane.

"Yes, yes," Akikane said, his eyes alive with amusement. "A wedding is not official without the officiant."

Gabriel gathered up the Sword of Unmaking and practice swords before Akikane teleported the three of them back to the confines of Fort Aurelius. As they headed their separate ways to clean up and dress for the impending nuptials, Nefferati caught Gabriel by the arm.

"Say nothing to anyone about what we spoke of today. Not even Ohin."

Gabriel reflected on that statement for a moment. He hated keeping secrets. He wasn't very good at it. Especially keeping them from Teresa. However, considering the magnitude of Akikane and Nefferati's proposal, it might be best to keep it between the three of them for the time being.

"Don't worry. I'll keep my mouth shut." Gabriel silently hoped the Council would give them no reason to act upon the intentions implied by their discussion.

"Good, good." Akikane nodded to Gabriel, his face once again serious. "We would not want rumors of a conspiracy to begin floating through the air like butterflies in search of nectar."

"Flower metaphors. Hmff." Nefferati shook her head at Akikane and headed toward her quarters. Akikane smiled after her and patted Gabriel on the back before walking to his own room.

An hour later, Gabriel, most of the residents of the fort, and small contingents from the eleven other outposts, gathered in the main square to await the arrival of the bride and groom. Gabriel walked among the celebrants looking for familiar faces, his recently showered hair still damp against his scalp. He wore a dark blue suit with a red tie, or at least he appeared to. Nearly everyone present had used their concealment amulet to alter their appearances in some way, most opting for a manner of traditional clothing from their own cultural histories.

Gabriel caught sight of Ohin in a white Ethiopian gabbi, a long cloth wrapped around his shoulders and torso. He stood next to Paramata, the two of them speaking quietly, their heads drawn together to better hear over the noise of the crowd. Paramata wore a magnificent embroidered dress of red and gold in the Indonesian style of her ancestors.

Gabriel hesitated. Ohin and Paramata looked to be enjoying one another's company, and he wasn't certain if he should insert himself into their conversation. Over the past year, Ohin had managed to find fewer and fewer excuses to avoid Paramata's affections, and her seeds of persistence finally seemed to be baring fruit. Gabriel frequently found the two in each other's company.

He turned his attention from Ohin and Paramata to scan the crowd again, looking for his teammates. One in particular. He caught sight of Sema and Marcus standing side by side near the front of the crowd. He hesitated again. He had already spent too many awkward moments with them that day. He scanned the faces around him once more, tempted to use Wind Magic to levitate above the mass of people in the square to gain a better vantage point. Unfortunately, such flashy displays of magic were frowned upon in the Grace Mage community. Besides, it would probably remind him too much of his last sight of Windsor Castle, hovering above the grounds as his magic turned it to ash.

Two hues of brilliant blue, one cobalt and one azure, captured his eye. Ling and Rajan stood next to one another, Ling in a long, sky-blue Chinese dress with a high-embroidered collar and Rajan in a dark blue Indian kurta. At last. Two people who wouldn't mind being interrupted. Not that Ling and Rajan didn't enjoy one another's company, but Gabriel could not imagine a spark of romance ever igniting between them. Ling seemed to spend most of her free time trying to set Rajan up with one lovely young Grace Mage woman after another. Then again, Gabriel had been clueless about Sema and Marcus for the longest time. Not as clueless as *they* often appeared to be, but surprised, nonetheless.

He nudged his way through the ever-compressing crowd to stand beside Rajan.

"Ah good, you got the memo about dressing in blue." Rajan looked at Gabriel's cerulean-colored suit and laughed.

"I can change the color if you like," Gabriel said, only half-serious.

"No, I always thought we should have team colors," Rajan replied.

"What happened to your hair?" Ling stared at Gabriel's head.

"It's wet." Gabriel ran a hand through his hair and found it still quite moist.

"You look like a larder," Ling said.

Gabriel frowned for a moment. "You mean a greaser."

"Whatever," Ling said as Rajan laughed. "What's the point of being able to use Fire Magic if you don't dry your hair?"

Ling had a point. He could have used magic to dry his hair, but it was something Teresa had taken to doing for him, and he for her. A gesture of intimacy.

"I'd dry it if I were you," Rajan said. "Before Teresa shows up."

"You wouldn't want to look like a Roman candle," Ling added. "Or has she forgiven you already?"

Familiar fingers entwined with Gabriel's as Teresa's voice filled his ears.

"Of course I've forgiven him. I can't be mad at him too long. It's like being mad at an oak tree. It can't help being dense and inflexible."

"What?" Gabriel wasn't entirely certain he liked being forgiven for doing what he had thought to be right while being compared to an unthinking mass of wood.

"*Forgiveness is the final form of love*," Rajan said to Teresa and Gabriel's blank stares. "Reinhold Niebuhr," he added as a hush fell over the wedding congregants.

"Wise words for a single man to quote," Ling teased. Rajan pointedly ignored her and she laughed out loud.

"I didn't realize you had forgiven me," Gabriel whispered to Teresa as he watched Akikane step before the crowd.

"Neither did I until I walked up beside you." Teresa squeezed his hand tightly as the bride and groom joined Akikane at the edge of the square. "Don't make me regret it."

"I won't." Gabriel looked into Teresa's eyes and then kissed her. As he closed his eyes for the kiss, Teresa embraced the imprints of her talisman bracelet and his scalp grew warm. She ran her fingers through his thick, dark hair.

"Better not." Teresa stared into his eyes and Gabriel felt as though he had taken some oath without quite reciting the words.

"Quiet, quiet." Akikane's voice boomed from the head of the crowd. "We gather here this day to unite two people in love and life."

Gabriel turned his attention from Teresa to the wedding, watching it unfold as the tension in his back and stomach gradually faded away. All the discomfort carried from his argument with Teresa seemed to evaporate. He sighed and smiled at himself, knowing it to be an expression of contentment rather than exasperation.

The bride and groom, Helga and Jin, seemed blissful and nervous at the same time. They held hands and stared into each other's beatific faces as Akikane guided them through the ceremony. Leah and Liam stood to either side of them, smiling so widely it seemed they might burst from happiness as they craned their necks back to look up at the adults.

Helga and Jin, both Earth Mages, had fallen in love while taking shifts together caring for the youngest orphans from the destruction of the castle. As their hearts had opened to embrace each other, so too had they expanded to encompass Leah and Liam. The ceremony Akikane led would not merely bind them together as wife and husband, but also make official their decision to adopt the two children into their lives.

Gabriel's throat tightened and his eyes misted as he watched Leah and Liam. He still felt a pang of guilt now and then when he saw them, knowing he had promised, yet failed, to save their parents from the Dark Mages who had attacked the castle. They had never blamed him, though. For weeks afterward, the two children had refused to be separated from Gabriel and Teresa. Even Sema and Marcus had been unable to console them. It took Helga and Jin to make the two orphans feel safe again. And loved.

Gabriel reached up and wiped a tear from his eye.

"That's why I forgave you." Teresa's voice drew his eyes to hers, where he found similar tears. "You can't help being you."

"Sorry."

"Just try to be a little less you when it comes to me."

"I may need better instructions than that."

"I'll put them in writing for you."

"That would be best. As long as they're not encoded in ancient Indus, I might have a shot at figuring them out."

Teresa laughed and then turned back to enjoy the conclusion of the ceremony.

Minutes later, Helga and Jin kissed and embraced, reaching down to pull Leah and Liam up into their arms and into their first hugs as an official family. Gabriel kissed Teresa again as they joined the receiving line, giving their best wishes to Helga and Jin before hugging and tickling and teasing Leah and Liam while the children giggled.

"We're so happy for you." Teresa adjusted Leah's flyaway red mane.

"Yes." Gabriel smoothed the wrinkles of Liam's small tunic.

"We're happy, too." Leah beamed with excitement.

"We have a new mommy and daddy." Liam glanced at Helga and Jin before turning back to Teresa and Gabriel. "And you can be our new aunt and uncle."

"That's exactly what we'll be." Gabriel hugged Liam again.

"You'll be careful, won't you?" Leah seemed suddenly concerned. "You're always on missions."

"And missions are dangerous," Liam added with a slight pout.

"We'll take care of each other." Gabriel smiled to reassure the children's fears. They'd lost enough people in their lives during the last year.

"We'll stick together and guard each other's backs." Teresa grinned warmly and threw her arm around Gabriel.

"Promise?" Liam asked.

"Promise," Gabriel and Teresa said together.

"Good," Leah said, her face brightening again.

As Teresa and Gabriel wandered away to enjoy the post-wedding meal set up on rows of long tables at the north side of the square, she turned to him.

"I'm going to hold you to that promise."

"Oh, I know." Gabriel stifled a sigh and replaced it with a grin as he tightened his grip on Teresa's hand.

Sometime after sunset, the two of them sat with the rest of the team at a table littered with the remnants of a Spartan, but varied and delicious, meal. Nearby, a trio of musician mages played a lively Cuban contradanza on violin, oboe, and sitar as couples danced around them in a clearing between the tables. To the surprise of Gabriel and the rest of the Chimera team, Paramata had joined them for the duration of the meal, only recently having excused herself to speak with a fellow member of her own team. Ohin seemed to smile more times during the course of the meal than he had in the past month. With Paramata's departure from the table, the seriousness of Ohin's natural disposition reasserted itself and the conversation returned to familiar ground.

"But how far back can they go if there are only a hundred and eight of them?" Marcus took a sip from his glass. He frowned reflexively, as he had every time that evening when taking a drink from the glass filled with cider rather than his customary wine.

"In her notebook, Elizabeth said that she thought they might go back as far as the birth of the planet." Gabriel played with his fork, poking at a piece of cake that had somehow escaped his voracious consumption during the meal.

"Then there must be more than a hundred and a handful." Ling leaned back in her chair, stretching her long legs under the table.

"I think they may be spaced geometrically." Teresa placed her elbows on the table and her chin in her hands as she ruminated out loud. "There may be a pattern to their placement. Possibly getting farther apart as they go back in time. If we can find enough of them, I might be able to work out an equation that will tell us when and where to look for the whole string of them."

"How many would we need to find for you to come up with this equation?" Ohin stroked his chin as he peered through the candlelight illuminating the table.

"I don't know," Teresa said. "Maybe ten. Maybe twenty. The more data points I have the more accurately I can define the constraints of the equation."

"Even if we know where all the anchor points are, it still doesn't explain how we can save the Barrier." Rajan stared at the book on the table beside him as though its cover might somehow provide the answers. Only Rajan would bring a book to a wedding party. "If it took Grace and Malignant magic to create, it might require both magics save it."

"Rajan has a point." Sema folded her hands in her lap. "If the Apollyons find the anchor points and start attacking them, we have no means to repair them."

"We have Gabriel." Marcus looked across the table to Gabriel.

"One mage who can use tainted imprints may not be enough," Ling said.

"Assuming we can figure out how to repair an anchor point in the first place." Gabriel realized now what he suspected to be the real intent behind Akikane and Nefferati's plan to ally with Kumaradevi. They would need a small army of Malignancy Mages to help repair the anchor points from an attack by the Apollyons. Another notion occurred to him, as well.

"There's always Vicaquirao."

"I'd sooner trust a rabid dog to guard me in my sleep," Marcus said with a snort of derision.

"He's been helpful in the past," Gabriel countered. "And he does seem to want the Great Barrier of Probability to remain intact."

"Simply because our goals may coincide on a few points of mutual security does not mean we can trust him on the whole." Ohin sighed. "Vicaquirao's motives are his own and as difficult to predict as the weather."

"Gabriel may be right," Teresa said. "We don't have to trust Vicaquirao to use him."

"More likely it would be he who was using us," Rajan said.

Unfortunately, Gabriel had to agree with this assessment. Vicaquirao might have helped them in the past, but that did not mean they could entrust the future of the Primary Continuum to him. But wasn't that, in part, what Akikane and Nefferati were suggesting to do in an alliance with Kumaradevi? Between the two, Gabriel knew which one he would place more faith in. But that faith would be a slender bulwark against an army of doubled Apollyons.

"We're assuming it requires only one form of magic to destroy an anchor point." Neither Ohin's voice nor tone reflected the optimism of his statement.

"The Apollyons could always capture Grace Time Mages and use Soul Magic to control their minds." Sema's face tightened with her words.

"So the real question is, how do we stop the Apollyons before they have a chance to find the anchor points?" Teresa said.

"And how quickly can we do so?" Rajan said. "They must have enough copies already. They can only be waiting because they don't know how to destroy the Barrier yet."

"And hopefully they will not have gained any clues from their last attack near the Great Wall of China," Ling said.

"Hopefully," Ohin said. He didn't sound hopeful.

A silence fell over the table, each person contemplating the possibilities and hazards that confronted them. Gabriel wished he could say something about Akikane and Nefferati's plan. There seemed to be no good options available. Embracing, even at arm's length, a viper like Kumaradevi could lead as easily to a poisoned bite as to the successful defeat of the Apollyons. And the embrace of Vicaquirao as an ally seemed even more unpredictable. Kumaradevi wanted power, and the more she had, the more she wanted. Vicaquirao had said that he wanted to be left alone, but his interference with Gabriel's life on repeated occasions seemed to reveal other desires. However, he had also saved Gabriel's life more than once. It would be hard to imagine Kumaradevi doing the same.

Gabriel slouched in his chair, his hand absentmindedly resting on Teresa's knee as his mind wandered from one woebegone thought to the next. Nearly a year after the destruction of their Windsor Castle, they still had no real plan for defeating the Apollyons. Akikane and Nefferati's suggestion of an alliance with Kumaradevi provided the muscle that might be needed to stop the Apollyons, but not the strategy. The Council didn't know where the Dark Mages were, and had been unable to track any of them down. The attack by the Apollyons near the Great Wall of China had been their first encounter with them since the attack at the house in Maine at the edge of the Great Barrier.

Remembering that house brought Aurelius to mind, and Gabriel wondered if the former Roman Emperor would have had any words of guidance for him and the Council in how to prosecute this particular battle in the War of Time and Magic. The only real strategy Gabriel could envision would be luring the Apollyons into a trap. However, the bait for such a trap would need to be sufficiently tempting to entice even a handful of the Apollyons out into the open. And he knew what that bait would need to be — The Seventh True Mage. However, given his promise to Teresa only moments ago, he didn't see how he could put himself forward as bait for an ambush when Teresa would want to be at his side.

As though sensing the direction of the thoughts ricocheting through his mind, Teresa placed her hand upon his, where it rested on her knee. Her touch brought him back from his mental meanderings and to the silence still suffusing the table. Gabriel noticed Ling staring at Rajan as he gazed again at the cover of the book sitting next to his glass. Gabriel could just make out the words on the spine of the book in the flickering candlelight: Stendhal — *De L'Amour*.

"You should spend less time with that book and more time dancing with Imelda." Ling gestured with her head to where a lovely young woman in a flowery, yellow dress in with a Victorian cut sat at an adjacent table. Imelda watched dejectedly as couples danced around her.

"That's…" Rajan looked flustered as he searched for words. "…Off topic."

"You'll catch more women with footwork than philosophy." Ling grinned, enjoying Rajan's sudden embarrassment.

"She has a point, lad." Marcus laughed and took a gulp from his glass, looking like he might spit it out as his tongue realized the drink held no alcoholic content. He coughed, and Sema smiled bashfully at his side.

"They both have a point." Teresa turned her eyes skyward, as though speaking to no one in particular. "A bright boy would ask the pretty girl to dance."

"What?" Gabriel looked at Teresa, then around the table, and then to the nearby couples dancing to the soft music. He always felt like a hobbled ox in a chorus line when trying to dance, but it would be an opportunity to hold Teresa close, even if he would need to pay more attention to keeping his feet from crushing her toes than to the smell of her hair. He gave Teresa his most confident smile. "Hey, would you maybe like to dance?"

"See, a bright boy." Teresa stood and took Gabriel's hand. "I would love to."

"Now see how easy that was?" Ling punched Rajan in the arm.

"I…" Rajan glowered at Ling, then sighed and stood. "Fine." He shook his head and wandered toward the table where Imelda sat.

As Gabriel and Teresa walked toward the music, he heard Sema's voice behind him.

"It is a lovely night for a dance."

"Ah, well then, would you do me the honor?" Marcus requested.

Gabriel and Teresa found a spot not too far from the musicians but which offered some small amount of privacy. As they held each other close and swayed to the gentle rhythm of the music, Teresa placed her head on his shoulder and Gabriel forgot all about where his feet needed to be. It occurred to him that dancing and swordplay had a great deal in common — if you didn't think about it too much, your body would know what to do.

Across the crowd, he caught glimpses of Rajan and Imelda dancing near Sema and Marcus. He saw Ohin and Paramata talking near the dessert table. Ling, he noticed, had disappeared from the party. He started to wonder where she had gone, but instead closed his eyes, held Teresa tightly, and forgot all about the cares of his life. No Apollyons. No Kumaradevi. No Vicaquirao. No Great Barrier of Probability. No Council of Magic. No War. No Seventh True Mage. Only him and Teresa, entwined and twirling slowly beneath the stars.

Much later that night, after more dancing, and a bit of surreptitious kissing behind the concealing leaves of a small tree, Gabriel walked Teresa back to her room and said goodnight. They held each other for a long moment.

"Don't forget your promise again," Teresa whispered in his ear.

"I won't." Gabriel kissed her and smiled as she closed the door to her room.

He walked to his own quarters, two barracks away. As he entered his room, he used a tiny spark of Fire Magic to light a lamp on a table near the window. On the table sat a small, wood-framed chalkboard, propped up against a stack of books.

Gabriel stopped and embraced the imprints of the pocket watch, looking around the room. A frigid wind seemed to dance along his neck at the sight of the chalkboard and the words scrawled across its black surface. Gabriel had never seen the chalkboard before, but he knew who had placed it there. He stepped closer, reading the message again.

"We must meet about an urgent matter. V."

CHAPTER 6

An oven-dry wind blew a small cloud of sand around Gabriel's face. He brushed the dust from his eyes and pulled the edge of his keffiyeh tighter to his nose and mouth. Heat radiated up from the dune he lay upon to scorch his stomach through the thick cotton fabric of the desert thobe he wore even as the harsh sunlight from above baked his backside. He adjusted the focus on his binoculars and scanned the sand-swept horizon again.

He saw the white canvas of a house-sized tent flapping gently in the wind. The tent stood a mile away. Behind it sat the nearly completed limestone structure of Great Pyramid of Giza, scaffolding surrounding the base of the construction site as workers climbed over it like ants swarming the body of a fallen beast.

Teresa sprawled beside Gabriel in the sand, a pair of binoculars held to her eyes. The rest of the team flanked them, with Nefferati and Akikane taking the outermost positions. They hid behind a sand dune in the desert of ancient Egypt in the year 2535 BCE because of the message Gabriel had received on the chalkboard two days prior.

Gabriel had overcome his initial apprehension and natural suspicion at the presence of the chalkboard in his room to investigate it before bringing it to the attention of Ohin and the rest of the team. He spent several minutes probing the chalkboard with his magic and space-time sense to discern whether any spells booby-trapped the antique childhood learning aid. He discovered magical properties present in the chalkboard, but not the ones he anticipated. The magic imbuing the chalkboard did not turn it into a weapon, but rather a means of communication. Gabriel's magic-sense reveled a weaving of Time Magic on the chalkboard, similar to the one used to enchant the teacups and other items that allowed the Council to communicate through space and time. Much like the original teacup Elizabeth had found in her study back in Windsor Castle that allowed people to listen to conversations through a twinned version of the cup elsewhere, the chalkboard did something similar.

Curiosity and a deep appreciation for the subtly of the magic used drove Gabriel to pick up the chalkboard and wipe it clean with a sock from his floor. He rummaged through his desk until he found an old piece of yellow chalk and then wrote a message on the black slate of the board.

"How do I know who you are?"

A moment later, as Gabriel watched, his words slowly faded from the board, rubbed away by an invisible hand. A new missive took form, lines making letters that became words to create a single sentence.

"You are finally learning."

Seconds later more words appeared.

"I cooked your favorite meal the first time we met."

Gabriel had no doubt Vicaquirao held the piece of chalk that wrote on the duplicated version of the chalkboard in his hands. Through a quirk of space-time physics that he could intuit better than explain, the two chalkboards were not really separate things. Having been magically doubled, they were inextricably linked. Words written on one would appear on the other no matter how far apart they were in space and time. Vicaquirao might be anywhere, even the cabin in the mountains in his private alternate reality where Gabriel had first met him.

Gabriel needed to know what Vicaquirao wanted, but a more pressing question drove him to erase the words from the chalkboard and replace them with his own.

"How did you get this chalkboard in my room?"

Gabriel waited as the letters vanished and others took their place.

"A simple paradox. You are going to put it in your room for me."

Gabriel had sighed again for what seemed like the thousandth time that day. He hated paradoxes. He erased the message and wrote another.

"What do you want?"

A pause while text disappeared and reappeared.

"I have found a band of Apollyon doubles. I need your help to attack them."

That had been the moment when Gabriel came to his senses and took the board to Ohin's room. Ohin had paused only briefly to admonish Gabriel for his tardiness in bringing the chalkboard to his attention before the two of them set out to rouse Akikane and Nefferati from their slumber.

After a short conversation, and longer consideration, Nefferati and Akikane agreed to a rendezvous with Vicaquirao. Via the chalkboard, Vicaquirao sent coordinates in space and time to where a relic could be found that would take them to the location for the conference. Fearing that the act of bringing the covert meeting to the attention of the Council might give its members the opportunity to scuttle the meeting, they decided to keep the details of the summit secret. With as much stealth as possible, Ohin and Gabriel had woken the rest of the Chimera team and assembled them for the impromptu mission.

Three hours after he had first seen the chalkboard, and an hour after quietly gathering up supplies from the fort storerooms, Gabriel, Nefferati, Akikane, and the others sat in the desert sand watching the tent Vicaquirao had designated as the location of their clandestine appointment.

"If it's a trap, then it's a trap." Nefferati stood up, brushing sand from the thick robes cloaking her slender frame. "Let's see what the old devil has to say."

"Yes, yes." Akikane stood to his feet as well. "I will wait here with the others in the event something goes astray. I think he will be more pleased to see you."

Nefferati laughed. "We'll see about that."

Gabriel and Teresa helped each other up and walked over to stand beside Ohin and Nefferati. Teresa had insisted on accompanying Gabriel to the meeting. Ohin and Nefferati were unimpressed with Teresa's reasons, but when Gabriel demanded her attendance, the senior mages relented. Ohin accepted the idea more willingly than Nefferati.

"You remember your promise, girl?" Nefferati's hard gaze gouged at Teresa.

"Eyes and ears open. Mouth shut." Teresa nodded to Nefferati, matching the seriousness of her stare.

"Good." Nefferati turned toward the others.

"Good luck, good luck." Akikane offered only a thin smile. "We will watch for...any abnormalities."

"Don't forget the signal if something is wrong," Ling said to Teresa.

"How could she forget setting the tent on fire?" Rajan asked with a laugh.

Gabriel nearly giggled at the thought. He caught the look Nefferati gave Rajan and felt glad he hadn't joined in the laughter.

"We don't want to be late." Nefferati turned toward the tent.

"I'll take us." Ohin embraced the four of them in Time Magic and transported them across the desert dunes to within a few yards of the large tent.

"Ready?" Ohin asked Gabriel.

Gabriel hesitated a moment, considering briefly the consequences of his actions in the next few minutes and how they might play out over the course of his life and the war.

"Yep."

"Good." Nefferati gave Gabriel a slight shove to the middle of his back with the palm of her hand.

Gabriel stepped forward, a pace ahead of the others, and strode toward the wide-open flap of the tent. They had decided it would be better if he appeared to take a leading role in whatever negotiations might ensue from the meeting. He slowed his pace briefly as he crossed the threshold of the entrance, allowing his eyes to adjust to the interior. While the canvas roof provided shade from the blazing sky above, it only blocked a fraction of its light. Gabriel's eyes adapted quickly to the even glow beneath the curved cloth ceiling.

Ornately-patterned rugs covered the sand, providing a floor of sorts to the tent. Large pillows of various colors surrounded a long, low table in the center of the space. On the table sat a stone pitcher of water, several glasses, and a bowl of pears. Behind the table stood Vicaquirao, flanked by two of the doubled Apollyons.

Gabriel removed his keffiyeh and walked to the edge of the table opposite the three Dark Mages. His companions did the same, Teresa standing to his left while Ohin and Nefferati stood to his right. He noticed a hint of amusement in Vicaquirao's eyes, but none in the lines of his face.

"Thank you for coming." Vicaquirao nodded to Nefferati. "It's good to see you again."

"Thank you." Nefferati's voice sounded uncharacteristically tight. "I never had the opportunity to express my appreciation for your role in my escape from Kumaradevi's palace."

"No need," Vicaquirao said. "You were helping me at the time more that I was assisting you."

Nefferati seemed about to say something in reply, but chose to simply nod to Vicaquirao in response.

"I see there's been a reunion." Gabriel looked at the Apollyon standing to the right of Vicaquirao.

"Yes." The Apollyon smiled briefly.

While the two Apollyons looked identical, Gabriel's instincts told him that this particular Apollyon had been the one he and Teresa had shadowed for days in Chateau Galliard in the Middle Ages. The one they referred to as the Rogue Apollyon. Neither man wore their customary black garb. The former Rogue Apollyon dressed in a simple white shirt with cream-colored slacks while the other man wore a long blue jellabiya.

"Yes." The Rogue Apollyon gestured toward Gabriel. "Thanks to you."

"Indeed," Vicaquirao said. "Very clever that bit of Soul Magic."

"I suppose I owe you an additional thanks," the other Apollyon said. "For not killing me in the Battle of the Somme."

"Too much chit, not enough chat." Nefferati looked impatiently between the Dark Mages. "Why are we here?"

"Because we need your help." Vicaquirao pointed to the large cushions around the low table. "We'll get to details shortly. Please, have a seat. And we should make introductions. Not that we don't know all of you, but my colleagues are not who they used to be."

"Hmmm." Nefferati narrowed her eyes at Vicaquirao and the Apollyons.

As Gabriel and his companions sat on the cushions near the table, Vicaquirao poured glasses of water for everyone.

"This is Cyril to my right and Cassius to my left." Vicaquirao placed drinks before Nefferati and Teresa first.

"I thought it best to return to my original name." Cyril, the man who Gabriel thought of as the Rogue Apollyon, accepted a glass from Vicaquirao.

"And I took the name of our father." Cassius took a sip of water. "There is already enough confusion with so many of us running around. We didn't need to be confused about what to call one another."

Gabriel reached for his glass of water, but Teresa's hand found it first, switching it with the one given to her. He glanced at her, but she said nothing. He doubted that Vicaquirao would try to poison him, but if he wanted to it would be easy to place something the glass before pouring the water.

"A fierce protector," Cassius said with a smile toward Teresa.

"You were protecting him the last time we met," Cyril added, his smile a mirror of his twin's.

Teresa opened her mouth to reply, looked to Nefferati briefly, and then firmly closed her lips.

"How is Semele?" The least Gabriel could do to address Teresa's discomfort in front of the two Apollyons would be to create a bit of his own.

"She is well," Cyril said, his smile fading slightly.

"Both of her," Cassius added, looking toward his twin.

"Yes, and as long as neither learns of the other's existence, they will stay that way." Vicaquirao looked reprovingly at Cyril and Cassius. "But enough of that. Let us talk about other business."

"Yes, let's do." Ohin squared his shoulders, eyes on Vicaquirao.

For a moment, Gabriel had a sense of how much like a strange family the three Dark Mages were — two contentious brothers sitting with an estranged father. He wondered what Vicaquirao's reaction had been to Cassius saving another version of Semele the way Cyril had done. He couldn't imagine the elder True Mage had been pleased.

"I will try to speak plainly and present our case as best I can." Vicaquirao took a deep breath before he began. "Cassius made contact with Cyril nearly nine months ago. I found them shortly thereafter. In the time since, we three have been attacking the duplicate Apollyons when and where we could find them, but only if they were alone or in a small group of two or three. Even with the element of surprise, more than three would prove risky."

"I thought you loved risk," Nefferati interjected.

"Calculated risk, not blind jeopardy," Vicaquirao answered. "I only gamble on sure bets."

"How many have you killed?" Ohin leaned forward as though expecting Vicaquirao to whisper the answer.

"None," Vicaquirao said.

"Then I see why you need us." Nefferati eyed Cyril and Cassius suspiciously.

"They are not dead because we chose not to kill them," Cassius said.

"We severed their connection to the other duplicates in the hopes of convincing them to join our efforts," Cyril added.

"And you were unsuccessful." Ohin leaned back on his cushion, clearly worried about the direction the conversation appeared to be taking.

Gabriel didn't blame Ohin or Nefferati for their apprehension. Although he had found it a comforting sign that the Apollyon twins, Cyril and Cassius, did not complete each other's sentences the way their duplicates always did, he knew them and Vicaquirao well enough to guess the destiny of the Dark Mages they had captured. He sensed Teresa's physical tension where she sat next to him and admired the restraint she so had far exerted in the face of a clearly overwhelming desire to join the conversation.

"Where are you keeping them?" Gabriel looked only at Vicaquirao. "And how many do you have?"

"They are tucked safely away where they cannot harm the Primary Continuum," Vicaquirao said. Gabriel understood this to mean Vicaquirao's private alternate reality.

"How many?" Nefferati's voice sounded like churning gravel.

"Nine," Cassius said.

"They are sequestered in a remote place with no access to imprints, imbued objects, or relics," Cyril added.

"You are like two boys who think they're playing with salamanders rather than crocodiles," Nefferati said.

Cassius nearly growled as he leaned forward and clenched his fists. Vicaquirao placed a hand on his arm and the man relaxed.

"The nine captive duplicates are securely removed from the Continuum," Vicaquirao said. "They cannot get back even if they ever escape the small town we have built them to live in. If they cannot accept their fate, if they attempt to return to the Primary Continuum, I will sever the world they inhabit."

"And kill them in the process when you worked so hard to spare them?" Nefferati's tone sounded both skeptical and sarcastic.

Vicaquirao seemed about to reply when he looked at Gabriel. He held Gabriel's eyes a moment before speaking. "No one knows what happens to alternate branches cut free from the trunk of the Continuum. Given roots, they might survive."

"Again…" Ohin's deep voice resonated in the warm air beneath the tent. "…What do you need us to help you with?"

"As I said, we have only been able to capture the duplicates in small numbers," Vicaquirao said. "We hope to slow them down and keep them from reaching that critical number we all assume will allow them to destroy the Great Barrier of Probability. We also hope to turn more of them to our side as allies."

"Unfortunately, many of us are stubborn," Cyril said.

"And by the time we are released, most of us have been driven half mad by having our minds blended together day and night," Cassius added.

"We believe the more time the captives have free from the voices, the more clearly they will see their errors," Cyril said.

"One of our most recent detainees has provided us with information that presents a valuable opportunity." Vicaquirao placed his hands in his lap as he spoke. "The Apollyons have spread themselves throughout time in small teams. Seven of them are on a boat suspended in a space-time bubble in the middle of the Battle of Lepanto in 1571."

"We believe that if we approach them through the battle and then establish a space-time bubble of our own near their ship, that we can catch them by surprise and capture them," Cyril said.

"But the three of us alone could never manage to take all seven of them, even if they are asleep when we struck," Cassius added.

"Which is why we need your help," Vicaquirao concluded.

A wave of dizziness washed over Gabriel. He took a drink of water to cover his confusion and concern. As he finished the long sip of cool liquid and placed the glass back on the table, he realized that everyone's attention rested on him. Everyone except Teresa, who glared at the three Dark Mages as though they were rabid dogs escaped from the leash.

"You want us to help you capture seven Apollyon duplicates so you can put them in some country rehab center where they can plot to take over the world again?" Teresa leaned so far forward she nearly fell off her cushion. "You are all insane."

Nefferati glowered at Teresa as Ohin frowned to himself. Gabriel, however, found himself unable to contain the laugher that bubbled up from his chest. Teresa was right, and he couldn't have said it better himself. He saw that Nefferati and Ohin agreed with her even if they didn't approve of her outburst. Teresa blushed and looked at Gabriel, seeming concerned by his sudden mirth.

Gabriel's laughter ended abruptly in a long sigh. It was a crazy plan, but he knew it might give them the first real prospect of dealing the Apollyons a major blow. The plan also provided them with another opportunity.

"If we help you, what are you willing to offer in return?" Gabriel didn't bother looking at anyone except Vicaquirao.

Vicaquirao laughed and slapped his knee. "You keep this up and I'm going to start suspecting that you are actually paying attention."

"The boy asks a good question." Nefferati raised an eyebrow in Vicaquirao's direction.

Vicaquirao held her eyes and stretched his own brow in mimicked response.

"What do you want?"

A brief silence entered the room like a hot breeze, wafting over Gabriel and the others, clinging to them like the sweat dampening their skin. He had not thought about what to ask of Vicaqauirao and the two reformed Apollyons in exchange for assisting in an attack on their brethren. What could he ask for? Was it even his place to make such a request? Vicaquirao's attention seemed directed solely at Nefferati. What would she demand? What would be worth the risk they were being asked to take?

"Nothing." Nefferati eased her shoulders back as she sat straighter on the cushion. "Not at the moment."

"But there will come a time..." Vicaquirao let his unfinished sentence hang between them.

"Yes," Nefferati said. "One day we will need something in return."

"How do we know the trade will be fair?" Cassius asked.

"You don't," Nefferati replied.

"And why would you trust us to hold up our end of the bargain if we don't even know what you will want?" Cyril asked.

"I don't trust you to keep your word," Nefferati said, turning her eyes from Cyril to Gabriel. "I trust him to keep it for you."

Vicaquirao contemplated this statement for a moment and then smiled as he looked at Gabriel. "Your terms are acceptable."

Gabriel couldn't quite figure out exactly what the terms were. Nor did he fathom why Vicaquirao seemed impressed by Nefferati's insinuation that Gabriel would enforce the agreement. Vicaquirao accepted the deal, and Gabriel felt a surging sense of relief that the negotiations were over. He would be happy to be away from the desert heat and Vicaquirao and the two non-Apollyons. Cyril and Cassius stared at him a little too intently, as though silently challenging the notion that he could force them to fulfill the terms of the accord.

"We will need a place to rendezvous," Ohin said, bringing the conversation to practicalities. "And we will need to formulate a plan of attack."

"We have thought of this." Cyril removed a slender silver brooch from his pocket and placed it on the table.

"It will take you to a small dock at the edge of Lepanto," Cassius said as Ohin took the brooch from the table and held it in his palm. "We can meet there before the battle starts and finalize the details.

"Yes, I see the place," Ohin said, staring down at the piece of antique jewelry in his hand.

"There is a night when the dock is empty but a white flag hangs from one of the mooring posts," Cyril said. Ohin squinted at the brooch a moment and then nodded his acknowledgment at having found the point in time described.

"Before you arrive, we will procure a ship to use in the assault," Vicaquirao said.

"A ship?" Nefferati asked.

"Yes," Vicaquirao said. "They will sense us if we use Time Magic too close to the vessel they have commandeered. However, if we approach them in our own ship, slowly, from a distance, we have a good chance of catching them by surprise."

"A good chance or a slim chance?" Nefferati scowled at Vicaquirao's words like she had ingested an unpleasant meal.

"If these seven Apollyons have their ship in a space-time bubble, then we will need to time the approach of our boat perfectly, so we can arrive at exactly the moment their bubble begins to suspend them in space-time." Gabriel stared at his glass on the table, working through the variables that would be involved. "And we'll need to do it the middle of a sea battle without using magic to conceal ourselves, or the Apollyons will sense it. So we'll need to know in advance what will and will not happen around their ship for the whole course of our journey to reach it."

"Precisely." Vicaquirao's white teeth shone brightly in the filtered light of the tent. He looked as pleased as if Gabriel had been his own apprentice Time Mage. "We will also need to identify the position of every ship, every arrow, and every volley of cannon fire."

"There is a reason the Apollyons have chosen Lepanto as a hiding place," Cyril said.

"Unfortunately, this is the only way to capture them," Cassius added.

Gabriel believed Cassius and Cyril were right. The Apollyon duplicates on the boat had hidden themselves very well. It would take a master Time Mage to successfully mount a surprise attack on their ship in a space-time bubble. Gabriel had no doubt who had conceived the plan. Only Vicaquirao would even consider such a mission feasible. Gabriel reconsidered that thought.

"You're plan is not a plan, it is a self-made trap." Nefferati looked as though she might spit on the carpet.

"There are too many possibilities for mistakes." Ohin placed the brooch back on the table. "It is foolish and impossible."

Foolish and impossible. Those words described Vicaquirao's plan exactly. But did that mean the plan would not work? Gabriel suspected at least one other Time Mage besides Vicaquirao could see past the foolishness, believe in the impossible, and attempt something so complicated and intricate.

"No." Gabriel's voice sounded odd in his own ears, as though his words surprised him as much as those around him. "Vicaquirao is right. We can do this. I'm positive."

Vicaquirao's smile seemed ready to ignite the tent with its intensity.

Beside him, Teresa cursed under her breath before uttering something only he could hear.

"Foolish and impossible. We should make a t-shirt for you."

A sea of excitement percolated within Gabriel. They had formed an alliance with Dark Mages that might prove crucial in defending the Great Barrier of Probability. They had gained essential knowledge about what Vicaquirao and the two reformed Apollyons had been doing since the fall of Windsor Castle. Most of all, they finally had a plan to attack their enemies and bring the war directly to the Apollyons.

CHAPTER 7

Gabriel and his companions left the tent a short time later, having reviewed the preliminary aspects of the plan and allocated responsibilities. Vicaquirao, Cyril, and Cassius would be responsible for finding a ship they could use in the attack and for recording all the events of the battle surrounding the Apollyons' vessel. Assembling and briefing five teams of Grace Mages fell to Nefferati and Akikane. Meanwhile, Gabriel and Ohin reviewed the events of the battle through relics collected after the end of the conflict. They used their space-time sense to probe the relics and double check Vicaquirao's navigation through the fighting. If they encountered even one wrong arrow, or worse yet, one stray cannonball, they might not merely suffer casualties but accidentally alert the Apollyons of their presence…or unintentionally create a bifurcation of the Primary Continuum.

As Gabriel stepped toward the glaring light beyond the entrance of the tent, a hand clasped his shoulder. His magic-sense told him who stood behind him even before he turned around to find Vicaquirao, holding a small, thin bundle wrapped in dark red fabric.

"You need to take this with you." Vicaquirao handed Gabriel the package. "I'm sure you'll know what to do with it."

Gabriel frowned as he accepted the item from Vicaquirao's hands. The hard slate of the chalkboard pressed through the cloth beneath his fingers. "This paradox doesn't make sense."

"Paradoxes by definition don't make sense," Vicaquirao said.

"You're giving me this slate so I can go back in time and put it where I found it yesterday, but how did you know yesterday that I would place it there for you in the future?" Gabriel had a better sense of the vagaries of time paradoxes than most, but this chain of events made even his head spin.

"There is only one way to really know what will happen in your own future." Vicaquirao's face held a blank expression as he stared at Gabriel.

"You crossed your own timeline?" Gabriel's mouth fell open in surprise.

"Some risks are necessary." Vicaquirao smiled. "And some conversations more interesting than others."

"I don't ever want to talk to my future self," Gabriel said.

"Ah, but your future self may feel differently about that." Vicaquirao laughed.

"I have a question." Gabriel realized this might be the only time to ask what he wanted to know.

"About?" Vicaquirao's eyes narrowed.

"Were you the one who discovered that the Great Barrier took one hundred and eight mages to create?" Gabriel asked.

"I discovered nothing," Vicaquirao said. "I found myself in need of advice and consulted with a shaman woman. Instead of helping me with my query, she mentioned the Great Barrier and the number one hundred and eight several times. Given her history of accuracy, I believed her. And, in a moment of unguardedness, I mentioned it to Elizabeth."

"I see." Gabriel nearly sighed. One mystery solved by revealing a new mystery.

"How is she?" Concern filled Vicaquirao's voice.

"The same," Gabriel said. "No worse, but no better."

"Her spirit is strong. She will recover." Vicaquirao appeared to be reassuring himself more than Gabriel. "If you need to reach me, use the slate. And thank you."

Gabriel didn't need to ask why. "Don't make me regret it."

"I will do my best." Vicaquirao nodded and Gabriel joined his companions outside in the sun. As they walked away from the tent, Gabriel stepped closer to Nefferati. "Why didn't you ask for something in return for helping them with this attack?"

Nefferati shielded her eyes from the sun as she looked at Gabriel.

"Sometimes, when the caravan master offers to trade you for your camels, you wait and see what he will have in his packs the following season rather than accept the trinkets he has on hand."

Gabriel nodded to himself. It made sense. Having Vicaquirao and the two rehabilitated Apollyons in their debt could prove useful at the right time. Assuming they would fulfill their obligation and that Cyril and Cassius had truly reformed.

"This entire endeavor fills me with unease." Ohin pulled his keffiyeh up to his face against the dust and wind.

"It is a danger, but also a great opportunity," Nefferati said. "A precedent that may lead to other things."

"What things?" Ohin asked.

"Things we will discuss at another time." Nefferati glanced toward Teresa.

Ohin shielded his eyes against the bright glare but said no more.

"Well if it works, we'll finally have an answer to at least one of our questions." Teresa ignored Nefferati's comment, openly elated to be able to speak her mind again.

"What question?" Gabriel asked.

"Whether Grace and Malignancy Mages can work together." Teresa grabbed Gabriel's hand as Ohin teleported them through space to where their comrades stood observing Vicaquirao's tent.

"How did it go?" Ling asked when they materialized before Akikane and the rest of the team.

"Better than expected," Nefferati said.

"Good, good," Akikane said. "Our expectations were unpleasant."

"The task we will be attempting is unpleasant enough," Ohin said.

"What task?" Sema asked

Nefferati and Ohin turned to each other briefly, but neither spoke. Gabriel held his words as well. It would not be an easy plan to explain, and their future partners weren't potential selling points.

"We're going to help Vicaquirao and a couple of rogue Apollyons attack a ship full of their duplicates in the middle of a sea battle so they can be captured and sent to a special town for wayward Dark Mages." Teresa appeared chipper and enthusiastic. "Gabriel thinks it's a brilliant plan, so I'm sure we have nothing to worry about."

Gabriel squeezed Teresa's hand so hard she yelped. His face burned as the others looked at him.

"Well, that's good," Marcus said, clapping Gabriel on the back. "Gabriel's plans never go wrong."

"They never go as planned either," Rajan said with a laugh.

"We should get back to the fort," Ohin said before anyone else could speak. "We have a great deal to accomplish in the next day."

"More than a great deal," Nefferati added.

Before another discussion about the proposed mission to the Battle of Lepanto might erupt, Ohin whisked them all through time and space and back to Fort Aurelius. Upon their return, Nefferati and Akikane handed out assignments for everyone. The two senior True Mages would assemble the assault force, choosing one team each from five different forts. As co-heads of the Council they had the authority to mount small military actions on short notice. Neither Akikane nor Nefferati had any desire to spend hours debating the advantages and dangers of the mission with the full Council and risk the plan being rejected. If the mission succeeded, they would have greater leverage in convincing the Council of the feasibility of a future alliance with Kumaradevi to defeat the Apollyons.

Ohin and the Chimera team were responsible for quietly assembling the supplies for the mission and collecting the concatenate crystals they would need from the vault beneath the Council Hall. Once they had what they required, the team would rendezvous with Akikane, Nefferati, and the other five teams at a remote location in Neolithic North America to review the plan.

Before doing anything else, Gabriel returned to his room. On his bed sat the same chalkboard that he held in his hands. His space-time sense buzzed like a nest of hornets. The same object in paradoxical proximity to its magically twinned and entwined copy disturbed the natural flow of space-time within the Primary Continuum. Keeping the two versions of the chalkboard in the same place could have unpredictable effects. Gabriel didn't need any more unpredictable things in his life.

He used the same tiny fossil that led through time to the fort in order to travel back in time one night and place the small chalkboard on his table. As he stood in his room, knowing that elsewhere in the fort his previous self danced with Teresa, he unwrapped the chalkboard, Vicaquirao's message already printed on the slate in white chalk. Gabriel shook his head. He still couldn't puzzle out how Vicaquirao had managed to put this particular paradox in motion, but however he had, it worked.

Gabriel jumped through time again into the future, to a minute after he had left. The chalkboard still rested on his bed. His space-time sense throbbed slightly as he picked it up. He packed the chalkboard in a backpack with a change of clothes, his copy of *A Time Traveler's Pocket Guide to History*, an empty canteen, a compass, binoculars, a Swiss Army knife, and a few other things he always took on missions.

He met up with Teresa and the rest of the team in the supply barn at the western end of the fort a few minutes later. Rajan and Marcus held two tents in their hands while Ling had a bundle of blankets and sleeping mats slung across her back. Sema carried a small canvas bag over her shoulder in addition to her backpack of personal equipment. Gabriel sensed the magic emanating from the bag and guessed that it contained dozens of concatenate crystals. Probably 49. Enough for each team member to carry seven.

"How are your physicians?" Teresa handed him a large canvas pack with water sacks as she shouldered a bag filled with dried fruit, nuts, jerky, and other dry rations.

"My what?" Gabriel adjusted the bag of water sacks on his shoulders, holding his backpack in his hands.

"Your pair-o-docs." Teresa grinned as Gabriel groaned.

"That's awful, even for you." Gabriel took her hand and turned to the others. "I put the chalkboard where I found it, but it still hurts my head when I try to figure it out."

"Non-sequential temporal binding artifact." Teresa frowned knowingly.

"You're making that up, aren't you?" Gabriel asked.

"I could show you the math to describe the phenomenon," Teresa offered.

"And you know I wouldn't understand any of it," Gabriel said.

"It must be difficult having such a small brain." Teresa smirked as her teasing tone dropped half an octave.

"Who figured out how to save you after you were dead?" Gabriel looked up to the rafters as though trying to remember the name that might answer his question.

"You're right." A look of admonishment fell over Teresa's face as she kissed him. "You have a glorious brain."

"Thank you." Gabriel's smugness dissolved with his next thought. "Let's hope it's glorious enough to figure out how to navigate a ship through a battle without getting sunk or creating a bifurcation."

"Glorious, but mad," Teresa said.

"Is everyone ready?" Ohin asked before Gabriel could reply to Teresa's comment.

The members of the Chimera team each voiced their assent as Ohin pulled a flint arrowhead from his pocket. A moment of deepest black followed by a burst of purest white, and the team stood in a flat clearing at the edge of a stream in the middle of a dense forest of fir trees. Gabriel turned to examine his surroundings, breathing in the scent of pine and wild flowers as the sound of swiftly flowing water filled his ears. The wide glade would make a perfect basecamp.

"It seems we are the first to arrive." Ohin sat down his packs. "Akikane and Nefferati and the other teams will be here shortly. Let's get started setting up camp. We'll have a briefing to review the mission, and then we're going to need to capture some of the sleep we lost last night before we begin tomorrow."

Gabriel watched the sun hanging low in the sky between the trees arching over the stream. They would have at least a few hours before sunset. Time enough to set camp, evaluate the operation, and have a meal.

The team set about preparing the basecamp. They had been on enough missions that each person had a role and knew what needed to be done. By the time Akikane arrived with the first team, they had their tents assembled, their supplies unpacked, and a perimeter established with magical barriers to alert them of the approach of any people. Gabriel and Teresa built a small fire in the center of the clearing and began cooking a meal for the others.

Within an hour, the camp hummed with activity as the 30 members of the five teams Akikane and Nefferati had assembled swarmed through the grass, helping complete the tasks necessary to establish the camp. As the sun fell behind the trees, glowing orange light cascading along the rolling water of the stream, the combined teams of the mission gathered for a briefing and a quick meal.

"So, so," Akikane said, his voice echoing amongst the tree trunks as he stood beside Nefferati at the center of the camp. "Most of you have come not knowing what we will ask of you. Now you will learn."

"We chose you because we trust you to trust us." Nefferati's voice floated on the still air and wrapped each person in its gentle tones. "When we explain this mission, your trust will be tested. Hopefully it will not fail."

To the credit of the various mages Akikane and Nefferati had assembled, none of them balked at the nature of the mission once it had been explained to them. They had questions and concerns, but no one flinched at the notion of allying with Vicaquirao to attack the Apollyons or the danger inherent in the plan. They were most concerned with the idea that the captured Apollyons would be held in a special prison guarded by Vicaquirao. However, their confidence in Nefferati and Akikane did not waver. They were personally loyal to the True Mages and completely dedicated to the war.

After the fires burnt down and guards were set around the parameter, most of the mages settled into their tents or spread out sleeping bags beneath the stars. Gabriel said good night to Teresa with a long kiss outside the tent she shared with Ling and Sema. He had intended to climb into the neighboring tent where he bunked with the male members of the Chimera team when he spotted Ohin, still seated before one of the few campfires kept burning to provide illumination throughout the night. The look on Ohin's face as he stared into the flames drew Gabriel across the low grass. He knew that look of concerned consternation all too well, and it meant one thing.

"Nefferati and Akikane told you their plan." Gabriel settled down beside Ohin, keeping his voice low in case someone passed nearby.

"You're beginning to read my moods as well as Sema." Ohin said. "You are correct. They have confided in me." He turned his eyes to Gabriel. "I think it poses a grave risk. To you, most of all."

"I've faced Kumaradevi before," Gabriel said. "We're not expecting we can trust her completely."

"She is only one part of the risk." Ohin said. "The greater risk is the Council."

"You think they will vote against the idea." Gabriel didn't phrase this as a question. He too doubted the plan would find the Council's support.

"I am certain they will reject it." Ohin paused as he looked Gabriel over. "You have grown quite a bit since we plucked you from your death. But I fear this is too much to ask. To accept the mantle of leadership at your age is one thing, but to assume leadership by wresting power from the Council is quite another."

"I'm not so keen on that part of the plan myself." Gabriel avoided Ohin's stare and turned his eyes to the dazzling sea of stars above the forest canopy.

"You run a dual risk." Ohin reached his hand up to stroke his chin as he followed Gabriel's gaze toward the twinkling heavens above. "If you are to lead, you must truly do so. To receive advice from Nefferati or Akikane or myself will be acceptable, but you cannot be seen as a puppet. You must assert your own will and not simply be the conduit for someone else's. And if you do lead, you bear the burden of that leadership and all the mistakes and triumphs that might result from it."

"We succeed together, but I fail alone." Gabriel had been trying not to let these same thoughts take charge of his mind.

"It's not quite as stark as that," Ohin said. "However, if the Council rejects this alliance with Kumaradevi and you do try to assume the role of leader, you had better believe in and support that alliance completely. Nefferati and Akikane are right. The Grace Mages will nearly all follow you. But once they do, any plan of Nefferati and Akikane is no longer theirs. It is yours and you must own it."

"I know." Gabriel sighed. Then he sighed again in exasperation at allowing himself to sigh. "If I had a better idea, I'd mention it."

"Sometimes there are no good ideas, merely the best choices among bad options." Ohin placed a comforting hand on Gabriel's back. "Like the alliance with Vicaquirao and his twin protégés."

"I think we can trust Vicaquirao." Gabriel thought for a second and then amended his statement. "At least about this."

"Him, possibly, but what about the newly rehabilitated Apollyons?" Ohin asked. "You spent time with them both. Do you think they might betray us?"

"I don't know." Gabriel furrowed his brow, pulling his eyes down from the stars and back to the flames dancing along the pile of logs before him. "I don't trust them exactly, but I think they are sincere about wanting to stop their duplicates from destroying the Great Barrier. Especially the one Teresa and I met in Chateau Gillard. But once the Barrier is safe again, I don't know what they'll do."

"I don't think we have any choice but to find out." Ohin's voice took on a sad tone. "The Council does not see what Akikane and Nefferati do — we are simply too weak after the fall of the castle and the loss of so many mages to succeed in defending the Barrier without help. And we have little option in where we can turn for assistance."

"If this mission with Vicaquirao is successful, the Council may believe an alliance with Kumaradevi will work." Even as Gabriel spoke, he heard the sad, soft laugh in Ohin's chest.

"You are always so optimistic in the face of the unlikely and the impossible." Ohin let his laughter grow a little louder. "A good trait for a leader to have. As long as it is tempered by a dose of realism."

"I'm always realistic." Gabriel wanted to join in Ohin's laughter, but found it catching in his throat. "The problem is, I don't have enough experience to know when to stop being *optimistic*."

"You may rely upon me for that council," Ohin offered.

"I rely on you for more than that." Gabriel said.

There were many things Gabriel suddenly wanted to tell Ohin. Feelings and thoughts that had grown and shifted and coalesced over the years of his training under the elder mage's tutelage. Mostly, Gabriel wished to tell him that he had become a second father. As much a parent as those he had left behind with his death. Somehow, the words did not come to his lips. Maybe it was Ohin's reticent nature, or possibly his own adolescent embarrassment, or perhaps it was unnecessary to voice things already known and silently acknowledged.

"And I will always be there for you to rely upon." Ohin squeezed Gabriel's shoulder. "Now, we should get some sleep. We have a day of infinite impossibilities ahead of us tomorrow."

"That's perfect." Gabriel climbed to his feet and helped Ohin to his own. "I feel infinitely tired and impossibly sleepy."

Gabriel slept well that night and woke at first light. The teams gathered for breakfast and a quick review of the mission as the rising sun gradually burned away the early mist of daybreak. They had no time for extensive training. They needed to rely upon their collective experience and skill to make the operation a success. After their meal and briefing, the teams struck the camp, removing all signs that anyone had ever been there, Earth Mages blending ash from fires into the ground, while Heart-Tree Mages coaxed new growth from trampled or burned grass. By the time the thin morning fog had dissipated, the teams were ready to depart. They assembled in the clearing, surrounding Akikane and Nefferati.

"Is everyone ready?" Ohin pulled the ornate brooch from his pocket.

"Yes, yes," Akikane said. "Time to begin."

Gabriel sensed Ohin embrace the imprints of all seven concatenate crystals in the pouch at his waist, feeling both impressed and proud as his mentor shifted the entire assembly of 39 Grace Mages through time to the rendezvous point near the Gulf of Patras, off the western coast of Greece on October 7th of 1571.

CHAPTER 8

Infinite darkness gave way to impossible brightness that faded to reveal the teams still standing in a circle near a small, secluded dock. At the end of the mooring, a large galley ship rested in the water of the Mediterranean Sea. Aboard the ship, Vicaquirao, Cyril, and Cassius stood like statues set to guard against evil spirits.

A gangplank gave access from the dock to the deck of the galley. Akikane and Nefferati led the way and boarded the ship first. Gabriel and his team followed. In less than a minute all of the Grace Mages had boarded. As Cyril used Wind Magic to haul in the gangplank, Vicaquirao took Akikane and Nefferati to the raised sterncastle at the aft of the ship. Gabriel and Teresa followed. He had no intention of letting Vicaquirao out of his sight and she had no intention of letting Gabriel out of hers. Ohin and the rest of the Chimera team stayed below on the deck, but they kept their eyes trained upon three Dark Mages.

As Cyril lowered the gangplank to the deck, Cassius used Wind Magic to unfurl the lanteen mainsail down the tall mast at midship. The vessel looked to Gabriel to be a Venetian galley. It ran 138 feet long and had 24 benches for rowing on either side of the open deck with three cannons mounted in the forecastle of the bow. The arms of the long oars sat on the benches, the paddles protruding along the side of the ship from the oar holes. As Cyril helped Cassius use Wind Magic to unfold the foresail, Gabriel wondered how difficult the craft would prove to navigate into position alongside the Apollyons' vessel.

Vicaquirao's hand rested on the rudder as he guided the galley into the open water. Below, on the deck, Cassius and Cyril gave instructions to the Grace Mages on how to attend to the sails. At first, wary of the former twin Apollyons, the teams stood back, ignoring the requests until Ohin and the Chimera team took up the call for assistance. Gabriel's team had sailed on previous missions, and Ohin relieved Cyril and Cassius of their duties, pressing his fellow Grace Mages into service as an impromptu crew.

"Hopefully our two sides will work better together in battle," Vicaquirao said as Cyril and Cassius mounted the steps to the forecastle, standing alone above the main deck where the Grace Mages worked the sails.

"Yes, yes." Akikane steadied himself on the railing of the sterncastle. His smile seemed strained and he looked queasy. It appeared Akikane did not have sea legs. "We should be clear on our roles once the fighting begins."

"Agreed." Vicaquirao pulled the rudder to port, and the ship tacked to starboard as the sails filled with wind. "When we get closer, we'll need to lower the sails, and your people will need to man the oars until we are in position beside the Apollyons' ship. Once we board the other vessel, I think it best if your mages focus on maintaining a space-time seal and pressing the attack while Cyril and Cassius and I attempt to sever the connection that links the duplicates."

"Good, good," Akikane said. "I will make sure our teams know what to expect." He gave a nearly imperceptible nod to Nefferati and Gabriel before descending the short stairs to the lower deck.

"What about the space-time bubble the Apollyons have in place?" Nefferati looked out upon the open water of the Mediterranean Sea. "If they let it slip while under attack, we will need to be ready to replace it."

"Yes," Vicaquirao said. "They will likely drop the space-time bubble as a diversionary tactic. They know how rigid the Council is regarding accidental bifurcations of time."

"We've assigned Time Mages to create a bubble around this vessel and extend it around the other when we attack." Nefferati said.

"Good." Vicaquirao took a large rolled piece of paper from a canvas bag and spread it out across a small table nailed to the deck at the edge of the railing. Gabriel saw that the map marked the placement and motion of various ships on both sides of the battle with time markings next to each one. A dashed red line led a circuitous route through the ships. "I have charted a course through the battle that will allow us to arrive at the duplicate Apollyons' vessel without disturbing the Primary Continuum and risking a break in time."

"Where did you get this ship?" Teresa said as she watched the teams of Grace Mages take up positions to crew the vessel.

"We did as the Apollyon duplicates had done," Vicaquirao said. "We found a ship sunk during the battle, raised it, repaired it, and brought it back through time."

"That explains the stains." Teresa stepped back from the dark red blemish coloring the deck beneath her feet.

"I'll help navigate." Gabriel pulled out his silver pocket watch and set it near the map. "Where is your starting mark?"

"Here." Vicaquirao pointed to a circle drawn around a ship on the map near the southern horn of land inside the western edge the Gulf of Patras. "This ship will come under attack by cannon fire. When the first volley strikes, that will be our zero mark. Each event on this map is marked with a time signature. We need to cross each of these points at the time indicated to avoid being hit with cannon fire or rammed by other galleys from either side of the conflict."

"And how much leeway do we have at each event?" Nefferati leaned closer to examine the map.

"Very little." Vicaquirao pointed to the ships drawn on his diagram. "The closer together the events are, the less margin for error we have. We can be off by several seconds at the edge of the battle, but the Apollyons' ship is near the center of the conflict, meaning we need to hit each of these marks almost exactly."

"I'll remain here," Nefferati said. "With three of us extending our space-time sense, we may be able to improve our accuracy in following this course."

"Yes," Vicaquirao said. "A good idea."

Gabriel could not tell from the tone of voice whether he believed Vicaquirao's words or not.

"And what about me?" Teresa asked.

"There are plenty of oars that need rowing," Nefferati said.

"Hmmm," Teresa replied. This translated into a firm statement that she would remain at Gabriel's side.

"The maneuvers will be tight and close together and the air filled with cannon fire," Vicaquirao said. "You can stand at the railing and shout our instructions down to the crew on the oars."

"A perfect use of your skills." Nefferati smiled at Teresa.

"I'm sure I don't know what you mean." Teresa turned to the side, subtly ignoring Nefferati.

"I could explain," Gabriel said, dropping his voice so only she heard.

"Shush," Teresa said. "Look at your map."

Gabriel grinned as he studied the map, trying to get a feel for what to expect. The sounds of cannon fire, at first faint and hard to discern behind the flapping of the sails and the lapping of water against the hull, became evermore loud. Each gunpowder boom grew in volume with every yard closer they came to the battle. As the galley sailed around the tip of the isthmus creating the Gulf of Patras, the Battle of Lepanto came into full view.

Gabriel had taken a few moments the night before to read through the entry about the battle in *The Time Traveler's Pocket Guide to History*, but his research did not prepare him for the deadly chaos he witnessed on the waters off the coast of Greece. The combatants of the battle ultimately fought for the control of Cyprus, but also to determine how far and fast the Ottoman Empire could continue to expand through the western hemisphere. Muezzinzade Ali Pasha commanded the Ottoman fleet, assembling his 230 galleys in a crescent formation facing his adversaries. The opposing fleet, led by the illegitimate half-brother of the King of Spain, Don Jon of Austria, comprised 206 galleys and six galleasses, vessels larger and more heavily armed than the smaller galley ships.

Don Jon's forces represented a combined fleet with ships from the independent city of Venice, Hapsburg Spain, Genoa, and several smaller contingents from the Papacy, Savoy, and Malta's Knights of St. John. Christened the Holy League, Don Jon's fleet set sail to relieve the Venetian forces of Cyprus from attack by the Ottomans. Upon encountering Ali Pasha's ships, Don Jon broke his fleet into four squads. Eventually, Don Jon used his more nimble fleet to outflank Ali Pasha's galleys and crush the Ottoman armada. The Holy League suffered the loss of 8,000 men while the Ottoman's lost 20,000. The defeat signaled the end of the Ottoman Empire's westward expansion and conquest.

It would be a bloody day with men dying from arrows and swords and fire and cannonballs and shrapnel and downing. And at the center of the battle, at the height of the conflict, floated the Apollyons' resurrected ship, sealed in a space-time bubble and supplied with a wealth of negative imprints should they need them.

Gabriel saw why the Apollyons had chosen this particular hiding place. Virtually impossible to find, much less attack, the Apollyons would imagine themselves safely hidden within the Battle of Lepanto. That would be Gabriel and the attacking mages' lone advantage.

The sound of the cannons grew louder and the smell of sulfur on the wind reached Gabriel's nose. Through clouds of black gunpowder smoke, he followed the vague outlines of ships engaged in battle. Ottoman ships attempted to ram Holy League ships which in turn tried to aim their guns for maximum destruction.

"We're getting close." Vicaquirao pointed to a Spanish galley off the starboard bow. "Get ready to synchronize your watch."

"Right." Gabriel pulled the pin of the small knob at the top of the silver timepiece and turned it until all the hands had rotated back to the center at the number 12.

"Strike the sails and man the oars!" Vicaquirao's voice rose above the growing din of war echoing across the rolling waters.

"That's my cue." Teresa ran to the railing, leaning over and yelling at the top of her lungs like a pirate princess on the high seas. "Strike the sails and man the oars!"

On the decks below, Akikane and Ohin issued orders, breaking the teams into two units, the first setting out to lower the sails while the second divided into groups of three, settling into every other row of benches and easing the long red oars into the sea. There were not enough Grace Mages to crew all 47 oars, but once the sails were down they would be able to keep ten per side in the water. They could not move rapidly, but with the congestion of ships fighting around them, that would be of little concern. The greater problem involved turning the ship fast enough to avoid the events that Vicaquirao had marked on his map.

"Here it comes." Vicaquirao watched the approaching Spanish galley as a cloud of black smoke rose from the cannon of an Ottoman ship behind it. Seconds later, the deck of the Spanish galley exploded in a mass of shattered wood and limbs and flames. "Begin now."

Gabriel popped the setting pin back into the pocket watch and the second hand began to tick across the numbers of the watch face.

"The first turn is in twenty-five seconds," Gabriel said as he glanced between the map on the table and the battle they were swiftly sailing toward.

On the deck below, the crew had secured the sails and assumed the oars. Gabriel saw Sema and Marcus side by side with Rajan as they pulled at the long oars. Ling worked an oar with two members of another team, her long, muscular arms straining against the wood and water. She almost seemed to be enjoying herself.

"Pull…Lift…Down…Pull…" Ohin called out instructions to keep the rowers of both sides in unison and maintain a steady speed.

Gabriel reached out with his space-time sense seeking potential disturbances their presence might create. He perceived a wave of probable divergence from the Continuum to the starboard of the ship. Looking across the bow of the galley, and then down at the map, he realized the accuracy of Vicaquirao's drawings. He allowed a moment of hopefulness to kindle in his heart, and he then squashed it before he became distracted.

"Event to starboard in ten…nine…eight…" Gabriel called out.

"Hard to port!" Vicaquirao shouted as he yanked at the long wooden tiller.

"Hard to port!" Teresa yelled down to Ohin.

"Starboard oars up!" Ohin boomed. "Port oars down and hold."

Gabriel observed with his space-time sense, even more than his eyes, as the galley pulled to port, a cannonball exploding into the water off the starboard railing.

"Steady on," Vicaquirao said, pushing the tiller straight again.

"Steady on!" Teresa shouted.

"All oars up…all oars down…all pull!" Ohin yelled from the lower deck.

Nefferati let out a long, low whistle. "Close, but well done."

"Only twenty six more to go." Vicaquirao didn't grin, but his mood appeared unreasonably lighthearted.

Gabriel suspected the man actually relished the wild game of cat and mouse with cannon balls and bifurcations. He found that disconcerting. Moreso because he felt that same reckless excitement begin to build within his own chest.

"Another event coming soon," Nefferati said as she stared into the smoky battle beginning to surround them.

"Event to port in ten…nine…eight…" Gabriel said, checking the map and reaching out with his space-time sense as he followed the ticking of the pocket watch.

"Hard to starboard," Vicaquirao said as he pulled at the tiller.

"Hard to starboard!" Teresa yelled, seeming to enjoy their dangerous slalom through the embattled ships as much as Gabriel. No wonder he loved her.

Ohin shouted out orders, and the galley banked to starboard just in time to miss colliding with another ship that abruptly shifted course. Moments later, they pulled hard to starboard again before straightening out and then coming to a dead stop while a cannon ball whizzed off the forecastle where Cyril and Cassius still stood. They used hand signals to relay information on obstacles ahead to Vicaquirao on the sterncastle. Gabriel did not recognize all of the signals, but some were universal. Such as the wild gestures to indicate a capsized ship invisible to anyone at the aft of the galley.

With each near miss, Gabriel began to feel both a confidence and a grave concern growing and struggling in his chest like the two sides of the sea battle around him. The closer they came to their ultimate destination the better the crew became at issuing and executing the orders that would prevent their galley from entering the war and potentially altering the timeline of history. However, with every avoided incident, they came closer and closer to the heart of the battle, and the events they were trying to avoid fell nearer and nearer together. Orders to halt chased commands to turn to starboard, with orders to row full ahead coming right afterward, followed again by instructions to pull hard to port.

The sweat of tension and anticipation soaked Gabriel's face and back, but he had no time to wipe his brow as droplets of perspiration stained the map and he called out timings. His mind ached from extending his space-time sense farther and longer than ever before. Even with Nefferati helping do the same, and Vicaquirao manning the tiller as he too scanned for events he might not have noticed when he created his map, they were always seconds from an encounter that might destroy them or alert the Apollyons to their presence.

Through the joint efforts of their commands, the galley swung to starboard as a hail of arrows flew overhead. Screams rose up from the deck below, voices overwhelmed by the proximity the war cries, cracking hulls, and cannon fire of the battle on all sides. The galley wavered as the starboard oars fell still in the water.

Gabriel looked over the sterncastle railing to see that at least half of the Grace Mages at the oars had been struck by stray arrows. He recognized one face, clenched tight in agony. Rajan grasped at the arrow shaft sticking from his chest as he screamed.

Gabriel simultaneously forced his mind back to the map and outward in time and space.

"Event dead ahead in five…four…three…" Gabriel shouted.

"Hard to port, hard to port!" Vicaquirao roared above the clamor of war as he yanked against the tiller.

Teresa relayed his words to Ohin who managed to get the port oars dropped and held at the last second.

"This is too close," Nefferati shouted. "The events are too close together."

"We can recover," Vicaquirao insisted, his face a mask of passionate self-control. "We are too near our goal to waver now."

"I'll tend to the wounded." Nefferati growled her words, a wave of anger emanating from her. Gabriel could not distinguish whether Vicaquirao, or the battle, or even herself, might be the cause.

"Make sure there is no magic," Vicaquirao called out to Nefferati as she descended the steps to the main deck. "And get those starboard oars back in the water."

"Event to port in nine…eight…seven…" Gabriel's hand clutched the pocket watch so hard he thought he might break it.

"Hard to starboard," Vicaquirao said, Teresa's repeated words blending into one statement as she shouted to Ohin and the crew.

Gabriel saw Ohin, Akikane at his side, pulling at one of the starboard oars while shouting instructions. Nefferati knelt beside a wounded mage, an arrow in the woman's shoulder. Rajan lay on the deck, unmoving, Marcus at his side, pressing on the wound around an arrow shaft.

A thunderous crack crashed upon Gabriel's ears, and splinters of wood showered down around him. He looked up to see the top of the center mast falling into the sea, timber shards and rope and rigging cascading over the port side crew manning the oars. The stray cannon ball left little of the mast still standing.

Gabriel's space-time sense rang in his head louder than the cracking mast or the clanging battle that engulfed them. The map listed six more events, each too close for a successful reaction. They could not recover fast enough from their near-misses. Each mistake set them off schedule and nearer to colliding with an event, whether another ship or a cannon ball or a hail of fire-tipped arrows.

Gabriel could feel something else, as well — the space-time bubble surrounding the Apollyons' ship. He could sense it like a beacon shining through thick fog, intermittently revealing its position as they approached it. The bubble was in the future but not distant. And not far across the water, either.

"The next event." Vicaquirao's eyes, wild and fervent, locked on Gabriel. "When is the next event?"

Gabriel knew when the event would happen and that it would occur too soon for them to avoid completely. And the incident after it would transpire even sooner. Gabriel felt his insides burn like he had swallowed boiling acid as he realized they could not follow Vicaquirao's map. Not anymore. Their very presence was presenting opportunities of target for the ships on either side. If they were not careful they would become part of the battle. If they followed the map it would lead them to their deaths.

Gabriel looked up from the map, walking away from it as he lurched toward the forward railing of the sterncastle to stand beside Teresa.

"Gabriel." Vicaquirao's voice rang through the acrid air.

"What's wrong?" Teresa shouted from beside him.

Gabriel didn't respond. He slipped the pocket watch into his pants and grasped the railing with both hands, pushing his space-time sense in every direction and into every moment, decelerating the events around him like a slow-motion film. He needed a new map. A new path through the clashing ships to reach the Apollyons' space-time bubble. One they could survive.

Gabriel held his breath, and in the absence of air recognized a familiar sensation in a discordant form. He had honed his space-time sense with Ohin while training, but had always noticed that his best results in applying that special perception came when practicing the sword with Akikane. The sword and the senses and the mind needed to unify in each moment of battle to truly be effective. Gabriel sailed now into battle and he needed to make the galley he stood upon his sword. He might not be able to think his way through the events of the battle the way Vicaquirao had done, but he could fight his way across the battle and around the probable events just as he had fought Akikane and Nefferati in the field outside Fort Aurelius. He only hoped the result proved more favorable.

"Hard to port," Gabriel yelled.

"But the…" Vicaquirao began to respond.

"Hard to port," Gabriel shouted again, glancing over his shoulder, knowing his eyes where fierce like a mad man's as he stared at Vicaquirao. "The map is useless now. Hard to port."

Vicaquirao's jaw tightened in what could have been either concern or admiration as he shoved the tiller to the right.

Gabriel turned back to the bow as two cannon balls seared the air where the sterncastle deck had been moments before.

"I have complete faith in you," Teresa said, her voice panicked as she placed her hand on Gabriel's and squeezed it tight.

"Steady on for three seconds, then pull to starboard thirty degrees!" Gabriel shouted to the crew. He barely felt Teresa's fingers holding his own, but the sentiment of her words filled him with confidence as he probed the surrounding battle with his space-time sense. "Pull to starboard now!"

The galley eased past the prow of a sinking ship thrusting out of the sea as its aft section filled with water.

"Starboard again twenty degrees." Gabriel's voice strained to rise over the roaring wall of war sounds filling the air, but Vicaquirao and the crew heard and obeyed.

"Steady on for five seconds and then hard to port!" Gabriel shouted.

A storm of flaming arrows stuck the side of the galley, but none reached the crew on the decks.

"Steady on for four seconds and then hard again to port!" Gabriel's voice felt raw as much from yelling as from the emotions he struggled to keep in check. He needed his head clear to see the path through the battle. The space-time bubble around the Apollyons' ship would appear at any moment.

"The bubble is close," Vicaquirao said.

"I know," Gabriel said. "Hard to port."

The galley pulled to the portside as a cannon blast from a ship three feet away covered Gabriel and the crew in smoking debris.

"The teams need to be ready," Vicaquirao said.

"I said, I know. Tiller to port! Port oars down! Starboard full! Starboard full! Tiller steady ahead. Full Stop! Ohin! The time seal and bubble need to happen now. Be ready to board in five…four…three…two…there's the ship!"

As though materializing out of a distorted mirage of the air, the Apollyons' vessel, a long Spanish galley without oars or sails, appeared right beside the Grace Mages' ship.

Gabriel felt Ohin and a group of five other Time Mages join and blend their magic to impose their own space-time bubble, combined with a space-time seal, around the barrier keeping the Apollyons' ship from entering the Primary Continuum. Even as the space-time bubble and seal expanded to encompass the other galley, Cyril and Cassius threw grappling lines over the railing of the Apollyons' ship, pulling the two vessels closer together.

Gabriel could see Marcus removing the arrow from an unconscious Rajan and placing his hands across the bleeding wound. He felt the healing Heart-Tree Magic even from fifty feet away. Elsewhere, Heart-Tree Mages healed the other wounded as best they could.

"That was the second most impressive thing you ever done." Teresa beamed at him as Nefferati and Akikane led the Grace Mage teams below in boarding the Apollyons' vessel.

Gabriel let out a long breath. He had managed to accomplish the impossible, but he knew his success opened the door for even more danger as the Apollyons awoke to the assault leveled at their ship.

"Thanks. What was the first?" Gabriel wanted to kiss her, but a battle offered little respite for romance.

"You haven't done the most impressive thing yet." Teresa smiled mysteriously.

"You guided us through without a map," Vicaquirao's voice sounded both proud and possibly envious. "I don't know that I could have done that even if I had thought to abandon the charts."

"It was the only way I could of think to get us here." Gabriel could not untangle the oddly enjoyable feeling of both pleasing and outsmarting Vicaquirao. It created a peculiar dissonance to realize he had done something to impress the Dark Mage, even if he did not fully trust the man.

"Now that we are here, there is more work to do." Vicaquirao's eyes shifted from Gabriel to the Apollyons' ship.

Men in black began to pour out of the lower decks. Gabriel did not need to count the men to know that there were more than the seven Vicaquirao and the Grace Mages had expected. Far more than seven.

"And more work than we were told to expect." Teresa glared at Vicaquirao as her hands filled with arcs of blue-white lightning.

Gabriel grasped the imprints of the pocket watch and the Sword of Unmaking. He embraced the imprints of the concatenate crystals in his pouch as well, but the link to their sources felt weak, like tendrils of smoke caught in a stiff wind. The interference of the dual space-time bubbles distorted their connections to their imprints.

"Let's hope the second part of the plan works better than the first." Gabriel glanced toward Vicaquirao.

"Plans are meant to be revised." Vicaquirao seemed on the verge of smiling again. "As you just reminded us so well."

"Time for some more revising, then." Gabriel threw his arm around Teresa's waist and drew the Sword of Unmaking from the sheath across his back. He wrapped himself and Teresa in a wave of Wind Magic and carried them into the air and over the railing of the Apollyons' ship, into the midst of yet another battle.

CHAPTER 9

A furnace-like inferno of wind and fire whirled around the forecastle deck of the Apollyons' Spanish galley. Gabriel ignored the flames lapping at his body as Teresa and Ling countered the dark magic of the lone Apollyon the Chimera team had cornered. Gabriel concentrated on blending Heart-Tree and Soul Magic and attempting to sever the Apollyon's psychic link with his brethren. He focused his thoughts on the magic at his command and on pressing beyond the Apollyon's mental defenses as he assaulted the man's mind.

The Apollyon cried out as Ling, Rajan, Sema, and Marcus continued their various magical assaults in an effort to distract him. The Apollyons had obviously practiced how to protect themselves from the severing magic Gabriel had discovered at the Battle of the Somme. Other Apollyons sent magical energy through the link to defend it even as Gabriel tried to dissolve the connection. It felt like trying to cut down a tree whose trunk grew thicker with each swing of the axe.

Gabriel hovered at the precipice of the Apollyon's mental wall. Another second and the Apollyon would be a whole individual again. Still dangerous, undoubtedly still an enemy, but able to freely choose his own actions.

The air around Gabriel exploded in a ball of sinuous lightning, wrapping around him and the rest of his team even as an invisible hammer of gravity smashed down upon them.

Gabriel released his attack on the Apollyon, shifting his magical energy to help Ling and Teresa mount a defense against the Dark Wind and Fire magic suddenly assailing them. The wooden deck beneath Gabriel's feet turned to ash, and he plummeted into the darkness of the hold.

As Gabriel crashed into the galley's curved inner hull, one of the ship's deck cannons fell nearby, cracking the wooden planks. He saw that two other Apollyons had joined the one he and his team had been fighting. The Dark Mages assisted the first Apollyon in a simultaneous assault of multiple deadly magical attacks — hurling Soul Magic curses on Gabriel's mind as Heart-Tree magic assailed his flesh and flames combined with an invisible force attempting to causing the atoms of his bodies to fly apart.

Gabriel struggled to his feet as he fought off the attacks, pulling Teresa up as he pointed the tip of the Sword of Unmaking at the nearest Apollyon, preparing to use Wind Magic to send the blade flying through the air. Before he could do so, Ling's Wind Magic enveloped him and his companions, yanking them through the air and into the darkness of the galley hold. As they flew between the thick wooden beams supporting the decks above, an explosion rocked the ship from the bow, dust and flame filling the spot where the Apollyons had been. A team of Grace Mages had attacked the Apollyons on the upper deck.

"Some light would be good!" Ling shouted as she violently altered their course through the air to avoid striking a support beam.

"Got it." Teresa held out her hand as three small balls of milky-white light appeared beside her.

Ling guided the mass of dangling limbs to a clear spot beneath the shallow hold, near a ladder leading to the aft deck of the galley. Gabriel ducked in the cramped space, looking around, expecting an attack from every direction.

"There are too many of them." Marcus pulled Sema to her feet.

"And it is taking too long to sever their connections to each other." Sema pushed her fallen hair from her eyes.

"We need to get back above deck and help the fight." Rajan stared up through the hatch to the battle raging above them.

"We need a plan." Ling looked along the length of the hold as though expecting the Apollyons they had fled to follow them.

"No, we need a bigger army." Teresa wiped sweat and soot from her eyes.

"We don't need a bigger army. We need to make theirs smaller." Gabriel stared at the decks above the hold, reaching out with his magic-sense, trying to discriminate between which magics were being cast in what direction. More importantly, he strained to determine which magical attacks had their origins in malignant imprints.

"There." Gabriel pointed upward with the Sword of Unmaking to a spot in the deck boards. "There are two of them up there. Rajan, you take out the deck beneath their feet. I'll pull them down. Ling, you hammer their heads with Wind Magic. Marcus and Sema, you need to combine your magic and knock them out before they can fight back. I'll help."

"What about me?" Teresa looked upset that Gabriel hadn't assigned her a role in his strategy.

"We're going to need some smoke to cover their disappearance," Gabriel said. "When Rajan turns the deck to dust, you light the hole on fire and make the smoke as thick as possible."

"Right." Teresa's eyes seemed alight with enthusiasm in the shadows cast by her magical illumination.

"Get ready." Gabriel scanned the deck above with his magic-sense, waiting for a pause in the two Apollyons' attacks. "Now!"

A five-foot circle of wooden planks above turned to dust as two black-clad Apollyons crashed to the floor of the hold, driven downward at unnatural speed by Gabriel's Wind Magic, even as Ling use her own Wind Magic to send the heads of the two men slamming into each other. The wooden decking above burst into flame as smoke filled the air. Gabriel lent his Heart-Tree and Soul magic to that of Sema and Marcus, forcing the stunned Apollyons into unconsciousness.

"Now that's a plan," Teresa said as the Apollyons slumped forward onto their faces.

"You sever one of them and Marcus and I will sever the other," Sema said. The psychic severing required both Heart-Tree and Soul Magic to accomplish. Sema and Marcus had practiced for such a procedure, but never actually performed it.

"No, we need to even the odds a bit more first." Gabriel once again began scanning the deck above with his magic-sense. "The other Apollyons will feel the link being cut and know where we are. After what happened last time, we need to knock a few more out before it will be safe to try severing them."

"Where next?" Rajan asked, his eyes following the tip of the Sword of Unmaking.

"Here." Gabriel again used the blade of the sword to indicate the point of attack. "Two more right there. Get ready. Now!"

The second attack followed the same pattern as the first, leaving two unconscious Apollyons below and a smoking hole above. A sense of confidence returned with the success of his plan, and Gabriel moved to selecting a third target from the many opportunities on deck. As he raised the blade of his sword to point out the next unsuspecting opponents, the gravity beneath his feet reversed itself, rocketing him and his companions toward the wooden planks above his head.

Gabriel's shoulder struck the underside of the deck as wood exploded upward. He tumbled into the open air as more forces of gravity assailed him and his teammates, slamming their arms and legs and heads together. A wall of water fell on them, driving their tangled mass of limbs down to the open deck as the inky darkness of deep unconsciousness began to pour over his mind.

Gabriel's lids fluttered as he struggled to open his eyes. Water dripped from his clothes and hair. The world did not look right. He hung upside down, suspended in the air by invisible magical forces. His teammates dangled, inverted, in the air beside him.

Three Apollyons stood facing him. He suspected he had only been out for seconds. Although everything looked wrong side up, he saw that the contest to take control of the ship still raged around him. Nefferati and Akikane battled side by side near the main mast of the Spanish galley, their actions and magical assaults blending like the movements of two dancers anticipating each other's every motion. Even struggling to regain his senses, he realized he should not have been surprised at the combined skill of the two True Mages. They had, after all, been fighting together for centuries.

"That was an excellent..." one of the Apollyons said.

"Plan of attack," a second Apollyon finished.

Gabriel looked at the men, their faces seeming bizarre from the reversed angle.

"We hope you don't mind..." the middle Apollyon said.

"That we took it for our own." The first Apollyon chuckled.

Gabriel wondered why they had revived him rather than kidnap or kill him. What did they want? What advantage did they see in keeping him a prisoner in the middle of a shipboard battle?

"Order the surrender of your people now..."

"And we will spare your lives."

That answered Gabriel's questions.

"I can't do that."

Gabriel saw the Sword of Unmaking, its blade driven into the deck twenty feet away. He had no idea where his pocket watch or the pouch of concatenate crystals might be. He tried to focus his mind on accessing the imprints of his own body, but his head throbbed too powerfully to make such a thing possible. He hung helpless before his enemies.

"You can…"

"And you will."

A small inferno began to circle the unconscious forms of Teresa and the other team members, licking at their clothes, steam rising as water evaporated from the fabric.

"I'm not in charge," Gabriel shouted.

"They will follow your orders…"

"Just the same."

Gabriel watched as the flames first dried then singed Teresa's hair.

"Maybe if they were…"

"Conscious to feel the pain…"

"You might reconsider."

Teresa's eyes blinked open, and she let out a weak scream as the fire lapped against her cheeks.

"Surrender now…"

"Now, or you will all…"

"All burn."

Gabriel's mind froze as he watched the flames engulfing Teresa and his friends. The others woke from forced slumber and added their screams to hers. Those cries reverberated in Gabriel's head as he tried to formulate a response, some action that might turn the desperate situation to his advantage. He could not order a surrender even if the Grace Mages fighting the Apollyons might follow his instructions. He had no doubt the Apollyons would kill them all and hold him prisoner until they mined every bit of information about the Great Barrier from his mind. There were no good options. There was no secret passageway out of peril.

Gabriel cried out as the magical flames spread from Teresa's body to encircle his own. As his own screams filled his ears and began to drown out those of Teresa and his companions, a blur of motion abruptly overtook his vision.

Vicaquirao dropped from the smoke filled sky above to the deck between Gabriel and the Apollyons, thrusting forth both of his fists, striking the two nearest Dark Mages in the chest with the force of two crashing locomotives, sending them hurtling through the air to smash into the deck of the Grace Mages' Venetian galley.

The flames searing at Gabriel's skin winked out of existence as he and his teammates fell to the deck in a painful heap. He looked up as the remaining Apollyon turned his magical arsenal against Vicaquirao. The elder True Mage countered the lightning and gravity and curses on his body and mind, pressing the Apollyon with a physical assault, striking at the man's face and kicking at his legs. The Apollyon staggered back, attempting to recover from an unexpected hand-to-hand attack. Vicaquirao pressed the fellow Dark Mage hard, each blow landing like a wrecking ball. The Apollyon's fist connected with Vicaquirao's jaw, but the older mage shook it off, pummeling his adversary several times in the chest before a final punch sent the Apollyon sailing over the railing, out beyond the range of the space-time bubble and into the waters of the Gulf of Patras. Once outside the space-time bubble it would be difficult, if not impossible, for the Apollyon to return to the ship.

Vicaquirao knelt beside Gabriel and Teresa, inspecting their burns.

"We do not have time to heal you." Vicaquirao looked around at the battle spread across two ships. "Our forces are too narrowly matched. We will lose more than this engagement if we do not find a way to force their retreat or mount our own."

"Thank you." Gabriel stared up at Vicaquirao. "For saving us."

"It is becoming a habit with me." Vicaquirao smiled briefly, then turned to the others still holding their burned limbs. "You must ignore your wounds and fight. We have little time to turn this tide. Find your talismans and then help protect Ohin and the other Time Mages."

"No." Gabriel raised his voice as he pushed himself to his knees. "The opposite. You're right. We can't hold them, much less defeat them. But if Ohin drops the space-time seal and leaves the time bubble in place to hold us out of the Continuum, the Apollyons will run. They don't want to risk losing any more duplicates."

Vicaquirao considered this a moment.

"Yes. I believe you are correct. I will inform Ohin." Vicaquirao looked at Gabriel's teammates again. "Find your talismans and hide. Protect Gabriel. Once the time seal is removed, he will be a target again."

"We'll keep him safe." Teresa reached out and took Gabriel's hand.

Vicaquirao nodded to Teresa and then turned and leapt into the air, sailing through the smoke and landing on the deck of the Venetian galley near Ohin.

"I'm sorry." Gabriel looked to the others. "All of you. I'm so sorry."

"You did the right thing, lad." Marcus checked the burns on Sema's arms.

"We need to get out of the open, fast," Ling helped Rajan limp toward a hole blown into the lower chamber of the sterncastle at the aft of the ship.

"What about our talismans?" Sema asked, getting to her knees and crawling after Ling and Rajan.

"We'll have to hunt for them slowly until the Apollyons are gone." As the words left Gabriel's mouth, two Apollyons ran along the aisle between the rowing benches, pursued by Akikane and Nefferati.

As the Dark Mages turned to make a stand beside the main mast in the center of the ship, Gabriel perceived the space-time seal around the two vessels disappear. He snapped his head around to search for Ohin and the other Time Mages. Vicaquirao stood beside them and two teams of Grace Mages, fending off five Apollyons. Gabriel smiled to himself as the Apollyons began to vanish into time, fleeing the attack on their ship. He had been right. They were more concerned with preserving their numbers for the impending assault on the Great Barrier than in risking their lives inflicting causalities on the Grace Mages.

"Good call." Teresa winced as Gabriel helped her to safety beside the others in the captain's room beneath the sterncastle deck. They dared not risk being seen until they knew that no Apollyons remained on the ship.

"A lucky guess." Gabriel watched as the two Apollyons battling Nefferati and Akikane pulled relics from their pockets and vanished. The bone-like relics looked nearly indistinguishable. As Gabriel hid with Teresa behind a water barrel, he noticed one of the previously unconscious Apollyons struggling to his feet, holding his head as he took something from his pocket.

Gabriel's heart suddenly raced as he stared at the relic in the Apollyon's hand. It looked exactly like the relics the other Apollyons had used to escape. It might be a piece of a larger artifact that led them all back to the same location in time. If Gabriel got ahold of that relic, he could strand the still-dazed Apollyon from retreating and potentially gain the key to finding yet another Apollyon base with one small magical act.

With no talismans at hand, Gabriel quickly stilled his mind and focused on the imprints of his own body, acquired when he had given his life to save his former classmates stranded at the bottom of the river in that bus so long ago. He sensed the Apollyon beginning to warp space and time. As Gabriel united the subtle energy of his own body and mind, he concentrated on forming the Wind Magic he needed.

The Apollyon looked up in shock as the small piece of pale bone fled from his hand before he could make the time jump away from the ship. The shard of bone soared through the air toward Gabriel's outstretched palm. He squeezed Teresa's fingers in his other hand and smiled, knowing he had managed to turn a near catastrophe into a minor success. His smile died and withered as the fragment of bone touched the flesh of his hand and the blackness of time travel enveloped him and Teresa.

A sharp jerk pulled Gabriel's mind followed by another even more powerful tug at his inner awareness. Then the blinding whiteness of the time jump stung his brain, fading to reveal not the deck of a ship, but the dense undergrowth of a primeval jungle. Gabriel stared at the bone relic in his hand and gasped as it rapidly disintegrated into gray dust. He looked up again, seeing the terror in Teresa's eyes as she used her free hand to push a massive palm frond from her face.

"What have you done?" Teresa looked at the ashy substance spilling through Gabriel's fingers.

"I don't know." Gabriel stared around at the jungle towering above them. As he took in his surroundings and tried not to meet Teresa's gaze, a dreadful certainly filled his mind and leadened his heart. The booby-trapped relic had taken them somewhere far into the past before self-destructing. The potent jolts he had distinguished with his space-time sense told him something else, as well.

"We don't have our talismans." Teresa swallowed.

Gabriel thrust his hands into his pockets to find them empty. The relics he usually carried with him were likely scattered across the deck of the Spanish galley where he had hung upside down as the Apollyons' captive.

"Do you have a relic?" Gabriel's voice sounded horse and constricted with fear, already knowing Teresa's answer.

"No," Teresa said, patting her pockets. "Nothing." She touched her chest. "Not even my amulet." Gabriel had lost his as well.

Teresa winced with the pain of her burns, tears filling her eyes. "We're trapped with no way home."

CHAPTER 10

Insects flitted through the air, wings an imperceptible blur as they buzzed and darted and hovered.

Gabriel focused on his breathing.

"These insects are big." Teresa spoke between fire-blistered lips, head resting on a makeshift pillow of palm fronds spread across the thick vegetation that covered the jungle ground.

A dragonfly the size of Gabriel's forearm whizzed past his head.

"We must be in the Paleozoic era. Maybe the early Permian or late Carboniferous Period." Teresa panted as she spoke, coughing into her hand. "Insects can only get this big with enough oxygen. The oxygen levels dropped around 270 million BCE. We must be at least 300 million years in the past."

"Shush your big brain for a minute." Gabriel closed his eyes and held his hands just above Teresa's face where the worst of the burns had begun to blister. "You're in shock from the pain. I need to heal you."

"You need to leave and get back to the others," Teresa said, her head rolling to the side.

"Quiet."

Gabriel concentrated on his breathing. He imagined his subtle energy as a pure, clear light pouring into his heart from above and below with every inward breath and radiating down into his hands with every exhalation. With each breath his subtle energy, the ultimate source of his magical power, grew slightly. His heart blazed with the energy as he pushed it into his hands, but he knew it to be a fraction of the power available with a talisman.

Gabriel had been practicing this meditation for years, but there were limits to its effectiveness. He could use the imprints of his own body and consciousness like a miniature talisman to focus his subtle energy and perform magic, but it took great concentration and had imperfect results. He could manage enough magical power to make a time jump by himself, but not with someone else.

Teresa understood this. He might be able to travel safely away through time at any moment, but not with her.

However, he could muster the magical energy required to heal Teresa's burns. It might take hours and several attempts, but he could repair her flesh. If he didn't, she could die within days from her burns and infection.

"Don't worry about me." Teresa's voice cracked with the dryness of her throat.

"Shut. Up. Now."

Gabriel focused his subtle energy on the imprints of his body and called forth the mental frame of mind necessary to bend and shape reality to his will, that special way of seeing and sensing the systems of life known as Heart-Tree Magic. As Gabriel deepened his concentration, Teresa let out a gasp, the flesh of her face and neck and shoulders rebuilding itself with a burst of cellular activity beyond normal biological processes. The blisters faded, and charred skin fell away as new dermis replaced it.

Gabriel's energy faded, and he redoubled his focus, visualizing the subtle vitality again as a clear, white light flooding his heart. In that moment, he detected something that had escaped him in his previous practice of cultivating his subtle energy. Another energy existed beyond it. Or around it. Or they existed together, distinct, but not separate. Like a drop of water that was part of a wave as well as an ocean. Gabriel sensed a vast sea of subtle energy inseparable from his own, yet somehow inaccessible.

This insight intrigued him. Akikane had mentioned this energy once in a meditation session. *The fundamental essence of all reality*, Akikane had called it. Gabriel had never experienced it before. Knowing he lacked a mind skillful and sublime enough to touch this ever-present cosmic energy, Gabriel ignored it for the time being and concentrated again on Teresa's burns, willing them to heal with Heart-Tree magic. As the fire-red flesh of her forearms turned pink, then white, then brown, she reached out a hand and placed it on Gabriel's chest.

"Stop. I'm fine. Don't waist all of your energy on me. Save it in case something big and ugly and hungry shows up."

Gabriel released his concentration and opened his eyes to stare into Teresa's. Her skin still looked raw, but she would recover with only mild scarring. She smiled, leaning up on one elbow and kissing him. He held her in his arms, his heart swelling as an anxious tension fled from his shoulders. She was alive and they were together. All other concerns were secondary.

They parted from the kiss, Teresa cupping his jaw in her hand for a moment before they both leaned back against a tree.

"So, the Apollyons used your trick to booby-trap their relics if anyone except them touched one, disintegrating after it took us here." A look of annoyance clouded Teresa's face. "We need to stop thinking of clever things they can use against us."

"I'm sorry." Gabriel stifled an urgent sigh. "If I hadn't grabbed the relic, we wouldn't be here."

"How could you know it was booby-trapped?"

"I should have guessed."

"It doesn't matter." Teresa tightened her grip on Gabriel's hand. "The Apollyon you took it from probably got trapped and left behind on the ship."

"And we're stranded hundreds of millions of years in the past." Gabriel warily eyed another giant flying insect floating nearby that seemed intrigued by the size of the possible meal the humans represented.

"I'm stuck here," Teresa said. "You can get back if you find a relic. You can use yourself as a relic if you need to."

"I'm not leaving you."

"Don't be stubborn." Teresa reached her free hand up to pull his chin toward hers. "You can always come back and find me. We found Nefferati twice with relics. I might be a couple of days older, but so what?"

Gabriel said nothing.

"I can survive for a few days. You don't need to worry about me."

Gabriel remained silent.

"Even if you mess up completely and I become part of the Primary Continuum, we're so far in the past that it won't matter much if you pull me out. And you can always kill me and save me again." Teresa smiled.

Her smile gradually faded with Gabriel's continued silence.

"What aren't you telling me?" Teresa's eyes narrowed as she raised her chin.

"We're not in the Primary Continuum." Gabriel's shoulders began to tighten again.

"We're in an alternate branch of time?" Teresa frowned. "Are you sure?"

"Yes. But it's worse than that." Gabriel's voice rang with despair. "We're in an alternate branch of an alternate branch of time. We're two bifurcated realities away from the Primary Continuum."

"How could the Apollyons even do that? Create a bifurcation this far back in time?" A look of confusion crossed Teresa's face as she tried to puzzle out an answer to her question.

"I don't know." Gabriel thought about it for a second, applying what he knew and what he had intuited of the Primary Continuum. "If they destroyed a significant species it could create a bifurcation this far in the past. But they would need to do it again in the first alternate timeline to create the second one."

"Which means life could evolve completely different in this world." Teresa glanced around at the jungle foliage.

"Maybe." Gabriel wasn't certain how life in a tertiary continuum might develop. "Humans may still evolve the same way since the dinosaurs will probably still be wiped out."

"Why go through all that trouble?"

"Because it makes a safe hiding place…and a perfect prison."

Teresa looked away from Gabriel and sat in silence. She grasped the intricacies of time travel as well as any Time Mage. She understood what it meant to be lost with no relics in an alternate branch of time, much less what being marooned two branches of time away from the Primary Continuum implied. While a Time Mage could find someone with a relic by searching its past with their space-time sense, this became a much less predictable endeavor when using a relic from an alternate branch of time.

Alternate branches of time were, by their very natures, less stable than the Primary Continuum itself. This allowed them to absorb greater changes to events in their timelines without bifurcations easily being formed. History in an alternate reality would essentially rewrite itself to compensate for even serious variations. Events could change. People could appear or disappear. Alternate timelines were flexible.

However, massive changes in these secondary continuums would produce new bifurcations, creating tertiary alternate branches, like those of a tree trunk splitting outwards. These tertiary continuums were even less stable, able to absorb wild changes to their timelines, potentially altering the past and future in fluid ways. While this meant these timelines were less prone to bifurcations, it also meant that relics within them were unreliable for time travel. In a continuum where the future might change, a relic became an unpredictable method of finding a fixed point in time. More importantly, it made locating someone lost along the timeline of a relic in a tertiary continuum impossible.

"Cross-dimensional degraded chrono-coherency," Teresa finally said.

"Exactly." Gabriel had no idea what the words meant, but he knew she recognized their predicament.

"That leaves us with only one choice." Teresa's face hardened as she turned back to Gabriel. "You have to go back alone."

"What?" Gabriel blinked in surprise. "No."

"You have to." Teresa's voice sounded fierce. "They need you. The Council. The war. Saving the Great Barrier. You're essential to all of that. You need to go back, no matter what. I'm expendable. You know that."

"You're not expendable to me." Gabriel glared at Teresa, his eyes filled with anger and fear. The responsibility for the danger threatening her rested with him. He would not leave her behind.

"This is about more than you and me." Teresa grabbed his other hand to hold them both in her own. "We have to think of more than ourselves. You have to consider more than me. They can't save the Great Barrier without you. I know that like I know I love you. Without you, the Apollyons will win. You have to go back."

Gabriel sighed, emotions roiling within his chest and making his arms weak.

"Even if I agreed to leave you behind — which I won't — it's not as simple as that."

"You can manage enough magic to take yourself through time. I've seen you do it." Teresa's voice quavered with her passion. "You can use yourself as a relic."

"I doubt it." Gabriel shook his head. "Do you think the Apollyons chose an alternate world, two steps removed from the Primary Continuum, where I actually exist in some form? Whatever the future of 1980 CE looks like in this reality, I guarantee you, I won't be in it. And I can't imagine the amount of magical energy it would take to use myself as a relic to jump straight back to the Primary Continuum, or if that's even possible."

"You can find a fossil here in the past and then locate some relic in the future that exists in both this world and the Primary Continuum," Teresa said. "It may take a while but you can do it. It's not impossible."

"No, it's not impossible," Gabriel said. "That exactly what I'm going to do, only I'm taking you with me."

"You've never been able to take anyone with you on a time jump without a talisman, and you don't have time to learn how now." Teresa threw Gabriel's hands away and crossed her arms.

"I will practice until I am strong enough to take us both forward in time with a fossil so we can find a talisman and a relic we can use to get back to the Primary Continuum."

"And how long will that take? Six months? A year? Two? Ten? How do we survive that long? No, you need to go. Now."

Gabriel glared at Teresa. Why was she being so stubborn? Couldn't she see he had no choice, no matter how long his plan might take?

"You're the one who made me promise not to leave you behind." Gabriel's fear swiftly transformed to anger. "You're the one who said we have to watch each other's backs. I'm watching your back."

"This is not what I was talking about." Teresa's eyes narrowed as her nostrils flared. "I was talking about you leaving me behind to protect me while you went off to do something stupid."

"I was trying to leave you behind so you would be safe." Gabriel shook his head in frustration. "Now you want me to leave you behind so you can die."

"I am not a fragile thing to be protected in a basket." Teresa's voice began to rise in volume as it lowered in pitch. "I am not the Seventh

True Mage's girlfriend. I am me. I don't need to be protected any more than the Council needed to protect you by hiding you away."

"I wouldn't be hiding you away," Gabriel shouted. "I'd be letting you die to save me."

"Exactly!" Teresa got to her feet and started to pace along the jungle moss. "You would die to save me. I should be able to make that same choice. We all risk our lives fighting this war. People make sacrifices and they die. It's my life. I'm giving it to save you and to save the war. There's more at stake than my life."

"And what would happen to me if I leave you to die, have you considered that?" Gabriel stood up to face Teresa. "What would that do to me? How do I live with myself? How do I face down a hundred Apollyons knowing I killed you just so I could fight them? I don't want to be that person. I refuse to be that person. You may die one day, but it won't be because I didn't do everything I could to save you."

"You are so stubborn." Teresa threw her hands up in exasperation.

"Would you leave me behind to help the Council win the war?" Gabriel stomped toward Teresa and thrust his face next to hers. "Would you leave me to die here in this jungle if you could travel through time to save yourself?"

"Yes." Teresa's lower lip twitched as she wiped tears from her eyes.

"Liar," Gabriel growled, the ball of anger in his chest feeling like it might explode.

"I would. I would leave you if it meant saving everyone else. I would." Teresa bit her lower lip to cease its continual twitching.

Gabriel stared at her in silence, holding his breath.

"I would. I'd leave you behind to save everyone else."

Gabriel said nothing, his lungs holding tight to air that filled them.

"I would."

Teresa seemed to vibrate with anger, her hands clenched at her sides as she held her breath, the silence stretching out between them as they stared into each other's eyes.

"Idiot." Teresa's shoulder's slumped in defeat.

Gabriel released his breath in a long sigh, anger leaving him like water flooding from an upturned bucket. He held out his arms and

Teresa fell into them, wrapping hers tightly around his ribs as she buried her face in his chest.

"I'd never leave you behind. Ever."

"I know." Gabriel tilted his head down to hers. "We'll get back. Together. I know we will."

"I hope so." Teresa raised her lips. "I really don't want to play Little House on the Paleozoic Prairie."

They kissed as the insects hummed nearby, oblivious for a short time to their predicament. Many moments passed in perfect bliss before Gabriel's senses overwhelmed his concentration, pulling him back to the jungle as he pulled away from Teresa's lips.

"Did you feel that?"

"Feel what?"

The ground shook beneath their feet, vibrations running up along Gabriel's legs.

"Where have all the insects gone?" Teresa glanced around them.

"Something is coming." The ground trembled again and Gabriel tried to gauge the direction of its origin.

"You think maybe we made too much noise?" Teresa stood beside Gabriel, still holding his hand.

"No more yelling in the jungle."

"You were yelling. I raised my voice for emphasis."

The colossal leaves of the trees began to vibrate and sway as the shaking of the earth grew in intensity.

"I think something big and ugly is coming," Teresa said.

The leaves before them parted to reveal a long leathery snout.

"I think we should run," Gabriel released Teresa's hand as they spun on their feet and dashed into the trees, clasping hands once more as they raced between branches and bushes.

As they fled, Gabriel glanced back to see what looked very much like a dragon pounding through the jungle behind them.

CHAPTER 11

The spiny edges of wide leaves scraped Gabriel's arms and face as he and Teresa ran, hand in hand, through the dense jungle, leaping over fallen tree trunks, pulling each other along, racing to outpace the creature crashing through the underbrush behind them

Gabriel glanced back at the massive reptile-like monster closing the gap between them, the tall, spiny fin along its back whacking tree branches as its four squat legs propelled its nearly ten foot long body through the jungle.

"I think that's a Pelycosaur," Gabriel panted.

"Great!" Teresa knocked a tree branch from their path and pulled Gabriel to the left. "I think they're carnivores."

"Since we're the only mammals in sight for millions of years, that makes us an easy lunch." Gabriel tugged Teresa to the right, running between two close-set trees. "I hear something."

"More giant uglies?" Teresa glanced from side to side as they ran.

"No. Water." Gabriel heard it clearly, even over the racket they made rushing through the jungle foliage. The roaring sound of moving water came from straight ahead. A second later he spotted a turbulent blue river coursing between the vibrant green of the jungle.

"A river?" Teresa looked behind briefly before turning to run faster. "That giant reptile's ancestors were amphibians a few million years ago. What if it can swim?"

"I'm hoping the current will be too fast for it." Gabriel saw white crests of water in the river.

"We could always try to fight it off with magic," Teresa said.

"If I thought I could stop panicking long enough to focus my mind, I might try," Gabriel said. "But I'm not even sure how much magic I could manage."

"Neither am I," Teresa looked to Gabriel and gave him a wild, terrified grin. "I guess we swim."

Gabriel and Teresa burst from the thick jungle leaves and leapt blindly into the swiftly flowing waters, the churning current sweeping them in circular eddies as it carried them rapidly downstream and toward the middle of the river.

They surfaced together, still holding hands, spitting water from their mouths and trying to steer themselves with their free arms. The river stretched 100 feet from bank to bank and seemed to be at least 15 feet deep. Gabriel looked back to see the Pelycosaur rush from the jungle and flop half into the water as it tried to stop itself from falling in the river. The creature's powerful hind legs dug into the earth, pulling it back to the edge of the riverbank.

"It worked. It's staying out of the river." Gabriel thought the look on its face appeared almost dejected at being denied a succulent meal.

"Wonderful. Now all we have to do is keep from drowning." Teresa's legs kicked in the direction of the shoreline.

"We should stay in the river and put some distance between us and our lizard friend." Gabriel tried to match the stroke of Teresa's free arm. It would be easier to swim if they let go of each other but also more likely that one of them might be carried along the current alone.

"Good idea." Teresa bobbed in the water. "But the river is getting faster. We'll be safer near the shore."

As Gabriel paddled toward the slower, shallower water along the shoreline, he spotted something upriver behind them. Something in the water. Something that looked like a large log. A large log with four legs. Four legs and two eyes poking up above the water line. Eyes that were looking right at Gabriel.

"Bad idea. Change of plan. We need to get out of the water. Now!" Gabriel watched as the crocodile-like creature's legs churned the water, propelling it in their direction.

"Why?" Teresa glanced over her shoulder, swallowing a mouthful of water when she saw what pursued them. "Seriously? Do I have a sign on my back that says eat me?"

"Over there." Gabriel pointed between strokes of his free arm toward a slight clearing along the river's edge twenty feet away. If they timed their swim toward the shore correctly, the river's current would take them right to the clearing.

Gabriel looked back, seeing the eyes of the amphibious beast 15 feet behind them. They reached the shoreline, letting go of each other's hands and using low hanging branches to pull themselves from the water and up onto the soft grass carpeting the small clearing. Gabriel jumped to his feet as he looked behind to see wide, tooth-filled jaws snapping out of the water. He knew they had no time to run. They need to fight the creature and scare it off, if not kill it. He focused his mind to manifest the subtle energy of his body, calling it forth as the massive reptile's powerful claws tore into the wet earth of the riverbank, pulling it closer, its enormous mouth only a few feet away. He struggled unsuccessfully to get his energy to align with his will. Realizing he would be too late, he abandoned the effort and frantically scanned the ground for a fallen branch or rock he could use as a weapon.

"Run." Gabriel said, hoping to distract the prehistoric crocodile long enough for Teresa to escape.

Gabriel looked over toward Teresa just in time to see a slender filament of lightning arc from her index finger and strike the charging creature on its snout. The reptile skidded to a halt with a wild, guttural yelp of pain, shook it elongated head vigorously, and then turned to slide back into the waters of the river.

"Nice shooting, Annie Oakley." Gabriel grinned at Teresa. He knew she had been practicing cultivating her subtle energy, but he had never seen her manage more Fire Magic than lighting an oil lamp.

"I thought that thing was going to eat us." Teresa wiped water from her face and wrung her hair. "I guess a little fear helps focus my mind."

"It didn't do anything for mine." Gabriel shook the water out of his own hair. "I was preparing to hit it with a rock."

"You spent too much energy healing me." Teresa frowned at him. "Which I told you not to do."

"And if I hadn't, you wouldn't have had the energy to scare off that croco-saurous thing. So we're both right."

"Croco-saurous?" Teresa laughed at Gabriel's newly coined designation. "Is that the scientific term?"

"It's more scientific than *big ugly thing*," Gabriel teased.

"I'm a math prodigy, not a paleontologist."

"We're going to need a paleontologist." Gabriel looked around at the jungle surrounding them. "It'd be nice to have an idea of when and where we are and how to start looking for a fossil to get out of here."

"We need to establish a basecamp first." Teresa scanned the vegetation near the riverbank. "We can make this clearing a little bigger, push it back into the jungle more. That will give us the river on one side and the jungle on the other."

"We can build a fire and keep it going." Gabriel began to walk the clearing, pacing out how much jungle they would need to remove. "That should keep the big uglies away."

"These rocks are easy enough to use to fashion hatchets or blades." Teresa picked up a large stone from the river's edge and smashed it against a nearby rock, chipping off a small piece. "With a little sweat and a little magic, we can double the size of the clearing and have enough materials to build a nice lean-to hut. And we can fashion wooden bowls, and you can harden them with magic, so we can boil the river water until it's safe to drink."

"Then all we need to worry about is finding some *small* uglies to eat."

"I may become a vegetarian for the duration."

Gabriel walked over to Teresa and wrapped his damp arms around her wet waist and pulled her into a kiss. As they broke apart he touched his nose to hers. "There is no one I would rather be stranded in the far past of an alternate world with than you."

"This is not the romantic road trip I keep suggesting."

"I'll pick you some flowers."

"Make sure they're not poisonous."

"Which reminds me, we'll need to be careful about testing any fruit this far back in time."

"Hmmm, maybe we should see if there are any fish-like things in that river."

Gabriel looked up through the leaves of the trees above their heads, catching sight of the sun slowly setting from its zenith. He estimated they would have six or seven hours before sunset.

"If you start on a fire pit and a fire, I'll work on making the clearing bigger and collecting what we need to build a shelter." Gabriel let his eyes fall from the sky to Teresa's face. She looked almost happy. "What?"

"I wouldn't want to be trapped here with anyone but you either." Teresa gave Gabriel a quick kiss and then turned to point at a spot in the grass near the tree line. "I think we should cut those trees down and put the fire pit there."

"Without a giant crocodile-thing staring at me hungrily, I might be able to manage some Earth and Heart-Tree Magic," Gabriel said.

Setting up the base camp took nearly all of the remaining daylight hours before sunset plunged the jungle into darkness. Fortunately, they had plenty of experience establishing camps in hostile terrains from their numerous missions into the prehistoric past. Using his own subtle energy, Gabriel combined small amounts of Earth and Heart-Tree Magic, along with the sharpened edge of a rock, to fell several of the slender trees around the natural clearing. He dragged the fallen tree trunks to the edge of the glade, creating a barrier of timber, stripping free the large leaves to use in making a shelter. He sharpened the tips of two of the straightest branches, fashioning simple spears to use as weapons, if necessary. They kept them near to hand while they worked.

Teresa used the thick, sharpened edge of a large piece of dried tree bark to dig a hole in the ground deep enough for a fire pit. She then took large rocks from the riverbank and built up a small, circular stone wall around the pit, both to contain the flames and to retain the heat of the fire into the night. Lastly, she scavenged the nearby jungle floor for fallen branches and dried leaves. With the application of a tiny bit of sustained Fire Magic, generated from her own subtle energy, she soon had a sizable blaze roaring in the middle of the clearing.

Knowing the fire would keep away all but the most curious or ravenous predators, they began to feel a little safer. With the clearing expanded to give them a supply of wood and more warning if they were being approach from the jungle, they began building a shelter. With jungle vines for rope, and thick, roughly-hewn branches for support beams, they soon fashioned the frame of a simple, but sizable, lean-to. An hour of stripping and weaving leaves into a roof left them with a place to hide from the inevitable rain. A bed of long grass completed the homemaking for their little hut.

Near sunset, they set about finding something to fill their loudly complaining bellies, scavenging through the neighboring jungle in search of edible plant life. They discovered two different kinds of fruit they had never seen. Gabriel scanned them with the same Heart-Tree sense he used to heal bodies and pronounced them safe to eat. After a bite of each, under Teresa's skeptical gaze, he declared them delicious.

Making their way back to the river, they decided enough light still reflected over the water to attempt catching a fish. With Teresa standing watch over the depths of the river, her eyes scanning for any more croco-saurous creatures, Gabriel stood in the shallows, again reaching out with his Heart-Tree sense, trying to determine if anything lurked beneath the rapidly darkening waters. After several frustrating failures, one of which left him soaked to his waist, he eventually speared something the length of his arm that looked like a fish but fought like a water-borne rhinoceros. It even had a horn. He hauled it to shore and Teresa ended the battle with a well-placed rock to the fish's head.

By the time darkness cloaked the jungle and the brilliant stars of the later Paleozoic era filled the sky, Gabriel and Teresa sat comfortably beside their little hut, eating fish roasted on a jury-rigged spit while nibbling pieces of green-yellow fruit sliced with the magic-sharpened edge of a wooden knife.

"Not bad for two city kids." Gabriel plopped a piece of fatty fish into his mouth and wiped his hands on the grass next to him.

"We're going to need to come up with something to carry water in, but yeah, I'm pretty proud of us." Teresa pulled another piece of fish meat free from the inner side of the blackened carcass and blew on it gently before passing it through her teeth.

"I'm sure we'll find something with a big enough bladder to use for carrying water after we eat the rest of it." Gabriel took bite of fruit.

"I was thinking more like hollow coconuts than giant lizard bladders." Teresa's face twisted in mild disgust.

"Are there coconuts in the Paleozoic era?" Gabriel scrunched his face while considering the question. "We can find a ridiculously large seedpod and make it water-tight with dried tree sap."

"Or you could waterproof it with a little Earth Magic," Teresa said.

"Oh. Right." Gabriel felt silly. Although magic had become second nature to him, he still sometimes forgot how easy it made certain tasks.

"So, any idea how to find a fossil when fossils are only just being made?" Teresa asked.

"The river is probably our best bet." Gabriel had pondered this question while working to expand the clearing. Every era created fossils as a natural consequence of geological forces interacting with biological remains. As a result, the farther forward one stood along the timeline, the more fossils might be found. Conversely, the farther back in time one went, the fewer fossils were available for discovery. "If we can find a shallow spot of sandy shoreline, we might come across something from an earlier age."

"You don't sound very optimistic." Teresa turned from the fire toward Gabriel.

"Well, what we really need is a dry river bed. Something that was a flowing river a million years ago but dried out, leaving dead fish caught in the baking mud." Gabriel's elation at establishing the camp and preparing a satisfying meal ebbed away. "We could try hiking to someplace more likely to have fossils, or at least a little easier to dig for them. A desert maybe. Or an arid rocky land that might have had more life on it millions of years ago."

"How long do you think it will take?" Teresa's voice sounded hesitant, as though she didn't want to hear the answer.

"Weeks. Maybe months. I can't imagine it'll take more than a year. Or two at the most." Gabriel stared at the fire, afraid to look in Teresa's direction. She had been so adamant in arguing that he should find a fossil and leave her behind, and he so determined to convince her how wrong that would be, he hadn't had time to consider how long it might take to accomplish the goal of finding a suitable relic.

"Are you serious?" The pitch of Teresa's voice forced Gabriel's attention from the fire to her face.

"Well, if we're lucky it could be weeks."

"But it could be years."

"Yes." Gabriel smiled, trying to infuse as much optimism as possible into his next words. "But while we're working on finding a fossil, we can also start imbuing an artifact to become a talisman."

Teresa cocked her head at the idea. "I hadn't considered that. No one does that. It takes too long."

"With two of us it will take less time," Gabriel countered.

"How long?" Teresa asked.

"Well, I started imbuing a candleholder when I was held in Kumaradevi's palace, and it was slow work, but I'd say that with both of us, we might be able to imbue an artifact with enough imprints to use as a talisman within six months. A year at most."

"A year." Teresa's shoulders slumped.

"At most." Gabriel thought about it again. "Maybe eighteen months."

"You are pouring inky darkness all over my sunshine."

"Sorry." Gabriel felt bad about deflating the euphoric mood of establishing their basecamp and foraging their first meal while stranded. "I'll practice cultivating my subtle energy too. Between the two, and assuming we find a fossil, we might be able to accomplish a jump in four months. Maybe three."

"You're lying to make me feel better now, aren't you?" Teresa raised an eyebrow at Gabriel.

"Yeah." Gabriel laughed sheepishly at being caught out. "We're stuck here for a while."

"Well then, I suppose that means we should talk about the dinosaur in the room." Teresa's expression shifted to one Gabriel always found difficult to read.

"Dinosaur?" Gabriel looked to the jungle briefly, even though he knew Teresa's metaphor referred to something else. He wasn't certain what, but the heat rising in is face pointed toward one particular topic.

"We need to talk about The Promise." Teresa's eyes locked onto Gabriel's.

"Ah…The Promise." Gabriel had somehow managed to push the thoughts about The Promise and the implications of how hard it would be to keep it while trapped alone with Teresa in a tropical jungle to the back of his mind as he had worked to establish the camp. As Teresa stared at him the way she did just then, soft firelight painting the curves of her face, he found his thoughts consumed with The Promise, and moreover, how much he wanted to break it.

"I don't know if Sema and Marcus envisioned this kind of circumstance when they presented us with The Promise," Teresa said.

"Actually, this is probably exactly what they had in mind." Gabriel laughed. "They watch us like owls hunting mice most of the time."

"So the question is, do we honor that promise here, when we are away from everyone else?" Teresa leaned forward, waiting for Gabriel's response.

"Wait." Gabriel considered the problem and all the possible answers, wondering which one Teresa was looking for, and more importantly, what her answer might be. "Do you want me to tell you what I want to do or what I think we should do?"

"Those are two different things?" Teresa looked surprised.

"Well, it's all about the time frame," Gabriel said, clarifying his thoughts as he spoke them aloud. "The Promise makes a certain amount of sense, even if it is extremely old fashioned and wildly hypocritical. I mean, they want me to stage a coup and lead the Grace Mages like an adult, but they don't actually want me to be adult when it comes to you. But breaking The Promise does complicate things. Everybody says it complicates things. However, considering how many people break similar promises, it seems like a nice complication to have. Especially alone in the jungle, potentially for months, if not years. But there's another complication. The longer we're here the more sense it makes to break The Promise, because, well, we might be here a long time. But, there is a counter argument that the longer we're here the more important it is to keep The Promise, because breaking The Promise can lead to serious consequences that get up and walk away from you. Of course, if we are stuck here for years and years, those kinds of consequences are pretty desirable. At least that's what everybody who has mobile consequences says. And here's the real question, the one that makes the time frame so important — how long were the terms of The Promise to begin with? That was never very clear to me. This was probably intentional, now that I think about it. Is this supposed to be a promise that expires when we turn a certain age, or is this supposed to be a promise that we keep until we make some sort of special announcement that calls for invitations and cakes and dancing? I think there's a case to be made that the contractual basis of The Promise is invalid because the terms of duration aren't specified. Of course, it's not like we can take this to a judge. Especially not here. So we kind of have to make our own decision. Although we don't have to decide about it tonight if you don't want to. Obviously."

Teresa sat in silence for a moment, her face a mixture of confusion and appreciation.

"You seem to have given this a great deal of thought," Teresa finally said.

"I think about it a lot. Besides the Apollyons and Kumaradevi and Vicaquirao and the war and the Great Barrier, what else to I have to think about?" Gabriel realized that maybe he hadn't appropriately prioritized his thinking.

"I guess it's nice that you make the time." Teresa's face glowed with mirth the firelight.

"It's my favorite pastime." Gabriel knew this to be an understatement.

"So, what should we do?"

"What do you want to do?"

"If I knew exactly what I thought we should do, would I be asking you?"

"Good point."

"Wait."

"What?"

"Who wants you to stage a coup and lead the Grace Mages in the war?"

"Nefferati and Akikane. And Ohin. I wanted to tell you, but they made me promise not to tell anyone."

"Maybe you're too good at keeping promises."

"I know how to break a promise."

"Really?"

"Let me show you."

Gabriel leaned over and kissed Teresa, sliding his hand around her waist as his lips touched hers. They kissed and caressed by the light of the flickering fire beneath the blazing stars for what seemed like a small eternity — until the bushes behind their makeshift shelter rustled with the unmistakable sound of something large passing.

"What was…"

"That!"

Gabriel and Teresa leapt to their feet, grabbing their spears and shielding their eyes from the firelight. Gabriel focused his mind and channeled his subtle energy, preparing to attack whatever might emerge from the underbrush with a small blast of lightning.

They stood, spears clenched, magic poised, listening to the sounds of the jungle for several minutes. Finally, as though by silent agreement, they decided the danger had passed. Gabriel took Teresa's fingers in his own as he leaned the spear against his side, holding it with his free hand.

"We should take turns standing watch through the night." Gabriel glanced at Teresa and then back to the shadowed leaves shifting in the breeze.

"I suppose the jungle has decided what to do about The Promise." Teresa laughed softly.

"At least for tonight." Gabriel joined her in laughing.

"It's nice you know you think about special announcements and cakes and dances." Teresa stared deep into his eyes.

"How could I not?" Gabriel kissed her as the moon rose above the trees, painting their gentle embrace in soft, dappled light.

CHAPTER 12

They spent the night alternating shifts on watch every two hours, sitting with their backs to the fire, keeping an eye on the water and the jungle and each other. While most of the large reptiles of the age seemed to sleep at night, a few nocturnal denizens of the bush wandered close enough to camp that staying awake on watch did not present a problem. Splashes from the river, which Gabriel attributed to ancient crocodile-like reptiles hunting, also made it easy to remain alert. The creatures apparently ate day and night.

Gabriel took the last watch, letting Teresa doze late into the morning to compensate for the lack of sleep during the night. He felt tempted to forage some fruit for breakfast, but the thought of coming back to camp and finding a crocodile creature in the hut instead of Teresa tempered his growing appetite.

When Teresa woke, they freshened up in the cool waters of the river, taking turns keeping an eye out for anything that might want to eat them while washing their faces. They found more fruit of a slightly different variety than the night before, ate a quick meal, and began their quest to find a fossil that might take them away from their Paleozoic prison and into a future where they hoped to find a way back to the Primary Continuum.

Discovering a suitable fossil for time travel proved both easier and more difficult than Gabriel had anticipated. They found a sandy stretch of land along the water's edge, a little more than a mile upriver from their campsite. They discussed moving their camp closer to the dig site but decided against it. If the site didn't pan out, they would need to search for another location anyway.

After three days of digging with makeshift wooden shovels and sifting through the fine sandy soil with their fingers, Teresa discovered a tiny trilobite fossil. Gabriel's elation and excitement matched hers, until he scanned the relic with his space-time sense.

"No good." Gabriel tossed the fossil back into the hole they had been digging.

"What do you mean?" Teresa scowled at the fossil in the dirt and then up at Gabriel.

"It stays underground for the entire length of its timeline right up to the Great Barrier." Gabriel kicked earth over the hole. "Let's try here." He began burying the hole by digging another.

"Maybe we're going about this all wrong." Teresa looked around the river and jungle as Gabriel pawed at the soil. "We should be trying to find a fossil before it's a fossil."

Gabriel looked up from his digging. "You want to catch insects and critters and see which ones become fossils?"

"Is that crazy?" Teresa's tone of voice indicated she suddenly thought it might be.

"Only a tiny fraction of the remains from animals or insects become fossils," Gabriel said. "We could be here decades trying to do that."

"Oh." Teresa knelt down to help Gabriel dig. "You should at least check the bones of the fish we eat for dinner."

"That's not a bad idea." Gabriel thought about it. "It's also possible we might get lucky and find a fossil that will not only take us to the future but that also exists in the Primary Continuum. That would make our journey much easier. Any relic we find in the future that also exists in the Primary Continuum will be a shadow relic. Since it never really existed in the Primary Continuum, it won't directly link to it."

"Dysphasic quantum morphic resonance," Teresa said. "Spooky action at an impossible distance."

"Alternate realities will mimic the pattern of the Primary Continuum even if they diverge in significant ways," Gabriel said. "Like a shadow cast across multiple timelines."

"That's what I said."

"And aren't you impressed that I understood?"

"Can you even make a jump like that?" Teresa paused in her digging to look at Gabriel. "A jump between realities with a relic that isn't really a relic?"

"I don't know." Gabriel kept digging to avoid giving any sign of the doubts rapidly filling his mind. "I'm not sure if anyone has ever tried something like what we need to do."

"Oh good. We get to break new ground in time travel. That's always exciting." Teresa wiped the sweat from her chin with her shoulder. "So, here's a different question. If we're stuck here for months or years trying to find the right fossil, will we become part of this Continuum, and will it mess things up for us to leave?"

"I don't think so." Gabriel had also pondered this. "This world is a reality two branches away from the Primary Continuum. Even if we merge with it, the timeline will adjust to our being gone. And we're so far back in the past, I doubt it will matter."

"Unless future archeologists find our bones and think we're an alien Adam and Eve," Teresa said.

"You read too many sci-fi books." Gabriel wanted to laugh at the idea of his and Teresa's remains becoming fodder for alien conspiracy theorists in a future alternate reality, but the notion seemed less impossible the more he considered it.

They resumed digging, one of them always facing the water and the other constantly turned toward the jungle in the event that something large and hungry thought they might make a quick and easy meal.

Over the days, they had both gotten better at summoning the subtle energy required to produce magic, even if only slender streams of fire or electricity. Gabriel had also begun to master the method of combining Heart-Tree and Soul magics to convince curious creatures that he and Teresa were far less interesting than their tiny brains originally assumed.

Their fossil hunt went on like this day after day after day. While the sun stayed in the sky, they dug and sifted through the silky dirt along the river's edge, breaking for lunch and returning to camp for dinner. Days when it rained, they huddled in their hut to stay dry. After their first soaked day of rain under a leaky roof of woven leaves, Gabriel spent a few hours using Earth Magic to waterproof their dwelling.

In the evenings, they sat by the fire, eating roasted fish and the occasional large lizard. They talked and took turns trying to imbue a small, flint spearhead that Gabriel had fashioned to be a talisman. Even with their combined efforts, it soon became obvious that imbuing the spearhead with enough imprints to assist Gabriel in making a time jump would require months, at best. Their conversations ranged from the day's mundane events to what they missed from their lives at the fort to possible strategies for protecting the Great Barrier should they succeed in getting home.

Inevitably, the topic of The Promise arose, but it seemed moot, as guard duty occupied their nights and fossil hunting filled their days. Gabriel sensed they were both ignoring The Promise as it related to their circumstances, postponing the day when, whether bored while waiting for the rain to stop, or simply too curious to care about consequences, they would come to a mutual decision to abandon the pact. Their regular baths in the river and hours spent next to the fire while their clothes dried were the only times when abiding by The Promise felt like a near physical impossibility.

During the night, while taking his shift at guard duty, Gabriel practiced the meditation to increase his inner subtle energy. He found that it helped keep his eyes open and his mind alert to the potential dangers of the jungle. He made slow progress in cultivating the subtle energy available to him, and he knew it would take many, many months to develop his magical strength enough to take Teresa along with him on a time jump, even with the help of the talisman they sought to imbue.

As days turned to weeks, the footprint of their basecamp continued to expand in direct proportion to the amount of wood required to fuel their fire each night. This slow deforestation had the pleasant side effect of giving them a larger back yard, as Gabriel thought of it, putting potential threats that might emerge from the jungle at a greater distance from their hut. Furthermore, it allowed them to dig a sizable latrine within the boundaries of the camp, but still far enough away from the hut and the river to be sanitary.

One morning, after weeks of sunrises and sunsets had begun to blur into one interminable day, Gabriel woke at dawn to find Teresa seated by the remnants of the fire with a small, leaf-wrapped object cupped in her hands.

"Happy sixteenth birthday." Teresa kissed him as he crawled from the hut and into the pale sunshine.

"Thank you." Gabriel blinked away the sleep and accepted the delicately wrapped gift. He had forgotten his birthday.

"It's not the keys to a car, but considering the options, it's the best I could come up with." Teresa beamed at him, bouncing with excitement as he began to tease the leaves apart.

"This is extremely well-wrapped." Gabriel admired Teresa's handiwork while separating the interwoven leaves.

"Presentation is ninety percent of perception," Teresa said.

"You sound like an advertising executive."

"I've been thinking about opening a gift shop." Teresa laughed. "It would be good for the local economy."

"We could use a lemonade stand."

"A grocery store would be nice."

"Oh!" Gabriel untangled the strips of leaves enveloping his present, revealing it to the sunlight. "It's lovely."

In his palm sat a small stone, polished smooth by thousands of years on the river bottom. Across the face of the rock, Teresa had carved a simple message:

$G+T = Bliss^3$

Gabriel grinned and kissed Teresa. A long while later, he pulled away to look again at the stone in his hand.

"You've reduced our love to a mathematical equation." Gabriel laughed.

"I've *expanded* our love with a mathematical equation." Teresa beamed.

"You are such a geek." Gabriel kissed her again.

They decided, in honor of Gabriel's birthday, to take a day off from searching for fossils. Their single-mindedness in mining the slender strip of soil along the river's edge for the past several weeks had rewarded them with at least one fossil every few days, but nothing they could use to travel into the future. Teresa suggested a hike as a birthday celebration, which would also function as a chance to scout the area for a new potential hunting ground for fossils.

After a quick breakfast, they packed a lunch of dried reptile meat wrapped in leaves and a mix of colorful fruits. Teresa carried these in a basket she had made from woven palm fronds as they headed upriver. A large, dried seed pod filled with water hung from Gabriel's shoulder. Teresa's suggestion to use magic to make it watertight had turned out to be much easier than using a lizard bladder. And the water tasted clean. As long as they stayed near the river, they wouldn't need it, but they preferred to be prepared.

They followed the riverbank for several hours, talking quietly and moving as silently as possible, always on the lookout for any possible attack by crocodile-like creatures from the water, or land-based reptiles in the jungle. By the time the sun reached its midpoint in the sky, they had gone farther downriver than ever before. Having found the fossil hunting site on the first day of exploration, they hadn't had the time, or inclination, to do more scouting.

An hour later, the dense foliage began to thin out. Within another hour, the trees gradually started to give way to grassland. Soon they stood at the edge of a grassy plain stretching for miles, the river winding its way through the flat land like a rivulet of rain water on a window pane. A short hike brought them to a bend in the river where a low hillside had eroded away from flooding, exposing a wide stretch of sandy soil. They stopped to eat their picnic lunch and discuss their options.

"It's more exposed." Gabriel gnawed on piece of lizard jerky. "But it gives us a better sightline for any predators approaching."

"We can put the hut there on that rise." Teresa pointed to a nearby hill with the stick of meat in her hand. "But we won't have the trees to protect us from the wind and rain."

"We can reinforce the shelter after we move it," Gabriel suggested.

"We'll have to carry all the wood for the hut," Teresa said. "And for the nightly fire."

"There are a few trees here on the plains," Gabriel said. "And some dead braches we can salvage."

"We could build a small raft to haul wood downriver." Teresa bit into the jerky in her hand, speaking around the chunk in her mouth. "As long as we stay near the shore we should be fine."

"That's a great idea," Gabriel said. "And if we don't find anything here, we can take the raft farther downriver to hunt for a new place to dig."

"It's official then." Teresa smiled as she scanned the plains. "We have a new home."

Constructing a raft and moving their basecamp took several days. After establishing the newly reinforced hut atop the small hill near their new fossil quarry, they spent most of two days scavenging dried wood from the nearby plains and ferrying more firewood with the raft. However, returning the small craft back upstream for each load proved more time consuming than they had originally anticipated. The current ran too swiftly to make paddling or poling their way upriver viable methods of transport. Eventually, they fashioned a thick rope from jungle vines and used it to pull the raft from along the riverbank. They each took turns hauling the empty vessel while the other used a long pole to guide it from the river's edge.

A few days after their decision to relocate, they had reestablished their encampment along with an ample supply of wood for a new fire pit. They felt relieved to find the move more than justified as their first full day of digging exposed twice as many fossils as they had hoped to find. In the two weeks between his birthday and the date that made Teresa once again numerically older than Gabriel, they worked constantly, driven by the hope that a new location might bring them luck.

Gabriel enjoyed these days, mostly because they allowed him to think of himself as the same age as Teresa. It didn't bother him as much as it had when they first started dating, and he assumed it would matter less and less the older they grew, but being nearly a year younger than her still irked him in indefinable ways. In his mind, at least, it reinforced the impression of him being less mature. He had once mentioned this concern to Marcus, who had assured him that this perception was unlikely to change, no matter how old he became. He usually managed to forget about it. Usually.

The day of Teresa's seventeenth birthday proved momentous for more than merely the celebration of a milestone. Gabriel woke her with a kiss and present. Knowing he could not manage an intricate weaving of leaves to wrap his gift, he had instead wrapped it in a wide leaf and encased it in a layer of clay from the riverbed, letting it bake dry in the hot sun of the plains.

Teresa stared at what appeared to be a baseball sized clump of dried earth and laughed.

"A ball of dirt. How romantic."

"The romantic part is on the inside." Gabriel tapped the dried clay with his finger.

"Ooo. Like a clay chocolate truffle." Teresa dug her fingers into the clay and began to pull it apart.

"Lots of clay. Not so much chocolate." Gabriel held his breath as Teresa pulled the earthen crust from around the leaf-wrapped package.

She hesitated a moment and then tore open the inner leaf to reveal a small seashell, a delicate purple and white pattern mottling its ribbed outer curves. Inside the shell, she found the letters *G&T* etched into a tiny, red-painted heart.

"It's beautiful." Teresa threw her arms around Gabriel's neck and offered her appreciation in the form of a passionate kiss. When she broke away her face looked inquisitive. "Is it a relic?"

"It's not *that* nice a birthday present." Gabriel laid his fingers across the seashell. "It only lasts a few million years before getting pulverized by a rock."

"How did you find a seashell here?" Teresa asked.

"We must be close to an ocean." Gabriel had also wondered about that. "This whole area was probably under water at one time. That's why we've been so lucky finding fossils."

"Lucky?"

"Unsuccessfully fortunate."

"Now there's a phrase to rally behind." Teresa laughed.

"Shall we take the day off?" Gabriel asked as they stepped from their small hut to greet the day.

"Maybe we'll quit early. I have a good feeling about today." Teresa looked again at the inscription on the seashell before sliding it into her pocket.

"I thought I was the one who was supposed to have premonitions?" Gabriel said.

"It's more of a gut feeling," Teresa answered.

The premonition of Teresa's gut proved prophetic. Shortly after they returned to digging in the sand after a lunch break, she discovered the fossil of a miniature reptile. Gabriel examined the rock in her hand with his space-time sense and let out a whoop of joy.

"You were right!" Gabriel kissed her. "We found it."

"Will it get us home?" Teresa asked between joyful kisses.

"Not all the way," Gabriel said. "It doesn't link to the Primary Continuum, and it gets destroyed in a fire in someone's fossil collection in the late 1800s, but that means there are humans and that we can find more relics and make our way home."

"Humans. That's good news." Teresa sighed. They had both worried that the alternate universe they inhabited might evolve in a radically different way, producing another dominant species that achieved civilization, or worse yet, never producing one at all.

They stared at each other a moment, both knowing what finding the fossil meant but hesitating to speak it aloud. Gabriel saw the look in Teresa's eyes and spoke first.

"It won't take that long," he said.

"You said it might take a year or more." Teresa looked away.

"We're not going have this argument again." Gabriel's stomach began to churn uncomfortably.

"I'm only pointing out the obvious." Teresa turned away.

"It's obvious you're not thinking straight. I told you — I'm not leaving without you."

"That was before we had a fossil to get you home. You can leave now."

"You and I leave together."

"I'm the only thing keeping you here. Everyone else back in the Primary Continuum needs you more than I do."

"I need you more than they need me."

"You can find me again."

"I'm telling you, the variables make it impossible. You know that. This timeline is too unstable. Even travel into the future is unpredictable."

"I trust you."

"If I leave you, I can't get back. I might be able to use the fossil to come back to this time period, but I wouldn't be able to be accurate about it. I might find you decades later, if at all."

"I said, I trust you."

"I don't trust myself. I'm not leaving you here."

"You are so…ugh!" Teresa broke away from Gabriel's embrace and stood facing the river.

Gabriel stepped behind her, staring at her back for a long while before picking up his spear and walking down to the river to catch a few fish for dinner. He sulked and fumed as he stabbed unsuccessfully at the water. With each failed attempt to spear a fish, his ire clouded his concentration making success impossible. Finally he gave up, thrusting the spear into the sand and stomping off along the riverbank. He walked a few hundred feet away and squatted on a slight rise in the land. Even in his anger, he never thought of getting out of sight of Teresa, in the event a prehistoric creature found her appetizing while alone. She stayed near the hut, engaging in seemingly pointless and repetitive tasks, like cleaning out the fire pit three times.

Eventually, she walked downriver to join Gabriel.

"Sorry." Teresa sat on the grass beside him.

"Me too." Gabriel reached out his hand and Teresa took it.

"What are you apologizing for?" She pivoted to get a better look at him.

"For all the things I was thinking about you for the past hour." Gabriel sheepishly stared at the grass before him.

"Well, I'm only apologizing for the things I say out loud." Teresa tightened her grip on his hand. "But I am sorry."

"Let's catch a fish to celebrate your birthday and finding the fossil." Gabriel stood up, pulling Teresa to her feet.

"Excellent idea." She leaned in to kiss him, but he pulled his face back and caught her eyes with his own.

"And no more arguing about getting home together." Gabriel's brows furrowed with the seriousness of his emotions.

Teresa took a deep breath and exhaled slowly before making her reply.

"Deal."

Gabriel kissed her, and they walked hand in hand along the riverbank back to their campsite. While they did not argue again about the idea of Gabriel using the fossil to make the time jump to the future alone, the unspoken notion created an undercurrent of tension between them in the ensuing weeks.

With the possession of a fossil to take them forward in time to human civilization and, presumably, to shadow relics that might exist in the Primary Continuum, they spent the majority of their time focused on cultivating their inner subtle energy and imbuing the spearhead to use as a talisman. The level of concentration required for these two tasks limited their ability to engage in them. They could only focus their minds for so long before the effort brought about lapses in clarity that made the process untenable. Complicating this, they needed to remain on watch from the large reptile life inhabiting the tall grass of the plains. They each managed four meditative sessions a day. While one concentrated on the spear head, or intensifying their subtle energy, the other stayed on guard and prepared meals.

Three weeks after finding a useful fossil, Gabriel tried to assess their progress, as much to calm his fears as to counter Teresa's silent arguments that he should leave her in the alternate Paleozoic. He estimated that with his gradually increasing inner subtle energy and the imbuing of the spearhead, he might be able to manage a time jump with Teresa in ten to twelve months. If they combined their magical energy, they could potentially reduce that time to eight or nine months. This, of course, assumed that no serious injury befell either of them during that time. Not optimistic news, but he shared it with her, nonetheless, during an evening meal.

"Well," Teresa said, after a long pause. "That's better than two years."

"Yes," Gabriel said, trying to infuse the word with as much optimism as possible.

As the weeks continued to pass, the days grew longer and hotter, signaling a seasonal shift from a rainy spring to a dry summer. The grass of the plains became brownish and brittle, the river shrinking to half its former size. This newly expanded riverbank would have proved a boon if they had still needed to find a fossil. However, they deemed their time better spent trying to generate the magical power necessary to utilize the fossil they already possessed rather than hunting for something new that might take them farther into the future of the alternate timeline.

In the early hours before sunrise, nearly two months after Teresa's birthday, Gabriel sat by a small fire taking the last watch before dawn.

The dark clouds blotting out the stars had threatened all night to release a torrent of rain. Instead, as the sun rose behind a canopy of grey, lightning began to flash across the sky like brilliant, deformed spider webs. When the faint smell of smoke tickled his nose, Gabriel gently nudged Teresa to consciousness.

"It's still dark." Teresa groggily rubbed her eyes.

"I think we have a problem." Gabriel pointed to the western horizon. A pale orange light reflected against dark clouds that looked less and less likely to release their rain.

Teresa followed Gabriel's finger and then turned back toward the east where a hidden sun had barely begun to brighten the sky. She looked at Gabriel, her eyes wide with fear.

"Either the sun is rising in the wrong direction, or the world is on fire."

CHAPTER 13

"The lightning started a brushfire. And it's coming right at us." Gabriel stared toward the mandarin-tinged sky and tried to gauge the distance and speed of the wind. "I don't think we have more than an hour or two before that fire hits us."

"The river is low and the water isn't very fast, but if we take the raft downstream we might be able to get out of the fire's path." Teresa found Gabriel's hand with hers. The river ran downstream to the south. The fire approached from the west. They would need to cover miles and miles via the slow river in order to escape the approaching flames. "I think it's the best chance we have."

"It's the only chance we have."

They quickly gathered their few possessions and tied them to the raft. Gabriel checked to make sure both Teresa's stone birthday present and the small spearhead still rested in his pocket before helping her haul the raft into the water. Climbing aboard, they used the flat ends of their spears to push against the muddy river bottom and drift downstream.

They thrust their spears into the water again and again, alternating sides and timing their strokes to steer the raft and propel them as swiftly as possible downriver. They took occasional sips from the seedpod cistern but did not pause to eat. The closer the flames appeared the more creatures they saw fleeing from the grass and leaping into the water, seeking the supposed safety of the other shore. Even the crocodile-like beasts had abandoned the river for the overland flight from the flames.

"Maybe the lizards have the right idea." Teresa jammed her spear into the muck and pushed to steer the raft out of the path of a prehistoric reptile splashing through the water. "We could try to run east. The fire might not be able to jump the river."

"Look at the height of those flames." Gabriel pointed at the blazing wall rushing toward them. "It'll only take a few sparks to set the other side on fire. Then we'd have to try and outrun it on foot. I don't think these lizards can run that fast or that long and I know I can't."

After two hours of exhausting labor they saw the wave of flame approaching, the arid wind carrying its baking heat. The view downriver still offered no hope of sanctuary against the rapidly approaching conflagration. They pulled their tunics up over their noses against the increasingly black smoke, hoping the waterway might alter its course and turn east in time to save them. In defiance of their desires, the river continued to run due south.

Eventually the smoke became too thick for breathing and the heat too oppressive to continue laboring. With the fire now gorging on the grass of the plains merely a hundred yards from the river, Gabriel pulled his spear from the water and clasped Teresa's shoulder.

"We're never going to make it." Gabriel tossed his spear to the narrow deck of the raft. "Our best chance is to get in the water and stay low."

"Even in the water, the smoke is going to kill us if the flames don't." Teresa coughed as though to emphasize her point. "Maybe we should try to run east."

"We can use the imprints of the spearhead and combine our magics to make a shield against the fire until it passes." Gabriel stepped into the chest high water, holding the edge of the raft to keep it in place for Teresa. "Once the fire burns out, we can try to walk out of here."

Teresa nodded and jumped in the water beside him. While she held the raft in place, he took their two spears and shoved them into the muddy river bottom, angled against the flow of the water and just below its surface. If they survived, they would need their weapons for whatever they might encounter in the charred wasteland that remained. Teresa took their seedpod of drinking water and tied it to her arm as she released the raft, watching it drift away with the current.

Gabriel took the stone spearhead from his pocket and Teresa clasped her hands around his. He tried to still his mind even as he coughed to clear his lungs from the burning black air. He focused on his subtle energy, concentrating it in his heart center as he reached out to the meager imprints of the spearhead. They could not both simultaneously hold the imprints, but he could share their power with her. He sensed her magical energy and opened up his own, letting them blend together into to one magical force, like water mixing with water.

"You concentrate on shielding us from the fire and I'll try to create an air bubble for us to breathe." Gabriel looked into Teresa's eyes, seeing his own fear reflected back to him.

"Right." Teresa swallowed and her face hardened as she squinted.

As the wall of fire reached the river's edge, Teresa created a small sphere of magical protection against the inferno that lapped out over the water to engulf them. Gabriel established a similar bubble using Wind Magic to seal away what little smoke-filled air remained among the oxygen-devouring flames whirling around them. He watched the fire, blown by the strength of the wind, leap across the water to the kindling-like grass on the opposite shore. Within moments, both sides of the river blazed and roiled with smoke.

Gabriel sensed his magical energy waning as he struggled to maintain the bubble of breathable air. He could feel Teresa also fighting to hold in place her magical shield against the flames. While they had practiced cultivating their subtle energy, they had little training in prolonging its use while performing magic, and the holocaust threatening to consume them showed no sign of dissipating or even lessening in intensity.

"I don't know how much longer I can hold this," Teresa shouted over the roar of the firestorm. As she spoke, Gabriel sensed her shield against the flame shrinking.

"I'm not sure if I can last, either." His magical bubble of air began to become porous, noxious black smoke seeping through the barrier. "We have to hold our breaths under water."

"No." Teresa's voice sounded forceful and fearful at the same time. "You need to go. Now!"

"I'm not leaving you to die in flames." Gabriel's concentration wavered as the anger of the old argument gripped his mind. He struggled to hold his magical energy, and the air bubble, in place.

"You have to." Tears ran down Teresa's soot stained face. "I can't keep the flames away. You have to save yourself."

"No." Gabriel watched Teresa's sphere of Fire Magic protection begin to collapse. He took his hands from where they still clutched the imbued spearhead and placed them on her shoulders. "Breathe!"

Gabriel gulped a lungful of air and pulled Teresa down, his magical air bubble evaporating beneath the increased pressure of the water. Teresa glared at him as they clung to each other, the fire making the underside of the water a nightmare of orange and yellow and red and black. The water began to heat up, and he hoped they could hold their breath until the fire ate through its grassy fuel.

Teresa tried to break away from Gabriel, pointing at him with her free hand. He understood the gesture. He wrapped his fingers around hers and signaled with the stone spearhead, pointing to himself, then to her, then the spearhead, before pulling the fossil they had worked so hard to discover from his pocket. She shook her head. Gabriel pointed again, emphatically. Their only hope would be to combine their magical energies with the insubstantial imprints of the spearhead and try to make a time jump. Gabriel knew the futility of the idea. If they could not maintain the magic needed to shield themselves from the fire and smoke, it would be hopeless to try a time jump. But, if they had only one chance, they had to attempt it.

Teresa shook her head again. She reached out and cupped Gabriel's jawline in the palm of her hand. An icy wave raced through his body and mind. He grasped the significance of her gesture just as she opened her mouth and exhaled.

Air bubbles streamed upward from Teresa's mouth toward the fire cloaked surface of the river. As she willfully sucked in water the limbs of her body revolted, spasming wildly while she struggled against the instinctive urge to swim for the air overhead.

Gabriel nearly let the pent up air in his lungs explode forth, repressing the scream of rage building within him as Teresa began to convulse, her lungs filling with water. Gabriel held her close, tying to press his lips to hers and force the air from his chest into her own. She struggled against him, trying to pushing him away. As much as she fought against his attempts to stop her sacrifice, she never looked away from him.

Not knowing what else to do but unable to do the thing Teresa's actions attempted to force him into, Gabriel pushed the fear and anger and pain from his mind and embraced his inner subtle energy and the paltry imprints of the spearhead. He focused his space-time sense on the fossil he still grasped in his hand while holding Teresa close with his other arm. Her body ceased its battle against her will as her eyes closed and her limbs went limp.

The rancid air, hastily gulped down before his submersion, bit at his lungs, fighting for release. He remembered this sensation. He had experienced it before. In the bus at the bottom of that other river. He knew how long he could hold out before his lungs, longing to expel the air within them, overrode his need to retain it. He concentrated on merging the subtle energy of his own being with the nearly imperceptible space-time traces of the fossil, willing them to unite, as he had done so many times previously.

With his lungs aching to exhale, and his mind battered by thoughts of Teresa's death, the blackness that accompanied the warping of space-time began to shroud him. He closed his eyes against the sight of Teresa's still form and redoubled his efforts to make that sphere of warped space and time extend to include her. No matter how hard he pushed, regardless of the magnitude of his desire, he could not generate enough subtle magical energy to make the warping bubble of space-time embrace Teresa.

Gabriel had to choose. He could jump to safety in an instant, but he could not manage the magical power to take Teresa with him. He would need to leave her there in some unreachable alternate past — or he would die with her. His death would mean many things to many people, but he could not imagine that his passing could affect anyone as deeply as Teresa's sacrifice would touch him. She had given her life to save his own in the hopes that he might save the Great Barrier and the Primary Continuum from the Apollyons.

Gabriel recognized what he had to do no matter how much he would hate himself for doing it. He could not waste Teresa's death, her gift of life to him. He had to honor her death and her choice and the woman she had been and the memories of their brief time together, as well as their dreams of a future she would never enjoy.

CHAPTER 14

As he stared at Teresa's lifeless body floating a few feet beneath the water, crimson flames undulating along the surface above like a liquid sky of blood, a sudden clarity of profound depth fell upon Gabriel's mind. He perceived, all at once, the import and impact of Teresa's decision, and his own, rippling outward, a wave of immanent causality, colliding with every action of everyone else involved in his life. He saw the potential paths he might pursue, from wounded and vengeful tyrant forcing his will upon Grace and Malignancy Mage alike, to a mournful and disconsolate recluse hiding from duty and responsibility. In the midst of this clarity, he perceived the direction he would choose, the one that would have made Teresa proud of him, the one that might fashion him into a man from her martyrdom.

As this new wellspring of awareness continued to expand within Gabriel's mind, he reached out with the imprints and energy of his body and the spearhead, preparing to make the jump through time to the place he had identified along the course of the fossil's timeline. As his fingers loosened their grip on Teresa's arm and rose to touch the curve of her chin, he noticed something he had witnessed recently. With his consciousness more refined than ever before, Gabriel sensed the subtle cosmic energy pervading all existence. It seemed strange that he had not previously observed it so blatantly. Like only realizing that one breathed air once the temperature dropped low enough to make exhalation visible in small, vaporous clouds.

Gabriel tentatively reached out with his mind to touch this cosmic origin source. As his own subtle energy touched and blended with the unimaginably vast and profoundly powerful energy at the heart of all being in all times and places and possibilities, he felt humbled and emboldened. With this power, any imagined aspiration became conceivable. With this power, his mind and will could dictate reality in a way that made normal magic seem childish and superficial.

As wave of relief threated to upend the equanimity of his mind, Gabriel accepted a miniscule fraction of that cosmic energy. He bent down and placed the fossil in the mud of the riverbed. His plan had been to put it back exactly where he had found it. Only now did it occur to him that by moving the fossil downriver, he might have changed its timeline so much that it never again appeared above ground.

He would worry about that later. With the power coursing through him, he knew he could dig himself and Teresa out of any depth of earth they found themselves buried in.

He quickly scanned the fossil's path through history with his space-time sense, searching for a moment that would give them an opportunity to seek out more relics and begin their journey home. Instantly the blackness of time travel surrounded him and Teresa's lifeless body, carrying them to a point along the timeline of the fossil when a camel hoof would shatter it into crumbling dust.

The whiteness of time travel faded to reveal the jungle and grassy plains had long ago given way to a dune-swept desert. Gabriel lowered Teresa to the sand beneath their feet and embraced her not with Heart-Tree Magic but with the power of his will, amplified by the subtle cosmic energy of all things. As the water from their faces and hair and cloths soaked the sand, Gabriel used this newfound power to expel the fluid from her lungs and return her to life. It did not require magic, merely thought and desire coupled with the power he now wielded.

Teresa coughed and spat rancid river water from her mouth. Her eyelids fluttered as she looked up at Gabriel's face.

"What?"

"You're alive." Gabriel reached out to brush the water-soaked hair from her face.

"What?" Teresa propped herself up on one elbow.

"I managed a time jump with both of us." Gabriel stroked her cheek, elated that Teresa lived.

"What?"

Instead of an answer, Gabriel kissed her, holding her tight as tears filled his eyes. He thought of how close he had been to losing her. In this swell of emotion, he lost his hold on the subtle cosmic energy that had saved them and the special perspective that allowed him to perceive it. He didn't care. It didn't matter. Teresa lived. They had escaped from the jungles and plains of the Paleozoic Era to an age where humans lived. They would find a way home — together. Gabriel broke away from the kiss, grinning and wiping tears from his eyes.

"Who are they?" Teresa too brushed tears from her cheeks as she looked behind Gabriel.

He turned to see a small caravan of men and camels not twenty feet away. The men stood wide-eyed, curved swords drawn to defend themselves from the two people who had appeared from nowhere beneath the blistering midday sun. The men whispered among themselves in a language that sounded to Gabriel like some form of ancient Aramaic or Arabic. Without his magical amulet to translate, he had no way of knowing what the men said.

"Oops." Gabriel remembered sensing the presence of people when he had made the jump away from the firestorm, but he had been too concerned with reviving Teresa to care who saw them arrive from nothingness.

He stood up and faced the men. The camels warily shifted their feet at his sudden movement. The man closest to Gabriel raised his sword and emphatically shouted something unintelligible.

Gabriel sought that immaculately still frame of mind that had allowed him to sense the cosmic energy pulsing beneath all phenomenon, but found it elusive. It felt like trying to find a misplaced book in a darkened room. He thought he knew where it should be, but could not manage to clasp hold of it. Exasperated and knowing he had little time, he instead focused on his own subtle energy and the minor imprints of the spearhead, channeling what little he could muster into a focused burst of Wind Magic.

"I'm going to need your sword." Gabriel reached out his hand and the weapon leapt from the grip of the man before him. Gabriel managed to snatch the hilt of the blade from the air, more from his practice with Akikane than his magical control of the sword's flight.

The man screamed in fright and turned to flee, his companions following his lead, quickly mounting their camels and charging over the nearest dune, a miniature dust cloud trailing behind in their wake.

"I was looking forward to riding a camel again." Teresa's sarcastic tone said otherwise.

"Without an amulet to translate, I didn't think introductions would go very well." Gabriel knelt back down beside Teresa, placing the sword in the sand beside them. "Especially considering how we arrived."

"How did we arrive?" Teresa sat up, crossing her legs as she leaned toward Gabriel. "How did you make the jump? Even with the spearhead, how did you manage it all alone?"

"While I was trying to gather enough inner energy to make the jump with both of us, I accidentally found a deeper power." Gabriel frowned with the niggling suspicion that touching it again would not be so easy to accomplish. "With even a trickle of that energy, I could do anything."

"You worked magic by touching the primal energy of the cosmos?" Teresa's eyes widened in surprise. "I'd always assumed that was just a myth."

"No, it's real." Gabriel remembered the overwhelming sense of delirious joy and effortless authority the energy conveyed.

"Can you do it again?"

"I don't know." Gabriel's recent failed attempt came to mind. "I don't think it will be that easy to duplicate. You have to see things in just the right way. I tried when I took the sword, but I couldn't find it again. I had to use my own subtle energy."

"It's still amazing." Teresa grinned and took his hands in hers. "And you brought me back from the dead. Again."

"Don't ever try to kill yourself to save me." Gabriel clasped her hands so hard she yelped.

"Maybe I was trying to help you focus your mind so you could see the cosmic super sauce that would save us. Did you think of that?" Teresa yanked her hands back.

"You were trying to be a hero." Gabriel considered what she had said. Possibly the clarity of mind necessary to see the primal energy of the cosmos had required the intensity of focus that only came in moments near to death, or moments near to losing someone you loved.

"You do not get to monopolize the role of hero." Teresa raised her chin. "I did what I needed to make you leave me behind. If you had stayed and died with me, too much would be at risk. Had you bothered to mention the cosmic super sauce, I wouldn't have needed to drown myself. Which, I have to admit, you were right about. It is not a pleasant experience."

Gabriel stared at Teresa in silence, uncertain what to say and unclear of the emotions stirring in his heart. She had a point. He would have chosen to stay behind with her. By sacrificing herself, she had taken that option away, forcing him to save his own life. Moreover, he knew that if their situations had been reversed, he would have done the same thing. In the end, he decided that, however annoying she might be at times, having her around to be annoying far outstripped the alternative.

"Well," Teresa looked at Gabriel expectantly, steeling herself for another argument.

"You're right."

"What?" Teresa blinked in surprise. "I'm sorry, can you say that a little louder? I not sure I heard you correctly."

"I said you're right." Gabriel laughed as the emotions surrounding Teresa's near death dissolved along with the tension in his shoulders. "You did the right thing, and I would have done the same thing in your position."

"Now, see how easy that was?" Teresa smiled and gave Gabriel a quick kiss. "We're both right and we both get to be heroes. We saved each other."

"Hey." Gabriel grinned at Teresa, a wave of emotion rolling through him. "I love you."

"I've heard a rumor to that effect." A wicked curve came over Teresa's lips. "But then I wake up from the dead and there aren't any flowers, no box of chocolates, not even a camel to ride, just miles of empty desert."

"I hadn't realized camel rides were considered romantic." Gabriel feigned the tone of a wounded suitor.

"You haven't had a romantic evening until you've shared a camel ride under the stars."

"I'll get you a camel as a belated birthday present."

"Don't you dare. Those nasty things always spit on me."

"Then how about I find us a place where we can change clothes, take a real bath, have a romantic meal, and figure out how to get home?"

"What about the flowers and chocolate?"

"I can do either flowers or chocolate, but not both."

"Well, then, clearly it's chocolate."

"Done."

Gabriel picked up the sword as he stood to his feet, helping Teresa stand beside him.

"Hey."

"What?"

"I love you too."

Gabriel laughed and embraced the imprints of the sword. He had assumed that the desert nomad brave enough to challenge them would be the one with the most imbued sword. He had been right. The sword possessed more than enough negative imprints to use as a talisman. And even though it would no longer follow its original path through time into the future, remaining lost in the desert sands, it could still be used as a relic for a time jump into the past.

Gabriel scanned the sword's path back through time and tried to select a moment he could use to his advantage. It did not prove easy. The inherent instability of a tertiary continuum created immense difficulties for time travel. The timeline of the continuum could change, not only from events put in motion by time travelers in the past, but through the natural plasticity of the alternate continuum itself. Events might alter simply because they could. This made finding a specific moment in time an enervating endeavor.

Finally, hoping he would actually take them where and when he wished, Gabriel let the inky darkness of time travel blot out the desert sun. As the bright, clear light signaling the end of the time jump faded, they stood in a large tent at night, the past version of the sword hanging from a hook on the central tent pole. A young woman slept nearby among a pile of cushions. A small, wooden box sat beside her on a rug. Gabriel quietly opened the ornately carved cover the box, scanning the contents with his time sense for a relic. Selecting a simple necklace of glass beads, he focused on where and when it would reside in the future, embraced the imprints of the sword, and warped space and time to go there.

Two hours later, as Gabriel and Teresa experienced it, they sat at a small table outside a café in 1930's Paris, eating goat cheese smeared across pieces of bread, torn from a warm baguette, while sharing a glass of wine and watching the sunset. It had required ten jumps through time, using relics and imbued artifacts as they traveled, eventually collecting enough jewelry to trade in for cash and find a shop to purchase new clothes. As they happened to be in Paris, it seemed a shame to waste that pleasant coincidence and its proximity to Teresa's birthday. They had sought out a vacant hotel to bathe and change into their new outfits before heading out to find a meal.

The hue of their skin set them apart from other Parisians, but did not prove uncommon enough in such a cosmopolitan city to draw unwanted attention. They found a café with a street-side view of a massive stone sculpture where the Eiffel Tower would have been and immediately began ordering most of the contents of the menu. A subsistence diet of prehistoric fish and lizard and fruit for months left them ravenous for modern cuisine.

While this Paris superficially resembled its sister city in the Primary Continuum, there were enough differences that Gabriel suspected it could take a while to find a relic that might exist in both timelines. Moreso, because no object from the alternate reality would actually exist in the Primary Continuum. The only objects that might exist in the Primary Continuum and the tertiary reality would be fossils from before the bifurcation that the Apollyons used to create the first alternate reality. Finding such a fossil would take decades, or centuries.

However, objects similar to those in the Primary Continuum would still likely exist in the universe Gabriel and Teresa currently inhabited. Alternate and tertiary continuums could follow the general pattern of the Primary Continuum, the way a shadow naturally followed someone walking down the street. With the proper shadow relic, one that mimicked the existence of something in the Primary Continuum, Gabriel could theoretically establish a link between them and make a jump between the realities. Because the Apollyons would never allow a version of Gabriel to exist in their private reality, he could not use has own body as a relic. Without an established link between the continuums, making the jump using his body as a relic would be impossible.

Upon realizing they had jumped to Paris, he had initially been elated, assuming they would find an alternate Eiffel Tower he could use to cross back to the Primary Continuum. As he stared at the massive stone statue of a man he assumed to be Napoleon, or some alternate version of the French military commander and Emperor, he wondered how long it might take to find their way home.

"Now this is a romantic birthday present." Teresa leaned back in her chair, folding her napkin on the plate.

"It is beautiful." Gabriel stared down a broad avenue, watching the lights of the city randomly wink into life, gradually painting the metropolis with a vibrant tungsten glow. "But I don't know how easy it will be to get back to the Primary Continuum from this city or this world. We may have to go back pretty far in history to find something that exists in all three universes."

"I can't believe I'm saying this, but I think we need a history book." Teresa made a sour face.

"A history book in English." Gabriel's face soured a little as well.

"I can always translate for you. It worked for the menu." Teresa's French had been similar enough to the language spoken in the city of this alternate world to order food, but little more.

"I can't believe *I'm* saying this, but we should probably try finding a computer in the future and check the Interweb." Gabriel picked at the remains of something similar to crème brûlée, sliding the last bite past his teeth.

"Internet." Teresa laughed. "That assumes the future in this world has an Internet. Or computers."

"I miss the library at the castle." Gabriel sighed, expressing the nostalgia the memory of Windsor Castle evoked.

"We could see if this world has a Windsor Castle," Teresa suggested in a playful tone.

"If it does, I suspect St. George's Cathedral will not hold a library of history books and relics." Gabriel considered their options. "Maybe you're right."

"When is that ever in doubt?" Teresa raised her hands in mock confusion.

"It can't be that hard to find a relic that will take us to England or America so we can find a library." Gabriel took a drink of water to clear his palette and his head. The few sips of wine had made him cheery but had slowed his mind. "We'll have better luck looking for a building of some kind. Architecture can last a long time and is easier to track down."

"Once we make it back to the Primary Continuum, how are we going to find our way back to the fort?" Teresa asked. "Without your pocket watch it will be hard to meet the team at the usual rendezvous spot in that old antique store."

"That will be the easy part." Gabriel straightened in his chair. "Are you ready to be impressed?"

"More impressed than waking up from the dead today?" Teresa cocked her head sideways with curiosity.

"Okay, not that impressed." Gabriel slumped a little in his chair. "I have a special cache of relics and imbued artifacts that I hid near my house in my own timeline. I figured if I could make a jump using my own subtle energy, I could always use myself as a relic to get to someplace in my past. So I hid a box of things under the floorboards of the shed behind my house."

"That is impressive." Teresa smiled appreciatively. "It shows initiative and forward thinking. I may recommend you for a promotion."

"I have enough people recommending me for promotions." Gabriel unconsciously slid a little farther down into his seat. "At least while we were lost I could forget about the war and The Great Barrier and the Council and potential coupes."

"We don't have to go back right away." Teresa leaned closer and held Gabriel's hand. "We can hide here in the Paris of Bizarro World for a while longer."

"No." Gabriel took a deep breath, trying to permanently impress this moment upon his mind. He suspected he would need lovely moments to remember in the long and inevitably painful days to come. "We should get back. We have too many things to do and too many people counting on us. We can take a vacation later. Unless you want to rest. It has been a long day. We could spend the night in Faux Paris."

"I'm sure there will be plenty of daylight where ever we go." Teresa stood up from the table, pulling Gabriel to his feet. "Let go home."

CHAPTER 15

After an hour of searching, they found a relic to take them to Alternate Cherbourg, where Gabriel used the hull of a shipping vessel as a relic to carry them to Alternate Portsmouth in England. From there, they located a car that had been in Alternate London, and Gabriel used it to bring them to the center of town where they found the main library of the city. The building did not sit where it did in the Primary Continuum, and therefore offered no use as a gateway home, but it did remain standing for many years.

Gabriel took them into the future of the library's timeline to the year 2000, just before renovations turned it into a shopping mall. Teresa's suspicion that computers and the Internet might not have been invented in this world proved unfortunately accurate. The library did, however, have a large collection of history books. With the sun and a clear blue sky filling the massive bay windows near the reading tables, Gabriel and Teresa spread out several volumes outlining the history of the alternate world.

"I found some cave paintings." Teresa pointed to the page of the book resting in her hands. "Oh. Never mind. They're in Bulgaria, not France. Actually, it's not even called Bulgaria here."

"I was hoping we could use the Great Wall of China, but it's not so great in this world." Gabriel swung the book around to show Teresa the photo in the book. "It's more like a long pile of dirt."

"They have Pyramids in Egypt, but none of them seem to be the right spot." Teresa flipped a few more pages.

"What about ziggurats in Mesoamerica?" Gabriel stared at the ceiling trying to think of places and structures that might exist in this world and the Primary Continuum.

"I considered that. Same problem. The ones in the correct places don't look the way they should." Teresa closed the book and reached for another.

"We may have to start looking for smaller things," Gabriel said. "Works of art, like statues and paintings."

"I think I have something." Teresa excitedly tapped the page open before her. "Hadrian's Wall."

"Really?" Gabriel leaned over to read the paragraph next to Teresa's finger. "I got the impression that Roman history diverged too much from ours."

"Well Hadrian's Wall didn't diverge." Teresa grabbed another book and rifled through the pages. "Here. There's even a photo."

"It's worth a try." Gabriel smiled at Teresa. "Good work. Now we need relics that can get us there."

"If there's a British museum of history in this world, I guarantee you they will have relics from the wall. Possibly a piece of it." Teresa grabbed another book from the pile. A tourist's guidebook to the Alternate London.

She turned out to be right on both counts. Alternate London did have a museum of history, and it did have a piece of the alternate Hadrian's Wall. Unfortunately, the chunk of stone wall on display showed no signs of linking back to the Primary Continuum.

Undeterred, Gabriel took them back through time and space to the actual wall itself. He used the wall as a relic to jump along its length, searching for the oldest section of the great partition that separated northern and southern ancient Alternate Britain. In the Primary Continuum, Roman Emperor Hadrian had begun building the massive stone wall in 122 CE to keep the British tribes of the northern regions from raiding and battling with the Roman outposts in that far-flung part of the Empire. The wall served a similar purpose in this reality.

Gabriel eventually located a stretch of masonry older than the others that held a tenuous link between the tertiary reality they inhabited, and the secondary reality it had split from, all the way through to the Primary Continuum itself. The connection felt weak, as though the stones in the wall were not properly aligned with their companions in the Primary Continuum. The wall did not provide a perfect conduit back to their reality, but it would work well enough.

On a whim, he tried once more to shift his perception to reveal the cosmic subtle energy behind all existence, but the vision eluded him, as it had with every attempt since their escape from the fire-covered river in the Paleozoic Era. Unsurprised and undaunted, he gathered the imprints of the artifacts they had collected in their sojourn through the timeline of the tertiary alternate reality — a dagger, a necklace of prayer beads, a small bear carved from bone — and focused his will upon the Time Magic to take them home.

"Hold my hand tight." Gabriel wove his fingers between Teresa's. "This won't be like the trip we took to get here."

"Dysphasic quantum correlation degradation," Teresa said, nodding her head knowingly.

"If that translates as 'bumpy ride' then you're right." Gabriel grinned at her incomprehensible reiteration of his words. "The fossil that stranded us here existed completely in both alternate realities and the Primary Continuum. This section of wall exists in all three worlds, but there are subtle differences in each. I can't follow the timeline of the wall the way I normally would. I need to use it more like a guidepost and push us between the three realities. Like jumping from one branch of time to another."

"Shadow relics." Teresa frowned warily at the wall Gabriel's free hand rested upon. "Should we look for something else to use?"

"We're going to run into this problem with all the shadow relics we find that exist in all three worlds," Gabriel said. "I don't know how the Apollyons found that fossil they booby-trapped. It must have been by accident. It would have taken years otherwise."

"What's the worst that can happen?" Teresa asked in a rhetorical tone. "We end up back here looking for relics again."

"Or, we don't make the jump to the next branch and end up somewhere else." Gabriel's heart thumped faster at the notion.

"What's between the branches of time?" Teresa looked sideways at Gabriel as she puzzled through the question.

"I have no idea." Gabriel breathed deep to slow his heart. "I don't think anyone has ever tried this."

"Now that you've got my curiosity aroused, what are you waiting for?" Teresa grinned with excitement. "We're boldly going where no one has gone before."

"I cannot believe you just said that." Gabriel groaned. "Whatever you do, don't let go of my hand."

"I wouldn't dream of…"

An impenetrable infinity of nothingness consumed them as Gabriel warped the nature of space and time around them.

In that infinite absence of presence, Gabriel struggled to find his bearings, his space-time sense confused by the dislocation of the wall's temporal signature, unfolding differently in each continuum. He focused his mind on the variant points of reality expressed in the wall's ancient stone, willing himself to be in a certain place and time in the Primary Continuum. He didn't try to follow the path of the wall between worlds. Instead, he forced himself and Teresa into the absolute oblivion between all possible realities.

His mind reeled as a moment that could not exist stretched into eternity.

The Void between realities held not only the lack of all possible existence but also the endless probability of all potential occurrences.

All things were possible, and none could ever happen.

Nothing ever occurred, and all conceivable things took place.

Endless probabilities connected all potential realities in an infinite timeless *now* that extended to every imaginable past or present or future because none of these were anything more than the manifestation of the unmanifest underpinning of all reality.

In this existential implosion, Gabriel ceased to be Gabriel. In a place that could not be, no mind could be a mind. No thoughts found expression. Only awareness of the nonexistence of awareness existed.

Only the paradox of being the essence of all Being — being a being both probable and improbable — aware and nonexistent — nothing and everything — allowed for the collapse into the singularity of selfhood and will and desire and…

Alabaster light, intense and all-encompassing, gradually ceased as Gabriel's senses returned.

Teresa held his hand in a vice-like grip, legs shaking, her breath ragged, sweat dripping down her face.

Looking at her, he realized his own breathing came in short gasps, and perspiration drenched his weakened limbs.

"What the hell was that?" Teresa put a hand out to the stone of Hadrian's Wall to steady herself.

"I don't know." Gabriel tried to slow his breathing. "I think the Primary Continuum and all the possible alternate universes exist in some kind of infinite probability well. An endless and eternal void of potentiality."

"The ultimate paradox." Teresa wiped her damp forehead. "Let's not do that again."

"I'm not even sure how we managed to complete the jump." Gabriel scanned the stones beneath his palm with his space-time sense. "But we did make it back to the Primary Continuum."

"What's the next stop?" Teresa turned to Gabriel, still looking a little shaky.

"My parents' house."

They took a few minutes to recover and assure themselves that the jump between realities had not left any lasting effects on their bodies and minds. Then, Gabriel used the power of the three talismans he held and concentrated on using his own body as a relic. The connection between the talismans and the tertiary continuum were markedly weaker than before, but proved sufficient enough to allow a jump through time. A moment later, they stood in the shade of a hickory tree beside a small, wooden shed in the backyard of Gabriel's childhood home. The sun, rising over the edge of a neighbor's house, began to evaporate the dew still clinging to the grass beneath their feet.

"Is that your family?" Teresa gestured with her chin toward the largest of the windows.

Gabriel looked at his younger self and his parents seated around the breakfast table. "Yes."

"Where are we in your timeline?" Teresa asked.

"This is the morning I die," Gabriel said. "Ohin and I appeared outside the kitchen window last night and I stole my grandfather's pocket watch. The version of me, in there with my parents, says goodbye to them in a few minutes."

"Why so close to the end of your official timeline?" Teresa stepped forward to get a better look at the scene beyond the window pane.

"I didn't want to risk the chance that my previous self might accidentally find the stash of artifacts and relics in the shed." Gabriel watched as his younger self got up from the kitchen table and headed for the front door. "I hid the box just before sunrise a few hours ago. I figured I could always make it back here in case of an emergency."

"Do you want to watch yourself say goodbye?" Teresa turned to Gabriel, her face filled with gentle concern.

"No. This is as close as I want to come to seeing them again." Gabriel looked away from the window. Tears began to brim along his eyelids. "It's too painful afterward. Let's go. While my parents are watching the younger me at the front door."

Gabriel and Teresa snuck around the edge of the shed, lifted the wooden hinged lock, cracked open the door, and slipped inside. The shed held the family lawnmower, a rusted wheelbarrow, and a wide range of garden implements. They waited a moment for their eyes to adjust to the dimness within before Gabriel pulled the door closed behind them.

He took a hammer from a bench along one wall and knelt down. He began to pry up a floorboard at the back of the small structure. Beneath the floorboard lay bare earth. Putting the hammer back, he grabbed a garden trowel and started to dig.

"A little Wind Magic would be easier." Teresa looked over his shoulder as he piled dirt beside a rapidly-growing hole.

"Old habits." Gabriel sheepishly placed the trowel back on the bench and reached out with Wind Magic, moving dirt to expose the top of a narrow metal toolbox. He pulled open the lid revealing a small treasure chest of items — watches, rings, broaches, coins, shards of pottery, and many more.

"Think you have enough relics?" Teresa laughed softly.

"I wasn't sure what I might need in an emergency." Gabriel dug through the various items until he pulled a small yellow rock from the toolbox. He held it up to a slender shaft of light peeking through the wall of the shed. A tiny beetle glowed orange, suspended timelessly in amber. "This will take us back to Fort Aurelius."

Gabriel looked through the items in the toolbox again. He took three coins to act as relics and a silver necklace with a tiny gold cross as a temporary talisman. The imprints of the imbued items from the tertiary reality were too weak to be of much use in the Primary Continuum. Not knowing what else to do with them, he placed them in the toolbox next to the other relics, then closed the lid and used Wind Magic to replace the dirt around it. Finally, he slid the floorboard into place and tapped it down with an invisible hammer of gravity. As he did so, his space-time sense tingled briefly. He stopped and waited for it to reoccur, but it didn't.

"What?" Teresa looked around.

"Nothing," Gabriel said. "I thought I felt something. It could just be another version of me getting ready to use the stash in the toolbox."

"Then let's go," Teresa said. "As much as I love you, I really don't think I could deal with two of you."

Gabriel laughed. "Neither could I."

He wrapped them both in Time Magic and followed Ohin's established procedures, cautiously using the coins from the toolbox to leap to several locations in history before utilizing the chunk of amber to jump back to Fort Aurelius. Seconds later, and millions of years in the past, they appeared in the street outside the main barracks of the fort.

Ling and Rajan sat on the front steps. He looked up from reading a book while she continued whittling a stick of wood into the shape of a smaller stick of wood.

"Took you long enough." Rajan put down the book.

Ling dug the tip of the blade into the wooden stairs. "We've been waiting all day."

CHAPTER 16

"Where did you get those clothes?" Rajan asked as he hugged Teresa.

"Paris," Teresa replied. "Sort of."

"You look taller." Ling released her python-like embrace of Gabriel and peered over the top of his head. "How long were you gone?"

"Longer than we wanted to be, but not as long as we thought we would be." Gabriel smiled, happy to be back among friends.

"Come on," Ling said, heading off down the street. Rajan fell in beside her.

"Where are we going?" Gabriel jogged to catch up with Ling's long strides.

"Akikane and Nefferati asked to see you as soon as you got back," Ling said.

"That's very optimistic of them." Gabriel noticed other mages watching him and Teresa and their strange clothes. They stared but did not say hello or wave. That seemed odd.

"It was more about faith than optimism." Rajan lowered his voice and stepped closer to Gabriel and Teresa. "Vicaquirao managed to get a lot of information from the Apollyon you stranded behind on the galley ship. We knew you were lost in the past of an alternate reality."

"Ohin has been working all day on possible ways to mount a rescue mission," Ling said. "Without your pocket watch, we knew you couldn't make it to the rendezvous point in the antique shop."

"We were hoping that if you did escape, you'd come straight to the fort," Rajan added.

"Why is everyone looking at us but ignoring us?" Teresa stared hard at a mage across the street until the woman looked away.

"We couldn't keep the news of the mission from Council," Ling said.

"We lost a great many people on those ships." Rajan's face darkened at the memory of the sea battle.

"I suspect that's why Akikane and Nefferati want to see you." Ling stepped up the stairs of the Council Hall and opened the door.

Gabriel and Teresa walked into the Council Hall to find Akikane and Nefferati talking in one corner while Ohin, Sema, and Marcus sat discussing something at a long, wooden table.

A momentary silence fell upon the room as they entered, followed by a new conversation consisting entirely of questions.

Gabriel and Teresa accepted the hugs and congratulations from their companions as they tried to answer the inquiries as to what had happened to them and how long they had been gone.

"Months," Gabriel said to Sema.

"The Paleozoic. Probably the Permian or Carboniferous period," Teresa replied to Ohin.

"A tertiary reality," Gabriel said to Akikane.

"Paris," Teresa said to Sema. "I like this dress."

"I have a secret stash of relics and artifacts," Gabriel replied to Nefferati.

"Something to eat would be great," Teresa said to Ling.

Ohin jumped through space to the kitchens and returned a few minutes later with a basket of food and a small cask of water. They quickly assembled and then assimilated a meal of cold beef, bread, cheese, and fruit. As they ate, Gabriel and Teresa took turns recounting the story of how they had first survived and then escaped their ordeal of being lost in time.

When it came to explaining how Gabriel had made the fateful time jump to avoid their deaths in the firestorm, he left out Teresa sacrificing her life to force him into saving his own. He wanted that part of their story to stay between them. As for how he accomplished the jump itself, Gabriel made it sound as though he had miraculously managed to find a hidden reserve of inner subtle energy. He made no mention of touching the subtle cosmic energy at the heart of all existence. He didn't know if they would believe him or not, but he felt that this, too, did not need to be known by the others. Not unless he managed to successfully duplicate the feat.

He looked at Teresa when he finished his part of the story and recognized the look in her eyes. She, too, found it comforting that they shared secrets no one else knew.

They finished the account, explaining how they had used Hadrian's Wall to return to the Primary Continuum. Here, Gabriel did share all the particulars, describing in minute detail the terrifying experience of crossing the Void between the continuums. Ohin seemed both impressed with Gabriel's accomplishment and intrigued by the implications of what he had witnessed. As they concluded recounting their adventure, describing how they had used Gabriel's secret stash to return to the fort, he noticed Nefferati casting a sly smile toward Akikane.

"That's it," Gabriel turned to Teresa for confirmation. Sema and Marcus exchanged curious glances. He guessed the source of their silent inquisitiveness.

"An impressive tale," Nefferati said with obvious satisfaction.

"Yes, yes," Akikane said. "Well done. Both of you."

"Now that you have shared your happy news with us, it is time for us to share our unpleasant news with you." Nefferati placed her elbows on the table, resting the tips of her fingers together.

"True, true." Akikane leaned forward in his chair. "Your return is more important than you might imagine."

Gabriel sat quietly, knowing whatever would be said impacted him more than anyone else. He sighed in apprehension as Teresa slipped her arm through his. The looks on Nefferati and Akikane's faces, to say nothing of Ohin and the team, only added to Gabriel's accumulating anxiety.

"As you were told, your departure did gain us a captive," Nefferati said. "With Vicaquirao's help, we interrogated the Apollyon whose relic you tried to steal. He provided several pieces of very useful information in addition to gloating about how impossible it would be for you to return. Firstly, the Apollyons have not yet figured out how to destroy the Great Barrier, but they are close. This is the good news. Unfortunately, they beat us to our plan of an alliance."

"How so?" Gabriel suspected he knew what Nefferati meant, but hoped he had misunderstood her words.

"It seems that Kumaradevi's Dark Time Mage, the one who tracked you down at the Great Wall of China, was secretly working with the Apollyons," Nefferati said.

"Malik?" Gabriel asked.

"Just so, just so," Akikane said. "With the failure of that plan, the Apollyons offered the traitor up to Kumaradevi as a gesture of good will. An opening to negotiations for an alliance."

"The Apollyons are working with Kumaradevi now?" Teresa's voice came out in a strained whisper.

"They have reached an accord." Ohin's voice, too, sounded tense. "Kumaradevi will help them fight us, keeping us distracted while they destroy the Great Barrier."

"And when they are successful, they will divide history," Nefferati said.

"Divide history?" Gabriel asked. It sounded ominous.

"The Apollyons get the future beyond the Great Barrier in 2012." Ling shook her head.

"And Kumaradevi gets dominion over all of the past *before* 2012." Rajan looked like the words stung his tongue on the way out of his mouth.

"Is there any chance the captive Apollyon lied to create a diversion?" Teresa asked.

"I helped read his mind myself." Sema's face tensed at the memory. "He was very truthful."

"Where is this Apollyon now?" Gabriel wondered if a second, more personal interrogation might reveal better news.

"We honored our agreement with Vicaquirao." Nefferati glanced at Akikane. "We turned him over to be held in Vicaquirao's prison town."

"Which is when the real problems started." Marcus stared at his empty glass as though wishing it might transform into a flagon of ale.

"Indeed, indeed." Akikane said no more.

"What problem is worse than the Apollyons and Kumaradevi working together?" Gabriel swallowed back the fear building in his chest.

"The mission did not succeed as we expected." Nefferati scowled down at the table. "The mission failed on almost every level. We lost ten mages, twenty more were seriously wounded, and we only captured a single Apollyon. And we assumed that we had lost both of you. While Akikane and I possessed the authority to launch such a mission, we could not keep the results of it a secret."

"No, no," Akikane said. "We had to inform the Council."

"The other members of the Council were not pleased." Nefferati paused for a moment, turning her eyes toward Gabriel. "They have called for a special session tomorrow…to vote for new leadership."

"What?" Gabriel shook his head in momentary confusion. "The Council may vote you out?"

"Yes, yes," Akikane said. "There are many members of the Council who were displeased to learn of the mission. And even more displeased to discover that we had worked with Vicaquirao and the two Apollyons."

"Displeased is a kind word." Nefferati sighed. "They were livid about us working with Vicaquirao and his tame Apollyons. Your disappearances and the deaths of the ten mages enraged them. When we told them we had released the one prisoner we managed to capture into Vicaquirao's custody, Councilman Romanov called a special session. This was before we revealed that the Apollyons and Kumaradevi are working together. That led to a lot of shouting."

"Much shouting, much shouting," Akikane said. "And clear calls for new leadership to head the Council."

"But they will need the two of you if we're going to fight both the Apollyons and Kumaradevi to save the Barrier." Gabriel's fear gradually transformed to anger. The mission had failed, people had died, but they had obtained vital information. Information that could be their only hope for protecting the Great Barrier of Probability.

"That is the heart of the problem we face." Nefferati looked around the room before turning back to Gabriel. "There have always been members of the Council who have believed that our efforts to protect the Great Barrier were not worth the lives of the Grace Mages lost in doing so. And there are some who feel that after our losses with the destruction of Windsor Castle, we are too weak to fight a war on two fronts."

"What are you saying?" Teresa looked like she might leap out of her seat. "The Council can't expect us to run away and hide."

"I suspect there are those who would like that very much," Nefferati said. "At the least, I believe Councilman Romanov will suggest that we focus more on defending the Grace Mage forts rather than protecting the Great Barrier. He has always said that the Barrier was like any other wall. Destined to fall at some point."

"The Barrier isn't just another wall." Gabriel leaned over the edge of the table. "It's essential. It's like the membrane of a living cell. It's there for a reason."

"No one here disagrees with you." Ohin appeared sad.

"Then what can we do about it?" Gabriel looked around the table. From the way the others looked back at him, he suspected he would not like the answer. He turned to Teresa, watching as she bit her lip. It took him a moment to realize her anxiety was for him.

"It is not what *we* can do about the Council, it is what *you* can do about it." Nefferati's gaze bored into Gabriel.

In an instant he understood what they were asking of him and what he would need to do. If the Council chose a new leader who turned away from the war and protecting the Great Barrier, it endangered not only the lives of all Grace Mages but the Primary Continuum itself. He could not allow that to happen. He *would* not allow that to happen.

"When is this special session the Council has called?" Gabriel planned to be at that meeting, and he would either convince them to continue the course Nefferati and Akikane had set or — he considered that unexpressed notion — he would do what he needed to do.

CHAPTER 17

After the meeting with Akikane, Nefferati, and the members of the Chimera team ended, Gabriel found himself standing alone for a moment. His sudden solitude in the room did not result from any conscious decision on the part of his companions, but he experienced the separation deeply, nonetheless. He always stood apart from everyone else, but he rarely perceived it as literally as he did then.

The others had not formally asked him to assume the role of leader of the Council, nor had they voiced the suggestion that he fight the Council leaders for power if they would not see reason. They had not needed to. The long months in a distant alternate past spent digging in the dirt for a way home had given him plenty of time to consider his role in the war and his place in protecting the Great Barrier. He had a duty that no one else could fulfill. While he might want to be asked to make a choice, he knew he really had none. None that he could live with afterwards.

If the Great Barrier of Probability fell to the Apollyons, giving them access to an unsuspecting future, and if Kumaradevi came to rule the whole of the past and not merely her horrible alternate kingdom, and if Gabriel did nothing to stop these things, he would be abandoning the promise of the prophecy of the Seventh True Mage. He understood, as much from contemplation as instinct and experience, that his role, his destiny, lay in being a protector. He embodied this nature. It explained why he swam back down to the bus at the bottom of that river. It clarified why he did the things he did. Why he was who he was.

More importantly, he wanted to be this way.

But how did you protect someone from a threat they did not acknowledge? How did you convince people to fight when hiding seemed so simple?

As the others left the room to prepare in their own ways for the special council session the next day, Akikane asked to speak with Gabriel alone for a moment. Gabriel told Teresa and his team that he would meet them at dinner and then stepped into the small courtyard behind the Council Hall. The silver watch, once again safe in his pocket, and the Sword of Unmaking slung over his shoulder, Gabriel admired the flowerbeds between two wooden benches as Akikane stared at a particularly lovely bloom whose genetic descendants might one day evolve into a Calla Lily.

"Thank you." Akikane's lack of customary repetition brought Gabriel's full attention to his mentor's next words. "We ask a great deal from you. And because of what we ask, things will change between us. Between all of us."

"I don't understand." An odd unease settled over Gabriel from Akikane's words.

"You do, you do." Akikane's voice sounded gentle and soothing. "But you do not want to admit that you do. We cannot ask you to lead us all and expect you to follow us as you have. If you become our leader, you must be our leader. Myself, Nefferati, Ohin, we can advise you, but to truly lead, it must be you who chooses the path we all follow."

"You're right. I don't want to admit that to myself." Gabriel's legs were suddenly rubbery, and he sat down on a bench.

"No, no." Akikane smiled. "Neither will the rest of us. It is no easier to see the student as the master than to see the mentor as the follower. It will be difficult for each of us in our own ways. However, it is something we must make ourselves aware of and face directly."

"I'll work on it," Gabriel said. "Assuming I need to. The Council may come around."

"Yes, yes," Akikane said. "Hold to the optimistic mind as long as possible. It staves off the hopeless thoughts."

Gabriel laughed. He did feel hopeless, and feigning optimism helped, even if it seemed irrational.

"Now, now," Akikane said. "There is something I must ask you."

"What?" Gabriel asked.

"The jump, the jump," Akikane said. "How did you really manage the time jump with Teresa away from the fire?"

"What do you mean?" Gabriel tried to ignore the probing look in Akikane's eyes.

"The truth, the truth." Akikane smiled slightly. "I know you're training. You could not have managed that jump with only your own subtle energy. It would take more months than you were gone to learn to cultivate it so deeply. Years, maybe."

Gabriel grimaced. Sometimes Akikane proved to be entirely too observant.

"Okay," he said. "Here's what actually happened."

Gabriel described the true course of events that had led to him making the time jump with the fossil away from the fire. He told Akikane about Teresa's sacrifice and his near death and the state of mind that allowed him to perceive the subtle cosmic energy beneath all reality and how he had used this energy to make the jump. He also explained how he had been unable to sense even a hint of this elemental energy again.

"So, so." Akikane looked thoughtful. "I had suspected as much."

"I'm sorry I lied," Gabriel said. "I wanted to keep it to myself."

"Certainly, certainly," Akikane said. "You were right. Tell no one of this for now."

"Have you ever heard of someone being able to use cosmic subtle energy?" Gabriel asked. The question had been nagging at him since escaping that fire-filled riverbed.

"Once, once," Akikane said. "I touched it many years ago. By accident, much like yourself."

"Were you able to do it again?" Gabriel found himself surprised that he had not suspected Akikane of touching the subtle cosmic energy.

"No, no." Seriousness filled Akikane's voice. "I have never tried. Such power is too great a temptation. It is good to have limits to one's power."

"What do you mean?" Gabriel stared at Akikane in confusion. "If I could access that power, I could stop the war. I could save the Great Barrier. I could do anything."

"Just so, just so," Akikane said. "But might there not come a time when you would be forced to choose between allowing events to follow their natural course and forcing your will upon reality? Unlimited power requires unlimited wisdom and unimaginable restraint."

Gabriel fell silent as he considered Akikane's words. Without even being able to access the cosmic energy again, he felt the temptation of it. The more he reflected on it, the more that temptation frightened him. It would be easy to use for good. To protect people. But it would also be easy to misuse. Even accidentally. How many times had he used his magical powers in ways he thought would be beneficial only to find unintended consequences bloom like flowers after a spring rain?

Akikane was right. Unlimited power posed too many dangers for a limited mind. If Akikane did not trust himself with that power, how could Gabriel even consider it? What might he do with that power if he were angry? The thought sent a chill throughout his body.

"I understand." Gabriel looked up to Akikane's face. "I won't use it again. Ever. I won't even try."

"One day, one day," Akikane said. "You are not me. There may come a time when you are ready for such power, or a time when it is necessary to use it. Like saving Teresa and yourself with that time jump. Remember, hold the mind of optimism as long as possible."

"It doesn't seem I could sense the energy again, even if I wanted to," Gabriel said.

"Possibly, possibly," Akikane said. "It is elusive. Ever-present but ever-absent. When I first left my life as a warrior and began my life as a novice at the temple, I had a teacher I came to revere above all others. He was a novice monk who had remained a novice monk for decades. He had a weak memory. Buddhism is rife with lists and philosophies and theologies, and they seemed to slip through his mind like wind through one's fingers. He helped in the kitchens, year after year, making food and serving it to the men who arrived as novices and left as monks or abbots. But he never seemed jealous or unhappy with his place in the temple. In fact, he often seemed the most contented of my brethren. I asked him about this once, on a day I had struggled and failed to master my meditations. He looked at me and smiled. 'Cook, eat, serve, meditate, study,' he said. 'They are all the same. Cook, novice, monk, abbot, tree, sky, earth, all the same.' That was the first real lesson at the temple I fully realized."

"I see." Gabriel nodded in seriousness.

"Really, really?" Akikane looked curious.

"No. Not at all." Gabriel sighed.

"One day, one day." Akikane laughed.

Gabriel smiled at Akikane's eternal hopefulness. They spoke for a while longer and then Gabriel left to visit Elizabeth. Considering what he expected to occur the following day, he thought it would be good to talk with her, even if the conversation remained entirely his to carry.

When he stepped into Elizabeth's room in the infirmary, he found Nefferati seated by the bed, holding the other woman's hand.

"…you would be proud…" Nefferati looked up as Gabriel stopped by the doorframe.

"Sorry," Gabriel said. Someone always seemed to be there when he came to visit Elizabeth. "I can come back."

"Nonsense. Have a seat." Nefferati gestured toward the empty chair on the opposite side of the bed. "I have been filling her in on what she's missed the last few days."

Gabriel sat down and placed his hands in his lap.

"You spend a lot of time here at her side." Nefferati leaned back. "That's good of you."

"It helps sometimes to talk to her." Gabriel looked at Elizabeth's sleeping face. "Helps me, I mean."

"I understand," Nefferati said. "I have spent many hours in this room. Apologizing."

"Apologizing?" Gabriel turned his eyes from Elizabeth to Nefferati, curious at her meaning.

"Yes." Nefferati sat in silence for a moment, seeming to consider her next words and whether to speak them at all. "Apologizing for not being there when she needed me."

"The castle was under attack," Gabriel said. "No one is to blame but the Apollyons and Kumaradevi."

"No. She needed me before the attack ever took place. That was when I abandoned her. And you." Nefferati turned to gaze out the window at the trees in the courtyard.

"You had good reasons to be on retreat." Gabriel understood those reasons. Having recently returned from a forced retreat in the distant past of an alternate universe, he understood how pleasant it could be to separate one's self from the war for a time.

"Good reasons or good excuses." Nefferati turned to face Gabriel. "I am weary of the war. So weary that my bones ache from the centuries of fighting. I thought that if I stepped away from it, if I found a place where I did not need to think about the war, that I could be free of it. If only for a time. I had hoped to find some of the inner peace that Akikane holds so easily. Such peace is not so quickly found. Not for me, at least. I am still who and what I am. It may not have been a mistake to leave, but I certainly made a mistake in leaving for so long. Elizabeth needed me. The Council needed me. You needed me. I was very selfish. Simply because there are others to fight the war does not mean it is not my responsibility as well."

Gabriel sat with these thoughts for a moment while considering what, if anything, to say in reply. He knew these sentiments all too well. He understood why she had left, why she had returned, and the recriminations she heaped upon herself.

"We have a duty to protect them, whether we want to or not, because we can." An inner strength and certainty filled Gabriel as his words passed his lips.

"Them?" Nefferati raised her eyebrows.

"Everyone." Gabriel said. "We can't stand aside when people need protection."

"No." Nefferati sighed. "That is why I apologize. For forgetting this."

"You didn't forget." Gabriel's voice sounded as firm as his conviction. "You can't protect everyone all the time. Sometimes you need to protect yourself. I think she understands that."

Gabriel looked down again at Elizabeth's closed eyes.

"I hope so," Nefferati said. "I..."

Her thought remained unfinished, her face hardening as she stood up. Gabriel leapt to his feet, as well. He, too, had sensed the distinctive warping of space-time that indicated the arrival of several Time Mages.

Alarm bells sounded a moment later.

An explosion shook the walls of the infirmary.

"Get Elizabeth to safety," Gabriel said.

Nefferati looked for a moment as though she would argue. She had more familiarity with giving orders in battle than taking them. However, whether due to Akikane's influence or her own judgment, she nodded in agreement. "And what are you going to do?"

"Protect the others while we all escape." Gabriel claimed hold of the imprints in his pocket watch and the Sword of Unmaking. They had built the forts not to be defended but because they were easy to abandon.

To help everyone else flee, he would need to fight, and to fight, he would need more imprints.

"We'll meet at the rendezvous point." Gabriel watched as Nefferati disappeared with Elizabeth before warping space around himself, leaving the infirmary room for the final time.

CHAPTER 18

Gabriel appeared in the armory as more explosions outside rocked Fort Aurelius. By design, the armory appeared to be nothing more than a storage shed containing sacks of grain and other dried foodstuffs.

He lifted a false floorboard to reveal a small cache of concatenate crystals in a wooden box. He flung aside the dusty lid. There were not as many concatenate crystals present as he had hoped. He grabbed a leather pouch and slid the remaining five crystals inside, embracing their imprints as he did so.

Gabriel knew he needed to provide enough of a distraction to allow the other residents of the fort to follow their pre-planned escape routes. He needed to do something else, as well. He needed to find Teresa.

Hoping to combine both goals in a single action, he teleported through space to hover two hundred feet above the fort. The sight below appeared all too familiar. Black-clad Apollyons attacked in groups of twos and threes as Grace Mages defended each other and tried to retreat. Kumaradevi's soldiers, in teams of six, were assaulting everyone not under attack by the Apollyons. It reminded him of the worst of the two battles that had caused him to destroy the Council's Windsor Castle.

Fireballs, arced upwards in the dozens, like some magical anti-artillery fire, exploding around him. He had no more time to look for Teresa or consider a plan. He need to attack until everyone else could find a Time Mage to help them escape.

He projected himself through space to land between two teams of Kumaradevi's soldiers and a pair of Apollyons, each fighting different groups of Grace Mages. The Apollyons and the Dark Time Mages sensed his arrival but did not have time to do more than turn before he focused all of the imprints he held on a creating a vortex of Wind and Earth and Fire Magic.

The ground beneath himself and the Dark Mages around him plunged downward in a churning well of and rock and fire. A sinkhole of extraordinary gravity and flames sucked the Apollyons and Kumaradevi's soldiers down into the bowels of the earth.

Gabriel remained floating above the sinkhole only a moment, long enough to yell to his Grace Mage comrades.

"Everyone to the evacuation points!"

He did not wait to see if they followed his instructions. He caught sight of another battle and jumped through space to appear in the middle of it. With the Sword of Unmaking in hand, he threw himself between two Apollyons attacking Ohin and the Chimera team. Ohin slashed at the Apollyons with his sword, leaping through space around them as Sema and Marcus assaulted their minds and bodies with magic, while Ling and Rajan simultaneously tried to crush them and turn them to ash.

Gabriel immediately noticed that Teresa did not fight alongside the rest of his friends. He engaged the Apollyons, with both sword and magic, forcing them to fall back. The imprints he held left him almost evenly matched with the two Dark Mages. He nicked one of the Apollyons in the arm with his blade, and the two suddenly vanished.

"Where's Teresa?" Gabriel looked between the others.

"We were looking for her when we ran into the Apollyons." Ohin turned to follow the sound of a nearby explosion.

"We need to…" Gabriel's words and thoughts vanished in a roar of wind and exploding arcs of lightning as gravity pulled him upward into the sky. He saw Ohin and the other members of the team trapped with him, spinning in the tornado of electricity and debris. He tried to undo the magic creating the whirlwind around them, but it held fast against every attempt to dissolve it. Seeing his companions suffering as blue-white bolts encased them, Gabriel did the one thing he could think of — concentrating all of his power in the form of Wind Magic, he pushed them out of the cyclone and into the empty sky beyond its walls of turbulent air.

Unfortunately, the sky did not prove to be entirely empty. Six Apollyons hovered in the air around the windstorm of caustic energy they controlled. They spotted Gabriel and pushed the maelstrom of lightning toward him. He did not try to fight. He jumped through space, taking Ohin and the rest of his team with him.

He appeared with the team a moment later in the main square of the fort in front of the Council Hall. Ohin staggered and fell to the ground. The others already lay there. Gabriel's legs wobbled, but he managed to keep his feet. He watched a Time Mage near the street corner take a small group of Grace Mages away from the fort. The Council Hall marked one of the eight evacuation sites where everyone had been trained to assemble in the event that they needed to abandon the fort.

"You have to take the others away." Gabriel reached out a hand to help Ohin to his feet. "I'll find Teresa."

"There are too many of them for you to fight," Ohin said, gasping for breath.

"I'm not going to fight unless I have to." Gabriel looked up as he felt magical energy forming in the sky above. He didn't wait for it to coalesce. He leapt through space again, taking Ohin and the team with him as the Council Hall exploded in a flash of brilliant light.

Across the square, Gabriel watched as the Council Hall crumbled in smoke and ash. The Apollyons were never very inventive with their magical assaults, but they were quick to adopt any innovations. They were employing the same type of gravity lens created by Wind Magic that Gabriel had used against them in defending Windsor Castle.

"Go now," Gabriel said to Ohin, before turning and running into the middle of the square. He knew the eight Apollyons above would target him. He was the reason they had attacked the fort in the first place. He needed to distract them long enough to allow everyone else to flee. And he needed to find Teresa. And, if there was time, he needed to retrieve something from his room.

He raised his hands to the sky, shouting to the Apollyons above, trying to draw their attention. One of them turned his head in Gabriel's direction, their eyes locking for a fraction of a second. Gabriel jumped through space to the top of the fort wall as the earth in the square exploded in light and heat.

They found him again quickly enough, the wall of logs erupting in flames as he leapt through space to the rear of the fort near the main gate. He deliberately picked places that were far from the designated escape sites, hoping to give the residents of the outpost more time to retreat. He noticed Akikane appear briefly behind one of the Apollyons, hovering in the sky. Both suddenly disappeared, a cloud of dust billowing into the air from a bone rattling impact outside the fortress walls.

Gabriel leapt through space again to avoid the impossible heat of the gravity lens. He appeared near the barracks and saw Teresa crouched behind a fallen wall. He gathered his magic to jump to her, but the direction of her gaze and the intensity of the look upon her face drew his attention toward his side of the street. Leah and Liam hid beneath the bed of an empty wagon. He sensed the magical lens shifting toward his new position. He teleported to the roof of a nearby building as the ground he had occupied melted into black char, the building behind it going up in flames.

He watched Leah and Liam run down the street even as he noticed two of Kumaradevi's Dark Mages turning the corner. They grabbed the children, and Gabriel yelled instinctively. He nearly allowed the distraction of the children's capture to delay his next jump through space. He appeared atop another building with a view of the street, his hair singed and the back of his hands burnt.

He watched as Teresa launched a volley of lightning balls at the retreating Dark Mages. One of them, obviously a Fire Mage, deflected the assault while the other used Wind Magic to throw an overturned cart in Teresa's path. Teresa rolled and dodged the flying wooden wreckage, bounding to her feet, both hands blazing with beams of white-hot plasma. The two Dark Mages disappeared around the corner of a building, an energy beam clipping the Dark Fire Mage's leg.

Teresa screamed curses as she ran after the Dark Mages who had captured Leah and Liam. Gabriel leapt through space again as the roof he stood upon became a scorched hole of cinders. He appeared on the other side of the fort, hoping to draw attention away from Teresa and her attempt to free Leah and Liam. While he needed get Teresa away to safety before the Apollyons or Kumaradevi's soldiers captured her, he also could not risk appearing anywhere near her or the children until he had figured out how to deal with the Apollyons who were trying to incinerate him from the sky. To do so would jeopardize all their lives. He could only afford to do that if they were near enough together that he could try to jump away through time with all three of them.

He magically pushed himself through space again as the heat of a thousand suns vaporized the ground where he had stood. A second later he appeared where he assumed he would see Teresa battling the two Dark Mages of Kumadevi's troops. Instead, he found Leah and Liam huddled together in the street. He saw no sign of either Teresa or the Dark Mages. Then something odd prickled his mind. The warping of space-time above him.

He looked up to find that the six Apollyons who had doggedly attempted to incinerate him had disappeared. He sensed several more twists in the fabric of space-time close together. With the last of these, a strange silence fell upon the fort. Explosions no longer reverberated through the air or shook the ground. People shouted and called for help, but the sounds of battle had retreated. How could that be possible?

"Teresa!" Gabriel looked around frantically as he ran toward Leah and Liam. They saw him coming and rushed to cling to his legs.

"Where's Teresa?" Gabriel placed his arms around the two children. "Did you see where she went?"

"They took her." Liam sobbed in terror.

"She tried to save us and they took her." Leah buried her face in Gabriel's shirt.

He held the children tight as he stared around at the burning buildings. He perceived space-time bending slightly and tensed, ready to fight. He relaxed as Akikane appeared before him.

"What is it, what is it?" Akikane asked, seeing the stricken look on Gabriel's face.

"They've taken Teresa," Gabriel said. "I think she was who they wanted."

"Yes, yes." Akikane shook his head. "Easier to capture, easier to interrogate, and better as a hostage."

"She knows everything we've discovered about the Great Barrier." Gabriel's head spun with dizziness.

"Indeed, indeed." Akikane placed a hand on Gabriel's shoulder to steady him. "We will find her. But for now, we must leave this place."

Gabriel nodded and gently pushed the still weeping Leah and Liam into Akikane's arms. "Take Leah and Liam with you. I'll meet you at the rendezvous point. I need to get something I'm going to need to save Teresa."

CHAPTER 19

"The Council majority has spoken. You are both hereby officially stripped of your titles of office. New elections will be scheduled immediately to secure replacements for your seats. There will now be a vote to determine the new temporary Head of Council. Please clear the Council chamber."

The words echoed among the wooden rafters of the high-ceilinged room as they resounded through Gabriel's mind. He stood between Nefferati and Akikane facing a long oak table in the middle of an octagonal room.

The ten remaining council members sat behind the table. Councilman Romanov, the one whose words still rumbled through Gabriel's head, struck a gavel to the table, emphasizing the finality of the Council's judgment.

Gabriel did not move to leave. He instead stepped forward. Akikane and Nefferati had accurately predicted how the Council's review of their tenure would proceed. They had formally requested his presence to give testimony on their behalf. He had barely been allowed to offer answers to a few leading questions. There had been no opportunity to speak in defense of Nefferati and Akikane's actions.

Convened in Fort Madison in the middle of the Triassic Period, 210 million years in the past, the council members had nearly universally savaged the results of the mission with Vicaquirao and had been especially unforgiving of the recent loss of Fort Aurelius. All the survivors of the attack had been safely evacuated six hours previously. However, five Grace Mages had lost their lives to the Apollyons and Kumaradevi's troops. The Council placed the blame for the loss of Fort Aurelius directly on Nefferati and Akikane, even though Gabriel had tried to suggest that *he* might be responsible for the Dark Mages finding the stronghold in the first place.

He could not be certain, but he suspected that the slight space-time distortion he had encountered while retrieving the artifacts and relics from his secret stash in his parents' backyard shed might not have been some future version of himself. In the wake of the attack on Fort Aurelius, it seemed more likely that either the Apollyons, or Kumaradevi's Time Mages had been staking out his past in a space-time bubble.

The last moment he saw his parents before his death had a potent emotional pull. The Dark Mages would know this and could have been waiting for him to return, ghosting his time trail back to Fort Aurelius. He had tried to accept responsibility for the attack, but the majority of the council members appeared intent upon placing the blame with Nefferati and Akikane. In the end, only Councilwoman Jones, an Earth Mage and former farmer from Wyoming in the late 1800s, provided the lone vote against deposing Akikane and Nefferati.

Standing between the Council and his two mentors, Gabriel cleared his throat, as much to give himself another moment to consider his course of action as to draw the council members' attention.

Councilman Romanov turned from speaking with Councilwoman Patel to glare at Gabriel. A pointed beard accented the narrow features of his face. Gabriel remembered that the man had been a minor aristocrat in the Russian court of Catherine the Great. A Time Mage, he was the most likely candidate to become the new Head of Council.

"I asked for this room to be cleared. The Council has business to attend to."

"I have business with the Council." Gabriel swallowed, breathing deeply to calm himself. He expected that what was about to happen would go badly, but it might go horribly. Part of that depended on how well he kept his anger under control. Watching the Council remove Nefferati and Akikane from power for doing what he believed needed to be done had left a bonfire of animosity burning in his chest. He could not afford to let that blaze get out of control.

"You may address your concerns to the Council at the proper time through the proper channels." Councilman Romanov made to turn back to Councilwoman Patel.

"That will be too late." Gabriel raised his voice to ensure the ten people seated behind the table turned to him as one. "I must petition the Council now."

Councilman Romanov waved his hand dismissively, but Councilwoman Jones leaned forward to speak first. "What petition do you seek?"

"This is irregular and counter to procedure," Councilman Romanov said. "It is not following the rules of this chamber that has led to our present circumstances."

"As we are in a situation where there is no Head of Council, it is within the authority of any one of us to pursue this petition and determine its nature." Councilwoman Jones turned away from Councilman Romanov.

"She does have a point, and there is precedent." Councilman Kim folded his hands on the table and looked at Gabriel. He had died in China in 632 CE to be reborn a Wind Mage. In his previous life he had been an ambassador of the Tang Dynasty under Chinese Emperor Tai Zong. He had adapted better than anyone to the politics of the Council of War and Magic. "What is the nature of your petition?"

"As the Council is aware, one of my teammates has been kidnapped by Kumardevi and the Apollyons." Gabriel inhaled rapidly, focusing on beating down the flames in his chest. "I seek the Council's support in mounting a rescue mission."

"You mean you want the Council to risk even more lives than were already lost in order to save your girlfriend." Councilman Romanov placed his hand on his chin in evident exasperation. "Just minutes ago you tried to convince this council that the attack on Fort Aurelius was likely your responsibility. Now you ask us to reward that lack of judgment by mounting a rescue mission that would undoubtedly cost additional lives. I might blame you for not seeing the folly of this request, but you have obviously been poorly tutored in these matters."

Gabriel opened his mouth but closed it hastily, refusing to give in to the irritation within him, even as he refused to look back toward Akikane and Nefferati.

"She is more than my girlfriend," Gabriel said. "She knows more about the Great Barrier than anyone. With her knowledge, the Apollyons may finally be able to destroy it."

"And what special knowledge does she possess that the Council has not been made aware of?" Councilwoman Patel placed her palms on the table as she straightened in her chair. She had been a merchant in India in the late 1990s running a small electronics company. A Time Mage like Councilman Romanov, she also happened to be his strongest supporter and a constant critic of Nefferati and Akikane.

Gabriel hesitated. Under the advice of Nefferati and Akikane, he and Teresa had kept the full information regarding the Great Barrier to a trusted circle. There had been leaks and betrayals from within the Council before, and they had not wanted to risk such treachery again.

"She knows how the Barrier was created," Gabriel said.

"What specifically does she know?" Councilman Romanov asked. "Does she know more than you?"

"No, Councilman," Gabriel said.

"Then tell us what she knows that is so important," Councilman Romanov said.

"Yes, we have been in the dark concerning these matters for far too long." Councilman Kim slapped the table for emphasis.

Gabriel looked at the ten faces behind the long table before speaking. He might not like them, might not agree with their decisions, but that did not make them traitors.

"The Great Barrier of Probability was created using both Grace and Malignancy magic, and it is held in place by one hundred and eight anchor points throughout time. If the Apollyons can find these anchor points, they may be able to destroy The Great Barrier. They have been copying themselves for this very reason. We need to know what they have learned from Teresa and how close they are to locating the anchor points."

The council members did not respond immediately. They seemed shocked by Gabriel's information.

"You say the Great Barrier was created with both Grace and Malignancy magic?" Councilwoman Patel looked skeptical. "Are you certain?"

"Yes," Gabriel replied. "I've inspected several of the anchor points, and they definitely possess traces of both magics."

"If this is the case, I do not see the cause for concern." Councilwoman Patel sat back in her chair. "Does it not stand to reason that the Barrier would also require both magics to destroy it?"

"No." Gabriel had deeply hoped the same, but close examination of the anchors points left that notion untenable. "Any Time Mage, Grace or Malignant, with enough imprints at their command could destroy an anchor point."

"How can you be so certain?" Councilwoman Patel asked. "We should inspect one of these anchor points ourselves. We should have had the opportunity to do so already."

"I'm positive," Gabriel said. "It may take dozens of people to build a house, but it only takes one person with a match to burn it to the ground."

"A frightening metaphor, but completely inappropriate." Councilman Romanov looked down his nose at Gabriel.

"Not if what he says is true," Councilwoman Jones said.

"Let's assume that *everything* he says is true." Councilman Romanov turned to Councilwoman Jones with a long sigh, as though speaking to a particularly dense child. "If the Apollyons know about these so-called anchor points, and they have made enough duplicates of themselves to attack them all, then there is very little, if anything, we can do to stop them. We simply do not command the forces necessary to defend so many points in time."

"Are you suggesting that we capitulate?" Councilwoman Jones shook her head in dismay.

"I am suggesting that we accept the facts before us." Councilman Romanov's voice grew louder and more passionate. "We are weakened to the breaking point, and we must focus our limited resources where they provide us the greatest security."

"Are you forgetting what Nefferati and Akikane told us about the alliance between Kumaradevi and the Apollyons?" Councilwoman Jones asked.

"Not at all," Councilman Romanov replied. "It is the one piece of news in our favor."

"I don't quite follow that line of reasoning," Councilman Kim said.

"Neither do I," another councilman said. Gabriel couldn't remember the man's name, but he looked as confused as Gabriel felt.

"If the Barrier comes down, the Apollyons have agreed to abandon the past for the future beyond the year 2012." Councilman Romanov looked between Council members Kim and Jones. "That leaves one less enemy to fight here in the past. And if we can locate Kumaradevi's alternate reality and sever it, we may find an end to the war."

"And we are to leave the future beyond 2012 to the Apollyons' desires?" Councilwoman Jones asked, her voice breaking slightly with emotion.

"We cannot protect everyone," Councilman Romanov said, his tone emphatic.

"Yes, but the Barrier is there to protect the future," Councilman Kim countered.

"That is a myth for all we know." Councilwoman Patel raised her voice. "In truth, we have no idea why the Great Barrier exists. In spite of the suggestion that it was created using both magics, it may actually be a natural phenomenon. Or a mistake. We simply do not understand enough to say with any certainly how the removal of the Barrier will affect the Primary Continuum."

Gabriel gasped in disbelief at Councilwoman Patel's statements. More frightening than her words were the looks on the faces of the other council members. Most of them seemed relieved that she had spoken aloud thoughts they had been harboring for years.

He had not realized how difficult his task in the room would be. He glanced back quickly at Nefferati and Akikane, impressed they still managed to refrain from interjecting. While Akikane seemed placidly concerned, Nefferati looked like she might explode from the attempt to contain her opinions.

"This is nonsense," Councilwoman Jones exclaimed.

"This is reality." Councilman Romanov pounded the table with his fist. "We have a responsibility to protect the people who elected us, and we cannot hope to lead them into a peaceful future if we are all killed fighting to stop something that may not only be inevitable but harmless in the long run."

"I don't see how the Apollyons' ruling the future of the Continuum could be called harmless." Councilman Kim seemed surprised at the suggestion.

"Again, we must face facts, and the fact is that even if the Apollyons make changes to the Continuum in the future, it will not affect us here in the past." Councilman Romanov had grown tired of the argument. "Regardless, this is not the matter before us at the moment. First, we need to choose new leadership before we consider the actions the Council will take moving forward."

"What about Teresa?" Gabriel had remained silent throughout the discussion in order to see how the various council members responded. He also feared what he might say in response to the ideas being presented. Now it seemed time to refocus the Council's attention.

"Your petition is denied." Councilman Romanov gave a perfunctory wave toward Gabriel, Akikane, and Nefferati. "Now, all of you please clear the room."

"We haven't voted on it." Councilwoman Jones looked indignant.

"Fine. All those in favor of mounting a rescue mission for the girl, raise your hands." Councilman Romanov looked back and forth down the table as Councilwoman Jones's hand shot into the air. It hung there alone until Councilman Kim's palm tentatively joined it.

"Two in favor. Those against?" Councilman Romanov stared at Gabriel as he raised his hand along with the seven other remaining council members. "Petition denied."

"Then I will rescue her myself." Gabriel let his voice deepen even as he struggled to keep his internal inferno of anger under control.

"You will do no such thing." Councilman Romanov glared at Gabriel, his voice brimming with indignance. "You are under the authority of this council and you will do as instructed. Now leave this chamber."

"I will leave, but I will not abandon Teresa." Gabriel fought back the urge to step closer to the table and the council members. He wasn't sure what he might do if he got too close to Councilman Romanov.

"I know it is hard to understand and accept." Councilwoman Patel's voice filled with something that might have sounded like compassion coming from anyone else. "There is little possibility the girl has not told Kumaradevi and the Apollyons everything she knows. And there is even less of a chance that she is still alive. You must let her go."

"Kumaradevi would never kill Teresa when she could use her as a hostage against me." Gabriel knew this to be his only hope that Teresa still lived.

"Then you would be a fool to play into her plans with a rescue attempt," Councilwoman Patel said.

"And we would be fools to risk dozens of lives to save one girl," Councilman Romanov added. "And we would be doubly foolish to allow you to risk your life in such an endeavor."

"It is my life to risk," Gabriel said.

"All of our lives are in service of the greater good," Councilman Romanov said. "Yours more than most. What little prospect there is of surviving the coming years may very well rest with you. In my opinion, you have been allowed far too much freedom to place yourself in harm's way. The first thing I will be suggesting to the Council upon your departure from this chamber will be assigning you a new mentor to apprentice under. Someone who will not allow you to carelessly put yourself and others at risk."

"I have a counter offer." Gabriel allowed himself two steps forward but restrained himself from moving any closer toward the table. He didn't think the firestorm building within him could tolerate any nearer proximity to Councilman Romanov and Councilwoman Patel.

"You have no status to make any offers of any kind. Your petition has been considered and rejected. Now leave this room immediately, or I will have you removed." Councilman Romanov nearly leapt up from his chair.

"Attempting that would be unwise." Gabriel clenched his fists, ignoring the desire to claim the imprints available to him.

He sensed what Councilman Romanov attempted even as the man claimed the imprints of the prayer beads wrapped around his wrist. Gabriel felt space-time beginning to twist around himself and Akikane and Nefferati. Romanov intended to teleport them from the Council Hall and into the street.

Gabriel did not reach for the imprints of his own talisman, opting instead for those held by Councilman Romanov. Focusing his mind as he had practiced so many times, he reached out with his will and magic-sense to wrest the imprints of the prayer beads from Councilman Romanov's control. Space-time around himself and his mentors collapsed to normality.

"What!" Councilman Romanov jumped to his feet, pointing at Gabriel in barely controlled rage. "What have you done? How dare you!"

Gabriel felt Councilwoman Patel reaching for the imprints of the necklace at her chest and took control of them from her before she had time to notice. She looked surprised that whatever Time Magic she intended did not work.

"How?" Councilwoman Patel began to say something that the fear in her voice strangled.

"I am not going to harm anyone." Gabriel raised his hands in a gesture of peace. Several of the council members did not believe him and claimed hold of the imprints of their talismans. As the council members rarely took part in field missions and hardly ever encountered battle conditions, it did not take Gabriel long to forcibly relieve them of their imprints. In a matter of seconds, he held the imprints of eight talismans. Councilman Kim and Councilwoman Jones had refrained from trying to hold any imprints.

Gabriel stared at the council members in silence for a moment. Councilman Romanov seethed with anger but appeared speechless in the face of Gabriel's display of magical ability.

"Here is my counter offer." Gabriel lowered his hands. "I suggest you listen closely."

"You are in deeper trouble than you can imagine." Councilman Romanov found his voice. "You have attacked the Council. This is treason."

"I was merely defending myself. Had I attacked you, we would not be speaking now." Gabriel allowed himself a momentary smile at that last statement, then quickly stifled it. "Here is what I propose. I will go to Kumaradevi's world and rescue Teresa. When I leave that world, I will sever it from the Primary Continuum. Hopefully with Kumaradevi in it. Upon my return, I will ask to be made Head of Council."

A stunned silence filled the room until Councilman Romanov laughed out loud. "I understand you are young and under the influence of those with no respect for the law, but you must realize how ridiculous that all sounds. You assume you will find Kumaradevi's world, that you can rescue this girl, Teresa, and that you can escape. But, more than this, you assume you could be Head of Council, even if we all voted for you. You are not of age to vote, much less hold a seat on this council. You are proposing to become a tyrant. We are a democracy. If you wish to rule this Council, you will need to wait until you are of age, get elected by the people, and voted into that position by the Council majority."

Gabriel listened to his breathing in the silence after Councilman Romanov's words. They had been the only things that he had so far agreed about with the man. He needed to be careful with what he said next. It would be important not only to him, but to all those who decided what to do about those words and his subsequent actions.

"I will not be a tyrant." Gabriel released the imprints he held. He did not need them. He doubted the council members would try again to use magic against him. As a caution against possibly being wrong, his pocket watch and several concatenate crystals sat in his pants pocket. "I will not try to force my will upon this council any more than I will try to force my will upon the people it represents. However, I will not yield to your shortsightedness, cowardice, and poor judgment. I will do as I have said. And when I have dealt with Kumaradevi, I will stop the Apollyons. All I ask is that you do not try to stop those who wish to join me."

Councilman Romanov looked to his fellow council members on both sides before speaking. "Let me be clear. Any threat to the authority of this Council will be dealt with severely."

"And let *me* be clear." Gabriel starred at Councilman Romanov and grasped hold of the subtle energy and imprints within himself. He did not need much magical energy for what he wished to do.

"Any attempt to stop me will be dealt with severely."

From the reactions of the council members, Gabriel knew he had managed the Soul Magic necessary to place his words in their minds. Aloud, he said something different.

"I am unlike anyone in this room. I am unlike any of our enemies. Ever since I was revealed as the Seventh True Mage, this Council has thought of me as a weapon. All I am asking of you is that you stand aside while this weapon destroys those who threaten us all. What I beg of you is that you do not make the mistake of turning this weapon against yourselves."

"You cannot threaten the Council without consequences." Councilwoman Patel's voice was not as loud as she probably hoped it sounded.

"I will make you an additional offer." Gabriel had not previously considered what he said next, and therefore spoke slowly. "If I accomplish all I have stated, and I am not dead as a result, I will submit myself to the Council's judgment and accept wherever consequences it deems just, provided no one who follows me is prosecuted."

"You threaten us *and* dictate terms of some future surrender?" Councilman Romanov shook his head in disbelief. "Does it not occur to you that those who follow you may not live to be held accountable by this council?"

"I am very aware of that possibility." That thought had hounded Gabriel for years. "I am also aware that they may all die, purely by allowing your incompetence to continue."

"I will not..." Councilman Romanov's thought got shouted down by Councilwoman Jones.

"How will you find Kumaradevi's world?"

"Vicaquirao knows how to find it." Gabriel had made sure to rescue the enchanted chalkboard from Fort Aurelius before he had destroyed the compound in a wave of Earth Magic.

"The same man who you led you into a trap that cost a dozen lives?" Councilwoman Patel laughed in derision. "You are a fool, boy."

"Possibly." Gabriel stepped forward again, noticing how many of the council members unconsciously leaned back in their chairs. "I may be a fool, and I may die with the things I propose to do, but I will not be fool enough to hide while the world is threatened and I can do something about it."

Gabriel did not wait for more words or arguments or discussions. He spun on his heel and walked from the room. Akikane and Nefferati fell in behind him. No one made any effort to stop them or use magic to impede their departure. When the doors of the Council Hall had closed behind them and they were halfway across the main square of Fort Madison, Gabriel let out the breath he had been holding since turning away from the council table.

"That went better than I expected." Nefferati patted Gabriel on the shoulder. "You were right about how to approach it."

"Yes, yes." Akikane's smile returned. "Very good political theater. Especially when you snatched their imprints."

"Threatening them in their own minds might have been a step too far," Nefferati said.

"Nonsense, nonsense," Akikane replied. "A counter threat is hardly a threat."

"It wasn't a threat." Gabriel glanced between the two True Mages at his side. "It was...an assurance."

Nefferati laughed and slapped him on the back again. "I may enjoy taking orders from you after all."

As they reached the far side of the square, Ohin and the rest of the team stood up from the benches where they had been waiting.

"How did it go?" Ohin looked straight at Gabriel, his face filled with concern.

"As expected." The anger that had propelled Gabriel evaporated, replaced by a growing weight piling upon his shoulders.

"What happens now?" Rajan asked, looking between Gabriel, Akikane, and Nefferati.

"Now I rescue Teresa." Gabriel tried to fill his voice with confidence, barely managing to convince himself that it didn't sound suicidal.

"Not alone, you're not." Ling spat into the dirt of the square. "We're a team, and she's ours as much as yours."

Gabriel began to say something, but Marcus raised his hand. "Don't even think of going alone, lad."

"We'd never let you go unaided, and you know it." Sema crossed her arms and nodded her head for emphasis.

The indefinable weight pressing down upon Gabriel began to lift as he looked into the faces of his teammates. He could not express how much it meant that that they would follow him. He knew they each cared for Teresa, that they would do anything to save her, but knowing they supported not just his rescue attempt but his confrontation with the Council hearted him.

"At least I won't have too many decisions to make now that I've decided to lead." Gabriel enjoyed the laughter that followed his words.

"What's first?" Ohin asked.

"First we need to talk with Vicaquirao."

CHAPTER 20

Leather boots splashed through mud and slid across rain-slicked moss. A continuous curtain of droplets cascaded through layers of conifer needles to soak the forest floor. The smell of wet pine and rain-drenched earth filled the air.

Gabriel might have enjoyed the scenery of the mountainside he and his companions clambered through were it not for the wetness that saturated his rain poncho and seemed to be working its way past the barrier of his flesh and into his bones. As he sidestepped a low branch, swinging with Vicaquirao's passage, his feet give way beneath him. The mud of the forest floor offered no resistance to the tread of his boots as he began to slide down the mountain.

He instinctively reached out for something to arrest his descent only to find Ling's long arm, her hand firmly clasping his own.

"Careful." Ling pulled him back to the thin path through the dense pine forest. "You're no good to Teresa in a heap at the bottom of the mountain."

"Thanks." Gabriel wiped the water from his face with a muddy hand.

"We're almost there," Vicaquirao called over his shoulder. "Not far."

"I don't see why we couldn't have come on a day when it wasn't raining." Rajan groused from behind Ling.

"Because I've been here on all the sunny days." Vicaquirao smiled. "Unless you'd like to meet two of me today."

"Hmff." Ling said. Her thoughts on the subject remained unclarified.

Ohin, Sema, and Marcus trudged along silently behind Rajan, Akikane bringing up the rear. There had been a great deal of discussion as to how to mount a rescue mission and who would comprise the team. They had considered recruiting mages from other teams to complement their forces, but Gabriel had been swayed by Ohin's argument that a smaller team might be less likely to attract notice.

Gabriel had tried to convince Nefferati to join them as well. He preferred to have as many True Mages as possible on the mission. However, she wisely pointed out that if the mission failed, a True Mage would be greatly needed by the other Grace Mages. In confidence, she also admitted that she did not trust herself to be near Kumaradevi. The goal of the mission was to rescue Teresa, not to seek revenge upon the woman who had held Nefferati in agonizing captivity for years. Instead, she remained behind to rally support for Gabriel among the Grace Mages of the eleven remaining forts. He had also agreed with her assessment that the mission needed a narrow time limit. The risk posed by the alliance between Kumaradevi and the Apollyons demanded rapid and conclusive action. Additionally, Gabriel entrusted the Sword of Unmaking to her care in his absence. The blade would only draw attention to him in Kumaradevi's palace.

After an exchange of messages via the enchanted chalkboard, Vicaquirao had met Gabriel, Nefferati, Akikane, and the Chimera team in the ruins of a Spanish monastery in 1876. There, Gabriel had reminded him of the debt still owed from the joint mission to attack the Apollyons in the Battle of Lepanto. Surprisingly, Vicaquirao had agreed to the plan, even though it revealed all of his patiently-acquired information about Kumaradevi's world. He did not merely know of a relic which existed in both the Primary Continuum and Kumaradevi's alternate world that could be used for transit between them. He had also discovered the moment in history where she had created her dark reality.

If Vicaquirao could lead them to Kumaradevi's alternate domain, then they could sever it from the Primary Continuum upon their departure. But they did not have weeks or days to find and rescue Teresa. The alliance with the Apollyons, coupled with the information Teresa had surely been forced to surrender, would leave a limited window of time for action. The Apollyons would immediately begin an attack on The Great Barrier, and Kumaradevi would no doubt aid them by assaulting the Grace Mages with the full might of her army. They gave themselves no more than twenty-four hours from the time of Teresa's capture to affect her release, or retreat and sever Kumaradevi's world.

Gabriel cupped his pocket watch in his hand, droplets smearing the glass that shielded the slender metal hands beneath it. They had a little more than six hours left. The hike through the forest had taken nearly an hour. Far too long. Unfortunately, they had no choice. Vicaquirao had protected his discovery with what he referred to as 'exceptional force.' If space-time near the area was disrupted in any way, the relic they marched toward would magically disintegrate. The location could only be reached on foot.

"Vicaquirao." Gabriel tried to keep the anxiety and impatience from his voice but largely failed.

"I know." Vicaquirao pointed ahead, just beyond a small outcropping of rock. "When I laid down the magic to protect this place from intrusion, I had not anticipated needing to reach it so swiftly."

"Normally I would be comforted by the fact that you failed to anticipate something," Gabriel said. "It's nice to see some cracks in the façade."

"There is no facade," Vicaquirao said. "However, the cracks are real enough. Over here."

Vicaquirao climbed over a boulder and reached down to help Gabriel up. Gabriel took his hand and jumped up to the top of the large rock. Beneath them, he saw that the side of the mountain had long ago given way in a mudslide. A massive set of bones protruded from the dirt, resting high along the edge of the open pit of earth.

"A Sauroposeidon," Vicaquirao said as he and Gabriel helped the others up. "It took me years to find it, but perseverance paid off."

"When in time are we?" Ohin asked as the group began to climb across the giant fossilized skeleton.

"Around 50,000 BCE," Vicaquirao said. "Fortunately, Kumaradevi is lazy. She created the bifurcation to spawn her alternate reality in around 10,000 BCE, right at the birth of human civilization. She took the people who existed there and made them her own. To secure the world, she hid it with magic on this side, in the Primary Continuum, and systematically destroyed all relics that might link back to it from her side."

"That seems like a lot of work to me," Gabriel said.

"Yes, yes," Akikane said. "But not as much work as creating a bifurcation before humans existed and then trying to build a kingdom with people kidnapped at the moment of their deaths. It would take years and years to find so many people and generations for them to multiply into a nation she might enslave."

"Exactly." Vicaquirao looked back at Akikane with a wary eye. "That constant smile is deceptive."

"I have seen the worst that humans can do." Akikane's smile did not falter. "I did much of it myself once."

"How do we get to the future in Kumaradevi's world after we reach it?" Ohin slid down the embankment, coming to a stop at the edge of a massive hipbone. "How do we even know when in the future to appear?"

"Kumaradevi's paranoia works to our advantage there," Vicaquirao said. "She never allows anyone to cross personal timelines, especially hers. I suspect she doesn't trust herself to meet herself. She certainly doesn't trust her soldiers to cross her timeline. The soldiers who attacked your fort will have returned to her world after exactly the amount of time they were personally gone. From what you've told me, they would have been back in less than an hour. That gives us a fairly precise window for your arrival, which is helpful considering how much time remains for you to complete your mission."

"The sooner we leave, the quicker we'll be back." Ling said, her voice sounding like a growling jungle cat as she stared at Vicaquirao.

"There are details to attend to in your departure." Vicaquirao bent to touch a jagged, cream-white femur bone. He turned his gaze from Gabriel to Ohin and Akikane. "In Kumaradevi's world, I have covered this dinosaur skeleton so it will not be found. The only part exposed is the small end of this bone. It is hidden under a hollow tree trunk. You should be able to place yourself near it easily while still remaining in touch with it."

"What time frame are we jumping to?" Ohin skeptically looked between Vicaquirao and the skeleton.

"This is where things get a bit tricky." Vicaquirao smiled and pointed to a nearby rock. "There will be a blue flower growing from a crack in that stone. I planted the flower there, and it will bloom for thirty days, and only once. Go to the very end of its bloom."

"How did you find a flower that blooms only for thirty days, and only once?" Marcus seemed professionally intrigued by the notion.

"I had some free time on my hands," Vicaquirao replied. "So I made one. Now, when you arrive, you will need to go to the tree standing directly behind the rock with the flower. At the base of that tree you will find a box buried two feet beneath the soil on the west side of the trunk. Within the box there are several pieces of brick. Any one of them will take you where you need to go. Unfortunately, the box is protected with certain enchantments. You'll need to look inside the box with your space-time sense and teleport one of the pieces out. I'm sure Akikane can manage that."

"Yes, yes," Akikane said. "Once we have a piece of brick, where will it take us?"

"To a cellar in the city outside Kumaradevi's palace," Vicaquirao said. "And here's where you must pay attention. You'll need to go to a time when you see a lantern in the room that is always lit. The lantern casts light on a chalkboard with numbers written on it. The number on the right is the year. You'll go to year twenty-one. The middle number is the month. Go to the ninth month. The set of numbers on the right indicate the day. Go to the tenth day. Finally, there is an hourglass near the lamp. It takes a day for the sand to drain once. The top glass bowl is marked from one to twenty-four on the side. Go to the point where it marks off the number ten."

"You've known about Kumaradevi's world for twenty-one years?" Rajan shook his head in wonder.

"The better question is…how often have you been going there?" Ling asked, placing her hands on her hips.

"And to what purpose?" Sema brushed her rain-sodden hair from her face.

"I have gone as often as possible." Vicaquirao addressed his answers to Gabriel rather than his interlocutors. "And my purpose in doing so will be clear upon your arrival."

"We should get to arriving." Gabriel leaned over to touch the ancient tusk protruding from the muddy soil.

"Not yet. There are still a few things to explain. And you'll need these." Vicaquirao took three small concealment amulets from his pocket and handed them to Ohin. "I only have three, so distribute them as you feel necessary. They will invert the appearance of magic."

"Invert how?" Ohin asked, looking at the amulets in his hand, their slender silver chains dripping between his fingers.

"They will make Malignant Magic appear as Grace Magic, and the reverse." Vicaquirao seemed pleased with the slight gasp from Sema.

"Yes, yes," Akikane reached out to touch one of the amulets. "This clarifies much." It explained how Vicaquirao had managed to infiltrate Windsor Castle more than once while pretending to be a Grace Mage.

"Thank you." Ohin handed the three amulets to Akikane, Ling, and Sema, the three most likely to have need of magic on the mission.

"Now, the last thing is a password." Vicaquirao looked directly at Gabriel. "There is always someone in the cellar with the lamp. Always. You need to give them the pass phrase. Otherwise, they are likely to kill you."

"It's sounding more and more like a typical mission." Marcus looked skyward as he spoke, running his hand across his rain-sopped bald pate.

"What's the pass phrase?" Gabriel squinted through the rain at Vicaquirao, unable to escape the intuition that he had become a pawn in yet another of the man's intricate strategies.

"Rejoice. Your day of liberation is upon you." Vicaquirao clasped Gabriel's arm. "Tell the person there that Istol has instructed him to take you to a man named Gerrad. Repeat the pass phrase to him and tell him what you need. He will help you. You must also ask him for the key. That is a relic that links back to the bifurcation that created Kumaradevi's world. It took the two of us years to find it. Now, you must go. Time is short." He glanced at his watch. "I will meet you at the bifurcation point in 9,823 BCE in exactly six hours. If you do not return, I will sever the world as we agreed."

"You're sure you don't want to come with us?" Ling's voice had a teasing note to it.

"Someone must ensure that the world is severed if you fail," Vicaquirao said. "Among other things."

Gabriel noted the tone of Vicaquirao's reply and suspected he knew what those other things might be. If Gabriel failed to return to the Primary Continuum before Vicaquirao sealed Kumaradevi's world safely away, he and the reformed Apollyons might represent the best hope of saving The Great Barrier of Probability.

"You should go." Vicaquirao stepped back.

As the others placed their hands on Gabriel's shoulder and he reached out for the imprints of the pocket watch, a question that had been nagging at him slipped out.

"If you've known where the branch that created Kumaradevi's world was for over twenty years, why didn't you sever it?" Gabriel noted a moment of hesitation before Vicaquirao replied.

"That will become obvious to you, I suspect," Vicaquirao said. "I assure you, I had good reasons. Now go. I'll see you in six hours. I hope."

Gabriel nodded and expanded his space-time sense, scanning the timeline of the colossal dinosaur skeleton for a blue flower. He saw it bloom in his mind and then wither and fade. He picked the day before its final discoloration and warped space-time to go there with his companions.

CHAPTER 21

Finding the box beneath the tree near the blue flower in Kumaradevi's alternate world proved easy enough, and Gabriel watched with rapt attention as Akikane used a subtle blend of Soul, Wind and Fire magics to determine the location of a shard of brick within the box before teleporting it to his open palm with Time Magic. A wave of sadness mixed with Gabriel's curiosity. He controlled a great deal of magical power, but he still had so much to learn about how to use it.

The piece of clay brick took them to the cellar as Vicaquirao had said it would. Gabriel counted off the years and months and days and hours until they arrived at exactly the correct moment. As the blinding haze of time travel faded, Gabriel noticed a woman with long blond hair standing beside the old oil lamp, a large revolver in her hand pointed directly at his head.

"Who are you?" The woman hissed, raising both hands to hold the gun.

"Rejoice. Your day of liberation is upon you." Gabriel stared along the barrel of the firearm, hoping he had gotten the phrase correct. It had not occurred to him to write it down until he saw that cold steel cylinder aimed at his skull.

"Who are you?" The woman lowered the pistol, her eyes going wide as she looked at Gabriel more closely.

"I am Gabriel Salvador."

The woman's eyes lit up with a sudden wild excitement. "You're younger than I thought you'd be."

Gabriel didn't know what to make of that statement. "Istol said I should ask for a man named Gerrad."

"It really has begun." The woman held two fingers to her heart moving them in a circle. She holstered her gun and looked around the room at the others. "Is this all of you?"

"Yes, yes," Akikane said. "We are few but mighty."

"Yes," the woman smiled. "That makes sense. I am Hevra." As she ushered the team out through a small wooden door and into a narrow stairwell, she turned to Gabriel again. "I had lost faith that this day might come in my lifetime. Thank you."

Gabriel didn't know what she might be thanking him for, but as he brought back to mind Vicaquirao's parting words, a vague notion of her meaning began to form in his mind.

"I will take you to Gerrad." Hevra picked up a second lamp from the table and lit it with a match.

As she turned and walked to the brick wall of the circular chamber, Gabriel realized for the first time that the room had no exit. Hevra pushed three random bricks into the wall and a metallic click rang throughout the cellar. She leaned against the wall and it pivoted inward, creating a doorway into darkness.

"This way." She raised the oil lamp and stepped into a narrow tunnel of stone and reddish clay mortar.

Gabriel and the team followed Hevra in silence as she led them along the curving corridor and through another secret door into an adjacent cellar. She paused a moment to close the concealed door of wood and stone before opening another just like it on the opposite wall.

Wooden crates of various odds and ends filled the room. Chipped vases sat with rusted daggers beside dusty necklaces on top of grime-caked bracelets. A room of relics, Gabriel guessed. He had little time to ponder the meaning of the room before they crossed into the next passageway.

They followed Hevra's lamp, its light casting twisted shadows back along the stone walls. The next cellar they came to appeared to function as a pantry. Bottles of wine filled a rack next to small casks of whiskey. Sacks of grain sat beside crates of apples and burlap bags of nuts.

"Stay here." Hevra hung the lamp on a hook near a set of steep stairs. She ascended the stairs and pushed open a trap door, exiting into a brightly lit room. Smells of roasting beef and boiling vegetables escaped down to the cellar before she closed the hatch. Gabriel's stomach rumbled with the scents. Even though they had eaten rations on the hike through the forest with Vicaquirao, he had discovered over the last year that he could nearly always ingest another meal.

"Odd greeting, but at least they are providing refreshments." Marcus ran his hand idly along the edge of a bottle of wine.

"We have better things to do just now." Sema shook her head.

"Don't tell me you're not thirsty after that march through the rain?" Marcus said.

"Eat an apple." Ling plucked a yellowish-red apple from an open barrel and tossed it to Marcus.

"Should we be stealing their provisions?" Rajan gave Ling a skeptical look.

"This world won't exist in six hours." Ling took an apple and bit into it. "What does it matter?"

"We should keep that knowledge to ourselves." Ohin frowned as Ling pitched Gabriel an apple.

"I've been wondering about…" Gabriel's sentence halted as the trap door above swung open again. He resisted the urge to bite into the apple, holding it at his side instead.

A man with bright red hair and ocean blue eyes descended the stairs. When his feet reached the packed earth of the cellar floor, he stopped and took in the sight of Gabriel and the team. He brushed flour from his hands, rubbing them against the side of his woolen breeches. Turning to Gabriel, he extended his hand with a smile.

"I am Gerrad. It is a pleasure to finally meet you."

"Thank you." Gabriel gripped the man's hand firmly, returning the powerful pressure against his palm as best he could. Gerrad stood a good six feet tall and had the build of a man used to hard labor with heavy objects.

"You wish to tell me something?" Gerrad maintained his grip on Gabriel's hand.

Gabriel observed that Gerrad's other hand rested behind his back in what might have been a formal pose…or a means of concealing a weapon. He expected something. It took Gabriel a moment to realize what.

"Rejoice. Your day of liberation is upon you."

Gerrad relinquished his grip and brought an empty hand from behind his back. "We have waited many years for this day."

"Yes." Gabriel thought a vague statement best, since he had no idea what the proper response might be.

"How may we help you as you help us?" Gerrad continued to stare only at Gabriel.

Gabriel glanced to Ohin and Akikane, but neither made as though to speak. He wondered again how wise it had been to assume the role of leader so soon. Surely the mission would have a better chance of success with one of his mentors in command. Fortunately, he'd have their advice, whether he wanted it or not. Just then, he wished he could have openly requested their help. Instead, he plunged ahead on instinct.

"A friend of ours is being held captive by Kumaradevi in the palace," Gabriel said. "We intend to rescue her. We need your help to gain access to the palace and any information you have on her location."

"A young girl about your age?" Gerrad asked.

"Yes." Gabriel's throat went dry.

"We have informants throughout the palace. We heard of her arrival. It caused a great deal of commotion among the palace hierarchy. I will try to find where she is being held."

"Thank you," Gabriel said. "We must hurry, however. We have less than six hours to locate her."

"So little time." Gerrad looked thoughtful. "I had expected more. Six will have to suffice. I will return momentarily. Stay here."

Without waiting for a reply, Gerrad turned and retreated up the stairs and through the trapdoor. Gabriel turned to the others, unable to mask his confusion.

"Very strange, very strange." Akikane gazed after Gerrad. "They seem to be expecting you." He turned to face Gabriel.

"Yes," Ohin said. "And your presence seems to be a signal of some sort."

"Sounds as though a rebellion is afoot," Marcus said.

"How would Gabriel be connected to a rebellion in Kumaradevi's world?" Ling took a bite of her apple.

"Vicaquirao," Gabriel said. "He's known of this world for decades."

"Plenty of time to build up a native resistance to Kumaradevi's rule." Rajan added.

"But why?" Sema asked. "They're both malignancy mages. This world posed no threat to him."

"Balance." Gabriel said, seeing clearly Vicaquirao's motivations.

"Just so, just so," Akikane said. "Where there is darkness there must also be light."

"A light that will be snuffed out along with everything else when we sever this world." Ohin stroked his chin. "Why would he sacrifice this world and his plans in order to save Teresa?"

"No, no," Akikane said. "Not Teresa. The Great Barrier."

"If Teresa has told them everything she knows, rescuing her won't save the Barrier." Ling looked at her half-eaten apple, appearing unsure whether or not she wanted to finish it.

"No." Gabriel felt nauseous as clarity settled across his mind. "Saving her saves me, and Vicaquirao thinks I am the key to saving the Great Barrier. He thinks the grief and anger of losing Teresa would hinder me from saving the Barrier. And to avoid that, he is willing to destroy this world."

"Maybe he realized this world is too dangerous with the alliance between Kumaradevi and the Apollyons?" Rajan offered.

"I don't think so." Gabriel considered Rajan's thinking. "He's spent more than twenty years organizing this rebellion. If it succeeds, Kumaradevi's power would be crippled anyway. He is very good at planning. He wouldn't set it in motion if he didn't think it could succeed."

"How could these rebels succeed against the magic Kumaradevi commands?" Marcus asked.

"With magic of their own," Ohin said. "I'd swear Gerrad is a Time Mage."

"Rebel Malignancy Mages?" Sema said.

"No, no." Akikane said. "Rebel Grace Mages. I sensed the power in him as well."

Gabriel had thought he sensed something but had assumed it to be a reflection of Ohin or Akikane's subtle energy.

"Then why set this rebellion in motion now?" Ling asked.

The trap door swung open and Gerrad descended the stairs again, carrying a bundle of clothes in his arms and a small sack in one hand. Hevra followed him with a similar burden. They stopped at the bottom of the stairs, and Gerrad looked directly at Ling.

"His presence here is the spark that ignites the flame." Gerrad turned to Gabriel. "We have been setting the tinder for many years, but we could not light this fire ourselves." Gerrad placed the clothes on a nearby crate. "Now hurry. These uniforms will give you access to practically the entire palace. You're concealment amulets would be detected by the sharper Soul Magic guards."

He handed Akikane the uniform of a captain while Hevra helped the others. Each team member took the uniform that held the symbol of their particular magic. Gabriel took the one with a red flame embroidered on the breast. He would pretend to be a Fire Mage.

"We have asked all our sources, but we do not know where your friend is being held," Gerrad said. "She has been moved several times. I wish we could help you, but we have other matters to attend to. We can offer you these."

Gerrad opened the sack to reveal seven daggers and a collection of concatenate crystals. He passed Gabriel and each of the team members a dagger. Gabriel's eyes widened as he sensed the Grace imprints upon them. "These daggers are common for elite troops. Don't let anyone touch them. As you can no doubt tell, they bear imprints of Light, not Darkness. These also carry imprints you can use." He handed out a single concatenate crystal to each person except Gabriel. To him, Gerrad handed three different crystals. Gabriel's magic-sense told him the crystals linked to several others, each in turn linked to numerous malignant imprints.

"Stolen from Kumaradevi's own armory," Hevra said when Gabriel looked up from the crystals in his hand.

"We would offer you more, but we will need many imprints ourselves this day." Gerrad watched as Gabriel and the team changed into the black woolen palace uniforms. Sema and Ling stepped behind a stack of crates for privacy.

"I thought Kumaradevi killed every Grace Mage as soon as a child showed signs of magic." Gabriel buttoned the tight fitting jacket over his shirt.

"She does." The muscles of Gerrad's jaw tightened. "But she does not find all of them. Those we can locate before her troops sniff them out are hidden away in a secret village. There we are trained to conceal, and to use, our magical abilities."

"There can't be enough of you to defeat Kumaradevi's armies." Ohin sounded sad to raise the point.

"Few of the armies have mages within them." Hevra said as she helped Akikane into a jacket. "The soldiers battle to create imprints for the Empress's mages. They have no love of her and no loyalty. They fight because they and their families will be slaughtered if they refuse."

"The Empress has many mages at her command," Gerrad added. "But there are many who have defected against her. There are even some within her inner ranks waiting to turn against their comrades."

"We each have lost people we love to the Empress's nation of Darkness." The passion in Hevra's voice gave weight to her words. "There will be losses, but we will prevail."

"The Light will triumph. And balance will be restored." Gerrad touched two fingers to his chest and Hevra mimicked his action. "Now you should go. There is not much time and the palace is large. I have a map to help you."

Gerrad made to reach for the cloth sack again, but Gabriel raised his hand to stop him. "I know the palace well."

"Yes, I'm sure you do." A thin smile crossed Gerrad's lips. "This way."

Gerrad led Gabriel and the team through yet another secret passage.

"May you find you the one you seek." Hevra closed the door behind them.

Gerrad guided Gabriel and the others though a series of tunnels branching off into other passageways, past doors that did not seem to have been opened in years, up flights of stairs and back down again, along narrow crawl spaces, and finally up a wooden ladder and through a false stone door. He ushered them into a small room of black stone walls with large boxes stacked in neat rows.

"You are in a storage room on the lower level at the western end of the palace." Gerrad held the lamp up, illuminating his face. "If you go left along the hallway, you will find yourself near the entrance to the dungeons. That was the last place your friend was sighted by our spies. I apologize for not sending someone to accompany you."

"You have helped greatly." Ohin said.

"Yes, yes," Akikane added. "May we both swiftly find success."

"You will need this." Gerrad handed Gabriel a tiny statue of a bull carved from cream-colored bone. "This will lead you back to where you came from."

Gabriel rubbed his thumb along the edge of the small bull's horns before slipping it into his pocket. He reached out and offered Gerrad his hand. He admired a man who could plan for so long for such a sacrifice. "Good luck."

"You as well." Gerrad shook his hand briefly and smiled.

With a quick nod to the others, Gerrad disappeared through the secret passage, closing the false stone wall behind him. The hidden door closed the lamplight from the room, plunging it into darkness.

Gabriel waited for his eyes to adjust enough to see the light seeping from under the door leading to the hallway.

"Let's go." He reached for the handle of the door. "We have less than five hours left."

CHAPTER 22

To Gabriel, the search for Teresa began to feel more like a forced march to a guillotine rather than a rescue mission. Each passing minute brought the next one inexorably upon its heels, time seeming to compress and flow more swiftly. The sharp blade of their potential failure hung above their heads, threatening to decapitate them with the compiling list of false leads and dead ends. Hours passed in a haze of anxiety, fear becoming a palpable companion to their footsteps through the polished marble corridors of the palace.

Gabriel took the team to every tower and dungeon he knew of, Akikane pretending at each check point and guard post to be leading a random inspection team under Kumaradevi's direct orders. Gabriel at first worried he might be recognized, that maybe he should try to alter his true appearance with his concealment amulet. However, he had grown so much since his time in the palace that no one gave him a first look, much less a second.

As the quest continued and each successive failure to find Teresa accumulated, they fought the impulse to run to the next potential holding cell. Any unusual action might draw unwanted attention to them and foil the whole rescue mission. As the minutes became hours and the hours accrued, it became clear they needed to adopt another search method if they were to have any hope of locating Teresa.

As Gabriel climbed the stairs of the final dungeon cell, he sighed, letting the despair that had been building within him crest and burst uncontrollably. He had no idea where Teresa might be and no notion of how to find her. He glanced at the hands of his pocket watch. They had less than an hour to locate her before they needed to leave. Then he faced as difficult a decision as the one he had surmounted fleeing the firestorm in that distant alternate reality where the two of them had been trapped. He would need to abandon her, knowing she would cease to exist along with the rest of Kumaradevi's world when Vicaquirao severed it from the Primary Continuum. The alternative would be to stay and hope this universe somehow survived the severing so he could rescue her or perish in the attempt.

"Where next, where next?" Akikane whispered from where he led the short column of mages along a darkened corridor.

"I don't know." Gabriel's feet began to slow. "That was the last cell I remember. There are thousands of rooms in the palace. If she's in a regular room, we'll never find her in time."

"We'll find her, lad." Marcus placed his hand on Gabriel's shoulder from behind him.

"Maintain formation." Ohin looked back from where he marched with Ling ahead of Rajan and Gabriel, who walked before Marcus and Sema. "We can't afford to attract attention to ourselves. Not now."

"Is there someplace you might have missed?" Sema wondered aloud. "Someplace where she could be guarded but not in dungeon cell or tower room?"

"Someplace outside?" Ling suggested.

"Or in Kumaradevi's private chambers," Rajan added.

"Maybe." Gabriel considered all the alternative locations where Kumaradevi might keep a captive as prized as Teresa. "There are too many places to choose from and they are all over the palace. It would take too long to search them all."

"We could try splitting up," Ling said.

"No, no," Akikane said. "We would be too noticeable if not seen as a team." Nearly everyone they had passed in the preceding hours had been part of a team of six mages, or a team of no fewer than seven if servants. Kumaradevi did not trust people to act alone.

"There might be another way." An idea formed suddenly in Gabriel's mind and he latched on to it in desperation. "Wherever Teresa is, Kumaradevi will want to gloat over her capture. Yes. Why didn't I think of that?" He resisted smacking his hand to his forehead. "She'll want Teresa close at hand. She might even move her to remain nearby. She may have been moving her this entire time."

"How do we find Teresa if she's being moved constantly?" Ling's voice rose in annoyance.

"We don't have to." Gabriel nearly smiled. "All we need to do is find Kumaradevi. She'll lead us to Teresa."

"But will she lead us there in time?" Sema asked.

"The sooner we find Kumaradevi the sooner we'll know." Ohin said. "Where do we start?"

"Yes, yes," Akikane said. "Which way next?" They were approaching an intersection of corridors and Akikane needed to choose a direction soon. To be seen standing in the middle of the halls looking indecisive would bring the curiosity of passing eyes.

"Take a right," Gabriel said. "She checks on everyone with any real responsibility at least once a day. It's almost time for her evening meal, so she should be making her administrative rounds on the third level."

Gabriel quietly gave Akikane instructions to lead the team through the palace, following the route he had so often walked at Kumaradevi's side during his captivity. He had been attempting to sequester those memories for fear they might distract him from his task. Now they came back in a flash of sensory association, reminding him of his fear and anger and despondency during those months of servitude and abuse. He fought these feelings as they attempted to return in full, pressing them out of his mind, focusing on his need to locate Teresa with the dwindling minutes that remained.

It took them twenty minutes to discover Kumaradevi leading a throng of servants and advisors out of a meeting room and down a wide staircase. One of the Apollyons walked beside her, listening to her give orders to her servants with a look of bored resolution. Gabriel guessed this Apollyon had been selected to be an ambassador to Kumaradevi for the duration of the alliance. He wondered how well the psychic connection to the Apollyon copies in the Primary Continuum worked from within an alternate reality.

The speed of the procession offered little time for reflection or planning. They opted to follow Kumaradevi and her cohorts directly, falling in behind the last group of servants in the line and trying to appear as though they belonged there. Within minutes, Gabriel realized their ultimate destination and cursed himself for not considering the possibility earlier. As they approached the massive open doors of the throne and banquet room, a flash of electric light deepened his suspicions and his self-recrimination.

"Turn left before the door," Gabriel whispered to Akikane.

Akikane turned as instructed, their small unit breaking off from the main contingent following Kumaradevi into the throne room. Gabriel gave Akikane directions that eventually led the team through the kitchens and into a back hall that looped around to deposit them before a door at the rear of the massive audience chamber. Two guards stood outside the door.

"They'll accept no excuse for us to enter," Gabriel said to Akikane.

"Not a problem, not a problem." Akikane broke into a smile as he approached the two Fire Mage guards. "We have been sent to inspect you."

"Inspect our what?" The burly guard on the right asked with a menacing glare.

"You're reflexes." Akikane struck the two men so quickly and forcefully Gabriel did not realize what had transpired until both Dark Mages slumped to the ground.

"Pull them inside and out of sight," Ohin said, grabbing one of the fallen guards by the arms as Marcus claimed the man's feet.

Gabriel opened the door and peeked through, opening it partway while the others hauled the unconscious guards into the back of the throne room. A large screen partition hid the back door, covering their entrance. Rajan and Ling bound the guards with strips of their own clothing while Gabriel relieved the men of their malignantly imprinted talismans, adding their two daggers to the one already hanging on his belt.

Gabriel took one of the daggers and dug the tip into the thin wooden screen, placing his eye to the hole he had created. The colossal room had not changed since Gabriel's time there. A mosaic of marbled tile in a repeating pattern stretched 300 feet along the floor of the room, erupting into an image of seven crossed swords at the edge of a large throne sculpted from stone to resemble a huddled mass of suffering subjects. The hem of Kumaradevi's robes fell to the side of the throne, signaling her presence in the seat. Twenty advisors and soldiers knelt in supplication before her. More Malignancy Mages and soldiers entered the room in a constant stream, kneeling behind their comrades.

Gabriel looked around the hall, wondering if he had been wrong, if following Kumaradevi had been a mistake. Enormous columns rose up to support an arched ceiling three stories high. As Gabriel's eye tracked upward, he let out a soft gasp. Fears confirmed, he forced himself to look at where Teresa floated, fifty feet above the throne, encased in a cage of orange-white electric arcs. Beside her, another familiar face floated in the air, sheathed in lightning — Malik. Apparently, his punishment for betraying Kumaradevi involved being on display with her other trophy captive.

Gabriel pulled his head back from the screen to face Akikane and his team.

"Teresa is here, but it won't be easy to get her out." He placed his eye to the peephole again. More and more soldiers poured into the room. "We're going to have to wait until Kumaradevi is finished addressing her subjects."

Gabriel relinquished his peephole so the others could see the circumstances and the odds against them. Uniformly sullen faces turned from the hole to stare back at Gabriel. Even Akikane's smile had fled.

Gabriel placed his eye to the peephole again as the massive doors of the room shuddered closed. With the closing of the doors began the familiar cadence of Kumaradevi's pronouncements. The words were new to Gabriel, but not the tone of her voice — triumphant imperial narcissism. Bile climbed the back his throat as he listened to her speech.

"Above me rests a sign, a portent of what the future holds. A harbinger of the glories my empire will ascend to. As many of you know, I have decided to mend the rift that has divided the forces of Light for so many years. Our new friends and I have agreed that collaboration, rather than competition, is the key to our mutual advancement. With the information this pitiful girl has provided, and the assistance of my new allies, I am now in a position to take what has been denied me for so long. The promised war of liberation is upon us, and I will lead my armies to victory against those who have…"

"How long does the windbag usually go on for?" Ling looked ready to burst through the screen and attack the room full of Dark Mages.

"I'm not sure." Gabriel took out his pocket watch. "We've only got twenty minutes left."

"We can't grab her with a whole room of mages and soldiers watching," Rajan said.

"Maybe Kumaradevi will finish and clear the room before we run out of time." Sema tried to sound hopeful.

"I'm really wishing I had some of that wine about now." Marcus put his eye to the peephole and rubbed his head.

"We should wait as long as possible in case we get lucky, but we need a plan." Ohin settled his gaze on Gabriel.

"I have a plan." Gabriel had been giving the options considerable thought ever since glimpsing Teresa through the peephole. He could not abandon her now. No matter what the cost. The sight of her in agony stirred some irrational part of his brain that trampled all notions of caution.

"A plan to fight a room full of Dark Mages?" Fear and determination tinged the edges of Rajan's voice.

"A plan to distract a room full of Dark Mages," Gabriel replied.

"Yes, yes," Akikane's smiled returned, looking more devious than beatific. "Sleight of hand. Like a magic trick."

"Exactly." Gabriel began laying out his plan for the others, glancing down at the watch in his hand while trying to ignore Kumaradevi's voice still droning on behind them. He realized she'd never finish before their deadline. She loved to gloat and preen to her subjects too much for anything less than an hour, even with one of the Apollyon duplicates standing beside her throne. She would list off all the ancient illusory grievances, present her imagined injustices, parade her plans for revenge, and finally call for volunteers to lead the first assaults. She might go on for more than an hour. They needed to halt her oration and turn the attention of the room away from the throne long enough to rescue Teresa from her perch, suspended in the air above it.

When Gabriel finished explaining his plan, he handed Akikane the small bull statue — the relic key that would return the team to the Primary Continuum where Vicaquirao waited to sever the alternate reality. The others looked at Gabriel with concern and annoyance.

"I know what Teresa would say." Ling looked as though she might spit on the marble floor.

"Worst. Plan. Ever." Rajan looked to Akikane and Ohin, clearly hoping one of them would override Gabriel's newfound leadership decisions.

"Exactly," Ling said.

"It's risky, lad," Marcus said.

"We will lose more than Teresa if it fails," Sema added.

"That has always been a risk." Ohin placed his hand on Gabriel's shoulder. "This plan can work."

"Indeed, indeed," Akikane said. "And we should work it quickly. While we still have time."

Gabriel looked again at his watch. They had less than ten minutes now. He turned to Akikane and his teammates. He wanted to say something. Something encouraging. Something inspiring. Something heroic. He settled for something practical.

"If it goes wrong, don't wait for me."

Before anyone could respond, Gabriel slid out the back door of the throne room and into the service hall. As he walked, he stripped off the jacket with the red flame emblazoned on it. He needed people to recognize him now. Throwing the coat to the floor, he embraced the imprints of the three daggers and the three concatenate crystals. His stomach lurched with the assumption of so many dark imprints. He added the Grace imprints of his pocket watch to counter them. It did little to help. He focused his mind on his breathing, holding at bay the spark of rage being inflamed by the negative imprints. He could not afford to allow his anger to cloud his judgment in the coming minutes. Too much depended on what he was about to say and do.

He passed through the kitchens again, drawing little attention at first, but as his pace and his manner were gradually noticed, gasps of recognition began to compete with the noise of clanging pans and hustling cooks.

When Gabriel walked through the kitchen doors into the main hall, he encountered a team of six Dark Mages standing sentry duty. He knew they had drawn the responsibility as a penalty for real or imagined infractions. All of the soldiers with any social standing would be in the throne room with Kumaradevi.

Before they became fully aware of his presence, he reached out to them with Soul and Heart-Tree magic. Fortunately, as punishment, they had been given talismans that contained worthless imprints. Gabriel easily overwhelmed their minds and left them standing in a stupor as he strode between them. Had their talismans contained any significant imprints he might have stopped to collect them. Instead, he walked calmly and purposefully toward the towering twin doors that led to the throne room.

Two hulking Wind Mages stood guard on either side of the giant doors. As they saw Gabriel and realized who he was, they reached out toward him with simultaneous attacks of Wind Magic. Gabriel deflected their assaults as he concentrated on their talismans, stealing control of their imprints and robbing them of their magic. He cast the men aside with a flick of Wind Magic before turning that same power toward the doors looming in front of him.

The great doors burst inward with a momentum so powerful that they crashed against the walls, driving their head-sized brass handles into the polished marble walls in a cloud of dust. Gabriel marched through the doorway without pausing to think, without considering the ludicrousness of the path he had set himself to follow.

The sound of the crashing doors drew all eyes toward the entrance and onto Gabriel. Hundreds of Dark Mages turned to face him as Kumaradevi looked up to see the nature of the commotion that had interrupted her presumptive victory speech. Gabriel stopped just inside the threshold of the door, seeing the look of rage upon Kumaradevi's face and how it contrasted with the confusion clouding the continence of the Apollyon duplicate standing beside her throne.

Gabriel felt a space-time seal fall in place around him, held there by the Apollyon ambassador. He had expected this. It would give his adversaries a false sense of advantage. Now his plan fell into motion. His part needed to be convincing in order to provide the necessary distraction for his teammates.

He focused solely on Kumaradevi. Her dark eyes and beautiful, angular face floated above the fabric of the red and gold dress flowing off the throne and down the steps of the dais. The garment twinkled with reflected light from the many concatenate crystals sewn into the fabric. Gabriel continued to stare at her. He did not risk looking where Teresa floated above her head for fear of drawing notice to the very thing he need to lure attention away from.

"This seems so familiar. You before a room of incompetents, boasting of things you will never accomplish. No wonder you had to hide in this world." Hopefully those words held her attention.

"How did you find this place?" Kumaradevi's voice rang with anger. She remained seated, but her hands gripped the arms of her throne as though she might leap to her feet at any moment.

"You are not the only one to have made new friends." Gabriel nodded to the Apollyon ambassador with a smirk. "Vicaquirao says hello."

Gabriel observed a shift in the faces of both Kumaradevi and the Apollyon ambassador. The knowledge that Vicaquirao knew how to access Kumaradevi's alternate kingdom implied things neither Dark Mage found pleasant. Before they had time to consider the full ramifications of Gabriel's statement, he added another. One he hoped would prove even more provocative.

"I have come to offer terms of a truce."

A murmur swept through the kneeling soldiers, rushing outward like the wave of a pebble dropped in a still pond. Gabriel used this commotion as cover to sneak a glance toward the ceiling where Teresa floated in her cage of lightning. He discerned the faint outline of six bodies cloaked in the invisibility of Wind Magic, rising to meet Teresa near the ceiling. Ling used small amounts of Wind Magic to bend light around the team and avoid attracting attention while Akikane used a similarly limited amount of Wind Magic to fly them slowly to their destination above the throne.

They were almost there. Gabriel quickly flicked his eyes back to Kumaradevi.

"Silence!" Kumaradevi's bellowed word echoed throughout the marble walls, the room instantly falling quiet as the vibrations of her voice faded. "What truce do you speak of?"

"A truce that will provide all sides with what they desire." Gabriel resisted the urge to look upward again. His teammates needed another few seconds. And he needed to place a believable proposal before Kumaradevi and the Apollyon ambassador.

"The Council has authorized me to offer the following terms: we divide the Continuum among us. You may remain unmolested in this alternate realm while the Council will retain control of the past up to the year 2012. The Apollyons will have dominion over the future beyond 2012, but the Great Barrier of Probability will remain intact. All of the Apollyon duplicates will need to cross the Barrier as it is, sealing them away from the past."

It was, of course, a ridiculous plan, but Gabriel hoped it illuminated for Kumaradevi the Apollyons' true desires. If they only wanted to rule the future beyond the year 2012, they could do so at any time by crossing the Great Barrier. They would never be satisfied with anything less than control of the entire Continuum. He also hoped it provoked a few seconds of argument that he needed for his plan work.

"Your proposal is too little, too late," the Apollyon ambassador said with a laugh.

"I pronounce judgment here." Kumaradevi turned to glower at the Apollyon.

Gabriel used this moment to glance upwards again. As he did so, a cry rang out through the chamber. Gabriel turned toward the scream ringing against the marble walls to see a servant at the edge of the room, pointing toward the ceiling. The candlelit chandeliers hanging from the ceiling created a flickering illumination that Ling's low intensity Wind Magic could not easily disperse. The effect rendered her magical field of invisibility only partially successful. While the team would not be seen from anyone's peripheral vision, they were obvious if looked at directly.

As the eyes of Kumaradevi, the Apollyon ambassador, and hundreds of soldiers rose to follow the servant's outstretched arm, Gabriel blended Wind and Fire Magic to create an exploding shockwave of gravity, heat, and light. The growing ball of flame and force tossed the soldiers surrounding him outward in a rapidly expanding circle. Even before the edge of the surging fireball reached the walls, he gathered his Wind Magic and launched himself into the air. The space-time seal around him did not break, and his only hope of escaping the room alive was to reach Akikane and Ohin before they used the tiny carved bull to jump back to the Primary Continuum. The three of them together could disrupt the space-time seal and rescue Teresa and the team.

Screams of anger and pain and fear shattered the air as Gabriel soared to his awaiting companions. Even though his speed of flight might be fast enough to elude the eyes seeking him, halfway to his destination, fifty yards from Teresa and the others, he knew they could not make it away from this world. He felt a space-time seal fall around Akikane and Ohin and the team — a seal far too powerful for them to break though.

Pain began to wrack his body as dozens of unseen Wind Magic hands dragged him to the ground. He fought back as best he could, seeing Akikane and the rest of the team pulled to the floor as they tried to repel the magical violence allayed against them. Winning a fight with the Apollyon ambassador and Kumaradevi alone would have been improbable. Especially as the Empress commanded the imprints from dozens of concatenate crystals stitched into her ornate dress.

The hundreds of Dark Mages filling the room, angered now by Gabriel's attack, rendered his escape impossible. His plan had failed. If they did not find a way to elicit their freedom in the next few moments, it would all end when Vicaquirao severed the entire alternate world from the Primary Continuum and they ceased to exist.

The knowledge of Kumaradevi's irrevocable demise provided some small comfort to Gabriel as the dark magical forces compelled him, groaning, to his knees. He could barely see straight with the Soul and Heart-Tree Magic stabbing into his brain. His arms quivered as he tried to keep himself from falling face first onto the marble floor. The negative imprints he held were ripped away from him, and he clung to the Grace imprints of his pocket watch.

Akikane, Ohin, and the rest of the team slammed into the floor beside him, writhing and moaning in pain. Gabriel found his head forced upward to look directly into Kumaradevi's eyes, a fury burning in them that seemed it might set the room aflame with their intensity. Far above, still hovering near the ceiling, Teresa floated in a prison of electric arcs.

"You will find your future far different from the one you described." Kumaradevi's voice rasped with uncontrolled emotion. "Your future will be filled with pain and suffering beyond your feeble imagination until the day I grant you the mercy of perpetual servitude. Your punishment will be the cries of your companions and your rewards will be their deaths. You will witness everything you have ever loved destroyed and you will thank me for it as you help me destroy all else that you have held dear. Your life will be an endless misery compounded by the knowledge that nothing will ever reprieve you from your despair. This will be your future."

Tears of agony streamed down Gabriel's trembling cheeks, his besieged body quaking against the onslaught of magic. He wished he could look at his watch. To see how many minutes remained of this torment — how many seconds. There could not be many. Regardless, he would not allow what little time he had to be spent in anything other than defiance.

"There is no future."

Kumaradevi looked at Gabriel quizzically, opening her smirking mouth to reply as a voice sliced through the air. A voice filled with terror and disbelief.

"The palace is on fire!"

Gabriel could not see who had entered the room, but suspected one of Kumaradevi's attendants from the tenor and accent of the man's voice.

"What do you mean?" Kumaradevi appeared confused by the phrase, as though it could not possibly describe reality. Beside her, the Apollyon ambassador suddenly appeared anxious.

"The palace and the city are on fire." The attendant's voice came closer with each running footstep. "Mages are attacking soldiers and guards. The streets and halls are bedlam."

"What mages?" Kumaradevi's attention passed completely from Gabriel to the approaching attendant. He felt the pain ease, but not cease, with her diverted concern.

As if in answer to Kumaradevi's query, a familiar voice rang through the air.

"The true Mages of Light, tyrant!"

Gabriel's muscles worked well enough now to turn his head to where he beheld a sight so inspiring as to be nearly unfathomable. Gerrad stood in the towering doorway to the throne room, hundreds of men and woman rapidly filling the space behind him. All of them were armed with swords or short carbine rifles. Gabriel knew those holding swords to be the Grace Mages of the rebellion. He could see concatenate crystals glowing at their necks.

"How dare…" Kumaradevi's next words were forever lost in the tsunami of sound that crashed upon the room with the rebel Grace Mages' simultaneous assault. Balls of flame and arcs of lightning filled the hall as the sound of gunfire and clashing swords reverberated through the air.

The Apollyon ambassador fell to the ground as a bullet struck his leg. Kumaradevi screamed in rage as the side of her arm exploded with blood from a rifle shot. The ground shook with blasts that deafened, the air filling with sulfurous smoke. The rebels had grenades.

Gabriel felt the magics that had been impaling him with pain vanish in the ensuing cacophony. The space-time seal also evaporated. He quickly scanned the battle being fought around him. He and his companions seemed forgotten in the heat of combat as Kumaradevi and her troops defended her throne. The Apollyon ambassador had disappeared from sight behind a wall of soldiers pushing to reach the fight at the front of the room.

He turned to Akikane. The elder mage nodded, his panted breathing too quick for words. Gabriel pulled his pocket watch from his pants and cupped it in his shaking hand. They had less than a minute. He reassumed command of the imprints of the pocket watch, the tainted dagger, and the three concatenate crystals, forcing space-time to bend around him slightly as he readied the Wind Magic he needed. A moment later, he and Akikane and the rest of the team floated in the air near the ceiling. Teresa hovered only a few feet away in a web of lightning, her mouth open in a silent scream of agony, her eyes rolled back into her head with the pain of her magical captivity. Knowing he did not have the time, he didn't bother trying to figure out the magic necessary to release her.

The mêlée below them grew in intensity and violence, the rebel mages and foot soldiers gaining the upper hand as more of them poured into the room with every passing moment. Gabriel saw Kumaradevi standing in the center of a phalanx of her troops, dispensing deadly magic to the rebels seeking to unseat her from power. He wasted no more time or thought on what might happen. He had only seconds to escape.

Akikane held the small bull statue in his hand. The blackness of time travel filled Gabriel's mind. His space-time sense tugged and twisted as the darkness became brilliance, fading with their arrival among the clay and stone ruins of a small village.

Gabriel turned to Teresa, the magical sphere of lightning vanishing, as he had hoped, with the distance in time and space from the dark alternate world. With the sudden absence of the magical torture that had confined her, she collapsed into unconsciousness. He crawled to her, holding her head in his hands, pushing her hair from her face as he kissed her forehead.

"Your return does not leave much time."

Gabriel looked up to see Vicaquirao standing above him. "I will sever the world if you wish to observe."

Gabriel did not have time to wonder why he might want to watch Vicaquirao sever Kumaradevi's world, or why he would choose to do so rather than caring for Teresa, wounded and battered in his arms. Instead, the air became heat and light and sound and vibration. The power of the sun fell down upon the earth. A fiery hand pressed into his flesh.

Gabriel shielded Teresa with his body, encasing them in a barrier of Fire and Wind Magic, pushing it out to cover his companions until the wave of blistering brilliance faded. He raised his head to see Vicaquirao, fallen to his knees near the crumbled wall of a stone hut, trying to fend off an attack by the Apollyon ambassador. The Apollyon, his leg bloodied but healed, must have ghosted their trail through time. The two men fought, exchanging malicious magics, oblivious to all else around them.

Gabriel released his protective shield of magic as he rolled away from Teresa. His quick thinking had protected her from the worst of the Apollyon ambassador's attack, whatever it had been. Akikane and the others had not been so fortunate. Their clothes smoked and smoldered, blisters covering their faces and the exposed flesh of their arms.

A nearby tree shattered into flame, splinters raining down on Gabriel's head. Vicaquirao stood on his feet now, wounded, but still attacking the Apollyon ambassador, drawing him away from the others. Gabriel made to stand, intending to help Vicaquirao defeat the Apollyon.

Akikane moaned and stretched out his hand, the charred statue of the bull cupped in his blistered palm. Gabriel understood. They needed to dissolve Kumaradevi's world above all else. They had always planned for their return to coincide with the creation of Kumaradevi's alternate reality. Had they returned an hour earlier, they would have had sixty minutes to prepare to sever the world, or jump through time to accomplish it. Gabriel looked at the pocket watch, still in his fingers. They had only seventeen seconds to sever Kumaradevi's alternate world from the Primary Continuum.

He took the bull statue from Akikane and sat on his knees in the hardened dust. Embracing the imprints of the pocket watch, he reached out with his space-time sense to the small statue. They had chosen a place near where Kumaradevi had hidden the original bifurcation in time that created the alternate reality of her kingdom. Close enough to make severing possible but far enough away to avoid ever attracting her attention should she look.

Gabriel pushed the noises of Vicaquirao and the Apollyon ambassador's battle from his mind, casting away his concern for Teresa and Akikane and Ohin and the team. He concentrated on the seconds passing as he scanned the statue and its timeline, waiting for the moment he needed to strike out with his Time Magic. He calmed his breathing and tried to focus on gathering his own subtle energy imprints to add to the power of the pocket watch. It would impossible to try and use the imprints of the negatively imbued daggers and concatenate crystals from Kumaradevi's world to performing the severing.

Focusing his power as the moments passed, he sensed an elusive disturbance in the space-time continuum begin to build. The magic cloaking it would have made it imperceptible from any other place or time. So close to the origin of the bifurcation, the unique signature of the rent in space-time grew with each passing second in Gabriel's mind, an inner image slowly coming into focus.

As Gabriel waited for the moment to strike, his mind filled with thoughts of Gerrad and Hevra and the rebels fighting for their freedom in Kumaradevi's palace. He still did not understand how Vicaquirao could so callously ignore their sacrifice. These people, whom he had groomed for decades in order to overthrow Kumaradevi's tyrannical rule, would cease to exist when Gabriel severed their world from the Primary Continuum. All that they had worked for, the future they were bleeding and dying to forge, would be eradicated in an instant as the world ceased to have a past, making any present, much less any future, impossible.

Gabriel mourned their lost dreams and lost lives as he closed his eyes, expanding his space-time sense while the last moments before the bifurcation passed. He heard Vicaquirao scream something as the air filled with the sound of crashing trees. Gabriel found it ironic that Vicaquirao had fought so hard to ensure the destruction of a world he had struggled so long to save.

The bifurcation looming seconds away, something obvious occurred to Gabriel — Vicaquirao always thought through the possibilities and contingencies, and he always had a plan to alter his plans when the need arose. He would never have worked for decades to oust Kumaradevi from power if his work could be ended simply by severing her world from the Primary Continuum. He must have had another plan.

As the moment of the bifurcation blossomed in Gabriel's mind, he remembered Vicaquirao's offer to witness the severing of the alternate branch of time. As he thought about the act of severing an alternate world, he recalled something else — the Void between realms. A sea of infinite impossibilities burgeoning with potential possibility. Impossible possibility that might allow for the survival of a branch of time sliced free from the trunk. A branch that would become its own new continuum. A continuum that would still need a past. A past that might be fashioned by peeling a thin, bark-like layer of the original trunk right down to its roots.

Gabriel slowed his perception of space-time to a near absolute absence of temporal unfolding, suspending the moment of the bifurcation's creation in his mind, fashioning a mental blade of Time Magic to cleave the alternate branch of time from the Primary Continuum. He forced the separation back through time, a slender remnant of the original continuum improbably stripping away, clinging to the alternate world, a stable shadow-past solidifying as the alternate world broke free into the great Void.

Kumaradevi's world would survive. Its past, grafted from the Primary Continuum, would allow it to possess a future. Time Mages from that new universe would never be able to travel back before the day of its creation, nor could they likely ever leap across the Void between worlds to return to the Primary Continuum, but they would live.

Gabriel noticed the silence and opened his eyes.

Vicaquirao stood before him, a bloody gash across his forehead. The Apollyon ambassador, unconscious but still breathing, lay on the ground behind him. Akikane had healed himself and helped Marcus begin healing the others. Teresa breathed slowly in deep slumber.

"You severed the world?" Vicaquirao's tone sounded concerned.

"I did." Gabriel reached out to place a hand on Teresa's forehead.

"I made a mistake." Vicaquirao looked back at the fallen Apollyon, his voice rasping in anger. "I wanted to take him alive. I should have killed him. If I had, there would have been time for me to sever the world." He turned back to Gabriel, his eyes sad.

"I figured it out." Gabriel raised his head to look at Vicaquirao. "The world is safe. They'll still need to deal with Kumaradevi, but Gerrad and the others will have a future."

"Thank you." A smile broke across Vicaquirao's bloodied face. "I thought I was the only one who had discovered that trick."

"I almost didn't," Gabriel said. "It took me a while to realize you aren't as awful as I assumed."

"Few people ever realize that."

Gabriel looked to where Akikane and Marcus sat healing the rest of the team of their burns. He turned back to Teresa before speaking again.

"The Apollyons probably know everything now. They will know about the anchor points. It will only be a matter of time before they find them all and strike at the Great Barrier. We need to do something soon."

"I'll see what I can learn from this one." Vicaquirao gestured toward the unconscious Apollyon. "You know how to contact me when the time comes." Vicaquirao turned to go but then stopped, looking back over his shoulder at Gabriel. "You did well today. There are more hard days ahead, but you saved an entire universe. And you rescued Teresa. And your friends are all alive. As are mine. You should be pleased."

"Thank you." Gabriel experienced an odd sense of pride flush over him, realizing as it did so, that Vicaquirao had become a mentor to him in some ways. Still an adversary, but one he respected, and one who admired him. The confusion wrought by that thought and the sentiments surrounding it crashed against the hard emotions of fearing for Teresa, and his friends, and all that had happened in the past day. Before Gabriel could consider an additional response, Vicaquirao disappeared through time with his captive Apollyon.

"Is it done, is it done?" Akikane knelt beside Gabriel and Teresa as Ohin and the others gathered around them.

"Yes," Gabriel said. "But not the way I had expected. I'll explain later."

"Hello Bubbles."

Gabriel looked down to see Teresa smiling up at him.

"Are you stalking me again? How far does a girl have to go to get away from you?" Teresa offered a thin smile with her words.

"The ends of time." Gabriel stroked Teresa's cheek.

"We should all be getting away from here." Ohin helped Gabriel to his feet. "Kumaradevi may still have agents in the Primary Continuum."

"Where are we headed?" Ling asked, leaning on a branch as she favored a wounded leg. "We aren't going to be welcomed anywhere by the Council."

"They should give us a bloody medal for today." Marcus held an arm around Sema to steady her.

"We'll be lucky if they don't try to arrest us." Sema ran a hand through her disheveled hair to clear it from her face.

"They may not arrest us, but I don't see Councilman Romanov being grateful no matter what we have done." Rajan helped Gabriel pull Teresa to her feet.

"Ling is right." Gabriel put his arm around Teresa's waist as she leaned into him on unsteady feet. "We need a place to operate from. A new base."

"Yes, yes." Akikane's smile seemed more cunning than usual. "The thirteenth fort."

"What thirteenth fort?" Ohin asked.

"Ours, ours," Akikane said. "The one Nefferati and I have been building for the last month."

"What are you all talking about?" Teresa turned to Gabriel. "What have you done now?"

Gabriel's sly smile filled his own lips as he stared into Teresa's eyes.

"It's not so much what I've done as what I'm going to do."

CHAPTER 23

The fort had no official name, but names abounded for it nonetheless. The Hidden Fort, Fort Inevitable, Fort Rebellion, Fort Desperation, and the Fort of Last Resort. This last appellation originated with Teresa and became Gabriel's private designation for the outpost nestled 100 million years in the past.

The thirteenth fort proved larger than Gabriel had expected. Nefferati and Akikane's clandestine construction had produced a structure capable of housing at least a hundred people with barracks, a meeting house, a kitchen with functioning wood stoves, storehouses filled grains and dried goods, and even a small, well-stocked, two-room infirmary for Elizabeth in her perpetual coma.

Gabriel sat beside one of the beds of the infirmary, Teresa tucked beneath its crisp, cream-colored sheets. Marcus and Sema had been adamant that she remain in bed until she had time to recover from her captivity and abuse in Kumaradevi's palace. Like Sema and Marcus, Gabriel worried more about her mental recovery than the physical wounds that magic might heal. Heedless of their concerns, she insisted on giving a full report of her internment and interrogation. Akikane, Nefferati, and Ohin sat in chairs assembled around her bed and listened intently to her story.

After her capture, Teresa had been taken by Kumaradevi's soldiers directly to the alternate world. Although two Apollyons remained present, Kumaradevi had insisted upon conducting the examination herself. This seemed to have annoyed the Apollyons. Teresa tried being defiant, but the three Dark Mages had ignored her while they argued. In the end, Kumaradevi led the questioning via Soul Magic while the Apollyons used their own Soul Magic to observe Teresa's thoughts. Gabriel assumed that one of the Apollyons had eventually departed to inform their brethren of the information gleaned from Teresa's interrogation while the other had remained as ambassador to Kumaradevi.

Teresa had tried to hold off against the invasive magic Kumaradevi used to probe her mind. She tried to think of complex mathematical equations to limit Kumaradevi's ability to read her thoughts. These acts of insolence were met with unspeakable agony that made it impossible to concentrate. As the magic swayed her mind, she came to believe that Kumaradevi was her friend, her savior, preventing the pain wracking her brain, offering her the only solace available — a true confidant to whom she could, and should, share all of her secrets.

"I told them everything. Every last thing I know about the Barrier and how we learned it. Everything from the notebook. Everything we discovered and guessed from examining the anchor points. Everything we suspect about how the Barrier was created. Absolutely everything."

Teresa wiped the tears of remembrance from her eyes and coughed to steady her voice.

"The worst part of it was that I wanted to tell her. I felt like I needed to tell her. It's not that I couldn't stop myself, it's that I didn't even want to."

"There is nothing you could have done differently." Ohin reached out to pat her hand, squeezing it firmly, his voice gentle and reassuring. "You should be proud to have survived."

"I survived because she wanted a trophy to replace Nefferati hanging above her throne." Teresa's face tightened as she remembered the pain of the magical cage.

"She also likely wanted you as a hostage against Gabriel." Nefferati's face mirrored the anger of Teresa's. "Something to lure him to her."

"That worked a little differently than she had planned." Gabriel tried to put as much cheer as possible into his voice to lighten the mood. Listening to Teresa recount her ordeal proved more painful than he had anticipated. His own captivity in Kumaradevi's hands seemed pleasant and carefree in comparison. He had been abused, but never tortured.

"Yes, yes." Akikane leaned forward for emphasis. "You were very brave. Now you must be brave enough to let go of what has happened. Remember, pain is like a snake — if you hold it too tight, it will bite you. Better to set it back in the grass and walk on."

"Better to stomp the little creature with your heel." Nefferati snorted in derision at Akikane.

Teresa laughed, and the others joined her until the mirth faded from her eyes.

"There was something else. Something odd." Teresa drew her knees to her chest and stared at the ceiling in concentration. "Toward the end, Kumaradevi seemed convinced that I was holding something back. That there was some secret I had not yet divulged. Ultimately, she decided I knew nothing more. After that, things got bad, and I couldn't think about anything except the pain in that cage of lightning."

"She won't hurt you ever again." Gabriel reached out to brush a tear from her cheek.

"Maybe she's right, though," Teresa said. "Maybe I do know something I don't even know I know."

"If there is something rattling around in that brilliant head of yours, I'm sure it will make enough noise and eventually get your attention," Gabriel said. "Try to think of something else."

"You mean like how we can stop the Apollyons from destroying the Great Barrier now that they know about the anchors points and how to find them?" Teresa filled her voice with chipper despair.

"Exactly, exactly," Akikane said.

"We'll all be thinking of that," Ohin added.

"Among other things that need thinking about. And doing." Nefferati stood up, stretching the kinks from her back. "We should let these two spend some time alone while we get this fort up and running."

After Nefferati, Akikane, and Ohin made their goodbyes, Gabriel and Teresa sat in silence for a long time. He looked at her, at the sheets, at her hand in his, out the window at the tree in the back of the infirmary. He didn't know what to say. He didn't know precisely what he felt. Relief that she lived, that she sat next to him instead of trapped in whatever might become of the alternate world where she had been held hostage. Regret that she had been drawn into the trap that resulted in her captivity in the first place. One thought came to him again — that she would be safer if he did not love her, if he did not want her near him all the time.

"Let's get out of here." Teresa's voice brought Gabriel back from the inner reaches of his thoughts. "I can't sit in bed anymore. Let's go outside."

"There's a nice tree out back." Gabriel gestured with his chin toward the window. "It looks like the great-great-great-grandfather of oak trees. The branches seem really strong."

Teresa smiled. "How do you always know what to say?" Her mood lightened considerably at Gabriel's suggestion.

"I've memorized a book of prepared lines for every occasion."

Teresa laughed as Gabriel helped her out of bed. She changed out of the nightgown she had been wearing and slipped into black pants and a simple blue tunic. She slid on a pair of slippers, took Gabriel's hand, and led the way to the tree in the small square behind the tiny infirmary. A few minutes later, they sat on the widest, highest branch of the tree, holding hands as they interlocked their dangling legs.

"I don't like the way our ledger is working out," Teresa finally said after several minutes of silence. "You've saved me twice recently, and I haven't had the chance to balance things."

"You may be too competitive." Gabriel watched a small, acorn-like nut fall twenty feet from a nearby branch to the ground. "It's not a contest."

"You're the one always talking about balance in the universe," Teresa said. "I don't want our personal universe to get out of equilibrium."

"I could jump out of this tree and let you save me," Gabriel offered.

"And how would I save you from falling with Fire Magic?" Teresa dug her elbow into his side.

"Oh. Right. I could set the tree on fire and you could put it out."

"Stop being ridiculous. I'm serious."

"This is going to start a fight if we talk about it."

"You mean, you're going to start a fight if we talk about it."

"I'm sure there will be plenty of opportunities in the future for you to save my life."

"Only if I'm near you when they happen."

"Did you hear me suggest that you shouldn't be near me?"

"But you were thinking it."

"I don't read your mind, so don't pretend to read mine."

Teresa didn't respond. Not with words. Instead, she let go of Gabriel's hand, pulled her leg free from his, and leaned back, falling from the tree limb and plunging toward the ground.

Gabriel spun around, grasping the imprints of the pocket watch in his pants and wrapping Teresa's plummeting body in a cocoon of Wind Magic, arresting her descent, her hair hanging down to brush the blades of grass. Gabriel set her upright before using Wind Magic to lower himself to stand beside her.

"Are you crazy?" Gabriel asked before his feet even touched the ground.

"I'm making a point." Teresa brushed her hair back behind her ears.

"That you're crazy?" Gabriel tried to keep his voice from sounding hysterical. Seeing Teresa fall from the tree had set his heart to hammering in his chest and his blood banging in his ears.

"I'm making the point that you can do things I can't. That you can save me from things that I can't save you from. That there may come a time when I need to save you and I can't." Teresa's lip quivered as she held back the tears gathering in her eyes.

Gabriel didn't know what to say. He didn't even understand Teresa's comment. Against all better judgment, he decided to be honest.

"I'm not sure what you're talking about."

Teresa frowned and sighed.

"That wasn't the perfect thing to say."

"I haven't memorized the whole book yet."

"I think I mean that…"

"There you are."

Teresa and Gabriel turned to see Sema and Marcus stepping from the back door of the infirmary.

"I knew we'd never keep you in bed for more than an hour." Marcus laughed as he and Sema walked to the tree.

"You look flush." Sema raised the back of her hand to Teresa's forehead.

"We were up in the tree." Gabriel tried to compose his face, relieved that Sema and Marcus seemed oblivious to the tension between himself and Teresa.

"I'm fine." A thin smile crossed Teresa's lips. "I could do with a nap, though. Climbing the tree wore me out." She kissed Gabriel quickly. "See you later."

"I'll walk you in." Sema followed Teresa. "I want to check your mind again for any residual effects of the magic that vile woman used against you."

Gabriel tried to ignore the sudden discomfort in his stomach and the tightness in his chest. He couldn't guess what Teresa might have been about to say, and he didn't really want to know. She wasn't making sense. Maybe it had to do with her time spent as Kumaradevi's plaything. He knew what that could do to a person's thoughts. Maybe she'd feel better tomorrow. Maybe she'd feel better about *them* tomorrow.

"She'll be fine."

Gabriel jumped. He had been so consumed with his thoughts that he had forgotten Marcus stood right next to him.

"She's strong." Marcus gently patted Gabriel on the back. "Might take her a while, but she'll be back to her usual self. And the two of you will be back to normal as well."

"You heard what we said?" A vague wave of embarrassment warmed Gabriel's cheeks.

"No, but I can guess," Marcus said. "And, at my age, I've learned to recognize when a woman is upset about something. Not that I usually have any idea why, but I'm assuming that skill will come with advanced age."

Gabriel studied the wrinkles of Marcus's face and sighed. "That's not as comforting as you probably meant it to be."

"No, I suppose not." Marcus chuckled. "I also doubt it will be any comfort to tell you that you did the right thing by risking yourself to save her. You didn't need to. You could have stayed back and sent the team in without you. And the Council, for all its faults, is right about how important you are. But sometimes, being right is the best way to be wrong. If we don't risk ourselves for those we love, it can weaken us in strange ways."

Gabriel noticed Marcus had fixed his eyes upon the window at the back of the infirmary. Sema stood next to Teresa's bed. Marcus took a deep breath and sighed.

"I was engaged to be married once." Marcus winked at Gabriel's obvious surprise. "This was a long time ago. A few years after I had died and joined the castle. A lovely Fire Mage named Jazzel. My death had begun my reformation from rogue to physician, but she confirmed it. Surely no women so beautiful and intelligent and loving would have anything to do with me if I had not truly changed my ways."

"What happened?" Gabriel regretted that question as he saw the look in Marcus's eyes.

"She died." Marcus raised his wounded eyes up to the leafy branches of the tree. "There is a war on, after all. We were on a mission. Four teams acting as a unit. She and I were members of different teams. This was before I joined Ohin's team, of course. Things went wrong, as they usually do, and the teams got separated. And then events turned from bad to tragic. I knew where she was. I could see the Fire and Wind Magic hitting her position. But I couldn't see her or her team. Couldn't tell if they survived. All the teams were hit hard. Ours as well. Our leader ordered a retreat. He insisted the other teams were dead or had already escaped. My three surviving teammates said the same."

Marcus stopped and leaned against the solidity of the tree trunk behind him. He remained silent for so long that Gabriel began to suspect he might not finish the story. It clearly pained him to speak of his memories.

"I had a choice. I could disobey direct orders, ignore the experience of my commanding officer, and stay behind to try to find out if the woman I loved had survived. If I had stayed to locate her, I'd have stayed for good. I wouldn't have had a way back. The location in time made it impossible to send a team back later to look for survivors. My team leader, a Time Mage with twenty years in the field, had a point. Her team might already have fled, and, if not, they were most likely dead. It made sense.

"So I followed my orders. We returned to the castle. We were the only team to make it back."

"So she died in battle." Gabriel wasn't sure what else to say or how to phrase it. How did one console another human being for the loss of their loved one with mere words? Words seemed completely inadequate to the task.

"Oh, she died, I'm sure." Marcus's voice sounded anguished. "What I have no way of knowing is if she died there in that battle before I followed my orders to retreat, or if she died later of her wounds, or if she died years after that, abandoned by the people she had depended upon. Abandoned by the man she loved. You see, I followed my head and not my heart, and I will never know what happened. I managed to forgive myself only because I knew she would have wanted it. But it took years and years. Dark years. You made the right choice, whatever the risks. It's better to follow your heart and know for certain the fate of someone you love than to follow your head and wonder forever."

Gabriel said nothing. There were no rational arguments to counter the grief and self-loathing evident on Marcus's face. He placed his palm on Marcus's shoulder in comfort, hoping a simple human touch could say more than any words.

"I've become quite maudlin in my advancing years." Marcus patted Gabriel's hand and leaned away from the bark of the tree trunk. "Thank you for listening to an old man ramble."

"Thank you for helping to ease any doubts I had."

"Oh, I don't think you had any real doubts about what was right and what to do." A broad smile creased Marcus's face. "That's why we're following you and not the Council. Now, I should join Sema. We're supposed to be responsible for helping to organize dinner. I'll see you later."

Marcus clapped Gabriel on the back and headed into the infirmary. Gabriel watched him go, unsure of what to do next. There were plans to be made, options to be discussed, chores to be attended to, a fort to establish, and a battle plan to form. He knew he should seek out Akikane, Nefferati, and Ohin to discuss how to proceed now that the Apollyons had all the knowledge they likely needed to destroy The Great Barrier. He found he couldn't. Beyond the emotional turmoil aroused by his fight with Teresa, he had too many things to consider before thinking of the future.

Was it even a fight?

He put that notion aside. He needed to concentrate on the future.

Wasn't Teresa part of the future?

He looked up in frustration at his inability to focus his mind. His eyes came to rest on the southeast guard tower of the fort.

Sighing, then chiding himself for sighing, Gabriel grabbed the imprints of the pocket watch and jumped through space to the rooftop of the guard tower. He needed someplace to sit and think without being disturbed. The top of the guard tower also gave him a good vantage point to observe the fort and people manning it. He had been surprised upon his return from Kumaradevi's world to find that Nefferati had gathered nearly fifty Grace Mages from the various forts who were willing to follow Gabriel as their leader. She assured him more would arrive soon. As he looked down on the people rushing from one task to the next, fulfilling errands to complete the establishment of the fort, he considered what they had each sacrificed to follow him and what more he might require them to surrender of themselves in the coming days.

How many of these people would die under his *leadership*? Could he ask them to risk their lives in the hope that he knew what he was doing? What *was* he doing? What *should* he be doing? Stopping the Apollyons and protecting The Great Barrier, obviously. But how? And, assuming he accomplished that, would he then lead the people who had followed him and managed to survive back to face the punishment of the Council? Would the Council of War and Magic even be needed at that point? Might some other form of governing themselves arise? Might some other way of living their lives become possible?

Gabriel brought his mind back to the needs of the present. There were more than fifty people below who needed to believe that they had made the right decision. They needed to be reassured that their choices to follow Gabriel had not been a mistake. They needed to feel a sense of purpose when the chores of completing the fort were finished. They needed to trust him to lead them in the desperate days ahead. They needed to know he would have their backs as he asked them to have his.

He looked to where the sky met the earth, the sun sinking slowly toward the horizon. He felt the weight of his decisions beginning to pile up within his heart. He could not protect all of them. Seventh True Mage or not, it simply could not be done. Some would be wounded. Some would perish. Nearly all would lose friends and loved ones.

Knowing this, he realized he needed to make his leadership, his judgments, worthy of those sacrifices and sorrows.

Was this the sacrifice Teresa had decided to make?

How did she come back to his mind so easily?

Was that what her words had tried to imply? That she could not protect him as he could protect her? That her best means of protecting him would be to keep him from risking his life to save hers? Did she think that not being together would be the best way to protect him? The irony made his stomach sour. These had been his exact thoughts once.

He needed to talk to her. He needed, it occurred to him, to talk to the people whom he proposed to lead into an uncertain fate. He needed to convince both Teresa and the mages of the fledgling fort to believe in him.

Shortly after sunset, Gabriel stood at the head of one of ten tables spread throughout the small common square in the center of the fort. The outpost's inaugural dinner consisted of simple staple foods — roasted vegetables, fresh bread, and chicken grilled over open flames. The warm midsummer breeze carried the smell of hot charcoal and the soft chatter among friends.

He breathed deeply and listened closely. It all reminded him of the Fourth of July picnic his childhood town held every year. The mayor of the village always gave a short speech before the meal to set the mood and remind everyone of the reasons for their coming together. To emphasize what their ancestors had given for independence and the birth of a new country.

He cleared his throat loudly to draw everyone's attention. When the eyes of the mages who had assembled for the first meal in voluntary exile were on him, he coughed again to cover his nervousness.

Gabriel briefly looked at the faces nearest him — those of his own table: Nefferati, Akikane, Ohin, and the rest of the team. He let his gaze linger on Teresa's face a moment before turning back to the other tables. She looked as tense as he felt. He had not told anyone what he planned to say, only that he wanted to speak before the meal.

"I want to say a few words. This may be the only opportunity to speak to everyone together before things get complicated. And things will get complicated. And dangerous. So, before all that begins, I want to thank you. You have all come here because you believe, as I do, that stopping the Apollyons and saving The Great Barrier of Probability is an essential task that must be accomplished.

"While I would be setting out to pursue this goal, even if no one else believed in it, in all honestly, it would be impossible without all of you. You have risked a great deal to be here. Your presence here is a silent agreement to follow me into whatever dark future we all share. While I appreciate that, while it fills me with confidence to see you all here, it is not enough. I am going to be asking you to risk your lives and the lives of those you love. Some of you will die. All of us may die. This is what we face, and to face that, I need you to follow me, not simply because of some prophecy or because I am a mage who can use Grace and Malignant imprints. I need you follow me because you believe in me, and in the mission I have set for us. More than that, I need you to believe that I will do everything in my power to see that we all succeed.

"Most importantly, I need you to understand, in your bones, that any sacrifice I ask of you is a sacrifice I would bear myself. If I ask you to risk your life to protect our future, you must know that I have risked the same in the past, and will do so again and again until I am either dead or there are no more threats against us. You have all volunteered to be here, but that was before you heard what awaits you. If you wish to change your minds, you need to do so before morning. In the morning, I assume command of you. After that, there will be no turning back. For any of us.

"Thank you."

Gabriel nodded to the gathered mages, seeing for the first time the tears in Teresa eyes. He bent to sit when Marcus pushed back from the table and stood.

"You have my allegiance now, and always." Marcus placed his hand to his chest in a simple gesture of solidarity. A salute that felt more like a prayer.

A Fire Mage from the table nearby stood next, placing her hand to her chest, repeating Marcus's words. Others joined rapidly, by twos and threes and fours. He saw Paramata stand. Then Justine. Finally, Ohin stood with Sema, and Rajan, and Ling. Nearly last, Nefferati stood with Akikane.

Finally, with everyone else on their feet, Teresa rose to hers. The expression on her face suggested that she did not stand last to be defiant, but to add emphasis to her actions.

Gabriel raised his hand to his chest and swallowed the emotions threatening to make his voice crack. "You have my allegiance now, and always."

A cheer, led by Marcus, rose from the crowd and sailed upward into the star-filled night, carrying the hopes and fears of all assembled skyward to the heavens. When the toasts and merriment had faded and the dinner tables were cleared, Gabriel found a moment to speak with Teresa. He had asked the team and Akikane and Nefferati to remain after dinner to discuss their plans. He had a few moments before he needed to attend to matters of the state. He hoped it would be enough time to tend to matters of the heart.

"That was an impressive speech." Teresa stood several feet away from him, creating an invisible, but palpable, physical and emotional barrier between them.

"I thought it went okay." Gabriel restrained himself from stepping closer to her.

"Modesty is not as attractive as people think," Teresa said.

"I wanted to talk before things got too crazy," Gabriel said. "To finish what we were saying earlier."

"Ithinkweshouldtakeabreak." Teresa's rushed syllables seemed all one word.

"That's what I was thinking too."

"Really?" Teresa's eyes widened in surprise.

"That's what I was thinking you would say."

"Oh. That's still what I think."

"You think that if you can't save me that I shouldn't be risking my life to save you."

"Well, yeah." Teresa's eyes shifted from surprise to suspicion.

"And you think if we're not together I won't be as likely to be in positions to risk my life for yours."

"Are you using Soul Magic to read my mind?"

"No."

"You're not usually this perceptive."

"I don't usually spend time thinking about how other people will need to risk their lives on my orders."

"Ah."

"Do you really think I wouldn't risk my life to save yours, no matter what the circumstances?"

"I think you'd put me ahead of everyone else." Teresa seemed torn between keeping her distance and stepping closer. "If you had failed while trying to save me from Kumaradevi it would have left no one to defeat the Apollyons and save the Barrier."

"Vicaquirao would have led the fight against the Apollyons." Gabriel knew this counter argument didn't carry much weight with Teresa. "And Nefferati would, as well. And the people who joined us here would have joined her."

"I'm not saying I don't care about you." Teresa dabbed at her eyes with the back of her sleeve. "I'm saying I care too much to let you die trying to save me instead of everyone else."

"I understand what you're saying." Gabriel crossed the distance between them in a single step. Teresa flinched as he reached out to take both her hands in his. "I want you to know that you are wrong. Not that I think you are wrong. This isn't an argument. I can no more decide not to save you than you could decide not to save me."

"What if it's a choice between me and all those mages who came here believing you will end this war?" Teresa raised her chin defiantly.

Gabriel had no answer. He offered a question instead. "What if you had to choose between saving me and the rest of the world?"

"Which of us is more likely to face that choice?" Teresa raised their clasped hands between them, kissing Gabriel's knuckles. "It's not forever. But it has to be for now."

"You're only breaking up with me until after I save the world?"

"Until we save the world."

"And what if I die tying?"

"Then at least it won't be because of me."

Teresa kissed Gabriel's hands once more, then released them and walked to the table where the rest of the team had assembled after dinner.

Gabriel took a moment to compose himself, to set aside Teresa's decision and to push down the passions it had birthed — the anger, the insecurity, the fear, the confusion. He put them in a box and closed the lid and shoveled dirt over it, rolling a rock overtop for good measure. It would not hold back the emotions for long, but it would give him time to think straight while considering how to proceed in this new front of the seemingly endless War of Time and Magic.

He took a few deep breaths to clear his head and walked over to stand at the head of the table. Nefferati and Akikane sat on either side of him with Ohin opposite at the other end of the table. Rajan and Ling sat to his left and Teresa, Sema and Marcus to his right. Among all those who had volunteered to follow him, these were the only ones he had requested to give him advice. They were the only ones he truly trusted. He wondered for a moment if that might be a mistake. Not trusting them, but limiting his circle of confidants to them alone rather than extending it to some of the very experienced mages who now comprised his small army. It might be, but it would be a mistake he'd live with.

"So." Gabriel sat, trying to ensure that the air rapidly escaping his lips as he settled in the chair did not come out as a sigh. "Anyone have any brilliant ideas?"

No one spoke. Gabriel looked around the table at the faces of his friends. He placed his chin in his hands.

"Me neither."

"Well, they know what we know now." Marcus reached for the bottle of wine to fill his empty glass, but seemed to reconsider and pulled back his hand. "What would we do if we wanted to destroy The Great Barrier?"

"A good place to start." Ohin stroked the days-old stubble on his chin. "They can only find the anchor points one by one. That will take time."

"Two at a time." Teresa's voice sounded soft and distant. "If they start with the ones we know about, they can search forward and backward along the timeline."

"They will need to find a relic to take them to each new anchor point they discover." Nefferati focused on the flame of the oil lamp in the center of the table. "That will slow them down a little."

"Yes, yes." Akikane folded his hands on the table. "This may give us a few days."

"We need to attack them now." Ling dug the blade of her dinner knife into the wood of the table, unaware of her actions.

"With every passing day there will be more Apollyons at more Anchor points." Rajan placed his fingertips on his temples. "If we stop one or two, they'll only make more copies, and be we'll right back where we started, like Sisyphus rolling the stone to the top of the mountain each day. We don't have enough mages to attack them all."

The silence returned to the table but did not last as long as previously.

"There may be a way." Sema straightened in her chair slightly as she looked to Gabriel at the head of the table. "We could attack them the way Gabriel did at the castle. Attack the mind of one and use their psychic link to attack the others. Render them all unconscious at the same time."

"I've tried it again and failed." Gabriel's lips curled into a frown. "They have adapted their psychic link somehow. I could put them to sleep one at a time, but not all at once."

"Not you alone," Sema said. "I'm thinking of a linked circle of True Mages and Soul Mages. There are six Soul Mages here at the fort besides myself. With you and Akikane and Nefferati, that would make a circle of ten."

"Indeed, indeed," Akikane said. "With enough imprints, we might be able to press beyond their defenses."

"And do what with them?" Ling asked. "How long can you keep them unconscious?"

"Long enough for teams of Time Mages to locate and collect them." Ohin said.

"And put them on a shelf?" Teresa said. "What can you do with a hundred and eight madmen?"

"Ship them off to Vicaquirao's prison." Gabriel said.

"Leaving Vicaquirao in charge of a handful is one thing, but this many copies of that man cannot be controlled," Marcus said.

"It's that or kill them all in their sleep," Rajan said. "That doesn't sound very appealing, either."

"Vicaquirao's prison." Gabriel filled his voice with the tone of finality. "I'm not killing even the Apollyons while they sleep. Vicaquirao will keep them safe or sever his prison world."

"You put a great deal of faith in that man." Nefferati sounded skeptical.

"He doesn't want all of the same things I do, but I trust him on the things we do have in common," Gabriel said. "Saving the Great Barrier is one of them."

"Then he and his two companions should be happy to join us in making the circle," Nefferati said.

"Good idea, good idea," Akikane said. "Three more True Mages will make the circle even stronger."

"Three more Malignant Mages." Sema's voice sounded doubtful. "None of us have ever made a circle with a Malignancy Mage."

"You've made a circle with me," Gabriel said. "I'll act as a bridge between the two forms of magic."

"What do the rest of us do?" Teresa asked.

"We need to get one alone." Gabriel looked at Teresa and then the rest of the team. "You'll need to keep the other Apollyons distracted."

"Oh good." Teresa said. "I love being distracting."

"Yes you do," Rajan said.

"How many will we need to distract?" Ling asked.

"More than one and fewer than a one hundred and eight," Gabriel said.

"Well, as long as we know what we face." Marcus ignored a look from Sema and poured himself that glass of wine he had avoided earlier.

"This will require every mage in the fort," Nefferati said. "I wish we could wait for more to arrive. I'm certain more will."

"No, no," Akikane said. "We must not wait too long. If they find enough anchor points, they may be able to damage the Barrier beyond repair."

"We leave at dawn." Gabriel raised his voice to signal the end of the conversation. "Everyone will need a good night's sleep. In the morning, I will brief the mages and distribute the imbued artifacts. The concatenate crystals will go to the Soul Mages. They'll need them most."

Gabriel stood, leaning against the table to steady himself. This moment signaled the beginning of a new life for him. A life of making decisions. A life of giving orders. A life of leading others, people he loved, into danger and potential death. He could feel the sweat of his palms seeping into the dry wooden boards of the table.

"It's a good plan. I'm confident it will work. And I'm confident in all of you. Rest well. Tomorrow determines our future."

Another silence of quickly exchanged glances dissolved into a series of brief farewells for the evening. As much as Gabriel wanted to turn and walk into the night, seeking the solitude of his barracks quarters, he stayed until the others had left. He had watched Ohin and Nefferati and Akikane and Elizabeth leading in different situations over the past several years and he had learned that he needed to be both decisive and open to being swayed into changing his mind. He had also learned the importance of being the last one to leave the room. To guarantee that everyone felt their concerns had been heard, and to underscore the fact that he would also be the last to leave the battlefield. People could only follow a leader who remained present for them to do so.

Teresa lingered until she stood alone at the table with Gabriel, the warm glow of the oil lamp flickering in her eyes.

"We're all behind you."

"I don't want you behind me, I want you beside me." Gabriel struggled to resist the urge to reach out and hold her.

"Gabriel..." Teresa looked away into the darkness.

"You're right. This is good motivation. Once this is over, once the Barrier is safe and the Apollyons are locked away in some alternate prison world, you'll have to decide what you really feel and what you really want. I don't need that motivation. I already know."

Knowing it to be wrong, to be the last thing he should do, he turned and walked away from the light of the lamp, from Teresa, and into the cool summer night air. He didn't look back. He kept walking until he had reached his quarters in the barracks, where he collapsed onto his bed, tossing for hours before finally falling into slumber. With his last conscious thought, he wondered how many of the mages he now led, including Teresa, would survive the following day.

CHAPTER 24

The high pitched warble of a tiny, yellow-breasted bird floated through the air, competing with the din of small arms fire, booming cannons, and the screams of dying men.

Gabriel crouched near the ground as he leaned against a linden tree. The bark bit into his back as he watched the final skirmish in the Siege of Namur in Southern Belgium in the late summer of 1695. The fort of Namur, held by the French, sat on a hillside across the valley from Gabriel's current position, hidden in the nearby forest. Belgian and Danish troops fought against the fort from the low ground, as they had for months of the siege.

This battle marked the first anchor point that Elizabeth had discovered and the most likely place for the Apollyons to begin launching their search for the other anchor points spread throughout time. They assumed the Apollyons would hold themselves in a space-time bubble at the moment of the anchor point. The majority of the Apollyons would be elsewhere, seeking out anchor points or hunting relics to travel to them. Gabriel and his companions needed to find the place in time where the Apollyons were hiding and capture one of them before the others could react. The plan hinged on the hope that only a handful of Apollyons resided at this location.

Gabriel looked to his right, where Akikane sat next to Vicaquirao and Cyril, one of the two reformed Apollyons. These three men comprised his extraction team. To his left huddled two teams of Grace Mages. They would provide the distraction that would allow Gabriel and his fellow True Mages to capture one of the Apollyons. Other teams would be attacking any Apollyons at the anchor point in the Battle of Ceresole on April 11th, 1544. They would avoid any such diversion near the Battle of Shanghai Pass because of the overlapping timelines there already. The chances for paradox and bifurcations increased precipitously as more Time Mages visited each anchor point.

Gabriel watched the battle around the star-shaped fort.

He knew from his previous visit that the anchor point came into existence ten seconds after a cannon blast ripped the edge off one of the pointed battlements of the fort along the north-facing wall. They then had 37 seconds, the length of the anchor point's presence, to find the time bubble.

The cannonball struck the wall of the fort where Gabriel had been watching, a small cloud of crushed stone billowing into the air. He extended his space-time sense and glanced at his pocket watch, noting the placement of the second hand.

He sensed the presence of the anchor point several hundred feet away, but no impression of a possible space-time bubble registered in his perception. He looked to see Akikane and Vicaquirao standing and turning slowly in place, like radar antenna seeking an incoming projectile. Cyril stood as well, but none of the three faced the same direction.

"Nothing, nothing." Akikane frowned.

"They must be here." Cyril closed his eyes in concentration.

"They have hidden themselves well." Vicaquirao tilted his head to the side as though listening to a faint noise.

"Fifteen seconds." Gabriel raised himself to his feet, glancing at the two teams of crouching mages, waiting for the order to attack.

"They've done something different." Cyril smacked the side of a tree in frustration. "I should be able to sense their time bubble."

"We may need to find another location and return to this moment again," Vicaquirao said.

"Seven seconds." Gabriel strained to perceive something, to no avail.

"Nonsense, nonsense." Akikane drew his sword and closed his eyes, rotating where he stood, the blade tracing an intricate pattern in the air. The sword stopped, pointing to a clump of trees on a nearby hill.

"There." Akikane opened his eyes.

"Now." Gabriel gestured to the two teams of mages. They rose to their feet as Akikane warped space around all of them.

Blackness and whiteness mingled momentarily with a strange electric sensation — the effect of jumping directly into a space-time bubble. A moment later, Gabriel and his mages stood on the opposite hillside, a dozen or more pairs of identical eyes turning toward them in surprise.

The attack transpired swiftly, Akikane grabbing the nearest Apollyon in a vice of Wind Magic while Vicaquirao poured Soul Magic into the man's mind to disable him. Cyril and Gabriel attacked the other Apollyons with arcs of lightning while the two teams of Grace Mages offered similar assaults.

Two seconds after their arrival, Gabriel warped space-time, transporting himself, Akikane, Vicaquirao, Cyril, and the captured Apollyon away, into the past. The other Grace Mages would stay a second longer and then retreat.

After seven rapid jumps through time to ensure no one followed them, Gabriel deposited the extraction team on a hillside overlooking a lake two million years before the rise of the first human ancestor. Nefferati, Sema, and a team of six Soul Mages awaited them in the tall grass. The second reformed Apollyon, Cassius, stood somewhat apart from the others, looking out of place. Ohin and the rest of the Chimera team waited in a group behind the mages. They looked determined but decidedly unhappy.

Gabriel had specifically ordered them to remain with the Soul Magic circle to provide protection. The mages engaged in the circle and assaulting the Apollyons' minds through Soul Magic would be vulnerable to any attack. They could not defend themselves without breaking off the psychic assault on the Apollyons. Ling and the others had complained that anyone could fulfill guard duty and that the team's talents would best be used attacking the Apollyons at anchor points to create a distraction. Gabriel had disagreed, explaining that he needed someone to watch his back. Someone he trusted without question. A successful attack on Gabriel and the others while in the circle could end not only their hopes of attacking the Apollyons but also the battle to save The Great Barrier and the war itself. There had been no arguments to that logic.

"Quickly, quickly." Akikane lowered the unconscious Apollyon from his arms and down to the grass.

"Everyone in position." Gabriel crossed his legs and sat down near the Apollyon's head. He reached out to hold the unconscious man's skull in his hands. As he had the most experience doing so, he would lead the assault on the Apollyons' minds himself. Cyril and Vicaquirao sat on either side of him, placing their arms on his shoulders, doing the same with Nefferati and Akikane on each side of them. Akikane touched Sema and the circle continued back around to Nefferati and Cassius.

"Positions." Gabriel nodded to Ohin, and the Chimera team formed a loose ring around the seated mages, facing outward toward any possible attack.

Gabriel closed his eyes, embracing the imprints of the pocket watch and the Sword of Unmaking. He waited a moment and then embraced the negative imprints within the three crystals Vicaquirao and Cyril had provided. The circle needed all the magical power it could mount from both magics.

Holding the imprints, feeling them balance each other in his mind, he let his will float free, reaching out with his magic-sense for the presence of the mages nearby. He sensed Vicaquirao and Cyril initially, linking their magical energies with his own before merging it with the magic held by Akikane and Nefferati and Cassius. He heard the others breathing deeply, no doubt trying to acclimate themselves to the sensation of an unaccustomed magic flowing through them. This was the first time these Grace or Malignant Mages had experienced opposing imprints directly. Gabriel closed the circle, including Sema and the other six Soul Mages within it.

"Just follow my lead." Gabriel found speaking difficult with the magical sensations of everyone in the circle united with his own. "Focus on pouring your magical energy into the circle and into me. Don't try to control anything. If we struggle over the power, the circle will break."

Gabriel swallowed back the apprehension of the moment. He had held magical power mixed between Grace and Malignant magics before but never with others connected to it. He imagined himself as a warrior with twelve powerful horses hitched to his chariot.

"I'll need to wake him up to establish the connection with the others. It will be too hard to do from his dreams." Gabriel reached out with a blend of Soul and Heart-Tree magics and nudged the sleeping man back to consciousness. As the Apollyon's eyes flashed open,

Gabriel pushed his will into the man's thoughts. The Dark Mage gasped in surprise at the power behind the invasion of his mind.

"What?" the Apollyon said.

The Apollyon's eyes fluttered as Gabriel used Soul Magic to tame his thoughts, keeping him just above the level of unconsciousness, probing through the psychic connection linking the Dark Mage to his duplicate companions throughout time. Gabriel pushed a massive wave of somnambulant Soul Magic through that link, a spider web of minds woven together, each falling into the deepest slumber as his will touched and overwhelmed theirs. He sensed through that psychic link the panic and fury of the Apollyons he had not yet subdued. He pressed forward, pushing one Apollyon after the other into a coma-like sleep. He lost count of the number of men whose minds fell silent, but he judged by the decreasing sensations being fed back to him along the link that only a handful of them remained to find and pacify.

He sensed a space-time distortion nearby but ignored it and kept his eyes closed. Explosions and shouts followed, but he disregarded those as well. He could sense, through the psychic link, the elation of two Apollyons who had somehow managed to find the location of their attackers. Gabriel focused on these two men alone, knowing that if he could force them into unconsciousness, he would end their attack. He experienced, through the link, an emotion akin to deep satisfaction from the two as space-time warped nearby and the sounds of battle ceased. The elation lingered through the psychic connection for a moment. They had taken someone with them.

Cassius, the reformed Apollyon.

Suddenly, Gabriel found he could no longer locate the two Apollyons through the psychic bond. There could only be one explanation — they had severed themselves from the link to avoid falling prey to Gabriel's Soul Magic attack.

Gabriel turned his attention back to the other Dark Mages linked through the first Apollyon, still unconscious in his hands. He sensed a few more and redoubled his efforts to subjugate their minds into submission. As Gabriel felt the last of the Apollyons spread out across time fade from consciousness, the ground exploded beneath him, sending his body flying into the air.

He opened his eyes as he hit the grassy hillside, rolling with the inertia of his fall. The Soul Magic circle no longer joined him to the other mages, but he still held the imprints of his own talismans and the concatenate crystals. He looked around to see fellow mages lying scattered throughout the billowing grass.

He turned around, trying to survey the damage to his companions. Akikane and Nefferati lay unconscious beside each other as did Cyril and Vicaquirao. The Soul Magic seemed to have rebounded against them. Ohin knelt next to Sema, calling out for help, waving toward Marcus, who tended to Rajan's burnt arm. Gabriel ignored the ringing in his ears as he called out for Teresa, his voice sounding muffled.

He twisted in place and saw Teresa beside two of the fallen Soul Mages. The strange look on her face froze him. She shouted something and pointed, but Gabriel could not hear her words clearly. He spun to follow her finger, glimpsing someone for only a moment before following his instincts as they urged him to hit the ground and roll away. Heat blazed above him as he continued to tumble and leap to his feet to face his attacker.

"Here is my retribution."

Kumaradevi, dozens of glowing concatenate crystals ringing her neck and arms, raised her hands to attack.

"How could you escape your world?" Gabriel stepped sideways to draw Kumaradevi's violence away from the others and hopefully allow one of them to flank her position. With most of the mages around him wounded and Kumaradevi possessing numerous concatenate crystals, defeating her would be unpredictable. Those crystals would likely be linked to imprints in the Primary Continuum now that her dark alternate world had been severed.

"I escaped nothing." Kumaradevi paced through the grass toward Gabriel. "That foolish Greek is not the only one who can make copies of himself."

Gabriel struggled to hear her words through his ringing ears and to make sense of them as they resonated in his mind.

Kumaradevi had doubled herself.

"Your world is not dead, even if you can't touch it," Gabriel said. "I severed it in a way that allows it to survive." He saw movement from the side of his eyes. Ohin, Rajan, and Ling snuck through the grass.

"What would I care if I cannot make use of the imprints I harvested there?" Kumaradevi glared at Gabriel as she flicked a hand and the ground exploded nearby, sending Ling and Rajan and Ohin tumbling into the air.

"You are still alive there," Gabriel said. "Probably."

"She is not me. She is nothing. And now *you* will be nothing." This Kumaradevi did not want revenge for her lost kingdom, or the original version of herself. She wanted revenge for the loss of the power it had afforded her.

A stream of impossibly bright energy erupted from the twin Kumaradevi's hands and flashed toward Gabriel. He had no time to move and barely assembled his thoughts to form a shield of Fire Magic. He flinched as a thin wave of reddish energy struck the wall of blazing light before it could reach him. Kumaradevi's attack bounced away, ricocheting like light striking a mirror. He blinked, confused. He knew he had not defected Kumaradevi's magic. Her eyes flared, and Gabriel followed them to see Teresa standing twenty feet away. The Kumaradevi duplicate attacked again, casting her deadly Fire Magic toward Teresa.

Gabriel screamed and watched as Teresa created a thin wedge of blazing light, splitting Kumaradevi's bolt of energy and driving it to both sides, the overwhelming onslaught of power forcing her to her knees.

Gabriel threw a wave of Soul and Heart-Tree magic at the duplicate Kumaradevi, intending to cripple her. She ceased her attack on Teresa and deflected Gabriel's magic. She commanded far more imprints than he could access. He rolled to the ground again, hearing her shriek in rage. He lifted his head as a massive wave of light filled the world and temporarily blinded him.

As his eyesight recovered, a scream pierced the air and drew his attention briefly away from where he had last seen the duplicate Kumaradevi. Vicaquirao sat on his knees, his heat blistered face stricken in horror as he looked at a long pile of ashes scattering in the breeze — all that remained of the man who had been Cyril.

Gabriel turned back to see the twin Kumaradevi's open hands once again aimed at him. He unsheathed the Sword of Unmaking, preparing to jump through space and attack her directly, when the blade flashed from his hand, ripped from his fingers by an unseen force. He thought for a moment that the duplicate Kumaradevi had used Wind magic to yank the sword from his grasp, but the thought faded as he saw the hilt of his sword sticking from her chest. She blinked in wonder as she looked at the ancient blade buried in her heart. Then she toppled sideways, dead before she hit the soft grass below her feet.

Gabriel looked around, confused at what had just transpired. He saw Vicaquirao, eyes fierce with pain, nod to him and then turn back to the remains of the man he had raised like a son from the age of twelve.

Gabriel swallowed. Vicaquirao had used Time Magic to take the sword from Gabriel's hand and place it inside Kumaradevi's chest, killing her almost instantly. Or at least he had killed a copy of her. Gabriel swallowed again with that thought. He had never considered the possibility that Kumaradevi might have a double kept somewhere in case of an emergency. The duplicate Kumaradevi had probably been held in a time stasis field, like a permanent space-time bubble, and released when her alternate world was severed from the Primary Continuum. A cunning back-up plan. How many versions of herself had she hidden throughout time? And how had she found him? Through the Apollyons? Had they helped her knowingly, or had she ghosted their trails through time? How had she known which ones to follow? Had she made more than one duplicate of herself?

Gabriel ignored these thoughts. The wounded required assistance. They needed to find a secure place to regroup and assess what had happened. There were still the two Apollyons who had captured Cassius to deal with, as well as those trapped in magical comas. Someone had to get the Grace Mages organized and on their way. Someone needed to lead.

"This place is not safe." Gabriel raised his voice to carry across the hillside as he walked over to Teresa and helped her to her feet.

"Thank you."

He stared into her eyes, trying to forget the white-hot wave of energy that had nearly turned her to dust and cinders.

"She should have picked a different magic to try to kill you with." Teresa held his hand a moment longer than necessary. "We're almost even again."

Gabriel discarded the thoughts her statement caused to saturate his mind. He turned to the others. "Everyone gather here in the middle. We'll tend to the wounded once we're clear of this place."

He used Wind Magic to help carry unconscious mages, Akikane and Nefferati among them, to one of the few swaths of grass not smoking in the aftermath of the duplicate Kumaradevi's attack. Marcus carried Sema, still-unconscious but no longer bleeding, to the assembly area.

Gabriel strode over to where Vicaquirao gathered the ashen remains of Cyril into a small pouch.

"We need to go." Gabriel placed a hand on Vicaquirao's shoulder.

"I wanted to gather some ashes." Vicaquirao stood up, breathing deep and wiping muddied soot from his eyes. "For Semele."

"Thank you." Gabriel walked with Vicaquirao back to the others. "You saved me."

"No." Vicaquirao's voice sounded harsh, like metal rasping against stone. "I don't believe she would have beaten you in the end. But I also don't think you would have done what needed to be done."

Gabriel had no reply to that impression of events. He took a relic from his pocket, a small button from a coat he would never see, and began to bend the fabric of space and time to carry them all away to someplace safe. Someplace where they could evaluate their losses and determine how to secure their future.

Vicaquirao turned to him just as the first Cimmerian phase of time travel swallowed them.

"The two who are left will try to kill you now. That is their only remaining hope for destroying the Great Barrier."

CHAPTER 25

The smell of burnt wood and charred brick filled the air, stinging Gabriel's nose and clinging to his clothes. He crouched next to Nefferati, both of their hands resting on Sema's head as she lay on the soot-stained concrete floor. He had brought them through time to a bombed-out and abandoned building in 1943 London in the midst of World War II. While he trusted Vicaquirao more than his Grace Mage companions, he did not think it wise to let the man know of the existence of their new fort.

Gabriel probed Sema's mind with his magic-sense, assisting Nefferati in attempting to revive her. He had managed to easily waken Akikane and Nefferati from the effects of the blown-back Soul Magic that had thrust them into unconsciousness. Waking the other Soul Mages had also proved straightforward. However, Sema had been affected differently. As he focused on delving Sema's mind with Soul and Heart-Tree Magic, he felt a mounting frustration begin to consume him. There seemed no good reason for her continued slumber. It reminded him of the magical coma that had afflicted Elizabeth for more than a year. The cause appeared clear, but the cure elusive.

He thought through the last moments before the Apollyons' attack, trying to remember exactly how he had been blending the magic to infect their minds and put them into deep sleep. As he did so, the obvious occurred to him. He had not simply been weaving Soul Magic, he had been merging imprints of Grace and Malignancy to create that magic.

Gabriel opened his eyes to see Vicaquirao standing nearby, looking through a large hole in a wall, gazing out over London as the sun dipped behind the tallest of the buildings.

"I need one of the tainted concatenate crystals back," Gabriel said.

Vicaquirao turned from the cityscape, his face shifting from a look of curiosity to sudden understanding. He reached in his pocket to retrieve the crystal Gabriel had given back to him only minutes ago.

Gabriel accepted the crystal and embraced its imprints as he held to those of his pocket watch.

"Are you certain of this?" Nefferati opened her eyes.

"Certain of what?" Marcus asked, his face wracked with worry. He sat next to Sema holding one of her hands in his, stroking it gently.

"It makes sense," Gabriel said. "I was using both imprints for the magic that knocked her out. It might take both to wake her."

Gabriel closed his eyes again and returned his concentration to the task of examining Sema's mind with his magic-sense. Now that he embraced both negative and positive imprints, the play of the Soul Magic across Sema's mind appeared clearer. He could see how the different aspects of the magic folded around her consciousness. The two forms of imprints manifested themselves differently when worked together. He imagined them like a web of knots enclosing Sema's mind, and he fashioned a slender scalpel of Soul Magic to snip the threads that bound her in a state of unawareness. Unable to do more, he released the magic and the imprints as he opened his eyes.

"Anything?" Marcus asked, his eyes damp with concern.

Sema's eyelashes fluttered and she took a deep breath.

"Oh." Sema looked around at the faces of those beside her. "We're alive then. That's good."

"Very good." Marcus laughed, wiping his arm across his eyes.

Gabriel rose to his feet, helping Nefferati up and stepping away to give Marcus and Sema time alone. He walked with her to where Ohin stood with Akikane and the rest of the team.

"Ohin, I need you to go back to the fort and bring Elizabeth here," Gabriel said.

"You think using the two imprints may wake her?" Nefferati asked.

"Maybe," Gabriel said. "I was thinking that if Elizabeth had been attempting to use Soul Magic on the two Apollyons it might take both imprints to revive her."

"Why bring her here?" Ohin asked.

"I'll need Vicaquirao to help me," Gabriel said. "It's not about how many imprints I can control, it's about how subtly I can use them. He has much more experience. I'll need Nefferati's help as well."

"Ling, I will need your assistance." Ohin stepped back from the others.

"Of course." Ling joined Ohin at the edge of the group.

Ohin nodded to Gabriel and Nefferati before he and Ling winked away into time.

"We must speak."

Gabriel turned to the sound of Vicaquirao's voice.

"About what you said back on the hillside." Gabriel's eyes slid to the corner where the remains of the duplicate Kumaradevi's body lay in the shadows. The Sword of Unmaking rested on the floor beside the corpse. He had removed the blade from her chest but had not had time to clean it in the rush to revive the fallen Soul Mages. Near her body, the captured Apollyon laid slumbering, his hands and feet bound tightly as a precaution.

"Yes." Vicaquirao followed Gabriel's stare for a moment, then turned back.

"I'm sorry about Cyril," Gabriel said. "And Cassius."

"Cassius is why the Apollyons will try to kill you," Vicaquirao said.

"Explain." Nefferati crossed her arms and moved closer to Vicaquirao.

"He will likely be dead by now, but the two Apollyons who remain will have interrogated him." Vicaquirao frowned. "Cassius will have confessed the suspicions that I shared with him."

"What suspicions?" A familiar chill began to expand in Gabriel's stomach, a fear of revelations that would upend his world.

"About the true manner of how The Great Barrier of Probability was created." Vicaquirao's eyes fastened on Gabriel. "I do not believe the Barrier was created by a large circle of Dark and Light mages working together. I believe it was created by one mage, wielding both magics."

"What?" A dizziness overtook Gabriel's mind. He pushed aside the urge to sit on the floor.

"One mage, no matter how powerful, could never control the imprints necessary to create the Barrier." Nefferati shook her head dismissively.

"Not one mage." Teresa stepped up beside Gabriel, looking between him and Vicaquirao. "One mage who copied himself a hundred and seven times."

"Exactly." Vicaquirao still stared at Gabriel.

"That makes no sense." Gabriel's feet carried him backward several paces until he bumped into the remains of a wall.

"Wild conjecture." Nefferati's voice sounded uncertain.

"It would explain many things that are still unclear," Vicaquirao said. "It is the most elegant solution to the question of how the Barrier came into existence."

"He's right," Teresa said, her face pinched as she considered the implications of the idea. "It is possible."

"Possible, possible," Akikane had remained nearby, silent throughout the exchange. "But likely?"

"The Barrier has always existed." Gabriel's heart beat evermore quickly in his chest. "How could I be responsible for creating it?"

"It has always existed, but that doesn't mean it always existed in your personal timeline." Teresa scowled as she brought her fist to her chin in concentration.

"I don't have any idea how to create the Barrier, much less when to create it," Gabriel said.

"I'm sure you'll figure out how, but I suspect the when will need to be soon," Vicaquirao said.

"Why?" Nefferati asked. "Why soon?"

"Because of Cassius," Vicaquirao answered. "In his interrogation, he will no doubt have revealed my suspicions to the two remaining Apollyon copies. They will unquestionably realize that their best chance for destroying The Great Barrier now lies in killing Gabriel before he can create it."

"That assumes I did create it," Gabriel said. "Or do create it." The dizziness only increased the more they discussed Vicaquirao's wild idea.

"This sounds like the worst paradox ever." Rajan rubbed his forehead in obvious confusion.

"Maybe so, maybe so," Akikane said. "However, it may also make sense of the paradox presented by the Barrier itself."

"How would I know when to create the Barrier?" Gabriel asked, trying to figure it out in his mind. He usually had a good grasp of time travel and potential paradoxes, but this particular one, with him at the center of it, eluded his comprehension. "Do I wait for it to cease existing and then make it exist? Assuming I can figure out how?"

"Teresa may be right." Vicaquirao nodded slightly toward Teresa. "It's possible the Barrier will only cease to exist from your perspective."

"Chrono-quantum consciousness entanglement," Teresa said

"Mumbo jumbo," Nefferati huffed. "If the continuum of his mind is linked to the continuum of the Barrier, which in turn is linked to the Primary Continuum, it might be possible that only Gabriel would ever notice the Barrier not existing."

"That's what I said." Teresa gave a small pout of annoyance.

"So I need to camp out in a space-time bubble at the edge of the Barrier and wait for it to stop existing for me but not for anyone who's with me?" Gabriel frowned, trying to figure out how that might be possible.

"That could take years," Rajan said.

"No, no," Akikane said. "If Vicaquirao is right, and the Apollyons will be trying to kill Gabriel, then his future self would have tried to establish the Barrier as quickly as possible."

"You make it sound like this has all happened before," Rajan sighed.

"It's like the history of the Primary Continuum," Teresa said. "You can know what happened in the future of the Primary Continuum, but you can only guess at what happens in the future of your own personal continuum. Just because we're outside the timeline of the Primary Continuum doesn't mean we don't have personal timelines ourselves."

"The alternative is to find a point in your timeline where the Barrier does not exist," Vicaquirao said.

"And if I fail to create the Barrier, or the Apollyons kill me first…" Gabriel found he had no desire to complete that sentence.

"Paradox Armageddon." Teresa looked worried as she spoke. "It could unravel the personal timelines of nearly every mage, unmake and remake the War of Time and Magic, potentially change the future beyond 2012, create an unstable number of bifurcations, and hypothetically destroy the Primary Continuum and every alternate branch of time attached to it."

"Well, as long as there's no pressure." Gabriel leaned back against the blackened wall behind him.

"Or maybe nothing will happen." Teresa looked as though she might reach out to hold his hand, but didn't. "Maybe the Apollyons are right and it will be fine if the Barrier is gone. Either way, you'll have help."

"Yes, yes," Akikane said. "And with the Apollyons we have captured, we will know where many more of the anchor points are located."

"It will take time for me to collect them," Vicaquirao looked to where the captive Apollyon lay in a bundled heap. "Even with the help of your Time Mages, it will require a few days."

"From what I could sense through the connection of their minds, they had only found a third of the anchor points," Gabriel said.

"Then we will need to move swiftly to discover those still hidden," Nefferati said.

"And make sure Gabriel is safe," Rajan added. "I still don't understand how they found us on that hillside."

"Time projection," Vicaquirao said.

"I didn't think that was possible." Teresa raised her eyebrows in surprise.

"I've never had need to attempt it myself, but it is," Vicaquirao replied.

"I've done it once." Nefferati's voice managed to combine both pride and regret in the same tone.

"Yes, yes," Akikane laughed. "And nearly killed me."

"What is time projection?" Rajan asked.

"The idea is that a Time Mage can project another person through time to a particular place if they have been there before, or have a relic from it." Gabriel had assumed the notion to be purely theoretical. "The Apollyons could sense where we were through the connection with the one we had captured. They used him like a relic and pulled themselves through time to where we were."

Rajan glanced at the unconscious Apollyon.

"He'd need to be awake for it to work," Teresa said, her tone not as reassuring as she hoped.

"If Kumaradevi had found one of the Apollyons, she may have done something similar." Gabriel glanced at the body of the duplicate Kumaradevi. "She could have used Soul Magic to follow the psychic link the same way they did. It would explain how she found us."

"Yes, it would also…" Nefferati began to say as Gabriel felt space-time bending nearby. Ohin and Ling appeared a moment later. Elizabeth's unconscious form floated between them.

Nefferati's statement remained unfinished as they all moved to surround Elizabeth. Ling gently lowered the comatose True Mage to floor as Nefferati, Akikane, Gabriel and Vicaquirao knelt around her.

Reviving Elizabeth proved to be easier than Gabriel had expected. The combination of Soul and Heart-Tree magic of the four True Mages, blended equally between Grace and Malignant imprints, slowly lifted the curse infecting her mind and brain. A moment after the four released their magic, Elizabeth gradually opened her eyes.

"The castle…" Elizabeth's voice sounded horse and weak. She looked at the burnt and broken ruins of the stone walls above her. "Are we in the castle?" Her eyes drifted down and came to rest on Vicaquirao's face. He smiled gently. "Not the castle then."

"This is not the castle, but you are safe." Nefferati brushed tears from her cheeks. "And you are well."

"You're back?" Elizabeth smiled at Nefferati and then turned her head to take in the sight of those encircling her. "How long?"

"Quite long, quite long," Akikane said, patting her hand. "More than a year."

"Did you find it?" Elizabeth's eyes filled with intensity as she sought out Gabriel's face.

"Found it, lost it, found it again, read it, lost it, and destroyed it." Gabriel could not restrain the wide smile that spread across his face. To see Elizabeth well again erased incalculable doubt and worry and fear and regret from his heart. "It's a long story, and we're still working on the ending."

"It must be an interesting tale." Elizabeth raised her head, a skeptical expression pulling at the muscles of her face as she looked at Vicaquirao.

"There have been some beneficial changes." Vicaquirao's smile seemed in competition with Akikane's for most ecstatic.

"How did you convince the Council of that?" Elizabeth asked.

"We didn't, we didn't," Akikane said. "We have temporarily abandoned the authority of the Council for new leadership." He clamped his hand on Gabriel's shoulder.

"Maybe someone should tell me what I've missed." Elizabeth sat up on an elbow, her purposeful nature rapidly reasserting itself even in her weakened state.

Gabriel left the others to fill Elizabeth in on the events that had transpired during her prolonged sleep. He needed some time to work through the implications of what Vicaquirao had suggested and everyone else appeared to agree with — he would create The Great Barrier of Probability. Assuming he figured out how. If he didn't, or failed in the attempt, or ended up dead at the hands of the Apollyons, the damage to the Continuum might be irreversibly devastating.

He stood in a deserted upper floor of the building, rubble and blasted brick walls nearly indecipherable from one another. He stared out across the devastation of the neighborhood, past still-smoking ruins of houses and shops to watch the people of London going about their normal lives and trying to replace the chaos of war with regularity and stability.

"I hear you have to save the world again."

Ling's voice came from just behind his ear and he jumped at the sound. She still enjoyed sneaking up on him when she could, as though he were still in his first days of training.

"Yep. It's no big deal. All I need to do is create something that already exists before it exists but before I can get killed which would keep it from existing." Gabriel's voice sounded more weary than sarcastic.

"Teresa explained it to me." Ling stepped beside Gabriel, crossing her arms over her chest. "Makes my head spin trying to understand it."

"Mine too." Gabriel stifled a sigh.

"She's stubborn," Ling said.

"Tell me about it." Gabriel could not hold back the sigh that came with those words and the emotions behind them.

"I just did." Ling frowned.

"Sorry." Gabriel laughed, remembering a similar comment from Elizabeth back when he had first arrived at the castle. So much had happened since then.

"She knows she's wrong, but now that she's made a decision, she thinks she needs to stick with it to remain true to herself." Ling gave a derisive snort.

"Obviously she's wrong," Gabriel said. "She wanted to break up because she was afraid she'd put me in danger — and then she saves my life today. How much more wrong can she be?"

"In my experience, people have a limitless capacity for being wrong," Ling said. "Especially where love is concerned."

They listened to the sounds from the street — cars passing, people talking, hard heels clicking against pavement, birds calling to one another across the rooftops and ruins. Into these gentle noises of city life amid the dangers of war, Ling added her voice, soft and tentative.

"My husband left me once. After our first child was born. He fell ill with a sickness that had been killing children in the village. In order to spare me and our children from catching the illness, he fled into the forest. It took me two days to find him. When I did finally discover him, sleeping under the low hanging branches of a tree, he looked nearly dead. With the help of the other villagers, we got him home. I nursed him for a week while he slipped in and out of consciousness. When the fever finally faded, his first concern was for the children. I had given them to a neighbor to look after while I cared for him. I assured him they were safe. He was relieved, but angry I had endangered myself and the children when he had fled the house to keep us safe. I explained that if he had died in the woods, his children would have had no father, and they would be far less safe. Sometimes we do things we think will protect those we love, but that, in the end, will only endanger them more."

Gabriel reflected on Ling's story for a moment. "How do I convince her of that?"

"You don't." Ling laughed and punched Gabriel in the arm. "You let her convince you. She's across the street with Ohin and Rajan, hunting relics and books. I'd hurry. I can't imagine we'll stay here for long."

"Right." Gabriel turned to go, then stopped and quickly kissed Ling on the cheek before she could react. "Thanks."

Ling wiped her cheek in mock disgust and then laughed as Gabriel ran down the iron stairs. At the bottom of the landing he saw Elizabeth speaking in low tones with Vicaquirao. He slowed his pace to give them a few seconds more of privacy. He noticed Vicaquirao hand her something small that she held in her enclosed palm without examining.

"In case you change your mind." Vicaquirao glanced behind Elizabeth to where Gabriel descended the stairs.

"Still always planning three steps ahead." Elizabeth laughed and shook her head. She followed Vicaquirao's eyes toward Gabriel. "I hear that I have you to thank for my revival."

"I should have thought of it earlier." Gabriel realized for the first time that he had grown so much during Elizabeth's coma that he now stood nearly half a head taller than her.

"Well, I'm grateful it occurred to you it at all." She casually slipped what had been in her fingers into her pocket. Then she reached out and placed both hands on either side of Gabriel's face and kissed him gently on the forehead. "Thank you."

Gabriel suddenly felt bashful as the focus of his mentor's gratitude and attention.

"Vicaquirao is leaving us." Elizabeth withdrew her hands and stepped back. "He wanted a word before he went." She turned and walked away, striking up a pleasant conversation with Nefferati, like two friends who had just met on the sidewalk by accident after years apart.

"I am departing now to begin collecting the Apollyons," Vicaquirao said. "Akikane and the teams you assigned will be assisting me."

"Will you be able to get a message to Semele?" Gabriel refrained from looking in the direction of Vicaquirao's belt and the small pouch containing the remains of the man who had renamed himself Apollyon and started the nightmare Gabriel had been living for the last three years.

"Yes." Vicaquirao patted the pouch. "I will bring her his ashes. She deserves that much at least. Maybe she will agree to help them in their new world. She helped Cyril more than I had ever imagined possible. I made a mistake there. One that altered the course of all of our lives. I did not see how much he needed her to become the man he was meant to be. Instead, he became something else. A lesson I hope you take to heart, as I have."

"I'm sorry about Cyril. And Cassius." Gabriel did not know how to comfort Vicaquirao in the obvious anguish of his loss. It felt odd even thinking of doing so. He had considered Vicaquirao his enemy for so long that regarding him as an ally still struck him as strange.

"You did more for him than anyone. More for all of them. More than they deserved." Vicaquirao forced a smile. "I will let you know when I have them all secured. Keep the chalkboard handy. In case there is trouble."

"I will." Gabriel said as Vicaquirao walked to join Akikane.

Akikane waved briefly before he and Vicaquirao disappeared into time. Gabriel paused a moment to consider how odd the two of them looked working together, how different they were, and how much he had learned from each of them. Then he made his way outside and sought out the bookstore Ling had mentioned.

The used bookshop across the street had been spared completely in the bombing. It stood between a paper store and a haberdashery, a wide green canvas awning stretching out over the street to cover a table displaying boxes of books. The bookstore was a good place to locate books that might be destroyed in a future bombing. Books that could be liberated to provide useful relics for time travel.

Teresa stood alone under the awning, browsing through a pile of paperbacks on the table.

"Find anything interesting?" Gabriel asked as he approached the table.

"Not really." Teresa looked up and gestured toward the inside of the store. "Rajan is in heaven, though. Seems the whole building gets bombed out in a few months, and most of the books are destroyed. Ohin said some of them ended up in the library at our old Windsor

Castle. Rajan is trying to convince him to figure out which ones we could safely take."

"Where would we put them?" Gabriel looked through the open doorway to see Rajan, giddy as a child in a chocolate shop, running his hands over a stack of books.

"He mentioned the need for a new library for our new fort." Teresa picked up a book and looked at the cover. It had an odd spiral design of an ever-widening sea shell emblazoned on it.

Gabriel recognized it as a representation of the Golden Mean. Teresa had explained the mathematical concept months and month ago in the middle of some conversation where he had spent more time staring at the way her hair fell across her shoulders than attempting to comprehend what she said. He felt proud of himself for remembering what the drawing was called, if not what it meant. He had things other than mathematics on his mind as he looked from the cover of the book to Teresa's face.

"I wanted to thank you again." Gabriel tried to project a tone and appearance of nonchalance as he spoke. "For saving me today."

"I got lucky." Teresa looked back to the cover of the book.

"It got me to thinking," Gabriel said. "About what you said. About us. About the team. They nearly got killed today as well. And I'm not an apprentice anymore. I'm not following orders, I'm giving them. I think it would be best for the team to be a real team again, not my personal body guards. I have to be seen as being able to protect myself. I can't lead the mages at the fort if I look like the kid who needs to have his hand held by Ohin and you and the rest of the team. They need to believe in me. And as much as I don't like it, you're right. If you and the others are around all the time, I may put myself at risk trying to save you. And with this new mission of trying to create the Barrier, we'll need every team we have in the field tracking down anchor points. Unfortunately, it is safer for both of us, all of us really, if we aren't all in the same place at the time. I wanted to tell you before I told the others. To help me sell it to them."

Teresa's mood had darkened as Gabriel continued to speak, her jaw tightening, her eyes narrowing, her lip twitching slightly, with each new sentence. She stared at Gabriel with a fiery intensity, abruptly reaching out and poking him in the chest.

"You've been talking to Ling, haven't you?"

"What? Of course not." Gabriel cleared his throat to cover his surprise at the abrupt turn in the conversation.

"You have." Teresa poked him again. "This is all her tai chi psychology, trying to get me to convince you of something you're already convinced of yourself. I hate it when she does that."

"I don't know what you're talking about." Gabriel licked his lips trying to figure out how to redirect the discussion and Teresa's growing ire.

"Liar." Teresa smacked his arm with the book still in her hand. "You always lick your lips when you're saying something you don't believe in."

"I do not." Gabriel could not help himself. He licked his lips.

"I will not be manipulated." Teresa crossed her arms, holding tight to the book. "I make up my mind based on my mind and not mind games."

"Then make up your mind." Gabriel's embarrassment at being caught out trying to deceptively sway Teresa's decision regarding their relationship rapidly transformed into an anger assembled out of the frayed pieces of his heart. "What do you really want? Do you want me to die someday without you there to protect me? Or to die alone without you? Or do you want to die alone without me? If you're going to break up with me it should be because you can't stand me anymore, because I'm a jerk to you, because you don't love me…but not because you're afraid bad things might happen when we're together. Bad things always happen to us whether we're together or not, so we might as well be together."

Teresa pursed her lips, looking as though she might scream. Instead, she smacked him in the arm again with the book.

"Now why didn't you just say that to begin with?"

"I thought I was being clever." Gabriel's anger seeped away to be replaced by a surging sense of hope.

"Just because you're right doesn't mean you're clever." Teresa stepped closer to Gabriel. "When I was facing Kumaradevi today I thought I was going to end up dead. Or that you were going to end up dead. And I felt stupid knowing that I hadn't told you I love you. That one of us might be dead and you'd think I didn't love you."

Gabriel didn't wait for any more words or try to think of words of his own. Words were never going to convey the upwelling of emotions in his heart. His slid his hands around her waist and he kissed her.

They broke apart from the kiss an unknown time later, wiping tears from their eyes and holding each other close. The book had fallen from Teresa's hand and balanced precariously at the edge of the table.

"We should put that back." Gabriel held tight to one of Teresa's hands. "Wouldn't want to create a bifurcation."

"Right," Teresa frowned. "The cover reminded me of something, but I don't remember what now. You annoyed me too much." She made to place the book in an open slot among the others stacked on the table. As she did so, another book caught Gabriel's eye.

"Hmmm." Gabriel reached out to the book that had attracted his attention, sliding it carefully from the pile. The title read *Nostradamus — Les Propheties*. He flipped it open and fanned the pages. As he did so his space-time sense tingled. "No."

"What?" Teresa looked at the title of the book. "What's the matter?"

"I never told you this, but Nefferati didn't write the prophecy of the Seventh True Mage." Gabriel handed Teresa the book. "She found it in the castle library. In this book."

"Wait." Teresa looked at the book more closely. "If she didn't write the prophecy, then who did?"

Gabriel said nothing. The tingling of his space-time sense continued to vibrate in his mind.

"No." Teresa looked up to Gabriel in disbelief. "Even I can't figure out how a paradox like that would work."

"Do you have a pen? I have some paper." Gabriel fished a small notebook from his pocket and ripped a clean sheet free from the binding.

"If you write out the prophecy and put it in the book and this is the book that Nefferati finds, then where does the actual prophecy come from?" Teresa looked uncharacteristically confused as she handed Gabriel a pen from her pocket.

"The better question is, if I write down a different prophecy, whether I'll suddenly remember the new words, or whether it might change my entire personal timeline." Gabriel began carefully writing out the words that had been etched into his memory. Words that had defined who he had become. Words that would continue to define him.

"Write it down *exactly*." Teresa sounded adamant. "We don't want to risk changing our timelines and finding out we suddenly hate each other."

"Not a possible universe," Gabriel said as he finished writing out the prophecy. He looked at it for what he realized would be the first time in the prophecy's own timeline.

"He shall come without warning
And leave without sign.
His coming shall mark the dawn of the endless night.
He shall walk among them, but be not of them.
He shall bestride the night and day.
Twilight shall be his world,
And all lands shall be his domain.
He shall pick of both trees
And eat of all fruits.
He shall plant new seeds
And harvest new crops.
He shall be the Breaker of Time
And the Destroyer of Worlds.
And all things shall hang in his balance
Until he is no more and yet is again."

He slid the prophetic piece of paper into the book of Nostradamus's prognostications and placed it back in the pile of books on the table. The tingling of his space-time sense faded.

"This is too much paradox for one day, personal and otherwise," Gabriel said. "Knowing something before you know it makes no sense to me at all."

"Perpetually cascading causality loop," Teresa replied. She stopped. Turned back to the books. Touched the one she had held so long. Her hand trembled. "Is this what it feels like to be you all the time? It's terrifying."

"What's terrifying?" Gabriel felt Teresa's other hand tighten on his own.

"I know why Kumaradevi thought I was holding something back when she interrogated me." Teresa's eyes were wide with wonder. "I did know something. Do know something."

"What?" Gabriel's unease came not from his space-time sense but from the look on Teresa's face.

"I know how to locate all the anchor points for The Great Barrier." Teresa's voice came out as a whisper. "I know how to find them because I'm the one who discovered where to put them in the first place."

CHAPTER 26

Black smoke, rich with sulfur, stung Gabriel's eyes and nose as it drifted off the field and between the leaves of the walnut trees, full and green in the height of summer. With the smoke came the sounds of battle — cannon fire, Gatling guns, explosions, rifles, screams, cries for help, the wails of wounded horses, and calls for men's mothers.

Gabriel turned away from the scene. Gettysburg, Pennsylvania, July 2nd, 1863. The pivotal battle of the American Civil War. A place where many things happened at once. A place where events in the timeline of history could easily be changed. A place where a young man appearing nearby would never be noticed.

The American Civil War began in 1861 when seven Southern states seceded from the United States of America over the issue of slavery. These seven states, where the enslavement of Africans and their descendants remained legal and supported the dominant agrarian cotton industry, declared themselves a new nation called the Confederate States of America. Four more Southern slave states soon joined them. President Abraham Lincoln and the Northern government, referred to as the Union, refused to accept the secession or recognize the Confederacy. Fighting began on April 12, 1861, at the Union held Fort Sumter in South Carolina. By the summer of 1863, Confederate General Robert E. Lee's Army of Northern Virginia had invaded the state of Pennsylvania. Union Major General George Meade's Army of the Potomac first defended the town of Gettysburg, then defeated the Confederate forces, driving them back southward in a military rout that signaled the end of the war. By the time of the Confederacy's surrender on April 9, 1865, some 750,000 American soldiers had lost their lives, nearly 50,000 of them at the Battle of Gettysburg.

Gabriel looked from the horror of the battlefield before him down to the map in his hands and then up to the faces of Ohin and Akikane.

"This is going to take some time." Gabriel glanced again at the map. It detailed the battle taking place around him. It also marked off 107 places with events that all took place at the same time. Events that could be altered easily to create a bifurcation. Akikane and Ohin had spent considerable hours in a space-time bubble hovering over the battlefield to assemble its contents.

"Take your time," Ohin said. "We have thirty-seven hours. We can afford to use a few here."

"Indeed, indeed," Akikane added. "Better to be slow and careful."

"I know we've gone over this a dozen times, but it still feels wrong." Gabriel wiped his sweaty palms on his pants lest he stain the map. "This many bifurcations in one place at one time is exactly what the Apollyons were doing when we stopped them the first time."

"They made no attempt to sever their new worlds within thirty-seven hours." Ohin flinched as a cannonball exploded nearby. "We will. But we need to move quickly."

"Yes, yes." Akikane patted Gabriel's shoulder. "But not so quickly that we make mistakes. Take your time. You have the relic, yes?"

"Yes." Gabriel tapped his pocket with the brass bullet casing that would be used during the battle in a clump of trees opposite the field from where they stood. He took his pocket watch out and checked the time. "You should both go. We'll meet you back at the fort." He paused a moment, feeling again like the pupil before his mentors rather than the leader of an army of mages. "I'm not looking forward to this."

"Meeting yourself once would be frightening enough," Ohin said. He seemed to think for a second before amending his statement. "No matter who you were."

"Quite right, quite right." Akikane smiled brilliantly at Gabriel. "However, you are who you are, so I am certain it will go well between all of you."

Gabriel nodded silently, hoping Akikane's assessment of his character prove correct. Akikane and Ohin disappeared into time, back to the new fort, leaving Gabriel to begin his dangerous task alone. He checked the hands of the watch again. Not long. Not long at all.

The days since the attack on the Apollyons had been hectic and confusing. As much as the arguments presented to him made sense, his mind continued to rebel against them. It did seem plausible that he would create The Great Barrier of Probability. It also seemed reasonable that if the Apollyons could manage to kill him that the resulting paradox would not only destroy the Barrier but could also irreparably damage the Primary Continuum. He even acknowledged the need to make 107 copies of himself in order to simultaneously establish the anchor points that held the Barrier in place. While he accepted all these things, their cumulative improbability, and the inherent paradox for his own personal timeline, left him with a growing sense of unease.

He had stifled that disquiet by keeping busy. There had been much to do. Teams of Grace Mages worked around the clock to locate and retrieve the comatose Apollyons and deliver them to Vicaquirao. Gabriel feared that the two missing Apollyons might attempt to rescue some of their brethren, but that had not been the case, or at least not yet. As the days passed, more and more Grace Mages defected from the Council's authority to join the forces at the new fort. Each new Time Mage who arrived was dispatched to help in securing the slumbering Apollyons.

While the various teams engaged in prison duty, as it became known, Ohin and Akikane had begun their search for a suitable place in time for Gabriel to copy himself. Meanwhile, Nefferati and the newly recovered Elizabeth helped Gabriel in hunting down the relics needed to travel to all of the 108 anchor points. Finding these anchor points in the first place fell to Teresa.

The cover of the book that Teresa had clutched for so long outside that bookstore in London proved essential to understanding how the anchor points were placed in time and space. The image of the Golden Mean led her to realize that her long-standing suspicions about a geometrically expanding distance between the anchor points were accurate. The placement of the anchor points followed a widening spiral through time and space. Knowing of even one anchor point allowed her to predict where all the other anchor points should be located. The math involved completely escaped Gabriel, but he understood her excitement as each anchor point she calculated coincided exactly with those they already knew the location for. As she revealed each new anchor point, Nefferati, Elizabeth, or Gabriel were dispatched with a team of Grace Mages to track it down and locate a relic for travel to and from its location.

It required nearly two straight days of work, but Teresa finally presented a list of all the anchor points. All except the final point in time, which secured the Barrier. Teresa referred to this as the Alpha Point. Her calculations indicted that it needed to be placed far before the planet Earth had even evolved from the interaction of gas and debris and gravity. The Alpha Point seemed to rest at the moment of the universe's creation, at the beginning of time. At first, it seemed impossible to create an anchor point at the moment space-time came into existence. Even if he could project himself through time, as Nefferati suggested, the vantage point to do so would need to be outside the Primary Continuum. Then he remembered his experience escaping the alternate reality where he and Teresa had been trapped by the Apollyons.

Gabriel looked at his watch again, the hands counting down the seconds until he needed to act. He tried to forget for a moment everything implied by Teresa's math. There would be time to figure that all out later. At least a few hours. And he would have help.

As the second hand reached its designated mark, Gabriel embraced the imprints of the Sword of Unmaking and gestured with his hand toward the sky with a thin wave of Wind Magic. A cannonball, descending at a speed beyond sight diverted slightly, falling in an empty section of the battlefield instead of the cluster of Union soldiers it had originally been destined to kill.

Gabriel felt an uncomfortably familiar bending of space-time and knew he had created an alternate reality where he now stood. Because his personal timeline did not affect the Primary Continuum where he created the bifurcation, unlike that night so long ago in Venice when he had saved Ling from death, he shifted entirely into the new reality. He no longer stood in the woods beyond the Battle of Gettysburg in the Primary Continuum. This signaled the moment when he would change the course of his life by violating the central rules of time travel he had worked so hard to learn and obey.

He took the brass shell casing from his pocket and focused his space-time sense on the moment in its timeline that he needed. Warping space and time in a flash of darkness and brilliance, he returned from the alternate reality and back to the Primary Continuum. He appeared in a barn not far from the battlefield, close enough to where he had stood, but out of sight from any possible onlookers. He arrived, not at the moment of his departure, not an instant later, but a full minute beforehand.

As he appeared in the barn, hay strewn beneath his feet, the smell of horses filling his nostrils, his mind reeled with two simultaneously overpowering perceptions. The first impression impinging upon his consciousness was one he had encountered before — a jangling sensation within his mind, his space-time sense rebelling against paradox.

The second perception exceeded his previous expectations.

So this is what it's like.

Yes.

Odd.

Very odd.

I can't wait…

For more voices…

To join the chorus.

Gabriel perceived himself in the barn.

He also stood in the woods beyond the battlefield half a minute before he had deflected the cannonball to create the alternate reality from which he had traveled to the barn.

We need to hurry

I need to hurry.

Yes, I know…

Let's not go down…

That path.

Gabriel Prime, as he decided he should think of himself, the Gabriel who would not end up in an alternate reality, stared at the map in his hands, looking for the next location indicated by a red X and a number 2. A hilltop. He jumped through space to appear behind a bush, shielding his arrival from those on the battlefield. He checked the map again, seeing the instructions for the subsequent bifurcation. Looking down to follow the hands of his watch, Gabriel reached out with Fire Magic to cause the gunpowder of a Confederate soldier to fail to explode, his rifle sitting useless in his arm. Reality shifted as the expected bifurcation split away in a new continuum.

All the while, in the barn, Gabriel Number 2, as he thought of himself, watched the mental image of Gabriel Prime on the hilltop. A moment later, his consciousness wavered as Gabriel Number 3 opened the barn door and entered. With this third Gabriel came the shared memory of having arrived a full minute earlier a hundred paces from the barn. And more confusingly, the memory of having left the hilltop for the following location indicated on the map, a ditch to the north of the battlefield.

This is…
Going to…
Get very…
Confusing…
No wonder…
He went…
Mad.

Each new Gabriel from each new reality appeared a little farther from the barn, using the varied travel of the shell casing to ensure that each new arrival would not run into his other versions before entering the barn.

With every duplication, with every fresh voice added to the ever-expanding mental cacophony, Gabriel, the Gabriels, all of them, began to collectively wonder if this endeavor would prove a grand blunder. Only a fool or a madman would attempt what they were doing. Only a sense of duty, and the knowledge of how bad things could be for everyone else in the Primary Continuum if he failed, allowed him to proceed, time after time, to create one alternate reality after another.

The psychic connection between the shared thoughts and memories made concentration increasingly difficult for Gabriel Prime, the one who needed to do more than stand and wait in a barn for versions of himself to arrive. The thought finally occurred, simultaneously among them, that it would be easier if the duplicated Gabriels in the barn meditated, letting their minds rest in an ever-present awareness, rather than reacting to, or contributing to, the thoughts they now constantly shared.

Eventually, after nearly two hours of creating bifurcations, the last version of Gabriel stepped into the crowded barn. Gabriel Prime joined his duplicates a moment later.

We should…
Continue to…
Meditate as long…
As possible…
A few of us…
Doing what is…
Needed while the others…
Remain as they are…
So our minds…
Do not…
Drive us mad…
Mad…
With voices…
Voices…

They stood throughout the large barn, sat in piles of straw, teetered at the edge of the hayloft, all 108 of them, waiting a moment, enjoying the silence of their shared mind.

Okay…
Let's get…
To work…

CHAPTER 27

By mutual decision, the many versions of Gabriel chose those who would warp space and time to deliver them all back to the fort. They appeared in the central square of the new fort a moment later. Teresa sat on the steps of the barracks. They had arrived exactly as planned, and she alone waited to greet them. She stood up and approached the nearest version of Gabriel.

"Which one are you?" She looked him in the eyes, ignoring the 107 pairs of eyes turned toward her.

"Number fifty-two," the Gabriel she spoke to replied.

"You've numbered yourselves." Teresa smiled. "That's cute."

"We were thinking…"

"Of getting…"

"Baseball jerseys made…"

Two other versions of Gabriel had joined in the response.

"That, right there, that has to stop." Teresa crossed her arms. "Only one of you speaks to me at a time."

"That will be me." Gabriel Prime stepped from the small sea of identical faces.

I thought…
There was no…
Difference…
I guess…
I was wrong…
Is this how…
They went mad?
Meditate…
Focus on…
Your breathing…
And perceiving…
And seeking…
And not her…
Lovely eyes.

Gabriel Prime ignored the voices in his head, unsure even which ones had come from his own mind.

"Are you…you?" Teresa asked, her eyes flicking between the duplicate Gabriels.

"I pretty sure," Gabriel said. "It's a little confusing with the thoughts of the others in my head all the time."

"Are you feeling crazy?" Teresa reached out to place the back of her hand against his forehead as though checking for a fever.

"I just made a hundred and seven copies of myself," Gabriel said. "That is insanely crazy."

"I suppose you're right." Teresa laughed.

Gabriel laughed as well.

A hundred and seven versions of himself laughed along.

"Okay, stop that. That's freaking me out." Teresa pulled Gabriel away from his duplicates.

"What's our status?" Gabriel asked, trying to seal his mind away from the few stray thoughts still entering it. Having the others stay in a meditative state of awareness seemed to help a great deal.

A pity…

That the Apollyons…

Never learned…

To meditate.

"We're doing fine," Teresa said. "Ohin and Akikane returned nearly two hours ago. They have been briefing the teams. Nefferati and Elizabeth came back a while ago with the final relics we'll need to access the anchor points. I've finished making my map of the anchor points for you to follow. I've marked all the ones where we'll have teams in place to protect you in case the two Apollyons show up. I think we're in good shape. How many hours do we have left before you need to sever all the alternate worlds you created to copy yourself?"

"Almost thirty-five hours," Gabriel said. He pulled his pocket watch out to double check. "Thirty four hours and fifty-five minutes."

"I'm worried about the Alpha anchor point." Teresa led Gabriel around the corner of a building, looking back over her shoulder at the courtyard full of duplicates of her boyfriend with a slight shiver. "I know you said you had an idea of how to reach it, but you didn't say what that idea was, and that worries me."

"I didn't tell you because I knew you'd worry even more if I told you what I have in mind," Gabriel said. "Remember when we escaped the alternate reality?"

"You can't be serious." Teresa stopped and grabbed Gabriel by the shoulders. "You don't even know if that's possible."

"It's the only way it will work," Gabriel said. Oddly, having so many versions of himself meditating and psychically linked to his mind left him feeling calm and confident. "I have to find a moment when the Barrier doesn't yet exist so I can create it. That's only possible from one place."

"To do that you'd have to use subtle cosmic energy, not imprints." Teresa shook her head.

"Yes, but that would explain why the Barrier appears to be created with Grace and Malignant imprints," Gabriel said. "A Grace Mage would see it as Grace Magic and a Malignancy Mage would perceive it as Malignant Magic. Even I saw what I expected to see. But the Barrier can't be created before time, before imprints exist, using imprints. That may be the one paradox that can't work."

"You only managed to use cosmic subtle energy once," Teresa said. "Do you think you can do it again?"

"There are over a hundred of me practicing how to do it right now." Gabriel, and all of his duplicates, comprehended how ridiculous that sounded. Maybe he should have discussed this with Teresa before he copied himself.

"And if they…I mean you, don't figure it out?" Teresa asked.

"We've got nearly thirty-five hours. I'm sure we can figure it out." Gabriel realized the assuredness that came with having a hundred plus minds in meditation linked together might also lead to arrogant overconfidence.

"And…until then?" Teresa left the question hanging in the air like a cloud of dust between them.

"There are some things I need to do," Gabriel said. "I want to practice projecting myself through time again with Nefferati. That will be part of how I hope to remain stable in the Void between continuums while I find and create the Alpha point. I also want to discuss sensing cosmic energy with Akikane. He said he's perceived it once before. And I should review the relics that lead to the anchor points with Elizabeth. I should also go over the anchor point map with you. And a few other things. Maybe address the teams with Ohin."

"That will eat up more than a few hours of the time we have." Concern coated Teresa's voice.

"Not necessarily." Gabriel sensed several versions of himself walk away from where he had corralled his duplicates in the courtyard.

"That's really freaky and weird." Teresa glanced back to see two versions of Gabriel setting out on missions he had just described. Two more followed shortly thereafter. Teresa turned back around, clearly not wanting to see more. "You're enough trouble when there is only one of you."

"There will be one of me again soon."

"Let me show you the map." Teresa caught sight of yet two more versions of Gabriel crossing the lane between the barracks. "Wait. I want to try something." She grabbed him by the back of the neck and pulled him into a passionate kiss.

Gabriel closed his eyes into the kiss, but he could also see through the eyes of Gabriel 33 and Gabriel 89, watching himself kissing Teresa as she peeked around his head to watch the copies of himself stopped in the middle of the street just before they too closed their eyes. He could feel all the versions of himself that had been walking through the fort come to a sudden stop as their eyelids slid shut.

"Okay, that's cool." Teresa broke away from the kiss with a self-satisfied grin. "Really bizarre and kind of creepy, but very cool."

"You're gloating."

"A little bit."

"Because I can't kiss you and walk at the same time?"

"A girl likes to know she commands her boyfriend's full attention. Come on. I'll show you that map of the anchor points."

The different Gabriels made their way through the fort to different destinations and different conversations, some intended and some unexpected, but all happening for him simultaneously with the same mind, a mind of many parts, most of which still meditated on the problem of how to perceive the subtle energy of the cosmos, as they lowered themselves, in one unified motion, to sit cross-legged in the courtyard like the monks of an ancient monastery.

Gabriel Prime followed Teresa to the common room of the barracks where a large map consumed one whole table — while Gabriel 33 approached Akikane crossing a lane between buildings — as Gabriel 89 came upon Ohin standing beside the main gate of the fort, speaking quietly with Paramata — even as Gabriel 44 happened to find Rajan seated on a bench near a tree eating a sandwich — while Gabriel 12 stopped to help Sema taking a break from sorting through imbued artifacts and concatenate crystals with a group of mages — as Gabriels 77 and 23 found Elizabeth and Nefferati reviewing the collection of relics spread across the tables of the dining hall.

"If the Council saw this, they'd have our heads," Elizabeth said as Gabriel 77 and Gabriel 43 entered the room.

"Then it's a good thing they can't see…" one of the Gabriel's said, standing before a table of relics, each one baring a numbered tag.

"What's in the courtyard." the other Gabriel concluded.

"It's nice to see you both…"

"Working together again."

"It's nice to be working together again." Nefferati frowned as she looked between the two identical Gabriels.

"It might be easier…"

"If we spoke separately."

The Gabriels both smiled as one of them led Nefferati to the kitchen while…

"Have you reached an existential epistemological crisis yet?" Rajan took a bite of ham and cheese pressed between two slices of bread, mustard oozing out the sides.

"You're starting to sound like Teresa," Gabriel 44 said. "Making up words to confuse me."

"I feel more like I'm making up words to confuse myself," Rajan said. "I'm beginning to think, though, that a little confusion is healthy."

"Then I'm probably the healthiest person you know." Gabriel 44 chuckled. In the courtyard, a hundred paces away, a 101 Gabriels chuckled softly, as well.

"You probably are." Rajan looked down at his sandwich with sudden dissatisfaction. "I suspect I've spent so many years with my head in books looking for answers that I've forgotten the pleasure of questions that remain unresolved. I may need less reading and more doing."

"Then Ling is right," Gabriel 44 said.

"Ling?" Rajan said. "Right about what?"

"About dancing with Imelda." Gabriel 44 grinned.

"Yes. She might be right after all." Rajan laughed as Gabriel 44 closed his eyes and smiled blissfully as...

"The key to projecting someone through time without a relic is concentration." Nefferati took a sip of tea from the cup in her hand. She and Gabriel 23 stood in the kitchen at the back of the dining hall. "Without a relic, any distraction of thought could cause a deadly displacement."

"Odd that the Apollyons hadn't tried it before." Gabriel had wondered about that, and now he wondered about it with several minds at once.

"It's very dangerous," Nefferati said. "I was sending Akikane someplace I knew well and had been often. I imagine that for the Apollyons, seeing all the places the duplicates existed simultaneously made projection through time even more difficult."

"I see that now." Gabriel existed in too many places at once to be able to focus on any one of them easily. "Putting most of them in a coma actually helped those who remained to focus on the one we had captured."

"Yes," Nefferati said. "A result I should have anticipated."

"We can't anticipate every possible problem," Gabriel 23 said.

"Even when there are so many of you?" Nefferati asked.

"The more of me there are, the more problems there may be to anticipate," Gabriel 23 laughed at Nefferati's frown and closed he eyes and smiled blissfully as...

"So the psychic link works?" Sema asked as she stepped aside with Gabriel 12.

"A little too well," Gabriel 12 said.

"It's a great risk," Sema said. "Thank you for taking it."

"We all take risks," Gabriel 12 said. "You and everyone on the team have risked their lives by being near me for so long."

"That doesn't feel like a risk." Sema gently folded her arms. "Odd, I used to take risks all the time when I was younger. My childhood was filled with attempts to prove I could be as strong and nimble as my brothers. Marrying my husband risked my heart, and helping him build our small merchant stall into a thriving house of exchange risked our livelihood. In my second life, I seem to have forgotten how to risk my future."

"The future is always the future," Gabriel 12 said. "You can't really risk it because you don't really know what it will be."

"I suppose the heart is much the same, when you think about it." Sema tapped her fingers against her arm as she seemed to ponder her own words, and Gabriel 12 closed his eyes and smiled blissfully as…

Paramata parted from Ohin with a wide grin as Gabriel 89 approached.

"She seems very happy," Gabriel 89 said. "Did you accept her offer of a date?"

Ohin frowned. Looked down at the ground. Sighed. "Yes. When this is all over. Dinner. Someplace nice."

"Paris is very romantic," Gabriel 89 said. "At least the version of it I was in."

"I know a place," Ohin said, his tone mysterious. He looked askance at Gabriel 89. "You think I should have said yes earlier."

Gabriel 89 said nothing.

"Possibly, you're right."

Gabriel 89 remained silent.

"Loss is not easy. I've lost two wives. Two women I loved as much as I could love anything. I lived and they did not. But what is the point of being alive if you're afraid to love?"

"You're asking me?" Gabriel 89 looked around as though someone else might be present.

"I'm telling you," Ohin said, "so you can remind me if I forget again." Ohin looked off in the direction Paramata had gone and laughed as Gabriel 89 closed his eyes and smiled blissfully as…

"It's all coordinated with Teresa's map." Elizabeth gestured to the numbered relics spread across five tables. "She's done an amazing thing."

"Yes, I see the map." Gabriel 77 did see the map through the eyes of Gabriel Prime standing beside Teresa on the other side of the fort even as he talked with Elizabeth in the dining hall. "And she is amazing."

"She is not the only one to amaze," Elizabeth said. "You should be very proud of yourself. Or yourselves, as the case may be at the moment."

"I'm only doing what needs to be done," Gabriel 77 said.

"That is not always as easy as it sounds," Elizabeth said. "Especially when you are asked to lead others into danger and potential death."

"I try not to think about that too much." Gabriel 77 realized he now had far too many minds with which to contemplate such thoughts.

"Good," Elizabeth said. "You can paralyze yourself with doubt, and that can be more dangerous at times than callous disregard for others. The first battle I took charge of ended very badly because I did not heed this lesson. Our teams found themselves pinned down by twice their number and I delayed the inevitable retreat because I knew the only way to cover our exit would be to ask one of the teams to sacrifice themselves for the others. Instead, I tried to cover the retreat myself. I thought I was being noble. I was being foolish. We lost nearly everyone that day, and I only escaped because I could do things those who died could not. I'm sure you know that feeling."

"All too well." Gabriel 77 stared down at a small brass ring with a loop of string running through it, a number 20 written in clean script on the attached tag.

"I lost friends that day because I didn't know how to ask other friends to die for them," Elizabeth said. "What I didn't realize was that by being there, they had already agreed to this bargain. It turned out that I was the only one not to abide by that unspoken contract."

"I understand. I've made this same pack with all of my selves." Gabriel 77 closed his eyes and smiled blissfully as...

"There you are, there you are." Akikane walked from the small lane to the shade of a nearby tree. "Where are the rest of you?"

"Busy doing different things," Gabriel 33 said. "I wanted to talk to you about cosmic energy."

"Of course, of course," Akikane said. "Have you glimpsed it again?"

"I'm trying right now." Gabriel 33 gestured toward the courtyard beyond the buildings. "I remember how I saw it the first time, but I can't seem to find it again."

"Yes, yes," Akikane said. "Looking can be the problem. Remember: cook, novice, monk, abbot, tree, sky, earth, all the same."

"Hmmm." Gabriel 33's frown of concentration slowly melted.

"You cannot search for the thing you already possess." Akikane said. "A fish does not hunt for water any more than a bird seeks air for its wings."

"Ah." Gabriel 33 closed his eyes and smiled blissfully as…

"See how this tail grows longer and wider?" Teresa traced the line on the map as it turned from the center, spiraling outward in ever-wider arcs until the final line ran in a gentle curve off the large sheet of parchment. "I've done the calculations and it flows back infinitely. Well, not infinitely, but that tail is really long."

"Back to the beginning of time," Gabriel Prime said.

"Exactly," Teresa said.

"Each red circle is a place I need to create an anchor point?" Gabriel touched his finger to Teresa's where it rested on the paper next to a red circle with numbers beside it.

"Yes," Teresa said. "The first set of numbers is the year, and the second set is the longitude and latitude coordinates. The equations for progression of the anchor points follow the Golden Mean closely, but I needed to calculate the locations by altering part of that equation to account for the spherical shape of the of the planet, and then adjust again because the Earth isn't a true sphere, and then compensate for the rotation of the planet and the processional tilt on its axis as it orbits the sun, and the effects of the sun's gravity, not to mention the moon's gravity, and then I had to figure out a way to convert the result of all that into coordinates we could actually use."

"And you did all that in two days?" Gabriel's heart swelled with love and pride and emotions that had no words to describe them.

"I didn't sleep much." Teresa looked away, slightly bashful. "You're mooning over me again."

"You'll get used to it," Gabriel laughed. "None of this would be possible without you."

"I've been thinking about that." Teresa's eyes found Gabriel's and held them. "Thinking about the paradox of me being the one who figures out when and where the anchor points go and why. Being the one who helps you create the Barrier. The paradox of you creating something that already exists, but doesn't exist in your future. I realized I can't process it all. I can't make sense of it. All I can do is follow the path that I'm on. But the important thing is that it's the path that you are on. The path we are on together. We've both thought about leaving that path for one reason or another. Because we wanted to protect each other. Because we were afraid. Because…it doesn't matter why. What matters is that we are both together now, and I hope it stays that way forever."

"Forever is a very long time." Gabriel made no attempt to restrain the broad smile that filled his face. "So that's good."

Gabriel closed his eyes and smiled blissfully…as Teresa kissed him.

In the stillness of that kiss 108 minds that were really one mind fell silent, perceiving nothing yet perceiving everything, seeing their own subtle energy pulse within them, a reflection of a greater power coursing through all things in all times and all places throughout the entire cosmos.

As the kiss faded the vision remained, like water cupped in a hand, slowly draining away. Gabriel Prime stared at Teresa, seriousness mixed with sublime calm.

"When we try to create the Great Barrier, I going to need you to kiss me first."

CHAPTER 28

Duplicates of Gabriel stood in 107 places throughout time. He stood atop the Great Wall of China at the Shanghai Pass in 1644. He also stood at the edge of a pitched fight during the Siege of Namur in 1695. Another version of him stood in the middle of the Battle of Ceresole in 1544 while he also stood aboard the deck of a ship in the Battle of the Echinades in 1427. One of him stood on a lonely beach with unfamiliar trees lining the shore in the year 300 million BCE while two other versions of him also stood in an alien landscape 3.4 billion years into the past. In each place, the duplicate Gabriel stood in a space-time bubble sealing him away from the flow of time a moment before an anchor point would come into existence.

One final copy of Gabriel stood atop a roof in the city of Aleppo in Syria on October 28 in 2012. A space-time bubble separated him, Teresa, Ohin, and the rest of the Chimera team from the civil war raging throughout the city and the nation. They gathered at the very edge of The Great Barrier of Probability, the moment when the final anchor point blossomed into being.

"We are all in place," that particular Gabriel said to Teresa and the others. "We will begin shortly."

"Take care," Ohin said.

"He will. We will. I will." Gabriel, and the many versions of himself connected to his mind throughout space and time, briefly considered the conundrum of proper pronouns for their peculiar state of existence.

"Don't forget." Teresa squeezed Gabriel's hand meaningfully.

"I won't." Gabriel smiled with the confidence of 108 young men about to do something unimaginably dangerous and thrilling.

"And watch your back," Ling said. "We don't have enough teams in the field to cover all of you."

"Yes, and the Apollyons may have found more anchor points than we suspect," Marcus added.

The retrieval of the comatose Apollyons revealed that the Dark Mages had discovered at least forty of the anchor points. There were only sufficient teams to cover half that number of locations to protect Gabriel in the event of an attack. A few extra relics allowed the teams to jump to places where they might be needed, but there were simply too many anchor points and not enough Time Mages.

Of course, the Gabriels scattered across time were not defenseless. They had each claimed the Grace and Malignancy imprints of the locations near the anchor points. Many of the anchor points were situated on the site of a battle or some conflict likely to have generated numerous imprints, both positive and negative. Due to the psychic link created by the doubling process, any version of Gabriel could access any of the imprints. He had an abundance of magic with which to defend himself. Moreover, if he once again managed to embrace the subtle energy of the cosmos, he would have more than enough power to fend off an attack by the two remaining Apollyons.

"One more of me to put in place and we will be ready," Gabriel said.

"You're sure this will work?" Teresa asked.

"What's the worst that could happen if it doesn't?" Gabriel tried to sound flippantly confident, but the notion troubled all 108 of his minds.

"You and I cease to exist as the Primary Continuum becomes unstable in an attempt to correct for all the ensuing paradoxes and either rewrites history where every Time Mage, including you, had affected it, or collapses completely into something even I don't have the math to predict." Teresa looked sick to her stomach.

"Again, thanks for not adding any pressure to the situation." Gabriel managed a weak smile.

"Sorry." Teresa grimaced and squeezed his hand again.

"It's okay," Gabriel said. As he stared into Teresa's eyes, he also observed a different sight.

Nearly three-and-a-half billion years away, on a rocky outcropping above a turbulent sea in a world so strange even oxygen had not yet arisen, Gabriel Prime stood beside his duplicate, encased in an air bubble of Wind Magic. He held in his hand a fossil, one of the oldest ever found. The remains of a cyanobacteria from the dawn of life on planet Earth. He, the Prime, the first and in some ways most true version of himself, had insisted on being the one to attempt creating the Alpha anchor point. The others, knowing him as well as they knew themselves, recognized that an argument would be pointless.

This was the most difficult and dangerous part of the plan. The part Gabriel had kept to himself until he had made the duplicates that made it possible. The part that concerned Teresa and Ohin and the others. The part that justified their concerns.

The only way to create The Great Barrier of Probability that already existed was to find a moment before it existed. A moment before time itself existed. And the only way to find the moment before the time of the Primary Continuum universe came into existence would be to locate it from the Void between all continuums.

Gabriel Prime turned to his identical companion, and through his eyes to all the versions of himself, each one calming his mind, seeking a meditative state of awareness.

No need to speak.
We already know...
Exactly what...
You will say...

Gabriel Prime laughed at himself then nodded to the duplicate Gabriel standing before him.

The duplicate Gabriel reached out with his space-time sense as he claimed hold of the imprints available to him through the many copies. He imagined in his mind a place he had been. Not a time and a place, but an actual absence of time and place. He began to warp space-time in a slightly different way than usual, bending it as though creating a tunnel, twisting it in a fashion similar to a bifurcation.

Be ready...
Now...

A voice of many voices cautioned Gabriel Prime as his duplicate companion thrust him through time and space and into the Void — existing without existence, between and beyond all existence, the emptiness of all potential continuums.

In an instant, he hovered in the Void, his mind, all of his minds, reeling with the impact of the improbable nature of the experience. His previous exposure did not prepare him for his presence in the Void.

Each moment there did not resemble any other moment, yet resembled all possible moments.

Gabriel Prime did find concentrating in the Void to be easier with his continued connection to his duplicates, but thoughts did not flow there in any normal manner. Thoughts needed the passage of time to coalesce. Primal awareness and will power were all that functioned within the Void. Gabriel Prime examined the Primary Continuum, appearing not to his senses but to the essential awareness of his mind.

The Primary Continuum stretched around him, an infinitely tall tree growing out of an infinitely small seed. He sought that seed with his mind, willing himself to it, perceiving the exact non-spot where it would become, not an infinite potentiality, but an ever changing probability — that non-place, that non-moment which would become the place and moment where the Primary Continuum erupted into existence, where time would begin — the edge of eternity.

Knowing he had found what he sought, he next pursued the thing he needed in order to create the linkage of energy and potentiality that would become The Great Barrier of Probability. In 107 places throughout the timeline of the Primary Continuum, Gabriel after Gabriel stilled his mind, seeking to perceive the subtle cosmic energy flowing through the Void and all existence. Out of that stillness arose a realization regarding the nature of the creation of the Primary Continuum and the true purpose of the thing he intended to create.

"Now is the time for…" the 107th Gabriel said to Teresa where they hovered in a space-time bubble in 2012.

As Teresa moved toward him, he raised his hand to stop her. In his mind, the mind that held so many minds, he saw an assault upon himself at one of the anchor points. And then at another. And another. And then more.

"We are under attack," Gabriel said. "I am under attack. At ten…no fifteen…no at least twenty anchor points."

"How is that possible?" Ohin asked, turning his back to guard Gabriel.

"There is only one Apollyon." The Gabriel beside Teresa concentrated, seeing himself in twenty places fending off twenty attacks, more onslaughts occurring with each passing moment. "There are teams of Dark Mages. Some are Kumaradevi's soldiers. Probably trapped here when we severed her alternate world. Some are Dark Mages with no uniforms. Maybe Apollyon's old henchmen. They are at forty of the anchor points now. Our teams are fighting back. So are we. So am I. I am…wait…no…it was all a diver…"

Gabriel, standing next to Teresa went ridged, his head tilting back, his mouth opened in a silent scream.

All of the Gabriels throughout time fell into a similar pose, their minds gripped by a malevolent curse, struggling for continued consciousness against an onslaught of impending eternal darkness.

Outside time and space and all existence, hovering in a state of improbable probability in the Void, Gabriel Prime felt his mind freeze through the link with his many duplicates.

On a hillside on the Isle of Lewis in the Outer Hebrides of Scotland in 2500 BCE, the circle of the monolithic Callanish stones not far away, one of the Gabriel's stood, still encased in a space-time bubble, his head enclosed by the hands of the man who had appeared behind him. This Gabriel reached for the Apollyon's fingers around his skull, but made no progress in his motion — his limbs and body held fast in a rictus of pain.

"You will die now," the Apollyon whispered in his ear. "All of you will die. And with your demise the Barrier will come to an end, because it will never have been created."

Gabriel fought the magic assailing his mind, sensing a vast sea of imprints behind the Apollyon's power. The man held more negative imprints than Gabriel had ever encountered. The Council had always assumed that the army of Apollyon doubles would rely upon their psychic connection as the source of their imprints. They seemed to have learned at least one lesson from Vicaquirao. They had prepared for their plan to go wrong by amassing a storehouse of concatenate crystals linked to malignant imprints. The Apollyon remained unseen behind Gabriel, but he had no doubt the man held more than a hundred such crystals upon his person, each linked to six more.

Gabriel's own considerable power could not match that of the imprints the Apollyon wielded against him. He slowly lost ground to the dark Soul and Heart-Tree Magic invading his brain and mind. The

Apollyon employed a blend of magic similar to that which Gabriel had previously used against the man and his duplicate brothers. The Apollyon sought to use the psychic connection between the Gabriels to cast them into a deadly sleep, one so deep and so profound it would slow their bodily functions to the point of death.

While the Gabriel of Scotland struggled against the Apollyon pushing him ever closer toward permanent slumber, those of him under attack elsewhere could not defend themselves. Some of the Gabriel-duplicates had Grace Mage teams to protect them. Many were not as fortunate, their frozen bodies under assault by teams of Malignancy Mages while the Apollyon's magic seized captive their minds. The Malignancy Mages kicked and beat his various selves, adding an unwanted distraction to his attempts to alter his condition and regain some control in the fight for his minds.

"I have had a long time to learn the weaknesses of having more than one mind," the Apollyon with the Gabriel in Scotland said. "You taught me some of them. What I teach you now will be your last lesson."

Gabriel did not respond with words. His mouth would not move to form them. But he could still speak with his mind.

You will destroy yourself as you destroy me.

"I will survive any paradox to come from your death," the Apollyon said aloud.

You do not even know why the Barrier exists.

"It exists to be destroyed." The Apollyon tightened his grip on Gabriel's scalp.

No. It exists because it must.

"Nothing must exist," the Apollyon said.

You are wrong. The Barrier exists because it needs to. It is not a Barrier. That is only a side effect. Only an anomaly. It does not exist to create a wall between past and future. There would be no need for anchor points to accomplish that. The anchor points are the important part. They exist because the past is not stable. The creation of this continuum, this universe, this possible continuum of countless possible continuums, is not stable, could never be stable, without the support of the anchor points. They are like the splint a sapling relies upon to grow straight and true. Without it, this continuum will splinter, pulled apart by minor instabilities that will flutter and shift countless probabilities over the course of billions of years, until it collapses upon itself.

"You lie." Hesitation marked the tone of the Apollyon's voice.

No. I do not.

Gabriel did not lie. He had not realized the purpose of the anchor points until stepping into the Void and witnessing the creation of the Primary Continuum, finally apprehending that it was not primary at all, but merely one of countless possible continuums, some coming into fruition while others began but crumbled under their own weight, like trees split asunder as their branches grew too heavy and wide apart. He had not lied, but he had not told the Apollyon this truth in hopes of swaying the man's judgment. The man could not be turned from enemy to ally with a few words, no matter what truth they might reveal. But words of deep truth always required at least a moment's consideration before rejecting their validity, even by madmen. A moment would suffice for Gabriel's needs.

Kiss me.

"What?" Teresa, standing on the rooftop in Syria in 2012, nearly jumped at the sound of Gabriel's voice appearing in her mind.

Kiss me. Now. Please.

Teresa pulled Gabriel's mouth to hers as she closed her eyes.

Even through the pain of the shared experience of being beaten and his mind infected with noxious magic, Gabriel, all of the Gabriels, sensed Teresa's passion and love infuse that kiss. He surrendered himself to that kiss — to that passion, that love, that moment, letting it fill him, allowing it to still his mind in an endless moment of joy. In that stillness, among his many minds, he perceived what had previously been invisible, unknowable, but now appeared as ever-present.

Gabriel touched the subtle cosmic energy of all creation and non-creation, its power filling his minds all at once, granting them, and their collective will, an inconceivable potential. He twisted the Dark Soul Magic of the Apollyon attacking him on the hillside in Scotland, turning it against the man even as he cast the Dark Mages assaulting him throughout time into sudden and irrevocable unconsciousness.

He heard the Apollyon behind him in Scotland fall to the ground. As this occurred, he felt something else as well. Something sharp and painful. Something that dropped him to his knees. He turned to see a second Apollyon standing where the first had been, his hand bloody, his eyes wide with terror. The second Apollyon had been behind Gabriel the entire time. He had seen what Gabriel had done to his twin. He had, no doubt, sensed the manner in which Gabriel had accomplished the feat.

Gabriel's eyes fluttered as he sagged, the blade of the knife still sticking between his ribs, piercing his heart. The Apollyon began to warp space-time to flee with his unconscious duplicate companion. With his mind fading in the absence of a beating heart, Gabriel knew that the precious time it would take to heal himself would also allow the Apollyon twins to escape. Instead, he seized the warping of space-time the Apollyon had begun and refashioned it, projecting the two men to a place he had previously been and remembered well, a place where a fire raged above a river, at a moment after he had departed, in a world far beyond the Primary Continuum. As the two men flashed out of sight, Gabriel, every Gabriel, wondered if the two men would ever make it back from the alternate reality where they had once trapped him and Teresa.

A last thought filled his dimming mind. A desperate plea rather than a coherent idea. An entreaty none of his other selves had time to answer. An imploration echoing throughout the many minds of his duplicates.

Help me!

This last thought faded, replaced by no other, darkness shadowing his mind, the link to his other selves weakening, the voices fading...

We will need to...
Make another duplicate...
There is not...
Enough time...
We must try...
We cannot fail...
We...

The mind of the Gabriel in Scotland dimmed into darkest oblivion, a sense of joy pervading him, a euphoria that carried him upwards into a light more brilliant than any he had ever conceived.

"I am here."

Light became darkness and the darkness grew back into light and his eyes flickered.

"I am here. You are alive. Again."

The eyes of Gabriel in Scotland gradually focused on an image of an old man, face wrinkled but eyes still alight with life.

"Vicaquirao?"

"Not the young man you remember, but the man nonetheless."

"I was dead."

"Not quite, but very close. I healed you."

"You saved me."

"Although not the first time, it will be the last."

"I don't understand."

I don't...

We don't...

Understand...

Questions echoed through Gabriel's many minds.

"How did you know where to be, and when?" Gabriel accepted Vicaquirao's hand and stood up, slightly weak but far from death.

"I have had a long time to think about it since you last saw me." Vicaquirao smiled. "We can discuss technicalities later. You have a task to complete, I believe."

"Yes."

Yes...

Yes...

We should...

Begin...

Gabriel Prime, the version of himself existing outside all time, acted in concert with his other minds, willing the subtle energy of the Void and all potential universes to conform with his desires, touching the moment of his own universe's creation and plying a line of energy through its continuum. He anchored it in places that would hold it steady against its own inherent instabilities, a line of indomitable power stretching across 13.8 billion years, anchor after anchor, linked together, flowing through to the final instant of forced stability in the year 2012 when the energy curved back upon itself, twisting ever so marginally before breaking free of solid reality and once more entering the Void, joining itself at its beginning, creating an infinite loop of potentiality, existing in every branch of reality that might ever split away from the continuum it allowed to exist.

Gabriel Prime witnessed this act of creation as he and the others willed it into being, reveling in the resulting paradox of perfection and probability, his many duplicates marveling as they perceived their individual anchor points as both ceasing to exist and being born in the same instant. Gabriel Prime made one final, minor adjustment to the Barrier at a single moment in a particular place, altering it imperceptibly in one significant way. Then, his companion at the beginning of life on earth pulled him back from the Void and into the flow of time. As they smiled, they released their hold of the subtle cosmic energy, letting go of the state of mind that allowed its perception, turning their attentions to other things and other places.

"You can stop kissing me now." The Gabriel in 2012 grinned at Teresa.

"Did it work?" Teresa held her breath, waiting for his reply.

"We're all still here, aren't we?"

Teresa kissed him as cheers rose up from the members of the Chimera team. They slapped him on the back and hugged him in joy. Meanwhile...

Versions of Gabriel also gathered the unconscious Dark Mages who had attacked him, stripping them of their relics and talismans before projecting them one at a time to a place where another version of himself stood in a grassy valley in the year 52 million BCE. The Dark Mages would survive well enough until Gabriel Prime figured out what to do with them. Meanwhile...

A version of Gabriel also stood beside Vicaquirao, looking out over the arctic summer ice, a large wooden shed beside them. Vicaquirao had brought them there when Gabriel had allowed the space-time bubble to dissolve in Scotland.

"Where are we?" Gabriel watched snow blowing across the peaks of the nearby mountains.

"Robert Scott's cabin in Antarctica," Vicaquirao said. "Around 1929. It's abandoned from 1917 to 1956. A good place to find chalkboards if you need. Also a fine place to hide from the world.

Though make sure you arrive after 1929 or you might find other guests already here."

"I still don't understand how you figured out where and when to find me," Gabriel said.

"That would take far too long to explain, and, as usual, you wouldn't believe me until forced to." Vicaquirao laughed. "What is important is that you do not mention this the next time you see me. That would lead to confusion."

"I'm already confused," Gabriel said.

"This will help." Vicaquirao reached in his pocket and removed a small hourglass. He handed it to Gabriel. "Keep this with you. Always."

"What is it for?" Gabriel turned the hourglass upside down in the palm of his hand, but the sand did not flow, seeming glued in place.

"You'll know when the time comes." Vicaquirao winked at Gabriel. "Now I must leave you."

"Where are you going?" Gabriel asked.

"Someplace I've never been," Vicaquirao laughed cryptically. "You did well today. You should be proud. But don't let that pride cloud your judgment. You have much left to do. Returning to a state of singularity, for one."

"We're going to return to our alternate realities and sever the bifurcation shortly," Gabriel said.

"Might I suggest one last task for all of you?"

"What task?"

As Vicaquirao explained, a grin broke across 108 identical faces throughout time.

The many Gabriels had at least an hour left before they needed to cleave themselves from the Primary Continuum.

Plenty of time.

CHAPTER 29

Gabriel, the only Gabriel then inhabiting the Primary Continuum, walked hand in hand with Teresa, staring up at the stars, a blazing sea of light washing across the black of the sky, as they crossed the Upper Ward courtyard of Windsor Castle. Around them, men and women sang and danced and drank and ate and talked and laughed and cried and yelled with pride as they passed.

"This was a brilliant idea." Teresa kissed his cheek.

"I wish I could take credit for it." Gabriel waved to Leah and Liam as they ran past, holding sparklers in their hands and screaming with unreserved joy, as only children can do.

"Vicaquirao may have suggested it, but you figured out how to do it," Teresa said.

Moving a version of Windsor castle from one of the alternate realities and back to the Primary Continuum had been easier than figuring out how not to disrupt that particular continuum's timeline due to the castle's absence. The Gabriel Collective, as he later came to call the sum of his various copies, had decided to steal Windsor Castle during World War II and make it look like it had been bombed out of existence. Faking the bombing proved simpler than altering the residents' memories with Soul Magic to believe the story. As an alternate reality, the future of the world would adjust slightly to compensate for the loss of the castle. And the alternate world would have its own version of Gabriel to ensure that things did not stray too far from the original course of events. All of the severed alternate realities were gifted not merely with shadow-pasts grafted from the Primary Continuum, but also a duplicate Seventh True Mage to stand sentinel over their timelines.

As Gabriel looked down from the stars to Teresa's face, illuminated by the oil lamps and Fire Magic globes of light hovering around the court yard, he felt a pang of guilt for the copies of himself who would no longer have the benefit of Teresa's love. They had all known this, of course, but he had sensed their pain as he severed the bifurcations creating their new worlds away from the Primary Continuum. Cutting the worlds free in the same way he had Kumaradevi's alternate reality meant they would each have a stable, yet inaccessible, history prior to the moment the bifurcation had been formed. It also meant they would each have a future. 107 new universes with 107 versions of himself, each, he knew, pining for the girl they would likely never see again.

Unless, of course, they each chose to seek her out in their new worlds, bumping into her by accident sometime before her natural death, altering the course of her future slightly, the flexible nature of the alternate reality adapting to compensate, leaving her alive to decide if she might be interested in the boy who could teach her Fire Magic and introduce her to Time Travel.

Gabriel wondered how many times that choice would be made and how often Teresa would say yes to him in those different realities. He decided it would be best to worry only about the love of the Teresa who walked beside him.

"There they are." Marcus's voice carried above the din of revelry, guiding them to one of the many tables that had been brought from the castle and hastily splayed across the lawns of the Upper Ward. Marcus waved them toward two seats near the head of the table, food and drink piled along its polished surface. Gabriel saw Paramata seated next to Ohin, her hand holding his beneath the table. Gabriel smiled at Ohin, who returned the smile somewhat reluctantly, as though admitting his stubbornness. Paramata winked at Gabriel as he pulled a chair back for Teresa.

"We were waiting for you," Sema said as Gabriel and Teresa seated themselves.

"Yes, we have an announcement." Marcus rose to his feet, helping Sema up from her chair. The pair seemed flustered and unsure of exactly what they might want to announce. Their eyes scanned the faces around the table, then flicked to each other, then back to the table.

"We are…" Marcus began.

"We have decided…" Sema said.

"We have come to the conclusion…" Marcus coughed.

"It has become apparent…" Sema reached out and took Marcus's hand.

"Hopefully what's been apparent to the rest of us forever has finally dawned on the two of you and you're getting married." Ling shook her head in exasperation.

"Well…" Marcus coughed again.

"Yes." Sema blinked her eyes bashfully.

"I have asked Sema to marry me and she has, for some unfathomable reason, agreed." Marcus may have said something else, but any further words were lost in the uproarious shouts of congratulations from their friends and companions.

Marcus's face flushed a nearly-luminescent pink and Sema placed her hand across her mouth in embarrassment. As the two took their seats and the cheers died down, Gabriel realized he needed to wipe his eyes to see clearly. He clutched Teresa's hand beneath the table and grinned and laughed along with the others.

"When is the date?" Rajan asked.

"How would I know?" Marcus said. "It took me long enough to realize what I should do. I haven't had time to consider when."

"Sometime soon." Sema glanced around the castle grounds. "When things are back to normal."

"What we knew as normal is hopefully gone for good." Ohin stroked his chin in thought.

"And good riddance," Ling said.

"Yes, yes." Akikane placed his two hands upon the table as though to emphasize his thoughts. "We have an uncharted path to explore. It should be exiting."

"Indeed," Elizabeth dabbed the corner of her mouth with her napkin. "This is the first real peace we have had in centuries."

"Assuming we can make it last." Nefferati glanced around the table lamp at Gabriel. "There are still Dark Mages who may not wish a peace."

"The Apollyons for one," Rajan said. "They may eventually make their way back to the Primary Continuum."

"Hopefully they'll kill each other first," Ling said.

"I doubt we'll be that lucky," Teresa said.

"No," Gabriel said. "But I don't think they'll be concerned with The Great Barrier anymore."

"They will undoubtedly be trouble one day," Paramata said.

"And we should prepare for that," Ling added.

"Part of that preparation should be dealing with the Dark Mages Gabriel stranded in time," Nefferati said.

"Yes, yes," Akikane said. "But deal with them how?"

"Offer them a truce," Ohin suggested.

"Oh, I think we can offer then better than a truce." Elizabeth smiled pointedly at Gabriel. "I think we can offer them new leadership."

"New what?" Gabriel choked on the bite of cheese he had been eating.

"You've given us back the castle," Elizabeth said. "We will need to invite the Council to rejoin us. To reunite with us. It occurred to me that the best way to turn this sudden lull into a lasting peace might be to invite all mages into the fold."

"You may have suffered permanent damage while in that coma," Nefferati said.

"No, no." Akikane smiled. "The Dark Mages need a leader now. So do the Grace Mages. Who better than one who can lead us all?"

"Someone who is both a Grace Mage and a Dark Mage," Rajan added.

"No…that…hold on a minute." Gabriel waved his hands as though shooing dangerous insects or dangerous thoughts from the table. "I thought the Council would resume leading. As Councilman Romanov pointed out, I'm not even old enough to vote. How could I stand for a seat?"

"Rules are sometimes changed to benefit the whole of a society," Elizabeth countered. "I was thinking that new elections could be held. Elections open to the new citizens Gabriel could bring to us. Those we previously fought."

"Are you really Vicaquirao pretending to be Elizabeth?" Teresa squinted hard at Elizabeth.

"I am quite certain I am not." Elizabeth smiled slightly at the thought.

"It would be easier to keep an eye on them." Nefferati placed her fists beneath her chin as she contemplated the idea. "Unless we decide we're interested in genocide, the only other real choice is allowing them to form their own nation of Dark Mages."

"Just so, just so," Akikane said. "And how long before they decided to make war against us again?"

"It sounds insane, but it's really no more ridiculous than the idea of Marcus and me getting married." A sly smile spread over Sema's lips as she looked to Marcus beside her.

"Asking you to marry me is not ridiculous or insane, it's ironic." Marcus feigned offense by looking away from Sema until she relented and kissed his cheek. "It's also the smartest thing I've ever done."

"No doubt about that," Rajan said.

"But it does make one question Sema's judgment," Ling laughed as Marcus tossed a grape from a nearby bowl in her direction.

"See," Teresa said. "I am not the only one who starts food fights at the table."

"Food fights might be the least of our worries with Dark Mages sharing the castle with us." Ohin grabbed the offending grape as it rolled along the table, holding it in his hand. "It will take firm leadership to unite all mages, Dark and Light, under one roof." He plopped the grape in his mouth as he looked at Gabriel.

Gabriel found himself possessed by an overwhelming desire to run from his seat and flee the castle and everyone and everything it represented. Teresa's hand jerked him back into his chair as he realized he really had been about to stand and bolt. He glanced at her, then the others, then swallowed.

"Using malignant imprints with no grace imprints to balance them changes people over time," Gabriel said. "They will be angry and suspicious and lacking in basic human compassion after so many years of using dark magic. I can try to teach them how to control the emotions that come with dark imprints, but I can't change what it does to them. I can try to lead them, but I don't know if they will follow me anymore than if the Grace Mages will follow a Council that allows Malignancy Mages into the castle. And if we allow them into the castle, we have to allow them to vote, and they will vote for Dark Mages to sit in council seats."

"Sounds like a mess," Paramata said.

"A mess that may be better than the alternative messes," Elizabeth countered.

"Pairs," Teresa said, her voice bright and exited.

"Non sequitur?" Rajan said. "Why pears and not apples?"

"Not the fruit. Pairs. Like teams." Teresa looked to Gabriel, nearly bouncing in her seat. "Teams of Grace and Malignancy Mages. Everyone paired together. Grace Fire Mages with Malignancy Fire Mages. Joining their magic and balancing the imprints."

"That might work." Gabriel clenched his jaw as he considered Teresa's idea. "That might actually work. It would be hard on the Grace Mages, feeling the malignant imprints through their partner, but it's possible."

"Now all we need to do is convince the remaining Dark Mages that this idea is in their best interests as well as ours," Nefferati said.

"Not us, not us," Akikane said. "There is only one man who can convince them to follow such a plan."

"Vicaquirao," Gabriel said. Akikane understood the problem perfectly. Only someone the Dark Mages had once seen as an ally could persuade them to embrace new allies working together to build a better life.

"Would he want to stand for Council then?" Ling asked.

"I very much doubt that," Elizabeth said. "Vicaquirao has little interest in such things."

"You would know," Nefferati said in a low voice.

"So, we have a plan," Ohin said.

"An insane and ridiculous plan," Gabriel said.

"We're used to those." Marcus laughed.

"The Council is going to need a new name." Sema looked around the table. "The Council War and Magic won't fit any more."

"The Council of All Mages," Gabriel suggested. "Something for everyone."

"We could call the castle Mageopolis," Teresa said, her eyes twinkling with mischief.

"I rather think not." Elizabeth frowned.

"Magicville," Gabriel said, smiling at Teresa.

"Magetopia," Teresa offered.

290

"Magicland," Gabriel said, laughing.

"We could get a rollercoaster," Teresa said with a giggle.

"I think we should separate the two of them before they come up with any more ridiculous ideas," Sema said.

"Next thing you know, *they'll* be thinking of getting married," Marcus said.

Gabriel and Teresa's amused laughter ceased in unison as they looked at each other and then their friends around the table. They shifted uncomfortably in their seats. Gabriel felt his face burning so hot he nearly grabbed a glass of water to douse himself as first Marcus then Sema, then Ling and Rajan and Ohin and Paramata and Nefferati and Elizabeth, and finally, Akikane burst into laughter that filled the night air. As their embarrassment turned to amusement, he and Teresa's laughter joined that of their friends, lifting their hearts.

Sometime later, after more merriment and more food and more plans for the future, Gabriel and Teresa sat on a bench beneath an oak tree in the Horseshoe Cloister, holding hands and staring up at the moon rising above the Curfew Tower, its light bathing them in a soft, luminescent glow.

"We did it." Teresa shrugged her shoulders as though releasing a long held tension.

"Did what?" Gabriel asked, absentmindedly pulling the small hourglass from his pocket and checking it before the light of the moon.

"Put it all right," Teresa said. "Kumaradevi, the Apollyons, The Great Barrier, and us. That's the best part."

"Yes." Gabriel turned to Teresa, admiring her face in the moonlight. "That is the best part. The best part of the future too."

"A very long future, hopefully." Teresa turned to Gabriel seeing the hourglass in his hand. "Still no idea what that's for?"

"Nope." Gabriel flipped the glass upside down. A single grain of sand defied gravity to rest against the upturned base of the glass. "The sand only flows in one direction, and very slowly. It could take years to empty. Decades, even."

"So, you're supposed to do something years from now, but you have no idea what?" Teresa raised a finger to touch the hourglass. "That's so very Vicaquirao."

"He said I'd figure it out eventually." Gabriel slid the hourglass back in his pocket. "Looks like I've got plenty of time to think about it."

"Meanwhile, I could suggest something else to occupy your mind." Teresa's mischievous smile, the one Gabriel found so appealing, slowly spread across her lips.

"A game of chess?" Gabriel teased. "Or checkers? A hand of cards?"

"I'd beat you at all of those." Teresa leaned closer to Gabriel. "I was thinking of something where we could both win."

"A jigsaw puzzle?" Gabriel leaned toward Teresa, two magnets irresistibly drawn together.

"You can stop being clever to impress me, I'm already in love with you."

Gabriel closed his mouth and opened his mind as his lips met with Teresa's, his heart welling in his chest as his thoughts flew away, erasing all concern of castles and councils and mages and wars and dangers and problems and futures unseen as he simply kissed the girl he loved.

They stayed like that on the bench for a very long time.

And they remembered that night for the rest of their lives.

THE LAST CHAPTER

Vicaquirao emerged from the eternal brilliance of time travel to stand exactly where he had stood only moments, and decades, ago. Robert Scott's expedition hut from over a hundred years earlier still stood nearby. He looked past the shed at the mountains of Antarctica and shivered against the chill wind. He had timed his arrival perfectly. Only seconds remained.

Vicaquirao stood beside that artic ice on October 28th in the year 2012 at 4:44 p.m. Greenwich Standard Time. As the seconds passed, he looked around, taking in the last moments of time before what he had always considered the unknowable future. At the moment when the Great Barrier of Probability divided time, he shivered again, stamping his feet after crossing it. He stood in the same place, in a future separated from the past — separated from everyone he knew in the past, as well.

He took a small nail out from his pocket and held it in his hand. Twisting space and time around himself, he appeared a moment later behind a dilapidated house, weeds fighting with wild grass to fill the small backyard. Vicaquirao slid the nail back in his pocket and closed his eyes. His features shimmered, his flesh wavering as it transformed from one state to another. He stood taller, looked younger, and processed a different face with a similar shade of skin but much darker hair.

A second man stepped from the house to stand on the rickety wooden boards of the back porch. The man touched a hand to his curly grey beard, cropped close like the locks of his head. He seemed confused. He walked forward off the porch and into the tall weeds and stared at the first man.

"Gabriel?"

"Hello Aurelius."

"You look so much older."

"I am older. It's so good to see you again."

The man who had appeared to be Vicaquirao, the man the boy named Gabriel Salvador had grown to be, stepped forward to his old friend, Marcus Aurelius Antonius Augustus, former emperor of Rome, and embraced him in his powerful arms. Gabriel, who had been pretending to be Vicaquirao in order to save his own younger duplicate self from death, felt a sense of relief at the conclusion of that particular mission. It had taken him nearly a decade to realize the purpose of the hourglass and its implications.

Eight years after saving the Great Barrier of Probability a voice had pierced his mind while in the middle of a mission to recover a stolen concatenate crystal. A voice he knew speaking words he remembered all too well.

Help me!

He had ignored it, hoping his imagination might be playing tricks on him. Fifteen years later, while looking for a particularly important relic, he heard it again. He did not ignore the voice that time but did not know what to do about it. He realized that in both instances, he had been in the same time frame as an anchor point. The voice had been his own. A version of his own. His voice as he died that day in Scotland.

The third time he heard the voice came five years later as he stood near an anchor point in ancient Babylon, watching the final grain of sand empty from the hourglass. That could not be ignored, and he knew exactly what it meant — yet one more paradox haunted his life. It had not been Vicaquirao who had saved him. He had saved himself. Would save himself. And would give his younger self the tiny hourglass to ensure it.

Eventually, he had convinced himself to embrace the paradox, and his life, and do his duty. As it always had, contemplating his duty brought his mind back to the man from whom he had learned the most about the subject.

"I do not understand." Aurelius held Gabriel by the shoulders, a look of wonder and confusion filling his face. "I thought you couldn't cross the Barrier without being trapped here in the future. What are you doing here?"

"I thought you might be hungry." Gabriel smiled, wrinkles creasing the corners of his eyes. "I thought I would take you to lunch."

"Lunch?" Aurelius laughed. "I could use a meal, but…"

Time and space bent around them, a flurry of deep darkness and infinite illumination that left them standing atop a castle tower overlooking rolling fields. A thick wall connected the tower to another and another, encircling a small town. A woman sat on a checkered blanket spread across the stone floor of the tower. She looked exactly as she always had, only years older. She leapt to her feet and threw her arms around the former emperor.

"Aurelius! It's so good to see you." Teresa kissed Aurelius on his bearded cheek. "It's been too long."

"Yes," Gabriel said. "We would have come earlier, but we were busy."

"Earlier?" Aurelius said. "It's only been a few hours since I fell across the Barrier."

"Hours for you." Gabriel gestured for them to sit down. "Quite a bit longer for us."

"Where are we?" Aurelius asked, looking at the fields below the massive stone walls.

"The walls of Avila in Spain," Gabriel said.

"The year 2015," Teresa added.

Aurelius turned slowly from the vista beyond the crenellations of the tower and back to Gabriel and Teresa. "It is good to see you both still together. It is not often young love lasts so long."

"There were a few years where we became confused." Gabriel frowned slightly at the memory.

"Long, painful years." Teresa grabbed Gabriel's hand. "But that is the past and we are here for the future. And for you."

"Me?" Aurelius said. "You should not have worried about me. After all, I did lead a nation once. I would have managed. And now you are both trapped here with me in the future, away from your friends."

"Well, most people would be trapped." Gabriel said.

"You said someone could only cross the Barrier in the direction of the future," Aurelius said.

"He's very clever when he wants to be." Teresa began pulling cheese, bread, fruit, and a bottle of wine from a wicker basket at her side.

"Clever enough to listen to someone twice as clever as I'll ever be," Gabriel pulled three wine glasses from the basket.

"You mean we can go back, across the Barrier, into the past?" Aurelius took an empty glass from Gabriel.

"As Teresa pointed out to me, when you build a wall to keep people from getting in, it is usually wise to build oneself a secret passage in case you need to get out. Or back in again." Gabriel poured the wine.

"It's a long story." Teresa handed Aurelius a small plate of cheese and bread and dried sausage.

"We'll have plenty of time to explain." Gabriel felt bashful as he looked into the eyes of his old friend. "We need your help."

"In the future," Teresa said.

"About a thousand years in the future," Gabriel said. "Surprisingly, these walls are still standing."

"I don't know how I can possibly help you with anything, but if I can, I will," Aurelius said.

"Thank you," Gabriel said. "We'll explain as much as we can while we eat, but there is a great deal to do."

"There always is," Teresa laughed.

"Then may I offer a toast." Aurelius lifted his glass. "To old friends. And the future."

Gabriel and Teresa raised their glasses while repeating Aurelius's words. Gabriel sipped the wine, smiling at Teresa and Aurelius as he placed his glass down. There would always be a future, even though he would one day cease to have a future of his own. He had once thought that day to have come by drowning in a bus at the bottom of a river. He had been wrong. He had thought his future to have expired many times since, but each time, fate, and just as often, his friends, had pulled him away from the end of destiny to continue onward through life. He knew that eventually a day would come when fate would not save him, when no friend's hand could pull him back from the brink, when his future would finally unravel and come to an end. He could not know when that time might come. It might arrive in centuries as easily as seconds. All he could do was be thankful for the time he had. Time to spend with old friends. Time to spend with Teresa, the girl who had become a woman — a woman who had saved him more times than anyone — most often from himself. Time to live, to love, and to do the things that only the Seventh True Mage could do.

Time to save the future.

The End of *The Wizard of Time Trilogy*

ABOUT THE AUTHOR

After a childhood spent whizzing through the galaxy in super sleek starships and defeating treacherously evil monsters in long forgotten kingdoms, G.L. Breedon grew up to write science fiction and fantasy novels. He lives with his wife in Brooklyn, NY.

He is also the author of:
The Wizard of Time
The Sword of Unmaking (The Wizard of Time – Book 2)
The Dark Shadow of Spring (The Young Sorcerer's Guild – Book 1)
Summer's Cauldron (The Young Sorcerer's Guild – Book 2)
The Celestial Blade

For more information or to sign up for G.L. Breedon's mailing list, please visit:
Kosmosaicbooks.com

Word of mouth and recommendations are essential in helping an author's work find new readers. If you enjoyed The Edge of Eternity please consider writing a short review. Even a few words would be very helpful.